RUNNING OUT OF TIME

Next Time Book 2

... UNTIL NEXT TIME

RUNNING OUT OF TIME

Next Time Book 2

W.M. WILTSHIRE

NEXT TIME SERIES: RUNNING OUT OF TIME
First Edition

Copyright © 2019 by W.M. Wiltshire

Book Cover Design and Interior Formatting by Melissa Williams Design

Edited by Hugh Willis and Susan Strecker

ISBN: 978-1-9991134-2-1

To my Mom who always told me I had a vivid imagination and who taught me that I could do anything I put my mind to.

Thank you for always being there.

Part IV

In the Wrong Place at the Wrong Time

1

"THAT WAS HIM!" Dani shrieked. "That was Jack the Ripper!"

"I know, and that bastard will never pay for his crimes."

"Where are we?" Dani asked, trying to orient herself.

"Look out!" a child screamed from somewhere over Daric's left shoulder. Daric's prone form looked up. The front hooves of a reared horse were plummeting downward, directly toward him. He instinctively rolled away, taking Dani with him.

"That was close," Daric muttered.

"Grab them!" a man's voice bellowed from above.

Two men among the crowd gathered at the side of the road rushed forward and seized Daric's arms. They pulled him up onto his feet and wrenched his arms high behind his back.

"Hey, take it easy," Daric protested, unable to mask his grimace.

Another man from the opposite side of the road bent down and pulled Dani to her feet, pinning her arms as well.

"Hey!" Dani objected. As she peered over her shoulder to see who was holding her so tightly, she gasped. She was looking into a pair of wide-set brown eyes that were staring out at her from a shadow-draped face under a wide-brimmed black hat.

"Don't you be givin' me no evil eye, witch," he snapped.

"Where did they come from?" a woman asked worriedly.

"They must be witches!" cried a young woman from the back of the crowd.

"Here," the cart driver said as he tossed some rope to the men restraining Dani and Daric and who made quick work of securing their hands behind their backs.

"Can we get on with it? We'll deal with these two later. They're not going anywhere," a man on horseback shouted.

As the cart slowly passed, Daric looked at Dani to make sure she was okay. As he did, his eyes met those of the man holding her. At first he couldn't believe what he saw: a face with thin lips, a broad nose, and a thrusting pointed jaw. He would know that face anywhere, no matter what kind of clothes its owner was wearing.

Daric mouthed the words. Dani acknowledged with a nod. Another Uncle Richard.

Present Day—Saturday

2

RICHARD'S MIND WAS awash with the possibilities. *Time travel: could it be true? To be able to travel through time.* He would be famous, the envy of his profession; hell, he would be the envy of everyone. "Quinn actually did it!" he muttered. "The things I could do with those travel bands." There was only one problem: the bands were in England, in 1888, last he knew.

Richard was annoyed that Quinn had been reluctant to share his incredible breakthrough with him. At the same time, Richard knew he would not have understood the endless equations involved in Quinn's achievement. They gave him migraines.

Although annoyed, Richard would bide his time. He would leave Quinn to work out the still unresolved details. Once Quinn was finished with his work, Richard would make his move.

After parking his Abruzzi in the garage, Richard entered the house. He proceeded to the north wing where he had previously installed a fingerprint scanner locking device. Unlocking the door, he entered, yelling, "Hey, Eddie, I'm home!"

"You can't keep me here," a timid voice muttered back.

"Of course I can, you worthless piece of shit. Nobody even knows you're missing, or cares, for that matter. Besides, you have a roof over your head, a comfortable suite of rooms, and decent meals whenever you want them. A far cry from where you were two months ago when I scraped you off the street and kept you out of the hands of the law. So, be grateful," Richard spat.

Edward "Eddie" Jonathan Keys was a young man, small in stature compared to Richard. Weighing one-hundred-fifty pounds, with narrow shoulders, he stood six feet tall. He had sad jade-green eyes behind thick black-framed glasses. His short brown hair was a little longer on top. He had a small mole just above the left corner of his mouth.

Eddie had been in the foster care system since he was five-years-old. That was when he had lost both his parents in a terrible car accident on their way home from a party one stormy winter's night. His life had been turned upside down in a matter of seconds when the police had come and told him the news. Learning that he had no living relatives who could take care of him, the police immediately delivered him to the local child care authorities. When old enough, he had left his last foster family late one night, and had been taking care of himself ever since. Until two months ago, that is, when he was hacking into a convenience store's ATM and was caught by Richard.

"I have a little job for you," Richard sneered. He knew he had a good thing when he caught Eddie breaking into the ATM. Richard had stood in an obscure corner of the store and watched the young man. He was immediately impressed by the self-made gadgets the kid pulled out of his pockets, all designed to access the cash in the machine. He would have succeeded, too, if Richard had not grabbed him and hauled him away. So far, the kid had not disappointed him.

"See this little box?" Richard asked, holding up the metal chest he had taken from Quinn's lab. "I need you to open it."

"Why don't you open it yourself?" Eddie asked defiantly, seated comfortably in his desk chair.

Before the pain could register, Eddie found himself sprawled on the floor, his overturned chair beside him. He had not seen the abrupt backhand slap coming his way.

"Because, smartass, it has a very special lock. Open it!" Richard demanded, as he pitched the small box onto Eddie's chest. "Buzz me when you're done."

Richard stormed out of the room, locking the door behind him. He made his way to his office where he poured himself a stiff drink.

Richard knew he had to get back into Quinn's lab to get access to his work. But Richard would need a distraction first, something to draw Quinn's attention away from the lab. *What would possibly bring Quinn out of his lab?* Richard thought deviously. He took another deep belt from his glass when an idea struck him. A sinister smile edged across his pencil-thin lips. Tomorrow: all he had to do was make one quick phone call.

The pure genius of it, he thought.

3

EDDIE PULLED HIMSELF up off the floor. Using the sleeve of his shirt, he wiped away the small trickle of blood from the corner of his mouth, while clutching the small metal chest with his other hand.

"Jerk," he muttered, as he set the small metal chest on the desk. He bent down, righted his chair and wheeled it behind the desk. He sat down and examined the chest.

Eddie's suite of rooms occupied the upper floor of the north wing of the Case mansion. The building itself was two-hundred feet long and eighty-five feet wide, with one central turret that stood eighty feet high. The wall surrounding the five-hundred-sixty-six acre Edwardian estate had been built of local stone and had encircled the ten kilometres of roads that interlaced the estate. In its glory days, the estate had included a number of outer buildings. There had been sufficient resources, then, for the estate to operate like a small, self-contained village. It had a dairy, slaughterhouse, smokehouse, and cow stables. It also had a refrigeration plant, water storage tanks, grain silos, gardens, and servants' quarters. Now, all that remained were the stables.

The mansion's impressive exterior was matched only by the luxuriousness of its interior. Even though Eddie had been confined to his suite of rooms since his arrival, he had got glimpses of some of the interior as he was being escorted through the mansion by Mr. Case's manservant, who also filled the role of bodyguard. The entrance hall and dining room he had passed were panelled with rich golden oak. Most of the interior walls were panelled in oak and rosewood. The floors were teak. Specially made light fixtures hung throughout the mansion.

Eddie's main room was over two-thousand square feet, with large lead-paned windows along the west-facing wall. The walls were all panelled with rosewood; the floors were teak. A fireplace with a seven-foot hearth was on the wall opposite the suite's main entrance. The room's sparse furnishings included four burgundy leather wingback chairs and a matching sofa positioned around the fireplace. A mahogany coffee table sat in front of the sofa, with matching end tables complementing each pair of chairs.

Richard had previously cautioned Eddie, if he was entertaining the idea of trying to burn the place down. "You'll be found among the rubble and easily explained away as a thief; you do have a history to support that claim." That escape option had instantly fled Eddie's mind.

Eddie's office was in one corner of the main room. Its most notable feature was a large antique mahogany desk; its drawers packed with every kind of stationery imaginable. Behind the desk was a high-back maroon leather office chair. On the desk's surface sat a 3D printer, a scanner and an iMac computer with a twenty-seven inch monitor with Retina 5K display.

When Eddie had noticed the computer soon after his arrival at the mansion, his first thought had been to contact the authorities for help, but, unfortunately, he had no internet access.

Eddie had known from the outset that he was in a difficult situation. But he had decided early on that he would do what was asked of him, and, when the time was right, he would make his break for freedom. Until a few minutes ago, he had never been physically abused. And Richard was right; he was warm, dry, and well fed. It had been years since he had felt this well cared for. But being held against his will definitely diminished his appreciation for his lush surroundings.

Eddie picked up the small metal chest. He was amazed at how heavy it was. He gave it a shake and heard something move from within. He examined the locking mechanism. He had seen nothing like this before. It almost looked like a finger-print scanning mechanism. Pulling a hand-held scanner from the bottom left-hand drawer, Eddie took a scan of the lock. He then enlarged the picture on his computer, but the image did not reveal the lock's secret.

Eddie turned the chest slowly, examining it from all sides. He carefully checked each edge and each corner of the chest. He pulled a large magnifying glass from the top desk drawer. He re-examined the chest with a closer viewpoint. He wondered whether the chest could have been fashioned after one of those Japanese puzzle boxes that can be opened only through some complicated series of manipulations. The number of moves can range from two to over fifteen-hundred; the challenge is to find the right moves and to perform them in the right order.

Looking closely at the small chest, Eddie could not even see any joints or seams. It was as if the entire chest were made from one piece of metal. It remained a mystery to him. *Mr. Case is not going to be pleased,* he thought.

4

DANI AND DARIC were tethered to the back of the slow-moving horse cart as it trundled through town. The cart, flanked by guards and mounted officers, had left the prison, travelled down Prison Lane, and turned right onto the main street. It carried five women: two were elderly and frail, one a quiet housewife, one an impetuous and brazen woman, and another a belligerent vagabond. Some were well-to-do; others were in rags. It didn't seem to matter what walk of life they were from; they were all headed to the same destination.

The cart looked like a hay wagon. The sides were comprised of vertical slats, their sole purpose being to keep the hay or, in this case the occupants, from falling off while travelling the rough, dirt roads. The prisoners were shackled to a long chain that had been threaded through the slats and encircled the cart. Those who were too weak to stand lay crumpled in a heap on the floor of the cart. Those with resolve and determination, who had the strength to stand tall, gazed at the passing scenery for one last time: the planted fields of tall corn and drying hay, the lush summer foliage of the oak, ash, elm and maple trees, and the cool running water of the North River.

Dani was in awe of the majestic beauty of the trees, especially the elm and ash trees. She had never seen those two species before. Long before she was born, the Dutch elm disease and the emerald ash borer had wiped them from the world she knew.

The procession moved southwest, heading out of town and drawing the attention of onlookers. The road angled toward the river which curved abruptly as it ran between bedrock hills. From the height of the hills to the south, a stream flowed through a salt marsh pool until it eventually met the river below. The massing crowd crossed over a bridge spanning the stream between the pool and the river. The level of the water in the river was down this morning, much of the water having been drained away by the low tide.

Turning off the main road, the cart took a track that climbed the hill above the salt marsh pool. The track was lined on both sides with spectators, who threw insults and jeers at the cart's passengers as they passed. At the top of the hill stood one lone oak tree that grew out from the clefts in the rocks. It must have been seven feet in diameter at its base. The lowest branches were at least twelve feet above the ground. It was the perfect hanging tree.

5

STARING DOWN AT the sweating humans through indifferent beady, black eyes were five large crows, all perched on different branches in the oak tree and at varying heights. One deputy, who had arrived ahead of the cart, picked up a weather-beaten wooden ladder that lay at the base of the tree. He propped it against one of the tree's massive lower limbs. The resulting small vibration carried through the tree caused the crows to take flight, squawking their protests as they faded into the distance. From a bag, resting at the base of the tree, he pulled out a length of rope, then another, and another, until there were five laid out on the ground before him.

As Dani watched, it dawned on her that the ropes were nooses. She shuddered. The deputy flung the ropes, one at a time, over the lower limbs: two on the left side of the trunk and three on the right. On the left limb, hung the knotted remnants of a previous hanging.

Another deputy, meanwhile, had climbed into the back of the cart. The five condemned women were unchained, one-by-one, and helped out of the cart; one elderly woman had to be carried down. Once on the ground, their arms were tied behind their backs.

"Give me those," ordered the man who had captured Dani. He was pointing to the shackles just removed from the condemned and now lying on the cart's floor.

After catching the tossed shackles from one of the guards, he clasped one end onto Dani's right wrist. He then dragged her over and instructed, "Get in," indicating the back of the now-empty cart.

Dani knew there was no point in resisting. With her free hand, she pulled herself up into the cart; the man followed. He fed the free end of the manacles through the cart chain. "Remove that," he ordered, referring to Dani's bracelet.

"No," Dani said firmly.

"Fine," he grunted, as he roughly yanked Dani's arm. He pushed the band farther up her arm, making room for the manacles, which he securely fastened around her left wrist.

"Okay, you're next," he said, pointing to Daric. This time, however, two men provided assistance to make sure there wouldn't be any trouble from their prisoner. The man didn't even bother to ask Daric to remove his bracelet. He just gave him the same treatment as Dani.

They had chained Dani to one side of the cart and Daric to the opposite side. There was no way they could reach each other to attempt an escape. They would have to bide their time.

The cart driver had climbed down from the cart and had walked up to the tree, awaiting the arrival of the condemned, since he was not only the cart driver. He was also the High Sheriff of Essex County. In this latter capacity, George Corwin would act as executioner in the day's proceedings.

The condemned were forced to climb the steepest part of the hill toward the base of the oak tree. As they moved up the hill, so did the gathered crowd. From where Dani and Daric were, they had an unobstructed view of the proceedings.

"Where are we?" Daric whispered.

"Keep quiet!" one of the guards ordered.

"Later," Dani mouthed silently.

Present Day—Saturday

6

"COME ON, BEAR. Let's go get Quinn," Sandra called. As she held open the door, Bear charged through and headed toward the peninsula and Quinn's lab.

Quinn had been gone when Sandra woke up this morning and she hadn't seen him all day. Nevertheless, she knew where he was, having talked to him earlier in the day on the intercom. She also knew what Quinn had to do, so she had not wanted to disturb him unnecessarily. But it was time.

When Sandra arrived at the gazebo, Bear was patiently waiting there for her. Sandra opened the door, followed Bear inside, and made her way down to the lower level. She found Quinn slumped over his console with his head buried in his hands.

"Quinn?" Sandra spoke quietly. She didn't want to startle him.

"Hi, Dr. Delaney," Hermes greeted enthusiastically, as he suddenly appeared at the far end of the console, startling Bear and jolting Quinn from his thoughts.

"Hello, Hermes," Sandra replied.

"Quinn, it's past midnight. You've been out here all day and you haven't had a thing to eat," Sandra gently scolded. "At least Bear had the sense to come in for supper."

"Sandra, I have to get this done. I have to get our kids back," Quinn insisted.

"And you will, but you're not going to be any good to them if you don't take care of yourself. Now, come back to the house and get something to eat. You can grab a couple of hours of rest and, then come back here and continue your work," Sandra said firmly. She couldn't help noticing the dark circles under his eyes and she knew from his tossing and turning last night he had not gotten a good night's sleep. Neither of them had.

"Professor, Dr. Delaney is right. You need something to eat and you need some rest. Your vital signs are indicating you are on the verge of exhaustion and you are not performing at your optimal level," Hermes stated frankly.

"See, Hermes agrees. Now come on, Quinn. Just for a few hours. Please," Sandra pleaded.

"Okay, you're right. I am tired and hungry, now that you mention it." Quinn's stomach took that moment to concur. "Hermes, continue to run the computation algorithm tests and I'll be back in a few hours."

"Before you go, Professor, I completed the analysis on the entry system you asked for earlier," Hermes said.

"Report," Quinn ordered.

"My analysis revealed that an unauthorized key accessed the entry panel. The key contained an override program that infiltrated our system and activated the access code prior to our firewall detecting the intruding program and being able to shut it down," Hermes said.

"How is that possible?" Quinn asked, both astonished and perplexed.

"I'm not certain, Professor. I have never experienced, nor have I ever come across, any program that can circumvent a security system within milliseconds of initiation, because that's what would have had to have happened to bypass our system. It's unheard of,"

Hermes finished.

"It couldn't have been Daric. He's smart, but not that smart," Quinn surmised.

"I concur," Hermes replied.

"This could be a very serious problem. If what you say is true, which of course it is, the infiltrator could bypass almost any security system in existence today. Our system is state-of-the-art. If they could breach our system, then any system could also be breached." Quinn was genuinely concerned as he considered the broader picture. "This could be a national security threat."

"Quinn, you should notify the police. This is serious," Sandra urged.

"I can't, Sandra. I can't have the authorities snooping around here. Not now. I have to get Dani and Daric back first. Then, I'll tell the authorities," Quinn replied. "Can you trace the virus, Hermes?"

"There was no digital footprint. The virus had an automatic sweeping program that erased all details relating to the virus codes, origins, and time," Hermes said.

"Damn! Have you been able to eradicate the virus?"

"Yes. I have removed it from our systems. Everything is clean. I double checked after I scrubbed all of our systems," Hermes replied confidently.

"Professor, there's something else. I decided to run analyses on all of our systems and it seems that someone has used the rear emergency exit. The exterior exit valve has also been activated, flooding the emergency tunnel," Hermes said.

"Wait, you can run analyses without being given any command to do so?" Sandra exclaimed.

"Yes," Hermes replied proudly. "I am a cognitive computer. I am able to learn . . ."

Quinn interrupted. "Do you know when the valve was opened?"

"Yes, it was yesterday at approximately 6:14 P.M.," Hermes reported.

"It couldn't have been the kids. I sent Daric to find you around dinner time. Then I remember seeing him at his boat, and then with Dani at the beach. Neither of them could have gotten into your lab, found and accessed the lower level, and then exited out the emergency door. They wouldn't have had time. It wouldn't have been possible," Sandra said firmly.

"Then, who was it and more importantly, why?"

"Professor, maybe Daric and Dani didn't take the chest with the chronizium as you original thought. Maybe it was the intruder," Hermes speculated.

"That would make more sense. Either way, our lab security has been breached and my last supply of chronizium is gone."

7

LATER THAT EVENING, after having devoured a delicious prime rib dinner with gravy, Yorkshire pudding and a tossed mixed-greens salad, accompanied with a few glasses of cabernet-sauvignon, Quinn stretched out on the living room sofa. The lights had been turned down. The flicker of the flame from the fireplace added a warm gentle glow to the room. Prior to dozing off, he had left strict instructions with his wife to wake him in two hours. But before that could happen . . .

"Professor?"

"I was just drifting off," Quinn mumbled. "What is it, Hermes?"

Quinn pulled himself up into a sitting position and ran his fingers through his thick brown hair, which had started greying at the temples.

"The children have moved again," Hermes informed him.

"What? Where? When?" Quinn's cognitive receptors immediately snapped to attention.

"They've left London, England and 1888 and are currently at 42° 30' 58.7838' N, 70° 54' 44.2074' W."

"Where's that?"

"It's in the United States, Massachusetts, actually," Hermes replied solemnly.

"What year? What date?" Quinn asked anxiously.

"1692."

"Help me out here, Hermes. Did anything significant happen in that era? Could my kids be in any kind of danger?" Quinn was beside himself with worry and frustrated beyond reason for feeling so helpless.

Hermes had previously run an analysis of that time period and of one specific location. He was not thrilled with his results.

Sandra had heard voices in the living room and put aside cleaning the kitchen to investigate.

"Oh, hello, Hermes." Sandra smiled, as she took a seat on the sofa next to Quinn. She couldn't help but notice how agitated her husband appeared. She reached over and clasped his hand; it was clammy. Something was wrong, but before she could ask . . .

"Good evening, or should I say good morning, Dr. Delaney? It is, after all, 2:30 A.M.," Hermes replied.

"So it is," Sandra agreed, still holding Quinn's hand, cradled in her lap.

"Professor, as I was about to inform you. The children arrived in Massachusetts on July 19, 1692. According to historical records of that period, on that particular day, five women were hanged: Rebecca Nurse, Elizabeth Howe, Susannah Martin, Sarah Wildes and Sarah Good."

"Dear Lord," Sandra grimaced. "What crime did they commit to have warranted the death penalty?"

"They were all accused of witchcraft," Hermes replied, bracing himself for the eruption he knew was about to follow.

"Oh, dear God!" Sandra cried out. "Our children suddenly appear out of nowhere, in an era where people are hanged for witchcraft. Quinn, do something!"

"Sandra, you know I can't bring them home. I would if I could, but, at this moment, I can't," Quinn said despondently. "Besides, maybe they materialized in a secluded area, out of sight of everyone. Hermes, where are our kids, precisely?"

"They are in Salem, Massachusetts: Gallows Hill, to be precise."

"I need to get back to work," Quinn said impatiently, as he quickly left the house.

8

"I'M INNOCENT AS the child unborn," she cried as she was being dragged up the hill toward the old oak tree. "Oh, Lord, help me!"

Rebecca Nurse was a woman of seventy years. She was hard of hearing and had been frail for a long time. She looked cadaverous, probably because of her recent illness and having kept close to her home before being arrested. Or it could have been from having spent the past four months languishing in prison.

"Goody Nurse, it's not too late to confess," Reverend Nicholas Noyes pleaded. He was a short man of stout figure in his mid-forties. He had eagerly volunteered his services at the trials, often taking on the role of prosecutor, questioning and, at times, badgering the accused. "Confess now, so that your soul may be saved."

Sheriff Corwin helped Rebecca Nurse climb up the ladder; the noose dangled forebodingly in front of her. He climbed up a couple rungs and then reached up and slipped the noose around her neck. He tightened the knot.

It did not take Dani long to figure out just where and when they had arrived. Terror struck her to her very core. There could not have been a worse place or time to just suddenly appear . . . and in front of an entire town of witnesses, no less. *'This can't be good,'* she thought.

"Dear Lord, what sin have I committed that you should lay such an affliction on me in my old age?" Rebecca Nurse pleaded.

"Goody Nurse, save your soul. Confess!" Reverend Noyes repeated. But he knew it was useless. The old woman would never confess.

Rebecca Nurse gazed longingly down at her husband. He was standing in the front row of the crowd that had gathered to watch the executions. "Take care of the children, Francis," she implored.

The Nurses were held in high esteem by their neighbors. They owned a three-hundred acre farm and were one of the more prosperous families in the community. Francis and Rebecca Nurse had eight children who all lived in the area.

The sheriff placed a black hood over Rebecca Nurse's head.

"Oh Lord, help me! It is false. I am clear. For my life now lies in your hands . . ."

Sheriff Corwin gave Rebecca Nurse a push. Her feet slipped off the ladder and the rope went taut as her body spun in mid-air. Her body twitched, jerked, and convulsed. The fall from the ladder had not been sufficient to break her neck. She was slowly being strangled to death. It was a gruesome way to die. After several minutes, the body hung limply from the rope. Rebecca Nurse was dead.

9

ONE-BY-ONE, the other women were brought to the base of the tree, forced up the ladder and had nooses placed around their necks.

And one-by-one Reverend Noyes asked, one last time, for each of the women to confess, to save their very souls, before the black hood was placed over their heads.

Elizabeth Howe replied, "If it was the last moment I was to live, God knows I am innocent . . ." before she was pushed from the ladder.

Susannah Martin remained true to herself. She would not lie even to save herself from the hangman's noose. "I never hurt man, woman or child. I have no hand in witchcraft."

Like the women before her, Sarah Wildes faced her death in the customary fashion: in the spirit of forgiveness, asking God to forgive those who had wronged her. For if not, their souls would appear before Heavenly judgement brimming with hatred.

The last woman to face the hangman was Sarah Good. Reverend Noyes, again, asked for a confession. But he held Sarah Good in contempt and his manner reflected his loathing. She was, after all, a foul-smelling, pipe-smoking, filthy, homeless vagabond, who dragged her five-year-old daughter, Dorcas, around town, begging for handouts. She was vindictive and was often heard muttering curses when the charity of neighbors fell short of her expectations. No one had noticed, at the time of her and Dorcas's arrest four and a half months ago, that under the layers of filthy clothing, she was pregnant. She lost the baby in prison: it was stillborn. And this morning, she had been dragged away from her screaming daughter, who had been left manacled in prison and was now all alone.

Sarah Good was forced up the ladder, hands tied behind her back.

"This is your final chance to confess, Goody Good. You are a witch and you know it," Reverend Noyes stated.

"You are a liar," Sarah Good snapped from her precarious perch upon the ladder. "I am no more a witch than you are a wizard," she said. "And if you take away my life, God will give you blood to drink."

Sarah Good's outburst elicited a collective gasp from the crowd. Only a witch or a spiteful old woman would go to her death with a curse upon her lips. Reverend Noyes nodded to Sheriff Corwin.

The sheriff placed a black hood over Sarah Good's head and, then forcefully pushed her off the ladder. He climbed slowly down. He pulled the ladder away from the tree and lay it on the ground. He walked back to the cart. Before climbing aboard, he looked back at the large oak tree where five bodies swayed gently in the breeze atop Gallows Hill.

* * *

It would be twenty-six years before Sarah Good's prophecy or curse came to pass. In 1718, Reverend Nicholas Noyes died of a brain hemorrhage and most likely choked on his own blood.

10

"NOW TO DEAL with you two," Sheriff Corwin grunted, as he mounted the wheel step and climbed onto the driving board. After the hangings, the crowd slowly disbanded. For such a large group, they were surprisingly quiet as they returned to their farms, shops, and chores.

"Haw," Corwin said, as he snapped the reins causing the cart to jerk forward. The cart made its way toward town by the same route it had travelled earlier that day. Not a word was spoken by the sheriff, his deputies or their prisoners during the entire journey. It was only when they turned left off the main street onto Prison Lane that Sheriff Corwin started barking orders.

"Starling, go tell the magistrates we have new prisoners they'll want to interrogate in the morning. Ride over to Thomas Beadle's tavern; they're probably there." Constable William Starling left immediately.

"Dounton, get out here and give us a hand!" Corwin bellowed in the direction of the prison.

Within moments, the front door flew open and a stout man with a bushy salt-and-pepper beard came barreling down the walkway. William Dounton was the Salem Town jailer.

"Take these two into custody," Corwin snapped, gesturing

toward Dani and Daric.

"Aye," Dounton replied, pulling himself up into the back of the cart. He untethered Dani from the cart first, refastening her shackles before handing her down to Constable Joseph Neale. "Take her down to the cells. I'll be down shortly with this one," he said, turning to unchain Daric.

Once he had re-secured the manacles, Dounton led Daric into the prison.

The first thing that struck him was the stench. As Daric was led down the dark, narrow staircase, the odor grew in intensity. He wasn't sure what was assailing his nose; whether it was the smell of unwashed bodies, human waste, or tobacco smoke. He thought it was likely a combination of all three. He fought desperately to keep what little he had left in his stomach in place.

A memory suddenly came flooding back. When he and Dani were five-years-old, their parents had taken them to the zoo. When they had entered one of the pavilions, Dani had shrieked, covered her nose, done an about-face and left the building. Their mom had followed Dani outside, hearing her little girl protest, "I'm not going in there. It stinks!" To which their mother had replied, "Dani, remember when we had our cat, Tiger? Well his litter box used to smell, didn't it? All animals have different smells. So do people. Remember when we used to go over to Nanny's house and it smelt different from our own? We get used to different smells after a while. Just give it some time and you won't even notice it." Daric thought, *I wonder how Dani's faring now.*

At the base of the stairs, along the wall, hung a collection of fetters. There were leglocks, handlocks, neck irons, and bilboes, large and small. The last were iron rods with sliding shackles to hold prisoners' ankles.

Cells lined both sides of a long narrow corridor. Daric's head grazed the rough wooden beams supporting the floorboards above, as he was led down the aisle. At first glance, it appeared that the women prisoners were on one side and the men on the other. *That can't be good,* Daric thought.

Dounton stopped in front of one of the pitted metal cell doors. He snagged the keys off his belt. After finding the correct one, he opened the cell door. "In ya get," he said, giving Daric a push forward into the cell and quickly locking the door behind him.

"I'll start your bill for room and board," Dounton announced. "What're your names?"

"Daric Delaney and my sister is Dani," Daric said, as pleasantly as he could. He knew he had to keep his cockiness in check. This wasn't the time or place to start stirring up trouble. "By the way, where is she?" he asked.

"Over there," Dounton replied, throwing his left thumb over his shoulder to indicate the other side of the dimly lit prison where the women were being kept.

"You're not from around here, are ya? You have a strange accent and you sure dress funny," Dounton snorted.

"No, we're not from around here. We dropped in accidentally," Daric replied curtly; then wished he hadn't.

"Makes no never mind to me," Dounton muttered over his shoulder, making his way back up the stairs.

Daric looked down at his clothing. He had been sweltering under the summer sun all morning during the proceedings, dressed in his long-sleeved shirt, vest, tie, and overcoat. He was sure Dani was suffering from the heat, too. After all, they had been dressed for a late September evening in Whitechapel, England.

"Dani?" Daric whispered, after working his way toward the end of the cell block.

"Here," she replied quietly, slowly making her way over toward the cell bars.

"Do you have any idea where we?" Daric asked hesitantly. "The countryside looks more like home, but without all the industrialization."

"We're in Massachusetts," Dani replied definitively.

"How can you be so sure?"

"Look around you. These cells are close to overflowing," Dani snapped. "When we arrived, we were arrested on the spot: no questions were asked; no charges were laid. We witnessed the hanging of five women, all accused of witchcraft. It didn't take me long to figure out that we're in Salem, Massachusetts: 1692 to be exact."

"Salem? As in the famous witch-hunt Salem?" Daric asked nervously. "Or should I say infamous?"

"The one and only. And we landed right in the middle of the witchcraft hysteria that descended on this community. How are we going to explain our way out of this one?"

11

UNDER THE VEIL of a moonless night, a rowboat slowly made its way down the North River. The oars silently sliced through the glass-like water. When the boat pulled up to the shore, three men climbed out and hauled it up onto the rocky shoreline. They quietly crept up the side of the hill until they had a view of the old oak tree. They saw several wavering lanterns off in the distance and heard the faint drone of several male voices.

"Will you hurry up; my supper will be cold by the time you get finished," Sheriff Corwin urged his men from horseback.

The deputies were cutting the ropes from which the bodies of the day's hanging victims still dangled, silhouetted against the even darker sky. One-by-one, the bodies fell with a dull thud to the ground, the nooses still around their necks. The deputies grasped the stubs of rope and roughly dragged the corpses to a ledge at the brim of the hill. Once there, they unceremoniously rolled the bodies over the brim. The bodies fell into crevices in the rocks along the side of the hill below, forming one common grave. A few shovelfuls of dirt were thrown over the ledge. The hasty burial left parts of the dead bodies exposed: a foot from one, part of a chin from another, and one hand protruding, as if in a cry out for help, from a third.

"All right, let's go," Corwin ordered, when he felt the job was finished.

The deputies picked up their lanterns and shovels, mounted their horses, and headed back to town.

No graveside prayers had been spoken. These women had been convicted of a capital crime. They had, after all, been trying to destroy the Kingdom of God by working with the devil.

Caleb Buffum had been watching the activities atop the hill from his home nearby. After the sheriff and his men had left, he was about to retire to his house when movement along the side of the hill caught his attention. He cautiously made his way over to investigate.

"Francis, what are you doing here so late?" Buffum asked hesitantly when he recognized his distant relative.

"Caleb, I've come for my wife. We are taking her home and giving her a proper burial," Francis replied coldly.

"But, Francis, the church . . . they're not going to tolerate this. It's a sin . . ."

"I don't care," Francis interrupted. "My wife is no witch, and you know it! Samuel, go get your mother."

Samuel Nurse and his eldest son climbed along the side of the hill to find and retrieve Rebecca Nurse's body.

"She's going to get the Christian burial she deserves," Francis whispered mournfully.

Buffum did in fact know that Rebecca Nurse could not possibly have been a witch. She was one of the most virtuous people he knew.

It took Samuel and his son fifteen minutes, much longer than they had originally planned, to locate Rebecca's body among the rocks and hastily thrown piles of dirt. Once they had uncovered her body, they lifted her from her temporary grave. They carefully wrapped her body in a blanket. Samuel bent down and tenderly cradled his mother's body. With her secure in his arms, he followed his son's lead as they carefully made their way back to the boat.

As his son and grandson passed, Francis followed quietly

behind, with his head held low in mourning.

"Wait, let me help," Buffum offered, running after them.

"Thank you, my friend," Francis said softly.

When they reached the rowboat, Francis climbed in first, followed by his grandson. They took the body from Samuel and Buffum who passed her over the gunwale, being mindful of the oarlocks. Then she was gently placed in the bottom of the boat. Samuel and Buffum pushed the boat away from the shore with Samuel jumping in at the last moment.

"Thank you, Caleb," Francis said quietly, not wanting to draw any unwelcome attention to themselves or to what they were doing.

"Be well, my friend," Buffum replied as he watched the rowboat quietly float away.

The boat rounded the bend in the river and slipped silently downstream past the town. Thankfully the midnight tide was in, allowing the small craft to maneuver north up the shallow estuary to Crane River. The boat then snaked its way along the narrow river to the Nurses' land and Rebecca's waiting family.

That evening, Rebecca Nurse received a proper burial in the family plot down the western slope beyond the house. She was home.

12

DARIC HAD FOUND a small area in the crowded cell where he could sit. Loosening his tie, he placed his overcoat on the straw-strewn floor and sat down. It had been a long, hot and traumatic day. He was hungry and thirsty.

He knew Dani and he would be fine until morning, based on what the sheriff had indicated, when he ordered one of his men to tell the magistrates they would want to interrogate them in the morning. That said, he was not at all sure who the magistrates were; he was equally unsure what interrogation meant. But, for now, they were safe.

Dani, on the other hand, wasn't fine. She was in the early stages of dehydration. She was thirsty that was a given. She had been sweltering in the sun all day, extremely overdressed for this summer weather. Her mouth was dry, her tongue felt coarse, she had one hell of a headache, and she was also experiencing occasional dizziness. On top of all that, she was uncharacteristically irritable, having cut short her conversation with Daric earlier. She needed to rest, and she needed to get some water if that was even possible in here.

As Dani was looking for a place to rest, she overheard two women whispering in a dark corner. "If the authorities would still hang Goody Nurse, even after receiving the governor's pardon, what hope is there for any of us?" asked one woman.

"No one's safe from the hangman's noose," replied the other.

Dani had found an open area in the cell she could claim as her own. She removed her hat, threw down her coat, and curled up on top of it in a fetal position, with her arms covering her head. She closed her eyes in an attempt to shut out the world. But that didn't happen.

"You're not from around here, are you, dear?" an elderly woman remarked.

"No, I'm not," Dani mumbled. Her own voice intensified her headache.

"You don't look so good. Do you feel all right?" another woman asked.

"I need some water," Dani replied, still cradling her head in her arms.

"Here, dear. Sit up and have a drink of this."

Dani slowly opened her eyes and saw a woman holding out a canteen toward her. She looked questioningly at the woman, who simply nodded that she should take it.

"Thank you," Dani said as she took the canteen. She pulled out the stopper and took a small sip. It was cool. It was clean. It was crisp. And it made her crave more. But Dani didn't know what was available to these people, and she didn't want to take another drink even though her body was demanding it of her.

"Go ahead, dear. Have more. You look like you need it. Besides, I'll have some more delivered tomorrow," the woman assured her.

Dani tipped the canteen back and took several big gulps of refreshing water before lowering it.

"Thank you . . ." Dani paused, not knowing the generous woman's name.

"Martha," the woman replied.

Martha Carrier was a thirty-three-year-old farm wife from Andover and the mother of five children. She was strong-willed and articulate. Some of her neighbors thought she was far too independent for a woman of her station.

"Thank you, Martha. I'm Dani." After hesitating for just a moment, Dani asked, "Would it be okay if I offered some water to my brother?" Dani hoped Martha's generosity would continue.

"By all means. Come back and we'll talk when you're done."

"Thank you, Martha. I'll try to repay your kindness," Dani said, as she stood and walked over to the cell bars. Her headache was receding and her dizziness had ended.

"That may be a little difficult to do from in here," Martha said dismally.

"Daric?" Dani whispered, from the end of the cell block.

"Here," came a reply deep within the cell, before Daric appeared.

"Hold out your arms through the bars," Dani instructed.

Daric put his arms between two bars of the cell as far as his manacles would allow. Dani did the same.

"Now, catch." Dani tossed the canteen across the aisle. Daric easily caught it and wriggled it through the bars.

"Take a couple of gulps, not too much. I want to give some back to Martha," Dani explained.

"Who's Martha?" Daric asked between gulps, savoring the cool liquid.

"The lady who owns the canteen," Dani replied. "Sorry, about snapping at you earlier. I wasn't myself."

"I could tell." Daric's concern was evident. "Are you all right?"

"Just dehydrated, but I'm a bit better now."

Daric had gestured that he was ready to toss the canteen back. Dani caught it.

"Try to get some rest," Daric encouraged. "I'll see you in the morning. I think we'll have an interesting day tomorrow when we meet the magistrates."

"We'll need to explain our sudden appearance. We did just pop in from nowhere in front of an entire town. So, try to come up with a reasonable explanation for our being here, something that will make sense to these people," Dani whispered.

"I'll try," Daric replied. "Now get some rest."

Sunday, July 20, 1692

13

DANI HAD BEEN up most of the night. Either she had been talking with Martha or Elizabeth, the other woman who had shown concern over Dani's condition. Or she had been going over different scenarios to explain their sudden appearance in front of a full town of witnesses.

It was difficult to tell what time it was, for there was little light entering the over-crowded cells. Dani could faintly hear the creaking of the wooden stairs. She caught a quick glimpse of a small rodent scurrying away from the light emitted by the approach of a lantern as the dark recesses of the cell diminished.

"Daric and Dani Delaney, step forward," William Dounton bellowed. He was followed by the same two deputies whom Dani and Daric had encountered the day before: Constable William Starling and Constable Joseph Neale.

Dounton opened Daric's cell door and waited for Daric to step out. "Take him upstairs," Dounton instructed, as he re-locked the cell door.

"Come on, you, get moving," Neale said, giving Daric a shove as they followed Starling down the aisle and up the stairs.

Dounton walked to Dani's cell door. He unlocked it, waited for Dani to step through, and closed it firmly behind her.

"Come with me," Dounton instructed. Dani followed him up the stairs. He stopped in front of a wooden door.

"Give me your wrists," Dounton grunted. Dani held out her arms; he released her shackles. Dani's immediate reaction was to rub her sore wrists; it was only then she noticed how raw the left one was. The iron cuff had been rubbing against the skin all night. The chafing had been caused by the extra weight of the travel band sitting on top.

Dounton opened the door. He looked at Dani. "In there," he ordered, gesturing toward the open door. When she had entered, he closed the door behind her. There were already seven women and one man in the room.

"My name is Dr. John Barton. Remove your clothes," he said firmly.

"Why?" The word had jumped out of Dani's mouth before she realized she had said anything.

"Do as you're told, witch" an older woman snapped, as she roughly pulled at Dani's clothes.

"All right," Dani protested, as she batted away the old woman's hands. "I'll do it." These were the only clothes she had, and she didn't need some old biddy ripping them off her. Who knew when or if she would get any more?

Dani was still wearing her nurse's uniform: her ankle-length, deep-blue chambray dress with a white collar and cuffs. Attached to her dress by a gold bead at each breast and tied in the back was a white-on-white striped apron. Her detachable pink armband, signifying she was a new nurse, was around her arm. Her honey-blond hair was pulled up into a bun. Her starched buckram cap and overcoat remained in the jail cell below.

Dani slowly pulled off the pink armband from around her left bicep. She unbuttoned the gold beads and untied the apron, folding it and placing it at her feet. Next she removed her dress and her undergarments, the latter drawing perplexed glances among the women present.

Even though Dr. Barton had seen many naked bodies during his career, he couldn't help but stare at the figure standing before him. *The creator must have paid particular attention to his work that day,* he thought. From her gold-spun hair, to her azure eyes, to her voluptuous breasts, to her slim waist, to her perfect child-bearing hips, right down to her well-shaped legs: she was a vision of beauty.

The women all started to examine Dani's naked body, turning her this way and that. "What are you doing?" she asked nervously.

"They are looking for witch marks, my dear," Dr. Barton replied, as numerous hands continued to roam over Dani's exposed body. "Unnatural permanent marks on the body are indicators of your pact with the devil to seal your service to him. They're evidence of your guilt, if one is found."

This wasn't Dr. Barton's first witch mark examination, nor would it be his last, he feared. Accusations of witchcraft had escalated, especially here in Salem Town. He prayed that this wild hysteria would end soon so he could get back to his real practise. But until then, he was at the beck and call of the magistrates.

"Spread your legs," the old biddy barked. Dani looked pleadingly at the doctor, whose only response was a nod to indicate that she should comply.

After several more minutes Dr. Barton asked, "Well?"

"We see a lot of red marks on the right side of her body," the same old woman replied. "Have to be witch marks."

"More likely flea bites," Dani said sarcastically, knowing she had curled up on her coat for a short time during the night. The cells were infested with fleas, lice and some other small critters she had heard scurrying in the dark.

"I tend to agree," the doctor replied. "You may now get dressed."

Dani snatched up her clothes and quickly dressed before the doctor changed his mind. Once Dani had finished, Dr. Barton opened the door. Dounton entered immediately. He secured the shackles around Dani's wrist, but this time she managed to move the travel band down below the iron cuff to prevent further irritation.

"Come with me," Dounton instructed. As Dani left the room, the door across the hall opened and Daric emerged, accompanied by Constables Neale and Starling and Sheriff Corwin. Dani saw that Daric wasn't wearing his hat or coat, leading her to wonder whether he had left them in his cell. She also caught a glimpse of four men in the room Daric had just left. She assumed he had gone through the same humiliating search she had experienced, hopefully with the same results.

14

DANI AND DARIC were led out of the Salem Town jail by the sheriff and his two deputies. They proceeded with their escort down Prison Lane. Before long, they turned left on to the main street, heading in the direction opposite from where they had travelled the day before. The sheriff hurried ahead, disappearing down the street.

As the group travelled along the main street, Dani saw a few women doing laundry. Several men were cutting hay; which others bundled and carried away. Every step they took raised a cloud of dust. The ground was parched; there had been no rain in weeks.

Dani noticed that the townsfolk stopped what they were doing and gawked at the strangers being led past. She heard whispering among several groups, but couldn't make out any words.

Dani was also struck by the fact that everyone appeared to be dressed in the same dull dark clothes. There were no vibrant colors anywhere. Even the children were dressed in dark clothes. *Come to think of it, there isn't much color here,* Dani thought, realizing her blue dress and white apron stood out in stark contrast.

After several minutes, the group came to a two-story wooden structure. A sign hanging over the front door read Beadle's Tavern. The deputies quickly ushered Dani and Daric inside.

The tavern's interior was rather dark and musty. Its main room was large and included a big hearth with a generous fire burning brightly. The furniture consisted of several wooden tables, most with benches and the rest with chairs. For Daric, however, the most notable feature of all was the aroma of roasting meat. He couldn't remember the last time he had eaten anything.

There were only a few patrons at this time of the morning, making the place look very spacious. Dani and Daric were led to the table closest to the hearth. It was already occupied by six men. Dani recognized two of them: the man who had roughly seized her yesterday who looks like Uncle Richard and Sheriff Corwin. *So this is where he ran off to,* she thought.

Three of the other four men were all dressed alike: each wore a dark suit, with a white stiff wing collar with bands. The bands looked rather like a necktie, comprising two flat strips of linen hanging down the front of the neck, forming an upside down 'V'. Each man had a black robe draped over the back of his chair. The forth man was dressed like the other three, except his bands appeared longer than theirs.

The men with the shorter bands were three of the nine justices or magistrates that had been appointed to the Court of Oyer and Terminer *(to hear and determine)*. The governor had instituted this judicial body to deal with the growing number of prisoners accused of witchcraft, rather than having them dealt with by the Superior Court, which sat only at certain times and was becoming overwhelmed by the number of these cases.

Shortly after Dani and Daric were ushered to the table, the tavern door opened and a group of young women entered; all appeared to be in their mid to late teens. Dani noted that they were dressed much alike: a simple white shift under a bodice, a long skirt that came in below the bodice and hair tucked up under a white cap. Their dresses were either black or brown.

Accompanying the young women was Reverend Nicholas Noyes, whom Dani and Daric had run into yesterday. He had been the one asking the condemned to confess to save their souls.

The newest arrivals made their way over to the table next to the magistrates. Noyes sat down closest to the magistrates. He pulled out a pen and some paper in preparation for taking notes during the examination that was about to begin. The young women sat opposite Noyes; all stared wide-eyed at the strangers in their midst.

One magistrate rose from his seat and pointed at Daric. He then turned and walked through a doorway into another room. Constable Neale gave Daric a shove, directing him to follow the magistrate.

Daric entered the small room. Standing beside the magistrate in the middle of the room was Sheriff Corwin. He was holding two pieces of rope. Daric hadn't realized the sheriff had got up from the table.

"Lie face down on the floor," the sheriff instructed.

"What are you going to do?" Daric said as he complied reluctantly. He knew he had no choice in the matter. His shackled hands laid out in front of him.

Neale knelt in front of Daric and removed his fetters. Corwin handed Neale a length of rope, which he used to tie Daric's wrists behind his back. He used the second piece, the longer of the two, to bind Daric's feet together.

After securing Daric's feet, Neale yanked the rope upwards, lifting Daric's feet off the ground. He next looped the free end of the rope around Daric's neck and tied it off. Daric's head was pulled back to meet his feet.

"We use this to extract confessions," Corwin explained.

"It's torture, no matter what you call it," Daric gasped out. That remark earned him a swift kick to his ribs.

15

DANI WATCHED AS Daric had been led out of the main room. She stood alone, facing the three remaining men in black and the man who seized her yesterday that she labeled 'Uncle Richard'. Reverend Noyes sat at the adjacent table with the six young girls.

"You are not from around here," one official stated. "What's your name?"

"My name is Dani Delaney," she said firmly, as she stood erect in front of the men who were here for her interrogation.

"Well, Dani Delaney. Let me make the introductions. I am Judge John Hathorne. I am the chief examiner and will be asking most of the questions today," he said.

"To my left is Chief Justice Bartholomew Gedney. At the end of the table is Reverend Richeard Barak Case. And across from me is Reverend John Higginson."

Judge John Hathorne was fifty-one years of age and the only one at the table who wasn't clean shaven. He sported a well-trimmed handlebar moustache, which at this moment contained a crumb of bread from his recently consumed meal.

Chief Justice Bartholomew Gedney was a few years younger than Hathorne, but several pounds heavier. As chief justice, Gedney had to be one of a minimum of five judges to preside over these cases.

As the senior Salem minister at the age of seventy-six, Reverend John Higginson was in attendance to conduct the opening and closing prayers and to witness the proceedings. Except for his two deluded assistant ministers, Reverend Noyes and Case, he like many of his fellow clerics, did not approve of the witch trials.

As for Reverend Case, Dani was sure he was one of Uncle Richard's ancestors. The name was right; only the first part–Richeard as Hathorne pronounced it–was from Old English: *Ric* meaning ruler and *heard* meaning hard. And, in terms of appearance, the man in front of her could have been Uncle Richard's twin. It was uncanny. *But why do they keep appearing in our travels,* she pondered?

"You understand that you are charged to be guilty of sundry acts of witchcraft? How do you plead?" Judge Hathorne asked, snapping Dani back from her musings.

"I'm not a witch, therefore I'm not guilty," Dani replied boldly.

"Speak the truth," Hathorne pressed. Before Dani could answer, he turned toward the young girls at the next table. "And so you who are afflicted. You must speak the truth also as you will answer to it before God on another day."

"I do speak the truth," Dani insisted.

"Dani Delaney, what evil spirit have you familiarity with?"

"I have no knowledge or acquaintance with any evil spirits. I told you I'm not a witch."

"Have you made a contract with the devil?"

"No."

Before Hathorne could ask another question, the young girls screamed out in anguish. The sound had the same effect as fingernails on a chalkboard; it grated at Hathorne's every nerve. He turned his attention back to Dani.

"Why do you hurt these children?" Hathorne demanded, finding it difficult to concentrate amidst the anguished wails of the afflicted girls.

"How can I hurt them from over here?" Dani asked referring to the distance between herself and the screaming girls.

"Who do you employ, then, to do it?"

"I employ nobody. I told you I'm not a witch!"

"What creature do you employ, then?"

"I employ no creature. I am innocent!"

"Then, explain to this panel how you happened to suddenly appear, out of nowhere, if it not be by witchcraft magic," Hathorne demanded.

Dani had been waiting for this question. Actually, she had been dreading it. She had tried to come up with an acceptable answer all night. How does one explain suddenly materializing in front of an entire town and not sound utterly insane or bewitched?

"The devil holds her tongue," Case bellowed from the end of the table. A murmur arose among the magistrates in response to Case's accusation. The young girls wailed louder.

"Have you made a contract with the devil?" Hathorne asked again.

"As I said before, I have made no contract with the devil," Dani insisted. The conduct of the young girls was making her nervous. Dani was very familiar with what had happened during the Salem witch trials; she had majored in History, after all, and these trials had always intrigued her. She could never have imagined, in a million years, that she would actually be a part of them.

"Look upon her, all of you," Hathorne ordered the afflicted girls, who had reduced their anguished cries to muffled moans. "Is this the person who hurts you?"

The girls could only nod in response because they were still being tormented.

"Dani Delaney, do you not see now what you have done? Why do you not tell us the truth? Why do you torment these poor children?" Hathorne asked.

"I'm not tormenting them."

"Who do you employ, then?"

"I employ nobody."

Reverend Higginson was finding the line of questioning redundant and ridiculous. Nothing Hathorne was asking was directed at discovering evidence of guilt. A bunch of girls, most likely vying for some attention, were screaming out as if by Hathorne's own bidding; it was ludicrous. It felt more like a circus than an examination to him.

"How do they come to be tormented, then?" demanded Hathorne.

"I have no idea," Dani snapped back, losing patience on this merry-go-round of questioning. "Where's my brother?"

"He's being taken care of," Case jumped in, his pencil-thin lips spreading out into a savage grin across his smug face.

Reverend Higginson thought now would be the opportune time to check on what was happening with Dani's brother. He had been wondering why Dani's brother had been removed from these proceedings.

As he left the table, Higginson recalled how people from all over the countryside had journeyed to see the afflicted girls. With all this sudden attention, the girls seemed to have increased their strange antics. First it had been on street corners; then, one Sunday, there had been an outburst in church. Now, it seemed that not a Sunday passed without the girls having fits in church. It seemed peculiar to him, however, that the interruptions occurred only during a lull in the services, never during the sermons or the prayers.

16

IT DIDN'T MATTER how big or strong one was because it didn't take long for one's back to weaken. Once that happened, the legs and head would lower and the rope would tighten around the neck. The slow strangulation was agonizing.

Daric wasn't sure how much more he could take and they had yet to ask him any questions. It seemed almost as if they took great pleasure from watching others suffer. The tender flesh around his neck had crimped and bruised and was burning. His eyes bulged as if they were ready to pop out of their sockets. He felt a trickle of moisture run from his nose; when he licked his lips, he knew from the coppery taste on his tongue that it was blood.

Daric was struggling to catch each and every breath. He knew if he passed out, his legs would fall and the rope would crush his airway. He had to hold on, for Dani's sake. He heard the creak of a door opening behind him.

"Cut him loose at once," Reverend Higginson ordered, slamming the door behind him. He glared coldly at the sheriff who hesitated for only a moment before nodding to Neale. Higginson then spun and faced the magistrate.

"Judge Corwin, how could you let this happen? This is no way to extract a confession!" Higginson scolded.

"We almost had one, no thanks to you," the sheriff interjected, clearly irritated.

"Corwin? You his father?" Daric rasped, lying flat out on the floor, waiting for his hands and feet to be unbound.

"Uncle," the judge replied. Judge Jonathan Corwin was a thirty-year older version of Sheriff George Corwin and was a prominent fixture at the witch trials.

"Jonathan, you know very well that the *Body of Liberties* states that no man shall be forced by torture to confess any crime against himself nor any other, unless it be in some capital case where he is first fully convicted by clear and sufficient evidence to be guilty. Even then, it says that the torture cannot be barbarous and inhumane. This man hasn't even gone to trial, let alone been convicted," Higginson declared.

"We needed information. This was the quickest way to get it," the sheriff spat angrily.

Ignoring the sheriff, Higginson continued to attack the magistrate's lack of moral judgement. "Jonathan, this is no better than branding, burning, or racking. It's simply another means of torture."

"That's what I was trying to tell them," Daric rasped, earning another kick in his ribs for the remark. He couldn't contain the moan from passing his lips.

"Stop that at once! I won't stand for any further abuse of this man. Help him up," Higginson ordered.

The sheriff's expression darkened as he stared coldly at Higginson. "Do it," the sheriff growled, his gaze never leaving Higginson's. Neale knew the order was directed at him.

Daric was helped to his feet. He bent over to try to ease his aching back muscles. Neale grabbed his bruised and raw wrists and slapped on the shackles.

As he was being led out of the room, Daric leaned closer to the reverend and whispered, "They didn't even ask me one question."

17

"WOULD YOU HAVE me accuse myself?" Dani asked tersely. She had used her hypermnesia, her ability to recall anything and everything she had ever read, so she could muster an appropriate response. She thought it might serve her better if she sounded like a local.

"Yes, if you be guilty," said Hathorne.

"How far have you complied with Satan whereby he takes this advantage of you?" asked Judge Gedney, who spoke for the first time during the proceedings.

"I will say it again. I am innocent. I do not torment these girls," Dani persisted.

"But most of the afflicted here identify you as their tormenting specter. Here is the clear evidence," said Hathorne, pointing at the girls, who, as if on cue, wailed louder. Just then the door to the other room opened and Daric was led out, followed by the others. Dani took one look at her brother and ran to his side. Her dash caught Constable Starling flat-footed. He swiftly gave chase.

"Are you all right? What did they do to you?" Dani asked, as she reached up and wiped the blood from Daric's face.

"I would like a do-over," Daric rasped through his bruised throat. He was holding his left arm tightly against his side. His sore ribs were making it difficult to breathe comfortably.

Dani gave the sheriff a withering glare. "What did you do?" she thundered, lunging forward. She was like a mother bear protecting her cub.

"What's done is done, my dear," Higginson said, as he stepped between Dani and the sheriff to intercept her charge. Higginson hoped to temper her rage, which was mounting.

"Gentlemen, these two have had enough for today," Higginson stated flatly to the magistrates. "I'll have the sheriff and his men take them back to their cells."

"You have no voice here, Reverend. Let them continue with their questioning," Case barked defiantly.

Higginson knew he had no authority in the proceedings. "And neither do you, Reverend Case," Higginson countered. He turned his attention back to the magistrates, hoping they would agree to his request.

"This man has been tortured. Tying a man's neck and heels is an extreme departure from the usual methods used to get a confession in New England. It's torture. Confessions should be obtained through questioning. And the proceedings I've witnessed here today, I find suspect," Higginson said contemptuously.

"You . . ." Case started to interject again, but was abruptly cut off.

"As you wish, Reverend," Hathorne said coldly. "But these two will be held over for trial on suspicion of witchcraft. You may take them away." With that, Hathorne reached for his glass on the table. With two loud gulps, he downed its remaining contents and then banged it down on the table. A voluptuous bar wench appeared from nowhere and immediately refilled it.

18

WHEN THEY HAD returned to their cells, Daric realized that someone had stolen his overcoat and hat. Although the weather didn't call for a coat, Daric was hoping to continue using it as a makeshift bed. He had also thought he might be able to barter the items later for food and drink.

Daric searched his cell to see whether he could find his missing belongings. He found nothing. He would have conducted a more thorough search, but his ordeal this morning had taken more out of him than he had originally thought.

"What happened to you?" one of his fellow inmates asked, as Daric slowly made his way back to his corner.

"They tied my neck and heels, as Reverend Higginson called it. Me, I call it torture," Daric whispered. His throat was still badly bruised, and it hurt to swallow. He just wanted to lie down and take the pressure off his back and ease the strain on his sore ribs.

"Why did they do that?" the man asked, perplexed.

"I believe they were looking for a confession. Funny thing was, they never asked me any questions," Daric explained dryly, as he carefully eased himself down, flinching once from the pain.

"That's barbaric!"

"No kidding."

His fellow inmate extended his hand. "I'm John, by the way."

John Proctor was a brawny man and a tireless worker. He had to be in order to support his wife and eleven children, six from his two previous marriages. He had a seven-hundred-acre farm southeast of Salem Village. He had also been bequeathed substantial property in Ipswich from his father. At the age of sixty, he had the distinction of being the first man accused of witchcraft.

Daric started to pull himself up, but John placed his hand on Daric's shoulder. "Stay put. You need to rest. You've been through quite an ordeal."

"Thanks. I'm Daric."

"Pleased to meet you, Daric. I wish it was under better circumstances," John said sadly.

* * *

When Daric awoke, he wasn't sure what time it was. There was never very much light in the cell to begin with, so it was difficult to determine whether it was night or day.

"How are you feeling?" John asked, when he saw Daric stir.

"A little better . . . oy . . ." Daric groaned when he tried to sit up. "That hurt."

"It will for a while. Try to move slowly, give your back a chance to recover," John offered.

"Good advice," Daric sighed, as he leaned back against the cool stone wall.

"I saved this for you," John said, handing Daric a chunk of bread and a bowl with some pallid liquid. "You were asleep when they came to offer dinner."

Daric gratefully took the bowl and bread and wasted no time in devouring the lot. He wasn't even sure what he ate, or whether it was good, as it flew past his taste buds and into his empty belly. Even the protests from his sore throat couldn't stop the onslaught of sustenance as it barrelled past.

"Here, wash it down with this. That slop isn't fit to feed the pigs," John snorted.

Daric grasped the proffered canteen and pulled out the stopper. He took a huge gulp and immediately had to stop it from spewing out of his mouth. He swallowed hard and started to cough violently. Severe pain shot through his damaged ribs with every cough. He tried to ease the pain by holding his left arm against his side until the coughing subsided.

"Whoa," Daric gasped, as he fought to catch his breath. "I was expecting water, not whiskey. Not that it's not appreciated, but you could have warned me," Daric bantered.

"I thought it would help. It'll be good for your throat, too. Have another belt." John gestured to the canteen.

"Don't mind if I do." Daric took another drink, a more respectable amount this time.

"I need to go check on my sister," Daric said, struggling to his feet.

"Relax, she's fine," John said.

"How do you know?" Daric asked, somewhat baffled.

"My wife made sure she got something to eat and drink."

"Your wife? She's in here too?" Daric interjected, before John could continue.

"Yes, we've been in custody for about three months, still waiting for our trial. My wife also told your sister that you were resting comfortably," John continued. "Rest a few more hours, then go talk to her. Everyone will be asleep by then, so you can have a quiet and somewhat private conversation."

Daric's protesting back made the decision for him. *What's a few more hours,* he thought.

19

"DANI?" DARIC WHISPERED, hoping not to disturb those around him.

"Here," Dani replied, appearing at the bars. "How are you feeling?"

"A little better. Ribs are still killing me; it's hard to find a comfortable position. And my back's still in spasm, but then again, you always called me a pain," Daric said, trying to add levity to ease Dani's worry.

"Did you get something to eat?" they asked at the same time and then chuckled lightly. "Twin-thing," they both joked. It was a long-standing habit; whenever they spoke in unison, they would follow it up by saying 'twin-thing'. Growing up, they had also had a tendency to complete each other's sentences, a practice that irritated them both.

Dani and Daric spent the next few hours relating the events of their day. Dani carried the majority of the conversation. She had made a few new friends, allies, cohorts; it was hard to put a name to them under the current circumstances. But she knew they all had each other's backs. She had already been the beneficiary of this support. Martha had made sure Dani's coat and hat had remained right where Dani had left them; she had even fended off would-be thieves, including the sheriff's wife.

Based on Dani's own vast knowledge and what she had learned, she brought Daric up to speed. "Daric, these people are Puritans. The Bible not only serves as religious instruction, but as a legal guide as well. Churches are not only places of worship, they're also the seat of government. It's where men go to elect officials, debate laws, and review evidence when disputes arise. There is very little separation between church and state."

"As for the children, they're taught early on to fear the devil. They're taught to tremble before God. Puritans learn that there is no guarantee of reaching heaven, no matter how moral or righteous they are. They believe they are God's chosen. They believe God punishes every sin with illness, pain, suffering or worse. And it's this belief that has sparked this community's hysteria about witches and witchcraft."

"And to throw more fuel onto the fire, these people face many difficulties, such as crop failures, starvation, small pox, long frigid winters, dry hot summers, Indian attacks, and the war with the French. It's no wonder they think they're losing God's favor and that the devil has entered their community. Everything that goes wrong gets blamed on the devil and his minions: the witches. They're looking to eradicate the devil from their midst." Dani paused and took a moment to catch her breath.

"Well, I don't think they're going about it the right way," Daric added bluntly.

"And what lit the flame that started the fire was a book written by a Boston minister by the name of Cotton Mather," Dani explained. "It was a bestseller of its time. It detailed an incident of witchcraft back in 1688. It described in depth the symptoms and torments of witchcraft. That book just so happens to be in the house of Reverend Samuel Parris, the place where all this witchcraft hysteria began."

"Daric, before this is all over, hundreds will be arrested, lives will be destroyed, communities will be torn apart. Several of the accused will die in jail, nineteen will be hanged, and one man will be pressed to death. Even two dogs will be shot and killed because they were suspected of witchcraft," Dani added.

"But we'll be okay. We know how to get out of here. We just have to wait for the right opportunity," Daric assured her.

"I know," Dani said dejectedly. "It's just that the most important aspect of history is what we learn from it. As philosopher George Santayana said, *Those who cannot remember the past are condemned to repeat it.* But we didn't learn!"

"What are you talking about?" Daric could see that something was gnawing at his sister.

"We did it again. There was another massive witch hunt in the 1950s, during the so-called McCarthy Era. Thousands of Americans were dragged before the Senate Committee run by Joseph McCarthy. They were questioned about their political and religious beliefs. The entire process was in violation of their constitutional rights. Many had their lives and careers ruined because they were accused of being communists. Why didn't we learn?" Dani asked dejectedly.

"Dani, the only defence against witch hunts, past or present, is to educate people to be tolerant of those with differing beliefs. And until that happens, the uneducated will continue to be prey to those with their own political agenda and unfortunately witch hunts will continue," Daric said miserably.

"I suppose you're right," Dani mumbled.

"Look, since we're not going anywhere anytime soon, why don't we use this time to see if we can figure out how this time travel thing works," Daric whispered to Dani.

"Did you say time travel?" a groggy male voice asked.

"He said time travels quickly when you're in here," Dani offered by way of explanation.

"On the contrary, my dear," a raspy female voice from the shadows behind Dani interjected. "It travels as slow as a fish trying to swim upstream."

Dani shrugged helplessly, looked over at Daric, and whispered, "We'll talk later."

Monday, July 21, 1692

20

"YOUR DAUGHTER HERE," Hathorne began, "has confessed to some things that you did not tell us about."

"I did not know it," Ann Foster protested.

Ann Foster was a feeble, sick, seventy-year-old who had now been widowed for seven years. She had few friends she could call on for help.

When Ann Foster had first been arrested, she had claimed adamantly that she was innocent of the charge of witchcraft. Now, she wasn't so sure. She was confused. This was the fourth time she had been questioned.

Earlier in the morning, Ann Foster had been brought to Beadle's Tavern. She now stood before Magistrates Hathorne, Corwin, and Gedney and Reverend Higginson, just as Dani had the day before. At the end of the table sat twenty-year-old Mary Warren, the only one of the afflicted girls from yesterday who had returned.

"Oh, mother! We have forsaken Christ, and the devil has got hold of us. How shall we get clear of this evil one?" Mary Lacy cried.

Mary Lacy was Ann Foster's forty-year-old daughter. With her was her eighteen-year-old daughter, Mary Lacy Jr. It wasn't uncommon to name, not only male children, but, female children after their parents.

"Goody Foster, you cannot be free of this snare if your heart and mouth remain stubbornly closed," Hathorne cautioned.

Ann Foster muttered something under her breath, but no one caught the words.

"The devil whispers to her. Can't you see?" Mary Warren stated, alarmed.

"I did not see the devil," said Goody Foster. "I was praying to the Lord."

"What Lord?" Hathorne asked.

"To God."

"What god do you witches pray to?" Hathorne pressed.

"I cannot tell, the Lord helps me," replied Goody Foster.

Hathorne fell silent. His questioning of Goody Foster was getting nowhere. He gestured to her to sit down. She was glad to do so.

Hathorne and the other magistrates turned their attention to Ann Foster's daughter, Mary Lacy Sr. During an hour of intense questioning, she told them how she had flown in the devil's arms to Newbury Falls a few years before. She explained that, while there, she had witnessed the devil baptize six witches and declare Mistress Bradbury, Goody How and Goody Nurse his forever. She stated that she didn't know the other three witches who had been present, but she believed them to have been among the chiefs and higher powers.

The magistrates finally indicated they were finished with Mary Lacy Sr.; they had heard all they wanted to hear from her.

Next, it was Mary Lacy Jr.'s turn to be examined.

21

AS GOODY FOSTER and her daughter Mary Lacy Sr. were removed from the room, Mary Warren started to convulse violently.

Earlier in the year, Mary Warren and her family had fled the area to get away from the Indian attacks. Mary's parents, however, were both killed, leaving her with virtually no one. She found employment as a servant in the Proctor household. When the witchcraft hysteria first started in Salem Village, Mary became one of the afflicted girls. Mary's seizures had suddenly stopped when John Proctor had threatened to beat her. Mary then posted a note on the meetinghouse's notice board, thanking the villagers' for their prayers, which she claimed had stopped her seizures.

Posting the notice at the meeting house, the place where the villagers all gathered for worship, caused the other afflicted girls to declare Mary Warren as having joined the devil; it explained her miraculous cure. The afflicted girls had feared that they would be betrayed. On the day of Mary's examination, she claimed the afflicted girls were merely playacting when they had their seizures. But during the course of the examination, Mary became confused, contradicting herself. The magistrates simply ignored Mary's accusations regarding the afflicted girls' integrity. Seeing no other option and to save herself, Mary fell back into seizures, thus avoiding having to answer any further questions. After a while, the magistrates let her go. She was no longer a suspect.

"How dare you come in here and bring the devil with you to afflict this poor creature," Hathorne blurted out, glaring directly at Mary Lacy Jr.

"I know nothing of it," said Mary Jr.

"Deputy, take Mary Lacy Jr. over to Mary Warren," Hathorne ordered. As Constable Neale escorted Mary Jr. to the end of the table, Hathorne continued, "I want her to attempt a touch test on Mary Warren." Such a test had neither legal nor religious approval, but was often used in the examination of those accused of being witches. It reflected the belief, shared by Hathorne, that a tormenting specter caused an afflicted person's convulsions and that the specter would return to its owner if the owner touched the afflicted person. Hence, if an afflicted person's convulsions stopped at the touch of an accused, the accused was deemed to have caused the affliction and, therefore, to be a witch.

"Go on. Touch Mary Warren," Hathorne directed Mary Jr.

Mary Jr. extended her arm and touched Mary Warren. The convulsions stopped immediately.

"Do you acknowledge now you are a witch?"

"Yes," said Mary Jr., surrendering to the court.

The magistrates continued to ask Mary Jr. one question after another. Initially, she gave only short answers. Gradually, she provided more details. At times, she altered the details

"Mary Lacy Jr.," Hathorne advised, "you must freely confess what you know. By repenting, you may still escape the devil's power.

"The Lord help me!" Mary Jr. cried.

Through the onslaught of questions, Mary Jr. admitted that her mother often wished the devil would take her. She admitted to hurting, not only Mary Warren, but others as well. She said that Richard Carrier, Martha's son, encouraged her to avenge an earlier beating of Richard's younger brother, Andrew. Martha Carrier was currently in the Salem Town prison, accused of witchcraft.

As Mary Jr. continued to set out her confessions, Mary Warren started to convulse again.

"There!" exclaimed Mary Jr., pointing. "There, standing on your table; it's a specter of a man."

The men sitting around the table immediately pushed their chairs back and moved away from the table. "Do you know who it is?" Judge Gedney asked.

"Yes," Mary Jr. replied. "It's Richard Carrier. Oh wait, I see another. It's his brother, Andrew."

"Richard told me his mother gave him something that he must show no one," Mary Jr. said, as she carried on with her confession.

"What did Goody Carrier give him?"

"It is a writing," Mary Jr. explained, "that the devil gave to Goody Carrier. You know, she's been a witch ever since she lived in Billerica."

"What else can you tell us about this writing?" Hathorne probed. It was well known that the devil had a book he forced people to sign, making them his to command at will.

"I know only what Richard, that wicked wretch, told me, that it would make him as powerful as his mother," Mary Jr. replied.

Mary Jr. abruptly took her confession in another direction. "I flew to the Village meeting," she told the magistrates

"By anointing yourself?" Hathorne asked.

"No, perched on a pole carried by the devil," she clarified. Returning to her story about the Village meeting, she went on, "The devil was the only man there. No, wait, it wasn't the devil. It was Richard Carrier."

"But your mother and grandmother said a minister was there," Hathorne reminded her.

"That's right. There was one," Mary Jr. agreed, "and I think he is now in prison."

"Are you sure it wasn't Reverend George Burroughs?" Hathorne asked suggestively.

"I suppose it was," Mary Jr. conceded.

"I saw red wine poured into clay cups and brown bread being served. The devil called out seventy-six witches' names and pressed them to do his will. He promised that they would be given crowns in Hell and that Goody Carrier would be a Queen in Hell and George Burroughs, a pretty little man, would be King."

"Can the devil hurt in the shape of any person without their consent?" asked Hathorne.

"No," said Mary Lacy Jr., putting to rest any further doubts. This confirms the court's theory that the devil uses only willing persons to carry out his deeds.

22

THE MAGISTRATES CALLED for Ann Foster and Mary Lacy Sr. to join Mary Lacy Jr. and to be gathered before them. They wished to question all three generations together.

"Here is a poor miserable child, a wretched mother, and grandmother," Judge Corwin muttered, as he watched the two elderly women being ushered back into the room.

"Oh, Mother. Oh, Mother!" young Mary cried, when she saw her mother enter the main room. "Why did you give me to the devil?"

"I'm so sorry, my child. The devil tempted me to do it," Mary Lacy Sr. admitted.

"Oh, Mother, your wishes have now come to pass, for you have often wished that the devil would fetch me away alive. Oh, my heart will break within me. Oh, that my mother should have ever given me to the devil." Mary Jr. burst into tears. "Oh, Lord, comfort me, and bring out all that are witches."

When Ann Foster entered the room, Mary Jr. cried out, "Oh, Grandmother, why did you give me to the devil? Why did you persuade me? Do not deny it, Grandmother. You have been a very bad woman in your time."

Hathorne was starting to think that Mary Jr. was showing signs of repentance. '*She might yet free herself from the devil's snares,*' he thought. He could not say the same of Mary Jr.'s grandmother. He looked hard at Ann Foster. "You, old woman, you have shown something of relenting, yet you retain a lie in the mouth."

"Oh, Grandmother, you must speak the truth," Mary Jr. pleaded when Ann Foster was brought forward.

"I know Martha Carrier was at the great meeting and that her sister, Mary Toothaker, and her niece, Martha Toothaker, had been with the witches, too. I also know Richard Carrier is no good," Ann stated.

"Was he at the great meeting as well?" Hathorne asked.

"I don't remember," Ann replied.

"Remember, Grandmother. He was there," Mary Jr. encouraged.

"I suppose he was," Ann said reluctantly. She was very confused at this point in the proceedings.

"I hope he gets arrested," Mary Jr. chimed in.

"I knew Richard Carrier was a witch, because he claimed he could make cattle drop dead in their tracks, if he wanted to," Mary Sr. added.

While the last line of questioning had been taking place, Mary Warren had been watching Richard Carrier's specter as it moved away from the table. It came in closer: she recoiled in fear.

After another thirty minutes of questioning, the magistrates accepted the women's confessions as fact. The court looked upon any inconsistencies in testimony as simple evasions of their questioning. The three generations had confessed to being witches. And they had named others during the process; that's what mattered.

The confessed witches were led away to the Salem jail; meanwhile the magistrates issued an arrest warrant for Richard and Andrew Carrier.

* * *

During the entire examination, sitting alone in a dark corner, out of view but within earshot of the proceedings, was another man.

He had quietly slipped into town and found the perfect, obscure corner in the tavern. Reverend Increase Mather was fifty-three-years-old. He was long-faced with a high forehead. His dark cloak and the wide-brimmed felt hat covering his silver hair hid him well in the shadows, out of reach of the flicking light from the hearth fire.

Mather was one of Boston's most prominent preachers and scholars. Mather and his fellow ministers were considered the community's leading citizens. They were the main source of inspiration and education. It was their job to minister to the sick, pray for the dying, and preside over funerals. They were also involved in resolving disputes. Mather had come to witness an examination, first-hand. And he had seen and heard enough. He paid his bill and left the tavern.

Tuesday, July 22, 1692

23

THIS MORNING RICHARD and Andrew Carrier were brought from their farm in Andover to stand in front of the magistrates at Beadle's Tavern.

Richard Carrier was tall for his age of eighteen years. He would take after his father, who was well over six feet tall. The young man had a muscular frame with large calloused hands. He was proud, but quick, with a short fuse. Andrew was three years younger than his brother, Richard, whom he idolized. Andrew hadn't reached his growth spurt yet, and he had a smaller physique.

The brothers now stood before Magistrates Hathorne, Corwin and Gedney and Reverend Higginson. At another table sat Mary Lacy Sr. and Mary Lacy Jr., who had accused the Carrier boys of witchcraft. With them were six young girls, the same ones who had been at Dani and Daric's examination.

"Richard and Andrew Carrier, you are charged to be guilty of sundry acts of witchcraft. How do you plead, Richard?" Hathorne asked.

"Not guilty," Richard answered firmly.

"And you, Andrew, how do you plead?"

"Nnnnotttt guiltttty," Andrew stuttered; he was so nervous. He stepped closer to his brother for reassurance and comfort.

"Did your mother give you a book," Hathorne asked, staring hard at Richard, who refused to answer the question.

"Did you not hear me? Answer the question. Did your mother give you a book?" Hathorne raised his voice. Again there was no response.

"Look, there's Goody Carrier," said Mary Lacy Sr., pointing at the magistrates' table. "She's with the devil and they're preventing them from answering."

Hathorne decided to take another approach. He pressured Mary Lacy Jr. to recount what she had told the court the day before. Richard listened carefully, still refusing to acknowledge the accusation.

"Now, Richard Carrier," said Hathorne, "what do you say to this evidence?"

"It's a lie," Richard said resolutely.

At that moment, the six young girls started to scream in agony. Two were rolling on the floor in pain; one had blood dripping from her nose.

"Remove them," Hathorne ordered, gesturing toward the Carrier boys. Constable Neale and Sheriff Corwin took them into another room. Once the boys had been removed, the girls seemed to calm somewhat.

* * *

After forty-five minutes, the two Carrier boys were ushered back into the main room. Andrew was clinging to Richard; they had to be forcibly pulled apart.

"I'm sorry. I'm sorry," Andrew cried quietly, over and over.

"Richard," said Hathorne, when the young man was standing in front of him, "though you have been very obstinate, tell us how long ago it is since you were taken in this snare?"

Richard reluctantly agreed to tell the magistrates whatever it was they wanted to hear: being at the great meeting in the village, tormenting these young girls among others, having signed the devil's book. He also provided names of others who were at the great meeting, but he used only names of individuals who weren't already accused and awaiting trial. He avoided accusing anyone new.

While they had been in the other room, Richard had decided it might be better to plead guilty. He was convinced that it was the only way he and his brother were going to survive. He didn't want to see Andrew suffer any longer.

After the questioning was concluded, the brothers were held over for trial. They were escorted to the Salem jail. When they arrived, Andrew was still clinging to his brother, sobbing quietly.

Dounton took the brothers to a cell, opened its door and indicated that they should enter. He closed the door firmly behind them.

"Is he okay?" John Proctor asked when he noticed some blood on Andrew's hands.

Another man moved forward to provide assistance. "Come, sit over here," he said, showing the boys to a relatively quiet area of the cell. "My name is Reverend Burroughs. Can you tell me what happened?"

Reverend George Burroughs was small in stature, but much stronger than he looked. He was handsome with dark features at forty-two years of age. He was learned, articulate, brave, and fearless, for he was one of only two ministers brave enough to serve in the dangerous outer reaches of coastal Maine.

Daric had also made his way over to hear the boys' story. He gingerly eased his way down to the ground and slowly leaned his back against the wall. His ribs were a continual reminder of his own recent examination.

Richard told those who had gathered around how the brothers had been dragged out of bed, manacled, and brought to the town for questioning. "When I said we were innocent, they took us to another room. I was determined to stand my ground. Then they threw us down on the ground and tied our neck and heels," Richard explained, as he comforted his brother. "They tied Andrew so roughly that he started to bleed around his neck and wrists. And when he cried and begged to be released, I couldn't take it anymore. I would have rather died than give in, but I couldn't see him suffer anymore," Richard said looking down at Andrew's head in his lap. "After that, I agreed to say whatever the magistrates wanted to hear."

"How can they get away with using torture to get a confession? It's barbaric! It's unlawful," John erupted. "Something has to be done!"

Just then Andrew stirred and whimpered, "Mother?" But his throat was so sore that barely a croak came out.

"Mother?" Daric asked sympathetically.

"He thinks our mother might be here. She was arrested on May 31st," Richard explained. "But I think she might be in Boston."

"What's her name?" Reverend Burroughs asked.

"Martha. Martha Carrier."

Wednesday, July 23, 1692

24

JOHN PROCTOR HAD been stewing all night about the Carrier boys' abuse, as well as Daric's torment a few days earlier. "It's not right, it's just not right," he muttered over and over.

"Then do something about it," Daric prompted.

"What can I do about it from in here?" John replied despondently.

"You'll think of something," Daric encouraged. "You did last night, when you found the boys' mother and when you convinced the jailer to move Andrew over to her cell."

"A good man fights for his family, but a great man fights for the greater good," Reverend Burroughs said softly.

John Proctor had spent the best part of the day gathering his thoughts. Once he was sure of his course of action, he asked the jailer for pen and paper. Under the light of a solitary candle, and on top of an old wooden crate, John Proctor penned a letter:

'The innocence of our case, with the enmity (hatred) of our accusers and our judges and jury, whom nothing but our innocent blood will serve their turn, having condemned us already before our trials, being

so much incensed and enraged against us by the devil, makes us bold to beg and implore your favourable assistance of this our humble petition to his Excellency, that if it be possible our innocent blood may be spared, which undoubtedly otherwise will be shed, if the Lord doth not mercifully step in. The magistrates, ministers, juries and all the people in general, being so much enraged and incensed against us by the delusion of the devil, which we can term no other by reason we know in our own consciences, we are all innocent persons.'

'Here are five persons who have lately confessed themselves to be witches, and do accuse some of us being along with them at a sacrament, since we were committed into close prison, which we know to be lies. Two of the five are (Carrier's sons) young men, who would not confess anything till they tied them neck and heels, till the blood was ready to come out their noses; and it is credibly believed and reported that this was the occasion of making them confess what they never did, by reason the said one had been a witch a month and another five weeks, and that their mother has made them so, who has been confined here this nine weeks. My son William Proctor, when he was examined, because he would not confess that he was guilty, when he was innocent, they tied him neck and heels till the blood gushed out at his nose, and would have kept him so twenty-four hours, if one more merciful than the rest, had not taken pity on him, and caused him to be unbound.'

'These actions are very like the popish cruelties. They have already undone us in our estates, and that will not serve their turns, without our innocent blood. If it cannot be granted that we can have our trials at Boston, we humbly beg that you would endeavour to have these magistrates changed, and others in their rooms; begging also and beseeching you would be pleased to be here, if not all, some of you, at our trials, hoping thereby you may by the means of saving the shedding of our innocent blood, desiring your prayers to the Lord on our behalf, we rest your poor afflicted servants, John Proctor.'

John's letter was addressed to several Boston ministers: Increase Mather, James Allen, Joshua Moody, James Bailey, and Samuel Willard.

25

RICHARD WASN'T AT all pleased with the news that Eddie had failed to open the metal chest pilfered from Quinn's lab. But Eddie's incompetence wasn't going deter Richard. He had other means at his disposal.

Having put the thought of the chest aside for now, Richard put Eddie to a more pressing task. Richard needed to acquire Quinn's fingerprints in order to get access to Quinn's lower-level console. If everything went as Richard planned, he would have everything he could possibly desire. But, first, he had to make that phone call; then his day could begin.

Eddie had been up most of the night fabricating the means by which Richard would get a set of prints. Whose prints and why, Eddie didn't know, nor did he care. He was just putting the finishing touches on his work when he heard the door to his suite swing open.

"Well, is it done?" Richard growled, slamming the door behind him.

I wonder who shit in your Cornflakes this morning, Eddie

thought. "I'm just finishing up."

Having access to a 3D printer and an abundant supply of stationery, Eddie had made everything Richard would need for his mission today. Under different circumstances, Eddie would have really enjoyed this type of work. He loved trying to unravel problems and solve puzzles; working with the latest technology made it all the more gratifying. Sometimes the possibilities were endless.

"Show me," Richard demanded.

Eddie picked up a small bottle that had been sitting on the corner of his desk. "This is carbon powder. You need to sprinkle this lightly onto the surface containing the prints you want to lift." Eddie had made the powder by finely grinding a piece of charcoal from the fireplace.

"Right, go on."

"Then, use this brush to spread the powder, making sure the entire print is covered," Eddie instructed, while handing Richard a mop brush he had earlier taken from the art supplies in his desk drawer.

"Next, peel the back off this adhesive film and set it aside; you'll need it later. Then, carefully place the film over the print. Be sure you don't shift the film or you'll smudge the print," Eddie cautioned.

Eddie began to show Richard how to peel the back off the film, but Richard snatched the film away. "I can figure that out. What else?"

"Then use this rubber roller to roll the film, applying enough pressure to squeeze out any air bubbles under the film. That'll ensure you get optimum contact between the film and the print and it'll give you an accurate impression. The rolling will also pick up any grease markings from the prints and will transfer them onto the film."

"When you peel the film off the print, lift it by two corners and gently pull it up off the surface. Carefully place the film back onto its original backing. Roll it up and place it in here." Eddie demonstrated the last two steps by rolling two pieces of clean adhesive film and placing them in an eleven-inch-long, cylinder-shaped container. He handed the container to Richard.

"But before you do anything, make sure you're wearing these surgical gloves," Eddie instructed, giving them to Richard. "You don't want to risk contaminating the prints with your own."

"Is that it?" Richard was impatient to get started.

"That's it," Eddie replied.

"Good. Now start working on how you're going to lift the prints, once I get them, so I can use them," Richard ordered as he turned and left the room, locking the door securely behind him.

"You're welcome," Eddie muttered to the empty space.

26

RICHARD HAD MADE the forty-five minute drive to the Delaney estate in less than thirty minutes. "A new record," he muttered, as he got out of his Abruzzi. He chose to forego the social pleasantries of visiting the house first because he knew exactly where he would find his quarry.

When Richard arrived at the gazebo, he decided it best to announce himself. "Quinn, you in there?" he shouted from the front door.

"Come in, Richard," Quinn answered. He pressed the button under his console to unlock the front door and allow Richard to enter.

Richard made his way to the back of the gazebo and proceeded down the stairs. He found Quinn leaning on his console, staring at a wall full of mind-numbing equations.

"How goes the battle?" Richard asked genially.

"Slow, but we're making headway," Quinn said positively. "Hermes will run some final computer models while we're gone. If all goes well, we should be ready to bring the kids home by the time we get back from New Zealand."

Quinn finally pulled his gaze from the wall. Noticing Richard for the first time, he asked curiously, "What's with the trench coat, Richard? It has to be sixty-five degrees outside."

"It was raining when I left my place," Richard lied, as he carefully removed his knee-length coat and draped it over a nearby chair.

"Good day, Mr. Case," Hermes said, appearing to the right of Quinn.

"Hermes, wasn't it?"

"That is correct," Hermes replied. "What brings you out here today, Mr. Case?" Hermes was trying to mimic what a good conversationalist would say upon receiving a guest. He knew Quinn was too busy for such niceties.

"Well, first, I came to see how things were progressing and to tell you I'll have my jet fueled and ready to go by Tuesday. Does that timing work for you, Quinn?" Richard hoped Quinn would agree. He needed just a couple more days to make sure that his plan came together perfectly.

"That'll be fine," Quinn mumbled, going over the figures for the umpteenth time.

"Hermes, run these numbers again; we're missing something. I know . . ."

"Quinn?" It was Sandra's voice over the intercom.

"Yes, Sandra," Quinn replied, trying to keep the annoyance for this interruption out of his voice, but failing badly.

"You need to come up here now; the police are here," Sandra stated.

"What do they want?"

"I don't know. A police cruiser just pulled into the driveway."

"Be right there," Quinn replied. "Come on, Richard; let's go see what this is all about."

Quinn shut the console down by simply waving his right hand over it. He led the way up the stairs and out the door. Richard was right behind him. But before the door to the gazebo swung closed, Richard exclaimed, "Damn, I left my coat inside. You go ahead, Quinn. I'll catch up to you."

Quinn nodded absent-mindedly and continued toward the house.

27

RICHARD MADE HIS way back down to the lower level of the gazebo. He picked up his coat. Rummaging through the pockets, he finally found what he was looking for. He pulled out the bottle of powder. He took a quick glance around. *No Hermes, good,* he thought. *Probably busy working on that problem Quinn gave him.* Richard just hoped there were no active motion sensors down here.

Removing the cap from the bottle, Richard sprinkled the powder on the console. He couldn't believe his luck when he had first entered the lab. He had seen Quinn with both hands flat out on the console. Now, he would get full prints of both of Quinn's hands. Richard reached for the brush, then remembered, *Gloves.*

After pulling on the gloves, Richard lightly brushed the powder over the surface; two large handprints slowly materialized.

Richard pulled the cylinder from the inside lining of his coat. He removed the two pieces of film. He pulled the backing off one piece of film and carefully placed the film over the print. He did one print at a time so that if he were interrupted he might get at least one good impression.

Richard then rolled the film as he had been instructed. He grasped two corners of the film and delicately pulled it off the console surface. He carefully placed the film onto its original backing, rolling it up, and put it into the cylinder. He repeated the same process with the second print.

He made sure he wiped all traces of the carbon powder off the console. Then Richard gathered his tools. He grabbed his coat and tucked the tools back into their hiding place. Once everything was secured, he flew up the stairs.

As Richard headed at a brisk pace toward the house, he struggled to balance two conflicting concerns. He didn't want to arrive at the house winded, but he needed to arrive within an amount of time that would seem reasonable for having gone back to the lab to retrieve his coat.

Richard could see Quinn was just approaching the house. He had to step up his pace.

28

"BILL, I WISH you would have called before popping by for a visit; give a girl a chance to freshen up a bit, stash the bodies, that kind of thing," Sandra said laughing.

"Sandra, I'm sorry, but this isn't a social call," Bill Brown replied sadly.

William "Bill" Brown was the chief of police and a close friend of the Delaneys. He and Sandra had dated once during high school and had been close ever since. He was a strapping six-foot-three-inches, with broad shoulders that tapered to a narrow waist. He had large meaty hands, which had served him well during his college years when he played wide receiver.

"May I come in?" Bill asked, while stepping into the house and glancing around, looking for anything that might appear to be out of place. He had been to the Delaneys' enough times to know whether there was. He and his wife, Amy, had taken turns with a few other friends hosting dinner parties that gave them all a chance to unwind from their busy schedules and to reminisce over old times.

"If this isn't a social visit, Bill, what's it about? Is Amy all right?" Sandra asked, concerned that something had happened to her friend.

"She's fine, Sandra. Thanks for asking," Bill replied. "This is about an anonymous call the precinct received early this morning. The caller said Dani and Daric had disappeared under mysterious circumstances and that the caller suspected foul play."

"What? That's absurd," Sandra blurted out. "You can't be serious!"

"I didn't believe it for a minute; that's why I intercepted the officers who were on their way out here. I'm about to chalk it up to a prank call, but I do need to investigate the reason for the call and close the report," Bill tried to reassure Sandra. He was concerned by the fact that the anonymous call had been untraceable.

"So, where are they? It's been almost a year since I've seen Dani and Daric. It would be great to be able to turn this red herring into a quick visit. Amy is always asking about them. You know she has a soft spot for the twins."

"Uh . . . uh, they're not here right now, Bill."

"Oh, okay." Bill pulled his comm out of his pocket.

Today's society had long since stopped calling them cell phones, because the devices had evolved to be so much more than mere phones. Early in the 21st century, the cell phone wars had erupted. The market had been saturated with manufacturers of cell phone devices, a myriad of operating systems and more features on the phones than most people knew what to do with. As a result of the fierce competition, they had packaged cell phone plans based on the manufacturers' needs rather than on the consumers' and, consequently, prices had skyrocketed.

It was only much later, at the insistence of enraged consumers, that governments got involved and declared comms an essential service. They consolidated the cell phone industry under one common operating system and one standard device. As a result, the device was now so advanced that consumers could program the features they wanted. But the best part of the consolidation was that the devices were now a common everyday item that everyone could afford because they were free. When there were no longer any competition wars, the advertising money previously spent by the rival companies was pooled to produce and supply the standard communication device, or "comm". Most people preferred to wear their devices, but some still preferred to stick to the old practice of carrying them.

"Give me Daric's number and I'll just have a quick comm visit," Bill suggested.

"Uh . . . he left his comm here. He didn't take it with him," Sandra stuttered.

"Okay, then give me Dani's number," Bill responded, as he tried another tactic.

"She didn't take hers either."

"Sandra, what's going on?" Bill pressed for answers. Something wasn't right.

"Nothing. Why?" Sandra asked innocently, stalling for time. She could see Quinn approaching the house through the stained glass panel in the front door.

"You can't expect me to believe that two kids, who have been attached to their electronics since they could talk, would both leave their comms behind. It's the first thing everyone grabs when you get out of bed." Bill was beginning to think Sandra's behaviour was out of character. Something wasn't making sense here.

"Hey, Bill," Quinn said, entering the house and extending his hand. "What drags you all the way out here?" Quinn left the door open, knowing Richard was close behind.

"An anonymous call that the twins had disappeared and that foul play was involved," Bill revealed. "So where are they, Quinn? Sandra seems to be reluctant to give me a straight answer."

Quinn looked at Sandra for guidance. "I told Bill that Dani and Daric aren't here right now. And when I told him they had left their comms at home, he didn't believe me," Sandra explained, hoping Quinn could fill in any other details to explain their children's absence.

Quinn decided to go on the offensive. "Who called you? Did you trace the call?"

"It was an anonymous call from an untraceable source," Bill

stated frankly.

"Really, Bill. Come on, you know that has to be a prank call," Quinn mocked.

"Hey, Bill, what's happening?" Richard asked, when he entered the house, shaking Bill's hand.

"I'm looking for the twins," Bill said irritably.

"I flew them down to my private island in the Caymans, yesterday," Richard said loftily. "They wanted to get away and do a little scuba diving, so I offered them my place. I wasn't using it. Didn't you tell him?" Richard asked, as he glanced over at Sandra.

"I didn't get a chance to. He kept insisting on talking to them," Sandra responded, quickly picking up on Richard's deception.

"What's your number there? I want to call them," Bill pressed.

"You can't. That's the whole concept about a getaway: to get away from it all. There are no electronic devices on my island. But I'm going down on Friday to pick them up. You can come back here then," Richard suggested.

"Or we can have them call you when they get back," Sandra added.

"I'll call back on Friday," Bill agreed and saw himself out. He wasn't sure what was going on, but he could wait until Friday. Besides, in his heart of hearts, he knew that Sandra and Quinn would never put their children in harm's way.

29

"THANKS, RICHARD; THAT was quick thinking." Sandra sighed in relief, after Chief Brown had left.

"Think nothing of it." Richard smiled charmingly.

"Come on inside; I was just about to fix some lunch. We can discuss the trip and get all the details nailed down," Sandra offered, as she walked toward the kitchen.

"Sounds great; I'm starved," Richard agreed warmly.

"I can only spare an hour; then I have to get back to work," Quinn muttered.

"Come to think of it, why didn't the kids have their comms with them?" Richard asked, knowing they always had them on.

"Daric must have taken his off when he put on the travel band, because I found it in the lower lab," Quinn explained.

"And Dani left hers in the house before she went down to the beach to try to teach Bear how to swim," Sandra added, as she finished preparing a couple of submarine sandwiches for Quinn and Richard and a chicken wrap for herself.

They sat around the maple table on the semi-circular upholstered bench appreciating the heat from the sun filtering through the picturesque windows, while they enjoyed their lunch.

"I told Quinn that we would be ready to leave early Tuesday

morning," Richard mumbled around a mouthful of food. "Great sandwich," he added, as he finished wiping away the last remnants of crumbs from his mouth with his napkin.

"My jet will be fuelled and on the tarmac when we arrive at the airfield."

"Great," Quinn replied.

"I'll load my scuba gear into the SUV and swing by to pick you up at nine in the morning, Quinn," Richard announced as he got up to leave. "Thanks for the . . ."

"I'm going with you," Sandra interrupted.

"There's no need . . ."

"I'm going, end of discussion!"

"All right," Richard agreed reluctantly. "I'll see you both Tuesday morning." With that, Richard showed himself out and headed to his car.

"Damn!" Richard muttered, as he slammed the car door. *I can't let that happen. It won't happen! I have to think of something to make sure Sandra doesn't go to New Zealand, or the rest of my plan won't come together,* Richard stewed.

As Richard drove east along Highway 501 on his way home, he spotted to his left the Fastrax train racing into the city. When it had passed, Richard had a clear view of the lake beyond, where he spotted a lone white sail. In the peak of summer, the lake would be dotted with sails.

Then a wickedly wonderful idea came to him. *It's perfect,* he thought. But first he would have to get Eddie's full and willing cooperation. And he knew exactly how he would get it!

30

EARLIER, ON THIS unusually warm sun-bathed Sunday morning, Kerry and Mike Kennedy had pulled away from their private slip at Frenchman's Bay. Kerry had taken the week off work to help Mike prepare the "Kerry Blue" for the upcoming season.

The preparations had started the previous weekend. The marina's crane, called a traveller, had removed the boat from its winter storage cradle and had put it into the bay. After giving the hull and deck a thorough power wash and filling the water tanks, the marina staff had motored the boat over to its private slip.

During the ensuing week, Kerry had outfitted the cabin with fresh bedding, had washed the dishes and cutlery, and had stocked the cupboards with food and beverages. Mike had been busy bringing up the boom, attaching the sail, and inspecting–and, where necessary, replacing the mooring lines.

While Kerry and Mike had been plugging away with their seasonal tasks, the bay had been dredged, providing reasonable assurance that the gap leading out of the bay would be deep enough for the sailboat's running board

With all the necessary preparations finally completed, Mike and Kerry had decided to enjoy a perfect spring morning by taking the thirty-eight-foot Catalina sailboat out for a first-of-the-season sail. Using the Kerry Blue's diesel engine, Kerry had skillfully maneuvred the boat away from its slip; Mike, meanwhile, had been busy pulling in the fenders and securing the mooring lines

"Kerry what's the current wind speed and direction?" Mike asked, as he moved along the upper deck toward the mast. She couldn't help but admire Mike's athletic physique; from his slim waistline to his broad shoulders and to his thick wavy silver hair.

Begrudgingly Kerry pulled herself away from her pleasant distraction and checked the weather station. "Winds are out of the southwest at a steady fifteen knots," she replied.

As soon as the sailboat passed the mouth of the bay, Kerry pointed the bow into the wind and set a heading of 220 degrees. Using the winches, Mike unfurled the head and main sails. The fluttering of the canvas joined in chorus with a flock of squawking seagulls until the wind finally caught the sails. The engine was cut. The boat lurched forward, slicing through the half-foot waves as it gradually gained momentum.

Once Mike finished securing the lines around the winch, he joined Kerry at the wheel. She relinquished the helm to him and took her usual seat beside him. She reached for the two Thermos mugs of coffee held securely in their cup holders. Kerry passed one over to Mike, who was taking a quick glance at the weather station before settling in for a relaxing sail.

"Thanks hon'." Mike's smiling eyes clearly showed his adoration for the petite woman sitting to his right and who had agreed to share the rest of her life with him. They weren't just lovers, they were soul mates. He couldn't wait for Kerry to retire.

As they sailed along the shoreline, Kerry noticed the Fastrax train speeding toward the city. She rode that train every day to her psychiatric practice downtown. It ran every thirty minutes. It was the most efficient, economical, and reliable way of getting into and out of the busy downtown core.

During rush hour, Fastrax adds additional trains, called express trains. These express trains skip several regular stations stops on their way into the city. The special rush hour train schedule helped to manage the vast volume of commuters. Kerry preferred the express trains, which cut easily twenty minutes off her morning commute. Those twenty minutes were devoted to Mike. *Three more months,* she thought, *and then I can enjoy this lifestyle every day.*

Sunday, July 27, 1692

31

DANI AND DARIC had found a place where they could meet with a degree of privacy. It was toward the back of the cell block where the aisle separated their respective cells. Although not ideal, it allowed them to steal private moments together, provided they spoke only in soft whispers. They had found that any and all movement or conversation drew unwanted attention since there wasn't a lot else happening in the lives of their fellow prisoners.

This afternoon, Dani had arrived at her spot and sat down, awaiting Daric's arrival. She could see Daric moving slowly toward his spot by the bars of his cell.

Daric eased himself down onto the straw-strewn floor. He leaned carefully against the pitted metal of the bars to take some pressure off his aching side.

"Is your back still bothering you?" Dani couldn't hide the worry in her voice.

"No, it's my ribs. Guess they took a harsher beating than I thought," Daric said grimly.

"Do you think they may be broken?"

"No, I don't think so. I have some mobility," Daric explained. "It's only when I forget and move the wrong way that they remind me to take it easy."

"Then you need to listen to them," Dani cautioned.

Dani and Daric continued their idle conversation. They were waiting for those around them to lose interest in what they were saying; only then would they feel safe to get down to what they really wanted to talk about.

"I'm getting kind of tired of being cooped up in this pigpen," Daric grumbled. "What's it been now, over a week?"

"My clothes are so filthy, they could stand on their own. What I wouldn't give for a nice soak in a cool bathtub," Dani said dreamily. "I'm even offending myself."

The heat of the days had been making the prison cells feel like they were sitting close to the fires of hell. The air was thick and rank with the smell of tobacco smoke, human waste, and sweat. Then when the sun set, the temperature dropped. When you would have previously been fighting for a spot to lean against the cool stone wall to get temporary relief from the heat of the day, at night you would recoil because the stone walls would become damp and cold. It was always one extreme to another.

When their fellow inmates had turned to other distractions, Daric whispered, "So, have you given some thought to how these bands work?"

"We've never initiated travel with a destination in mind, consciously anyway," Dani said, stating the obvious.

"We've always been trying to save our necks. Excuse the pun," Daric chimed in.

"But we do know that, when the travels bands touch, we move to another place and another time," Dani continued, ignoring Daric's lame attempt at humor. "So, that has to be the activation trigger."

"And so far it's always been to the past. Each time, we've gone further into the past; never forward in time," Daric noted, he was feeling uneasy about any future travel.

"Well, that's a different theory," Dani mumbled absent-mindedly.

"What?"

"Einstein; it's a different theory of relativity. There was the special theory of relativity, which proved time travel to the future was possible. And then there was his general theory of relativity that proved time travel to the past was also achievable," Dani explained.

"So, maybe Dad has figured out one and not the other; maybe that's why we keep going backwards in time," Daric speculated.

"It's possible, I suppose," Dani acknowledged. "But how do we control where we go and to what time period?"

"Is it the way the bands touch?" Daric hazarded to guess. "Or is it how our bodies are positioned? Or is it what we do: is it what we say?"

"No, wait," Dani jumped in, excitedly. "Maybe it's what we think that determines where we go."

"Where are you going?" a male voice asked from deep within the cell.

"Sorry," Dani whispered, "got a little excited I guess."

"I'm going to the midden," Daric replied to his cellmate. The midden was the toilet. Basically, a hole in a wooden plank placed over a metal bucket.

"Talk to you later," Daric said, as he rose and went to carry out his business.

32

"I GOT IT," Richard announced, entering Eddie's main room. A quick glance around the room revealed that Eddie was gone. Richard was furious. He stormed angrily to the door on the left. Throwing it open, he marched through a massive library that would be the envy of any university. At the far end, he threw open another door and bellowed, "What the hell do you think you're doing?"

Eddie sprang at the unexpected intrusion. Still half asleep, he suddenly found himself on the floor beside his four-poster king-size bed. *Talk about being bounced out of bed,* he thought.

Eddie quickly pulled himself up off the floor and sat on the edge of his bed. Reaching for his glasses on the bedside table, he looked over at his very enraged host. "I was up most of the night getting the material you needed. I was tired, and thought while you were gone I'd catch a few zzzs," Eddie explained calmly.

"Well, get dressed you have work to do, and you haven't much time," Richard growled as he turned and left the bedroom.

Eddie just shook his head in disgust and started for the door at the other end of the room. The bathroom on the other side of the door was done in classic Italian marble. It had a walk-in shower and a separate bathtub.

Eddie had a quick shower, followed by a shave with an electric razor, since Richard wouldn't trust him with a blade. He pulled open his wardrobe and stood for a moment to admire his vast collection of new clothes. All the clothes he had ever owned in his lifetime wouldn't equal the number hanging in front of him. He slipped into a pair of black jeans, a slate grey sweater and a black blazer, before donning a pair of black loafers. He was finally ready to confront the agitated Richard.

When Eddie entered his main room, he found Richard hovering impatiently around the desk. "It's about time," Richard grumbled.

"Here are the prints," Richard said, handing the cylindrical container to Eddie. "I was able to get full prints of both hands."

Eddie carefully extracted the two pieces of film and placed them on his desk.

"So, genius, how are you going to make these prints mine?" Richard asked acidly.

"With the 3D printer, I can use bio-ink and produce a layer of skin that can go right over your own. You won't even know it's there," Eddie stated, not looking up from his task.

"You can do that?" Richard asked, unbelieving. *This kid is smart,* he thought.

"Sure. Dr. Tony Salla, the Director of the Oceans Institute for Regenerative Medicine, is using the same technology in his research. He says it's like printing paper with ink, except you'd be printing tissue with cells. His current work is focusing on growing new human cells, tissues and organs. His success would be a major breakthrough in the medical world. Imagine being able to create a human heart from a 3D printer; it's mind-blowing," Eddie expounded wondrously.

"Whatever; just get it done. I have a timeline and it can't be altered." With that, Richard left the room, locking the door behind him.

I need to look into this research, from an investment perspective,

Richard thought. *What am I thinking? With time travel at my fingertips, I'll be able to do anything. Travel forward in time, find the cure for any disease and then just find the right buyer.*

Friday, August 1, 1692

33

"THANK YOU ALL for coming," Reverend Increase Mather began as he addressed the other congregational ministers who had gathered at the Harvard College Library in Cambridge, Massachusetts. In attendance, besides himself, were Reverends James Allen, Joshua Moody, James Bailey and Samuel Willard, all from Boston, Reverend John Hale of Beverly, Reverend John Higginson of Salem, and Reverend Deodat Lawson of Scituate.

"And a special thank you to Reverends Hale and Lawson, for coming all this way to provide us with their insight into the trials," Mather added.

"It's my pleasure," Hale said courteously.

"Wouldn't miss it," replied Lawson.

"I have a letter here," Mather said, holding a paper aloft for everyone to see, "from John Proctor of Salem Village. He has been accused of witchcraft and is currently being held in the Salem Town jail awaiting trial."

"John Proctor is writing on behalf of himself and the other prisoners," Mather went on. "John's letter says they, the accused, believe they aren't receiving a fair trial. He goes on to say confessions are being extracted by means of torture; it happened even to his own son."

"I witnessed a torture myself," Higginson interrupted. "I put an immediate stop to the barbaric act."

"The letter further claims that five recently confessed suspects are now accusing others of being at a sacrament, yet those they accuse were in prison at the time," Mather continued. "It also states that many prisoners have already lost their estates."

"How can they proceed with confiscating the belongings of an accused person?" Allen asked. "That personal property is supposed to support the accused during their incarceration. Only when the accused have been pronounced guilty and their sentence has been carried out can their property become the Crown's."

"John Proctor has been accused of witchcraft, and the Bible, under Exodus 22:18. clearly states: 'Thou shalt not suffer a witch to live'," Moody recited.

"Scripture also requires that the innocent be spared," Hale countered sharply. "He hasn't gone to trial; nor has he been found guilty."

"Gentlemen, please. We're not here to debate the Scriptures," Mather interjected in a bid to keep tempers from flaring further. "We're here to address this letter and to discuss a course of action, if any."

"So, in summary, gentlemen," Mather continued, "John Proctor and his fellow accused are begging us to use our influence to either have the magistrates replaced or have the trials conducted in Boston, with us in attendance. Here, I'll pass the letter around so you can all read it for yourself." Reverend Mather passed the letter to his right, into the hands of Reverend Hale.

"I've been an observer at many examinations and a couple of trials," Hale disclosed, "and I find the proceedings dubious."

"As do I," Higginson added.

"How so?" Willard asked.

"Sometimes during the proceedings, whether it be an examination or a grand jury trial, the afflicted girls start to convulse and scream, blaming the accused for their torment," Hale explained.

"Yes, I've seen that for myself, recently," Mather admitted.

"Then, have you ever asked yourself: why would a witch reveal herself by using magic in court? It doesn't make any sense," Hale challenged.

"And if witches are so powerful that they can disguise themselves, then why don't they use that power to save their own lives," Higginson argued.

"Proof of any crime requires corroborating testimony from two or more witnesses," Moody offered, continuing to play the role of devil's advocate.

"Okay, let's consider the evidence admissible in the Court of Oyer and Terminer. First there's the self-incriminating testimony," Willard stated.

"And too many are jumping onto that boat. They believe that pleading guilty will save them from the hangman's noose," Hale interjected.

"That could be true. There hasn't been a confessed witch executed yet," Willard added.

"Then, there are the accusations of those who have already pleaded guilty to being a witch and who point out others in their midst," Bailey added, "as mentioned in the letter."

"So, let's say, as an accused, I confess to save myself. By doing so, I gain the ability and the power to accuse my neighbour, who may be someone I have a property boundary dispute with or someone I would like to exact vengeance," Mather hypothesized.

"The jails are overflowing. Every day, people–respectable, righteous, God-fearing people–are being rounded up, accused of witchcraft. I find it difficult to believe that so many in so small a compass of land should so abominably leap into the devil's lap at once," Hale proclaimed.

"Give no place to the devil by rash censuring of others without sufficient grounds, or falsely accusing any willingly," Lawson recited. "It was part of a sermon I gave a few months back in Salem

Village."

"Well said, Reverend," Allen offered. "Then, there's the inability to say the Lord's Prayer. It's believed that a witch cannot recite the Lord's Prayer properly because the devil intervenes."

"I have not witnessed this test yet," Lawson stated. "I was at the trials in Salem on June 29 and the only test I witnessed was the touch test."

"No one can trust the touch test, because the accused might be victimized by the devil as much as the afflicted are," Higginson said irritably.

"Then, there's the presence of the devil's mark and the pin test, both highly suspicious," Hale added.

"The evidence that seems to sway the courts the most is spectral evidence," Lawson stated.

"But even that evidence is unreliable," Hale retorted. "The afflicted are the only ones who can see the specters; as a result, they can say whatever they want. Who's to judge what is true or otherwise in the Invisible World, which only the afflicted can see?"

"Could the devil impersonate the innocent?" Mather asked.

"I believe so, but I think it happens only rarely, and isn't very likely in the cases that now stand before the court," Moody suggested.

"The devil had once disguised himself as the Prophet Samuel; so I believe he can impersonate anyone," Allen offered.

"Wasn't the Lord Jesus Christ himself accused of using Satan's powers to perform miracles?" Bailey asked.

"If the devil can masquerade himself under the identities of innocent people, then the Court of Oyer and Terminer may have just inadvertently executed six innocent people," Lawson stated starkly.

"So, do we have a consensus, gentlemen, that the devil can, in fact, falsely represent anyone?" Mather asked.

All the ministers present agreed.

"Then, spectral evidence alone isn't enough to prove a suspect's guilt, if we have all agreed that the devil can assume any appearance he pleases," Mather further clarified.

Again, the ministers all concurred.

"Then, what can we do about John Proctor and the others?" Willard asked. "We have no authority over the judicial system," he noted.

"What good can any of us do?" Bailey asked dejectedly.

"We have to do something!" Hale exclaimed.

"Our advice to the governor last month, when we cautioned against relying on spectral evidence alone, fell on deaf ears," Moody stated bluntly.

Mather reflected for a moment and then declared, "I believe it would be better that ten suspected witches should escape than one innocent person should be condemned."

"Why don't you write a composition on the use of spectral evidence in the Court of Oyer and Terminer?" Hale proposed, as he looked over at Mather. His fellow clergy eagerly agreed with the proposal.

"I can try," Mather muttered.

34

PRELIMINARY TESTIMONY BEGAN at eight o'clock. At ten o'clock, in the jail's upper rooms, a jury of nine women and Dr. Barton again searched the bodies of Elizabeth Proctor and Martha Carrier for witch's marks. The sheriff, with a few of his deputies, searched John Proctor. It was Grand Jury Trial day.

Before leaving her cell, Martha had placed Andrew in Dani's care while she was at trial. Andrew Carrier's fever seemed to be worse this morning. He had been curled up, with his warm head resting on his mother's lap, all night. Martha had been eternally grateful to John Proctor, who had convinced the jailer to allow Andrew into the women's cell, considering what he had endured during his examination.

"Don't worry, Martha. I'll watch over him," Dani had assured her. That was hours ago and Andrew seemed to be getting worse.

* * *

John and Elizabeth Proctor had already returned to their cells, around mid-day. Both had stood their ground and professed their innocence. But both had been found guilty and had been sentenced to death. Elizabeth, however, had pleaded for a delay of her execution, until after her baby was born; assuming she and her baby survived the ordeal of childbirth in the filthy, overcrowded Salem jail.

Daric worked his way past bodies strewn throughout the crowded cell and over to see John. "What're you doing?" Daric asked, as he sat down beside him.

"I'm changing my will," John said solemnly, "seeing that my wife and I will be hanged."

"Oh," Daric remarked. "What happened at the trial?" Daric was hoping to get some useful information to help prepare him for what was sure to come.

"It was a sham," John muttered. "The verdict was predetermined. It didn't matter what we said. When those girls screamed and started to twitch that was the only evidence the judges would recognize."

"You're kidding?" Daric grimaced.

"No, I'm not. They'd scream, roll on the floor and point somewhere in the room and say my specter was tormenting them. But the most shocking part was that the five trusted and well-educated judges believed the rantings of six self-serving young girls, all vying for attention."

"What about that letter you wrote? Did you hear anything back?" Daric asked hopefully.

"Nothing," John replied dejectedly. "We even had two petitions presented on our behalf. One was signed by twenty of our neighbors from Salem Village. The other petition was composed by Reverend John Wise and was signed by thirty-two of our friends and family from Ipswich, where I grew up. The judges saw only the afflicted girls, and that was enough to convict us."

"How can you defend yourself against that kind of evidence?" Daric asked desperately.

"You can't." John stared at Daric with unbelieving eyes. "It's their word against yours, and they are the only ones who can see into the Invisible World."

"Invisible World?"

"Where the specters live and where they are controlled and manipulated by the power of the devil," John muttered coldly.

"If those six girls are the only people who can see the specters in the Invisible World, has anyone ever considered that they may have been possessed by the devil and that they, in fact, are witches themselves?" Daric proposed.

Sunday, August 3, 1692

35

MARTHA CARRIER WAS again removed from her jail cell early this morning. This was the second day of her trail, which was being held at the Salem Town Meeting House. Prior to leaving, she had entrusted Andrew into Dani's care. Martha noticed this morning that he wasn't getting any better, in fact, he was getting worse. His fever was raging and his face was pale. He hadn't been taking any food and, now; he was refusing even a bit of water. Martha knew she was asking a lot from Dani, but she had little choice.

"They'll search me again this morning, for witch's marks," Martha said calmly. "I'll ask Dr. Barton to come down here to check on Andrew."

"I'll be here," Dani sighed, as if she could go anywhere. She felt so helpless. She knew, if her mother were here, she'd know exactly what to do. Thinking of her mother made her heart ache like nothing she had ever experienced before. She hadn't allowed herself to think about her parents in a long time, for just that reason. *Are you still trying to bring us home?* she wondered. *Or have you given up?* Dani refused to think her parents would ever give up on them, but she had to be realistic, too. *How long have we been gone?* If their dad couldn't bring them home, Dani prayed that; *time has eased your suffering over losing your children?*

Lost in her own thoughts, Dani hadn't realized how much time had passed, when the cell door opened and Dr. Barton entered. He held a bandana over his mouth and nose, but the impact of the stench that stung his eyes could not be hidden as tears rolled down his cheeks.

Dr. Barton knelt beside Dani to examine Andrew. He felt the boy's forehead, pulling his hand away quickly as if singed by the heat. The doctor then proceeded to check Andrew's body for the cause of the fever. The doctor noticed the red ring around Andrew's neck. He looked curiously at Dani.

"He was tied neck and heels," Dani volunteered. "The ropes cut into his wrists and neck. His wrists were bleeding when he was brought in here. I'm not sure how many days ago that was."

The doctor looked over the raw skin on both of Andrew's wrists, but the shackles were interfering with his examination. "Dounton, remove these," Barton ordered. Dounton, who had been standing at the cell door, entered and did as he was told.

Barton pulled up Andrew's shirt sleeves; Dani gasped in horror. From Andrew's raw right wrist, travelling up his arm, under the skin was a red line. Dani knew what it was: poison.

"The arm will have to come off," Barton said bluntly.

"Are you sure?" Dani asked sadly

"He's sure to die if it doesn't," Barton replied sharply, taken aback by Dani's questioning of his assessment. "I'll have to get my bag. I'll be back after dinner to perform the surgery." With that, Barton rose and left the cell, followed closely by Dounton.

* * *

A couple hours later, Martha came back from her trial. She felt Andrew's head and was instantly alarmed. "What did the doctor have to say?"

"It's poison. He said he'll have to take Andrew's arm off," Dani said despondently.

"Mother, I don't want to lose my arm. Please, don't let him take it," Andrew's pathetically weak voice pleaded.

"You rest now," Martha said, cradling Andrew's feverish head in her lap. "We'll worry about that later."

36

WHILE THEY WAITED for the return of Dr. Barton, Martha filled
Dani in on her court proceedings.

"The testimony began with my accusers, the group of six young
girls, who said I or my specter torments them," Martha said coldly.

"Then, Ann Foster and Mary Lacy Sr. and Jr. told the court
I was at the great witch meeting, but I couldn't have been there,
because I've been in custody since the end of May."

"After that, several neighbors testified about issues that happened years ago. The Abbotts told the judges about a boundary
dispute we had last March. Then, they blamed me for the death of
several of their cows, like I had anything to do with it."

"That's ridiculous," Dani said bluntly.

"Exactly! The cows were old and not well cared for. They were
always breaking into our yard and eating our crops. Maybe if
they'd looked after their beasts, they'd still be alive," Martha said
sharply.

"Then, John Rogers and Samuel Preston blamed me for their
animals' illnesses and deaths, too, and it was all because we had an
argument a while back. This was their way of getting even," Martha grunted.

"But where's the evidence of your being a witch? This is all hearsay, speculation. Where's the cold hard evidence? Don't they realize that calling you a witch is a bell they can't un-ring?"

"What?"

"What I mean is that their accusations could lead to your hanging. Can't they see that?" Dani was outraged.

"Even my own nephew testified against me. He blatantly lied in front of a room full of townsfolk. He said my son, Richard, had thrown him onto the ground and that my specter had sat on his chest and prevented him from getting up until he apologized. And all during the trial, those damned girls convulsed and screamed and continued to accuse me. But I stood my ground and declared my innocence," Martha added boldly.

"What happened after that?" Dani could see that Martha was a woman of character; she was determined and proud and would hold true to herself.

"The jury found me guilty as charged," Martha admitted sadly.

Dani was finding it extremely difficult to believe that whole communities believed that witches, working under the direction of the devil, were the cause of all their suffering and grief.

Their conversation ended when the cell door creaked open on its rusty hinges. A man entered the cell. At first, Dani thought it was a minister, with his long, dark cloak and wide-brimmed hat. But then, she noticed the calfskin bag in his right hand and, when he removed his hat, she recognized his even nose and dark eyes and cleft chin. It was Dr. Barton.

"I'll need your help to hold him down while I do this," Barton said, as he reached into his bag to extract the necessary instruments.

When Barton reached for Andrew's arm to prepare the area for amputation, Andrew pulled away and buried his arm as he curled into a fetal position. "No, you can't take my arm. Mother, please, don't let him take my arm," Andrew weakly sobbed.

Martha looked imploringly at Dani. She didn't want her son to lose his arm. Times were tough on the frontier; it would be nearly impossible for him to provide for himself or a family with only one arm.

Dani had been racking her brain ever since the doctor had given his prognosis earlier that day. She had been trying to think of something to help young Andrew.

"I'll give him something for the pain, but I need you to hold him still," Barton repeated.

"Mother, please, no. Don't let him take my arm. Please, no," Andrew kept saying those two words over and over again. "Please, no. Please, no." Andrew's moaning pleas were breaking Dani's heart.

"No, wait," Dani said, as she grabbed the doctor's arm holding the amputation saw.

"What are you doing?" Barton barked. He was appalled at her interference.

"I have a better idea," Dani said. "Bring leeches, lots of them, and some rosemary and hot water."

"Who do you think you are, telling me what to do?" Barton was infuriated. He felt his professional competence and reputation were being challenged. He struggled to contain his anger.

"I'm hoping to save this young boy's arm," Dani snapped back. "At least, let me try. If there's no improvement by morning, then take his arm, but let me give him a fighting chance." Dani looked over at Martha, hoping her determination was enough to convince Martha that her suggestion was the right course of action.

"Do it," Martha said determinedly.

"If he dies, it won't be on my shoulders; it will be on yours," Barton grunted. Still struggling to contain his anger, something made him wonder whether Dani's idea might just work and allow the boy to avoid a life of extreme hardship, that is, if he survived the next few hours. As these conflicting thought continue to swirl in his head, Barton left to collect the items Dani had requested.

"Dani?" Daric whispered from the other cell. He had heard the exchange between Dani and the doctor.

Dani made her way over to the end of the cell where her brother had found a quiet corner where they could talk privately.

"What are you doing?" Daric asked cautiously.

"I'm trying to save Andrew's arm," Dani replied irritated, as she looked back over at the frail young lad resting in his mother's lap. She was worried that her remedy might not be enough to save his arm and that the delay might cost him his life.

"Dani, what if history says he's supposed to lose that arm?" Daric asked. "Remember, we can't be tampering with history."

"If history says Andrew will lose his arm, he will, but not today and not if I can help it," Dani said stubbornly. "If I save it now, he may well lose it at another time; therefore, history will play out as it should."

Daric knew by the determined look, the thrown-back shoulders, and the tone of Dani's voice, that there would be no arguing with her. So he turned and went back to his place. He hoped his sister knew what she was doing.

37

DOCTOR BARTON HAD returned an hour later with the requested materials. While she had been waiting for his return, Dani had applied a liberal amount of salve to both of Andrew's wrists, a salve that Martha's husband had brought several weeks ago to treat Martha's own raw wrists. She had also fashioned makeshift bandages from the ties on the back of her apron. And, finally, she had taken a few moments to scribble something on a piece of paper, which she folded and put in her dress pocket.

Taking the requested items from the doctor, Dani wasted no time in administering aid to Andrew, whose temperature was reaching alarming levels. Dani knelt down beside Andrew. Opening the jar of leeches, she pulled one slimy, wriggling creature from the huddled black mass inside. Holding it carefully, pinched between two fingers, Dani placed the leech directly on the red line on the boy's arm, half an inch from the uppermost reach. The leech quickly latched onto its new food source. There was no reaction at all from Andrew. *For the better,* Dani thought.

Dani pulled a second leech from the jar and placed it half-an-inch below the first. She continued this procedure until the entire red line on Andrew's right arm was dotted with black leeches. Dani checked the jar and realized there was a problem. "Doctor, we're going to need more," she said, holding the jar up to him.

"But there's still plenty in there," he replied coldly.

"When the leeches on Andrew's arm have consumed enough, they will fall off, dead, killed by the poison. I'll need to replace them, if we hope to get all the poison out of his system," Dani explained. "And I don't know how long that will take." Just then, the first leech that Dani had placed on Andrew's arm fell off, dead, clearly proving her point.

"I'll be right back," the doctor said, as he turned and ran up the stairs. As he maintained his pace across the floor, dust shook between the floor boards from his pounding footsteps and floated down through the cells below.

"How do you think this infection started?" Martha asked, replacing the wet cloth on her son's feverish head.

"I'm not sure. Maybe it resulted from the torture he endured." Dani suddenly sprang to her feet and bolted over to the cell door. "Daric!" she cried out.

"Dani?" Martha called after her, not sure what was wrong. "Daric?"

"I'm here. Is it Andrew? Is everything all right?" Daric blurted out, disturbed by his sister's frantic calling.

"Roll up your sleeves and stick your arms out where I can see them," Dani said firmly.

Daric didn't argue, but did as he was asked. "What's up?"

Daric pushed his arms through the cell bars as far as he could. Dani strained to see in the poor filtered light. The dust particles floating in the air hindered her ability to see Daric's arm clearly. She strained for what seemed like an eternity before she leaned back and took a deep breath. "What?" Daric asked.

"I believe Andrew got blood poisoning from his torture treatment. I knew your wrists were raw, too, after your ordeal. I wanted to make sure you were okay," Dani said calmly.

"What about Andrew's brother, Richard? He was tortured, too, at the same time Andrew was," Daric reminded her.

"Can you check on him? Look for any pronounced veins

running up either arm. If you're not sure, bring him over here and I'll take a look," Dani instructed.

Dani pulled two items from her dress pocket. She unscrewed the salve jar lid and placed a corner of the piece of paper in the jar and twisted the lid back on, holding the note in place. "Take this," Dani directed, as she tossed the jar through the bars to Daric. "Rub some onto your wrists, and onto Richard's, too. I have to go," she said.

"What's with the note?" Daric asked.

"I couldn't do anything to help Martha or John, but maybe you can give that note to someone. It might help their case, but I know this for sure: it can't hurt." Then, Dani disappeared into the dark cell.

Daric took a moment to open the jar and remove the note. He unfolded it and read its contents. "Only you would be able to remember something like this," he muttered. And he knew exactly to whom to give it to.

Monday, August 4, 1692

38

DANI HAD BEEN up all night, replacing the dead leeches with live ones. She had crushed the rosemary into a pulp, using the lid from the leech jar. She had mixed the pulp with some hot water and had forced a bit down Andrew's throat several times during the night. She had watched expectantly for any signs of improvement, but she had seen none.

From pure exhaustion and emotional strain, Dani had fallen asleep a few hours ago. Martha hadn't had the heart to wake her, not after all she had done for her son. Besides, Martha knew the routine and had continued with the treatment while Dani slept. But it was time. Martha reached over and gently nudged Dani.

Dani groggily mumbled a protest at being disturbed and then bolted upright. "Oh, my God, Martha. I'm so sorry. I must have dozed off. Is everything all right? Is Andrew . . ."

"See for yourself," Martha said joyfully, a huge grin spreading across her dirt-smudged face.

Dani peered down at Andrew, still lying on his mother's lap. His color was certainly better. She grabbed his arm and examined it carefully. The angry red line that had almost reached his shoulder was gone. Dani felt his forehead and sighed in relief.

At Dani's touch, the young lad stirred, opening his eyes, which were clear and bright. "Mother, I'm hungry," Andrew announced weakly.

"I know, sweetheart. I'll get you something to eat in a minute; just rest. You've had a rough few days," Martha said to her son, who slowly closed his eyes.

Dani was overjoyed. She was so giddy she didn't know what to do with herself. "Hunger, that's a good sign," Dani said quietly.

"I don't know how to thank you," Martha said sincerely, tears etching a clean track down her cheeks.

"I'd say we're even," Dani assured her.

"Not by a long shot," Martha replied, "not by a long shot."

"Martha, let me watch him for a while," Elizabeth offered. "He's out of danger; besides, you and Dani could use some rest."

"Thanks, Elizabeth, I think I will. It's been a long night," Martha sighed.

* * *

Dr. Barton arrived an hour later and was shocked to see Andrew sitting up eating a bowl of soup. If he hadn't seen it with his own eyes, he wouldn't have believed it. Barton had been sure the lad was a goner, even if he had taken the arm, and especially under these abhorrent conditions. He took his time examining Andrew, purely to satisfy himself that the lad was, in fact, cured. Barton looked over at Dani, nodded once, and then left.

* * *

Out of the corner of her eye, Dani saw two women talking to Dounton, just before he locked the door and followed Dr. Barton out of the cellblock.

39

RICHARD'S PLAN HAD worked to perfection. The call to the police had been the ideal gambit to draw Quinn out of his lab and give Richard the time he needed to lift Quinn's prints. Now, before he could execute the rest of his plan, he needed to test the prints to make sure they would work. He knew he wouldn't be able to play the same trick twice, so he decided to sneak into the lab, as he had done a few days ago.

Richard had driven to the eastern edge of the Delaney estate and left his car hidden among a thick stand of pine trees. He crept through the shadows until he was close enough to the gazebo to see whether any lights were still on. They were. Quinn was still working.

Richard would just have to sit and wait. He hated waiting. He was the kind of man who, if he wanted something, he wanted it now. And he had the resources to make that happen. Those who worked for him would often find themselves tripping over each other to make sure Richard got exactly what he wanted, and as quickly as possible.

Earlier that day, Eddie had completed the set of prints for Richard. He had also given Richard a USB key to open the lower lab door, the same key Richard had used on his previous clandestine visit. But he needed something more. He needed a virus that would shut down Quinn's computer system. That would give him the time to get to New Zealand, find the chronizium and return. Then, Richard would remove the virus and finally get his hands on the travel bands.

Richard was jarred from his musings by movement in his peripheral vision. "Crap," he muttered. "It's the damn dog."

Bear had run out of the gazebo, stopped abruptly and turned to her left. She started on a heading that would lead her directly to Richard. Had he been found out? He had to do something before Bear discovered him, but he was afraid to move, because any noise he made would call attention to his presence.

Richard suddenly saw Quinn leave the gazebo. *Now what?*

Quinn had spotted Bear moving toward the eastern end of the peninsula sniffing out something. *A deer probably,* Quinn thought.

"Come on, Bear. Let's go get some dinner," Quinn yelled over his shoulder, as he made his way toward the house.

Bear stopped in her tracks upon hearing her name. She looked back at Quinn. She paused, but only for a moment, before continuing on with her investigation.

Damn, Richard thought, feeling nervous the closer Bear got to his hiding spot.

"Come on, Bear," Quinn called again. "Let's go see Mommy."

That did it. Bear turned and darted toward the house, with Quinn trailing behind.

"Finally." Richard sighed. He waited a good ten minutes before emerging from the shadows and making his way toward the gazebo. Getting in was child's play. The first door access code was the date Quinn's children had been born and the number of minutes apart. Richard punched in 031723 and entered the gazebo. The second door opened when Richard inserted the override USB key.

Richard now stood in front of Quinn's console. Wasting no

time, Richard reached into his coat pocket and pulled out the prints Eddie had fashioned into fine silk gloves. They slipped easily onto his hands. Taking a deep breath, Richard waved his right hand over the console, mimicking what he had seen Quinn do yesterday. It came to life instantly.

"Fantastic," Richard snickered.

"Oh, Professor, I have news. I am one hour and thirty-two minutes from completing the computations for forward time travel." Hermes' disembodied voice echoed in the room, before he materialized beside the console.

"Oh, I beg your pardon, Mr. Case, I was expecting the professor," Hermes admitted, looking around for Quinn.

"So, I see," Richard sneered, as he inserted the second USB key, which immediately planted the virus into the system.

"Ahhh . . ." Hermes said, as his image quivered for a moment and then vanished. Richard had made sure that Eddie's virus was also designed to disable Hermes. Richard didn't want Hermes reporting this intrusion to Quinn.

Richard pulled the USB key from the console, removed the gloves, shoved them in his coat pocket, and made a hasty exit. *Now, for the next step in my plan: keeping Sandra from joining our trip.*

40

AFTER RETURNING HOME from his little experiment at Quinn's lab, Richard had stopped by the kitchen to place a special dinner order for two with his personal chef. He needed to make sure the stage was set just right if his scheme was to succeed. Once satisfied that his orders would be carried out to the letter, he headed to his suit of rooms. Grabbing a quick shower, he changed his clothes, and then made his way to Eddie's room.

Unlocking the door, Richard entered quietly this time; there was no shouting. He found Eddie sitting on the sofa in front of the fireplace, reading a book he must have selected from the library in the adjacent room.

Richard walked over and made himself comfortable in one of the wing-backed leather chairs.

"Well?" Eddie asked, looking up from his book on ancient civilizations. "Did it work?"

"Perfectly; the prints and the virus. Thank you," Richard said sincerely. His gratitude caught Eddie totally off guard.

"Look, I need your help with something," Richard said, just as the door to the suite opened. Harry entered, pushing a dinner cart in front of him.

"Over here would be fine," Richard instructed.

Harry Bennett was Richard's manservant and bodyguard. He was built like a tank: six-foot-five-inches tall, two-hundred-seventy-five-pounds of solid muscle. He had broad shoulders and large meaty hands. He had dark brown hair, brown eyes and a no-nonsense disposition. He was the only other person Eddie had seen since his imprisonment.

Harry placed two wine glasses on the coffee table. Picking up the bottle of cabernet-sauvignon, he proceeded to remove the cork.

"What's this?" Eddie asked suspiciously.

"It's dinner," Richard replied amiably. "I ordered a special meal. I hope you like it." Richard reached for the glass of wine that Harry had just poured and took a small sip. "That's fine, Harry; you may pour."

Harry finished pouring the two glasses of wine. He placed a chafing dish on the table and then arranged the two place settings before being dismissed.

Richard held up his glass of wine. "To a long working relationship," he toasted.

"And why should I drink to that?" Eddie grunted. He wasn't sure what Richard was up to, but one thing was certain: he didn't trust him.

An intoxicating aroma from the chafing dish slowly began to permeate the room. Eddie's mouth watered. He didn't know what was under the lid, but he knew it had to be delicious.

"Let's eat first; then we'll talk," Richard said, as he watched Eddie drool. He had to admit, he was looking forward to this meal, too. It would be a little while before he could enjoy anything this extravagant again.

After each had devoured a porterhouse steak and three lobster tails, Richard and Eddie were now working on their second bottle of wine. Richard was ready to ask for Eddie's allegiance; he was confident that Eddie would be receptive, now.

"What if I told you I could make you rich beyond your wildest dreams?" Richard asked casually, picking up his glass and leaning back, sinking comfortably into the deep leather chair.

"Hell of a lot of good that'll do me, locked up in here," Eddie spat. "Money has no value when I'm still your prisoner."

"I can fix that, too," Richard responded, smiling faintly. "I want you to work for me, Eddie. You have some very unique skills that I can use."

"Aren't I doing that now?"

"Yes, but I want you to be a willing employee. I want you to embrace your work. I want you to excel in your assignments. I *need* you to execute my demands without question," Richard explained.

"Like your puppet, Harry. That's not likely going to happen," Eddie said coldly, taking another sip of wine from his glass.

"What if I offered you something you simply couldn't refuse?" Richard was enjoying the banter, the give-and-take. It was like trying to land a marlin. He was preparing for the final haul.

"Like what? I have nothing and I own nothing. There isn't much I desire, except for my freedom, and you're not about to grant me that, are you?"

"What if I told you that I could reunite you with your parents?"

"By killing me? I knew that had to come eventually," Eddie said.

"No, not by killing you; by bringing them back to life." *Wait for it,* he thought.

Eddie sprayed a mouthful of wine across the table and started to choke. Richard sat sipping his wine, patiently waiting for Eddie to regain his composure.

"That's not possible," Eddie spluttered, wiping his mouth with his discarded napkin. "My parents were killed in a car accident when I was five-years-old."

"It's very possible. What if I told you that I can go back in time and prevent the accident that killed your parents?"

"You're asking me to believe that you can travel back through time?" Eddie was stunned. *It's not possible,* he thought. Eddie was a smart kid, and he knew physicists had been working on Einstein's theories for years. Was it possible they had made a breakthrough?

"Yes, I am," Richard answered smugly. "As a matter of fact, you've been very helpful in my mission, so far, and, frankly, I'd like that to continue," Richard added.

"And you can go back in time to prevent my parents from being killed?" Eddie asked skeptically. Could it be possible? Could he have his family back? Could he finally be happy?

"Just give me the time and date and I'll save your parents' lives," Richard said confidently. Richard knew he had the right bait to reel in his catch. "So, are you interested in my offer?"

"If you're serious, I guess I have nothing to lose. I'll do whatever it is you want."

"To a long working relationship," Richard said, raising his glass. And, this time Eddie did, too.

41

AFTER DINNER, QUINN took a moment to unwind. He knew Hermes was still running computer models. He would go out to the lab in a couple hours to check on his progress.

Quinn and Sandra were snuggled on the sofa in their living room in front of the soft glow from the fireplace. Quinn had his feet up on the coffee table and his arm around Sandra's shoulder; she was leaning into his warm body. Bruno Mars's *Just The Way You Are* was playing quietly in the background. If this had been any other night, it would have been kind of romantic. But Quinn had too many things on his mind; foremost were his children. Quinn was the first to disrupt the mood, pulling Sandra from her thoughts.

"Hermes has been crunching information through every computer model I have, and still there's something I'm missing. I've spent almost every waking hour at this. I'm so close, yet there's something I'm overlooking; something I can't quite nail down." Quinn exhaled in frustration.

Sandra didn't move or comment. She knew Quinn had to vent; it was his way of releasing at least some of the unrelenting stress he was experiencing. He was blaming himself for Dani and Daric's disappearance. He was becoming increasingly frustrated by his lack of progress. Sandra didn't know how much more pressure Quinn could handle. She had to be strong for him. She would also have to be strong for herself. Every minute, every hour, every day that had passed since her children's disappearance had been agonizing for her. What were they going through, was the question that played like a broken record through her every-waking moment. She couldn't imagine what Quinn was feeling, piling blame on top of his trepidation.

"How many times will it take for me to get this right?" Quinn asked, not expecting an answer. "I feel like Atlas, with the weight of the world on my shoulders."

Sandra knew there was still more to come, so she waited.

"Sometimes it seems as if I'm going in circles, each day a repeat of the one before and with the same results: failure," Quinn muttered. "What do you do, when everything you've tried just isn't good enough?"

Now, it was Sandra's turn. "Success is seeing what everybody has seen and thinking what nobody has thought," Sandra offered, pressed against Quinn's side, reluctant to move from her comfortable spot.

"What?" Quinn asked, surprised by Sandra's remark.

"Why not try blending a little imagination with knowledge," Sandra ventured. "You said it yourself: you've tried everything you can think of. So think outside the box. If I can use a very old quote: 'go where no one has gone before'," Sandra said encouragingly.

Quinn reached over and lifted the bottle of wine, holding it up to check its contents. "How much wine have you had?" he teased.

Since Quinn had already disturbed her comfort, Sandra sat up, looked over at Quinn and smiled. "A wise man once said: 'it always seems impossible until it's done.' I have faith in you, Quinn. You just have to believe in yourself."

"I think this may just be beyond my capabilities. It may be impossible," Quinn responded, hanging his head in shame.

Sandra placed her hand on the side of Quinn's face, turning his head gently toward her. She stared deeply into those beautiful blue eyes she had fallen in love with so many years ago and said, "You've come this far, where others have failed before. I have faith in you, Quinn, and so do our children. You can do this," Sandra said firmly and, then, leaned in and kissed him passionately.

After a long moment, they broke apart, each a little flushed and short of breath. "I'm heading to bed; we have an early start in the morning," Sandra said, leaning in for another peck.

"Just let me check with Hermes, and I'll be right up," Quinn said as he picked up the empty wine glasses and bottle and headed for the kitchen.

Quinn didn't feel like heading out to the gazebo tonight. The emotional rollercoaster he was on had finally taken its toll. He was exhausted. He placed the glasses and bottle on the kitchen counter, and, then activated his comm. There was no response. *That's odd,* he thought.

42

THE GROUP OF prisoners was led down the main street, accompanied by Sheriff Corwin and several of his deputies. Among the ensemble were John Willard, George Jacobs Sr., Reverend George Burroughs and, distressingly, Dani and Daric.

The group approached a two-story brick building that stood in the town's center, just around the block from the jail. The prisoners were ushered into the Salem Town meeting house. The building was used for both civil and religious meetings. The first floor was the Latin grammar school. The second floor was converted to a courtroom where the Court of Oyer and Terminer was about to convene. The governor had instituted this judicial body to deal with the growing number of prisoners accused of witchcraft, rather than having the Superior Court, which sat only at certain times, handle the cases.

When the prisoners were led into the courtroom, they could see it was packed to the rafters with spectators. All the prisoners, except John Willard, were ushered to reserved benches at the back of the room and told to sit.

John Willard was led down the center aisle; males were seated on the right, females on the left. The seating order in the town's meeting house wasn't based on church membership, but on an individual's social standing. All the elite members of the community sat front and center, as was the case this day.

At the front of the courtroom to the right, was a gathering of six young women. All turned and stared wide-eyed at Dani and Daric, the new strangers in their midst. On the left, seated at a small table, were Reverends Case and Noyes. At the front of the room, at the end of the long center aisle, were five gentlemen seated behind a wooden table.

The gavel banged abruptly on the table, bringing a hush over the crowd. The Court of Oyer and Terminer was now in session. Chief Justice William Stoughton was presiding, with justices John Hathorne, Jonathan Corwin, Bartholomew Gedney, and Samuel Sewall rounding out the five.

Dani recognized three of the gentlemen sitting at the table; they had been present at her examination. The other two she didn't know.

Chief Justice and Lieutenant Governor William Stoughton had always sought a life of power and influence. He had a sharp mind and thought privilege was a birthright. His experience, however, had threatened to cast doubt on this thinking. When the people of Massachusetts had expelled their British-imposed governor, Edmund Andros, in 1689, Stoughton, as a member of Andros's ruling council, had found himself forced to leave Boston. His return to respectability took time. It began only when his friend, Cotton Mather, wrote to his father, Reverend Increase Mather. In his letter, the younger Mather explained that Stoughton was willing to make amends for the wrongs of the previous government; he ended his letter by asking that Stoughton be restored to favor. The letter had the intended effect. On the recommendation of Reverend Mather, the new governor, William Phips, appointed Stoughton lieutenant governor. Soon after, he also appointed him chief justice of the Court of Oyer and Terminer.

At sixty-one, Stoughton was a lean man with a narrow face and a long nose. He was an exceptional intimidator; people generally withered under his stare. He knew he was now in the ideal position to retaliate against the people of Massachusetts for running him out of town. He was convinced that the devil couldn't impersonate the innocent, so his job was easy. He would condemn every one of the accused. During the trials, he brushed caution aside and rushed the executions, even when the court's methods were being called into question. By October, William Stoughton would have presided over the largest mass murder in New England's history.

Justice and Governor's Assistant, Samuel Sewall, was a full-figured man, often found wearing the black apparel preferred by high officials. He had inherited his wealth, included mills, wharves, rental properties, and wilderness tracts, from his father-in-law. A good-natured man and one of New England's most influential figures, Sewall was a familiar face at Boston's elite dinner parties. He would become the first and only judge to apologize for his role in the witch trials.

Both Stoughton and Sewall wore black caps. The caps were not part of the standard judicial attire, but they had a purpose. They covered the two men's bald spots.

Reverend Noyes stood and gave the opening prayer.

43

DURING THE MORNING session, the Court of Oyer and Terminer first heard the case against John Willard.

John Willard was from Salem Village, a young man in his twenties. In the spring, it had been Willard's turn to be constable in the village. He had been the one who rode out to the homes of the accused witches, shackled them and taken them to jail. But when the number of accused witches had increased so rapidly, Willard had found he could no longer bring himself to arrest any more. He knew these people he had been ordered to arrest; he had grown up with them. There was no way they were the devil's minions. So, he had resigned as village constable. It was shortly thereafter that he himself had been accused of witchcraft.

Testimony began with his wife's grandfather, Bray Wilkins. He blamed Willard for the ill health he experienced after a Boston dinner party. He claimed that, after Willard had stared strangely at him, he could not eat or urinate. He further claimed that, after enduring the thirty-mile ride back to his home, he had found his seventeen-year-old grandson seriously ill. His grandson, he added in a shaking voice, had died a week later.

Next, Ann Putnam Sr. testified. She blamed Willard for the death of her newborn daughter. She stated that, when he had worked as a hired hand on Putnam's farm, she had occasionally left him to watch over her children and that her youngest had died before reaching her first birthday.

Willard hadn't helped his cause any when he fled the area upon learning they had accused him of witchcraft. This act alone was a virtual admission of guilt. They arrested Willard while he was tilling one of his fields in Lancaster.

The cumulative testimonies presented by his neighbors and family members, plus the sudden death of his nephew, and the fact that John Willard had run for the hills far outweighed all his pleas of innocence. But when he tried to recite the Lord's Prayer to prove his innocence, he stumbled. Not once, not twice, but five times.

"It is a strange thing, I can say it at another time. I think I am bewitched as well as they," he uttered with a nervous laugh.

The jury found him guilty of witchcraft. John Willard was escorted back to the Salem jail to await his day of execution. The next case was ready to be heard.

* * *

George Jacobs Sr. walked unsteadily to the front of the courtroom, supported by two handmade walking sticks he had whittled himself. Jacobs was a toothless eighty-year-old, from Salem, who suffered terribly from arthritis. Although his body made him appear frail, his mind was as sharp as a whip. He was forced to stand before the bench with his arms stretched out to his sides.

Sarah Churchill, his twenty-year-old maidservant, testified to Jacobs's mistreatment, saying he hit her with his canes. The afflicted girls suddenly cried out, "He's beating me; please make him stop." The chant went up among all the afflicted girls. Jacobs looked on in disbelief.

"Your worships," Jacobs said, facing the bench. "All of you," he turned to face the spectators. "Do you think this is true?"

"What do you think?" Hathorne fired back.

"Okay, Sarah, prove my guilt," Jacobs challenged his

maidservant. "Show me the marks, if I have struck you with my canes."

"Your specter accosted me at Ingersoll's Tavern," Sarah said bitterly.

"I saw your two canes; it was you," Mary Warren added. Back on March 31ˢᵗ, when the community had been praying for the afflicted girls, Jacobs had interrupted the session, doubting the integrity of the girls. As one of the afflicted, Mary had taken great offence to his accusations.

"May I sit, your worships, for I feel unstable?" Jacobs asked. He was finding it extremely difficult to stand without the support of his canes.

"You have enough strength to torment those poor children; you should have enough strength to stand," Hathorne grunted.

Jacobs took a moment to collect himself; he was determined not to beg. He would work with the hand he had been dealt. He took a deep breath and said, "The devil can go in any shape. The devil can take any likeness. Any person might be counterfeited." He had used this same argument during his examination back in May.

The judges simply ignored the old man's repeated protests. To accept that the devil could take on any likeness would be to doubt nearly all the evidence the court had heard to date. And such an acceptance would mean that they had been responsible for the execution of six innocent people.

After listening to the afflicted wail and bear false witness against him and seeing how gullible the judges were, Jacobs fell down on his knees. "Pray, do not accuse me," he begged. "I am as clear as your worships."

"There is your evidence," Stoughton stated, pointing at the suffering girls.

Sarah's testimony and the suffering displayed by the afflicted easily swayed the judges.

"You tax me for a wizard," Jacobs hissed. "You may as well tax me for a buzzard! I have done no harm!"

"You have lived a wicked life," Sarah shouted, but provided no further evidence.

The verdict was delivered: guilty as charged. When Jacobs was being hauled from the courtroom, he yelled one final message. "Well, burn me or hang me. I will stand in the truth of Christ!"

44

EDDIE HAD WRESTLED with his conscience all night. What Richard was asking him to do was insane, but then again he had always questioned Richard's mental stability.

If Eddie were to do as Richard asked, he would be responsible for killing or injuring hundreds of innocent people. Could he live with that guilt? Maybe, if he knew why, but Richard refused to explain the reason behind his request. On the other hand why should Eddie care? In his opinion, society had cast him aside. Those who were supposed to have been there to raise him and protect him had failed miserably. He didn't owe anything to anybody as Richard had so bluntly pointed out last night. And his reward for fulfilling Richard's request was beyond even his wildest dreams. He would be reunited with his parents after all this time.

When Eddie had finally agreed to carry out Richard's request, Harry had brought a wireless router and hooked it up to Eddie's computer. Harry stood, watching over Eddie's shoulder all night, making sure Eddie accessed only the information he needed to complete his task.

Even though Richard and Eddie supposedly had a working relationship now, Richard still hadn't returned Eddie's comm, which he had confiscated when he abducted Eddie. The message was clear: Richard didn't trust Eddie. Lack of trust was no stranger to Eddie, but he was fine with it because Eddie didn't trust Richard either.

Eddie hadn't been sitting idly in his suite waiting for Richard to shout his next order. Last night, after Richard had left, Eddie had quickly grabbed several pieces of adhesive film. Using the film and the leftover carbon powder, Eddie had lifted as many prints as he could from Richard's wine glass and cutlery and the wine bottle. He had hoped to get prints from both of Richard's hands. Since Richard was ambidextrous, Eddie wasn't sure which hand Richard used on the fingerprint scanner that controlled access to Eddie's room.

A few days earlier, Eddie had also hacked into Richard's security system. It was on the same network as his computer. *Amateur mistake,* Eddie thought. So, after Harry had collected the dinner cart, Eddie had reviewed the security footage of his room, stopping when he found what he was looking for. Eddie zoomed in on Richard's face and captured a digital image of Richard's eyes. Using his computer and 3D printer, Eddie fabricated a duplicate of Richard's retina, just in case Richard had a retina scanner as part of his security equipment. Eddie was determined to obtain his freedom. When the time was right, he wanted to leave nothing to chance.

45

RICHARD ROSE EARLIER this morning; it was going to be a very eventful day. He quickly pulled together the clothes he would need for his trip and headed down to the kitchen for a light breakfast. His jet would be fully stocked, so he could have a more leisurely meal once he and Quinn were airborne. Right now, however, time was of the essence.

Richard placed his thumb on the scanner and opened the door to Eddie's room. "Progress report," he demanded as he entered. He noticed Harry standing over Eddie's shoulder, just where he had left them six hours earlier.

"The kid has hacked into the . . ."

"If you don't mind," Eddie interrupted, "I can speak for myself. Besides, you have no idea what you're talking about."

Harry was about to clout the smart-mouthed kid, but Richard held up a hand, stopping any further conflict. Harry grunted and stepped away.

"Continue," Richard, directed to Eddie.

"After first educating myself on how the system worked and where I needed to go, I was able to hack into the Centralized Traffic Control System or CTC. The CTC controls train movements using interconnected track circuits and field signals," Eddie informed

Richard.

"Go on."

"The system is designed so that trains are given a series of progressive trackside signals that require the train crews to take action based on the signals displayed."

Richard remained silent; his face gave no indication as to whether he was understanding Eddie's explanation or not. Eddie continued. "Computer displays and controls are installed in the Rail Traffic Controller or RTC office. Computer screens indicate track occupancy between controlled locations. Train movements approaching controlled signals are governed by advance signals that are automatically triggered by the presence of a train located between two specific controlled signals." Eddie could see by the changing expression on Richard's face that the explanation was getting a little too technical, but he powered on.

"When the RTC requests controlled signals for trains, the signal system determines how permissive the signals will be. The displayed signal conveys information to train crews and dictates the speed at which the trains may operate and how far the trains are permitted to travel. Signals also provide protection against certain conditions, such as an occupied block, broken rail, or an open switch lined against the movement."

"I don't need to know how it works. I just need to know if you can carry out the required task," Richard snapped.

"Yes, I can," Eddie said confidently.

"Good. I'm leaving now. I'll be back in a few days," Richard stated tersely. "Harry will make sure the task is done."

Harry stepped forward, puffing out his barrel-like chest. Richard moved over to where Harry was standing and whispered some last-minutes instructions before leaving the room.

Since Richard wasn't interested in learning more about the system, Eddie didn't bother to mention that CTC doesn't provide any failsafe measure to slow or stop a train if it passed a stop signal or other point of restriction.

Tuesday, August 5, 1692

46

THE COURT HAD called a recess. The magistrates had retired to Beadle's Tavern for their noonday meal.

While waiting for the magistrates to return, three distinguished-looking men entered the courtroom and took seats at the back, beside Reverend Higginson, not far from the accused.

Reverends Increase Mather and Deodat Lawson from Boston and John Hale from Beverly had come to bear witness, personally, to these proceedings. After all, Reverend George Burroughs was one of their own. As a minister, he had been entrusted with the community's spiritual welfare. Now he was accused of conspiring with the devil to bring down the Kingdom of God, at a time when his community looked to him for strength.

A fourth man entered shortly afterwards and made his way to the front of the courtroom. He was Robert Calef, a prosperous merchant from Boston. In 1691, he had been appointed constable in Boston. During his time as constable, he hadn't been called upon to arrest anyone accused of witchcraft, since all those so accused lived in outlying areas, beyond his jurisdiction. Having served as a constable, he wanted to see, firsthand, what the witch trials were all about.

When the court reconvened, Reverend George Burroughs was called to the stand. Although not tall in stature, he walked sharply, holding his head high.

The testimony began with one of the afflicted girls, Susannah Sheldon, an eighteen-year-old from Salem Village. "Reverend Burroughs told me he was a conjurer and that he outranked the witches. He told me he had called them to his meetings," Sheldon said. "He pressured me to sign his book. When I said no, he kept tormenting me," she went on. "He even bit me on the arm," she added, holding out her right arm.

At that moment, as if on cue, screams erupted from the group of afflicted girls, each one grabbing her right arm and screaming in pain. "He bit me!" one of them screamed. Ann Putnam Sr., who had been sitting at the front of the courtroom, approached one of the girls. Pulling up her sleeve, Putnam noticed teeth marks on the girl's arm. She checked the rest of the afflicted.

"They've all been bitten," Ann Putnam Sr. reported.

"Would you be so kind as to approach the bench, Goody Putnam?" Stoughton asked.

Ann Putnam Sr. approached the bench as requested.

"You had a good look at the teeth marks?" Stoughton queried.

"Yes, I did," Putnam replied. "They were quite deep."

"Would you check the teeth of Reverend Burroughs and tell us what you think?"

Ann Putnam Sr. walked over to Burroughs. "Please open your mouth?" she asked politely.

Knowing he wasn't responsible for the afflicted girls' marks, Burroughs obliged. Ann Putnam Sr. stepped closer and looked into Burroughs's mouth. After only a moment, she stepped back and approached the bench.

"Well?" Stoughton asked.

"The marks on the girls' arms match the pattern of Reverend Burroughs's teeth," Putnam stated confidently.

"I am not responsible for those bite marks," Burroughs protested.

"Thank you, Goody Putnam, you may be seated," Stoughton said. Turning to Burroughs he asked, "Then who do you think is responsible?"

"I don't know," Burroughs answered angrily.

"Lying wench," Calef muttered. There was no way Goody Putnam could have determined that those bite marks were a match to Burroughs's teeth. *'No way in Hell.'*

One after another, neighbors were called to testify. "I knew Reverend Burroughs's first wife, Hannah," said John Putnam Sr. as he began his testimony. "The reverend, his wife and their two children boarded with us until the new parsonage was built. Hannah was a dutiful wife, but the reverend was always sharp with her. After his wife died in childbirth, I lent the reverend the money for her funeral. He never repaid me, so I sued him. My brother told me to have him arrested, so I did. That's when the Village paid him his overdue wages, deducting the amount owed to me."

John Putnam's wife, Rebecca, added that Burroughs had treated his late wives harshly, bringing them to the point of death and had then made any witness swear not to talk about it.

Mary Webber followed. "Sarah Burroughs, the reverend's second wife, was too afraid of her husband to write her own father, so I had to write for her. She described to me the apparitions she and her black woman servant saw in their Casco Bay house: a white calf that the reverend chased down the stairs."

"Did you say calf?" Hathorne asked for clarity.

"Yes, a white calf," Webber replied.

Next came the testimony of Hannah Harris, who was once a maid in the Burroughs's household. "The reverend would know what Mrs. Burroughs and I were talking about when he wasn't even there. When he returned home, he would repeat it to me, word for word, what we had said."

"Thank you, Goody Harris," Hathorne said, dismissing the witness.

"In my opinion, if Reverend Burroughs hadn't kept his wife standing at the doorway while they argued, when she should have been in bed recovering from childbirth, she wouldn't have died," Hannah Harris proclaimed, as she left the stand.

Thomas Ruck, Sarah Burroughs's brother, started his testimony. "We were strawberry picking one day. Sarah and I shared a horse. The reverend chose to walk. When he stepped off the road and went into the bushes, Sarah confided in me, describing how cruel Burroughs could be. Just as we were approaching home, the reverend suddenly appeared beside us with a basket full of berries. He yelled at Sarah; he knew what we had been talking about. He said he knew our thoughts. I said even the devil couldn't know that. And Burroughs replied, 'My god makes known your thoughts unto me.'"

"What do you have to say to this accusation, Reverend Burroughs?" Hathorne asked.

"My brother-in-law had left a man waiting for me while they went ahead with the horse," Burroughs replied, failing to explain how his reply altered the situation and clearly sidestepping the part of the testimony that dealt with his ability to read thoughts.

"That's not true," Ruck protested, "there were only the three of us."

"What was this other man's name, Reverend?" Hathorne asked, pushing for clarity.

"I don't recall," Burroughs replied dismally.

47

TESTIMONY AGAINST REVEREND George Burroughs continued when the court heard from nine militia men. "I heard that Burroughs aimed with only one hand a fowling piece that had a seven-foot barrel," one soldier stated.

"Did you see this for yourself?" Stoughton asked.

"No, I didn't actually see it, but I heard about it," the witness replied, "and I've seen the gun. I couldn't steady it with even two hands." Three other soldiers confirmed the story, but none had personally witnessed the act.

"I steadied the gun by holding it behind its lock and bracing the stock against my chest," Burroughs explained.

"Still, an incredible feat for someone of your stature," Hathorne interjected.

Other soldiers recounted a story they had heard where Burroughs had lifted a barrel of cider out of a canoe and had carried it ashore, all by himself. They had even heard that Burroughs said he had almost strained his leg on the slippery shoreline.

"That never happened," Burroughs countered. Although Burroughs was short for a man, he was exceptionally strong for his size.

Robert Calef couldn't believe what he was witnessing. "They

accuse their innocent neighbors, encouraged by blood-thirsty magistrates and ministers who have lured them in with bigoted zeal," Calef mumbled. The man sitting next to him gave him a scornful look.

Throughout the proceedings, the afflicted girls had been moaning and thrashing at the front of the courtroom. Suddenly, they all went completely still, as if frozen in place. They were staring in the same direction, at the same spot. They were focused on something between themselves and Burroughs.

"What's going on?" Stoughton asked, looking at the afflicted, waiting for an answer. But they didn't move: they didn't even blink.

"I said, what's going on?" Stoughton thundered.

A few seconds later, the afflicted girls seemed to be released from their trance-like state. They quickly huddled together, clutching each other in terror, their faces masks of terror.

"What is it? What did you see?" Hathorne asked cautiously.

"I saw four specters," Susannah Sheldon said, still trembling. "I saw Hannah and Sarah Burroughs. They told me that the reverend had murdered them. They said he had smothered them and choked them."

"I saw the reverends' wives, too," Abigail Williams added. "They told me he had stabbed them and strangled them." Abigail Williams was Reverend Samuel Parris's twelve-year-old niece. She had been living with Reverend Parris, his wife and their nine-year-old daughter, Betty, when this witchcraft hysteria had blown up in Salem Village. In fact, Abigail and Betty had been the first girls in the village to be afflicted.

"Who were the other two ghosts?" Stoughton probed.

"I saw Reverend Lawson's wife and daughter," Mary Warren said.

Lawson bolted upright from his seat, only to be hauled back down by Mather. "Let it be," Mather said. "It's of no consequence now."

"I see no ghosts," Burroughs stated, appalled by this testimony.

"Vile wenches," Robert Calef muttered.

Seizures again claimed the afflicted, choking them speechless, stopping any further testimony from the young girls.

"Whom do you believe hinders these witnesses?" Stoughton asked.

"It is the devil," Burroughs replied.

"How come the devil is so loath to have any testimony borne against you?" Stoughton demanded.

No answer came from Burroughs.

Amid the distressing spectacle of the afflicted, the magistrates overlooked or ignored the contradictions in the stories about the ghosts of Burroughs's wives.

"Those who give false witness, as those who do so here, are the devil's brokers," Burroughs said. He reached over and handed a piece of paper to Judge Sewall, who sat closest to him. Sewall unfolded the paper and read it to himself.

Where is it written in all the Old and New Testaments that a witch is a murderer, or hath power to kill by witchcraft, or to afflict with any disease or infirmity? Where is it written that witches have biggs (nipples) for imps to suck on . . . that the devil setteth privy marks upon witches . . . that witches can hurt corn or cattle . . . or can fly in the air . . . Where do we read of a he-devil or she-devil, called incubus or succubus that useth generation or copulation?

Sewall glared at Burroughs and passed the piece of paper to the next magistrate. It took only a few moments before they all had had a chance to read what it said.

"You copied this from a book," Hathorne accused Burroughs.

"No, I did not," Burroughs said emphatically.

"It's from a book called 'A Candle in the Dark'," Hathorne said frankly.

"I'm not familiar with that book," Burroughs responded.

"It came directly from Thomas Ady's book. I recognize it, too," Sewall argued.

"I did not get it from a book." Burroughs was adamant.

"Then, where did you get it?" Hathorne asked suspiciously.

"A young man gave it to me," Burroughs admitted.

Burroughs unwaveringly claimed his innocence throughout his trial, but to no avail.

Chief Justice William Stoughton spoke to the jury before they deliberated. "I want you to ignore the obvious good health of these afflicted young girls, even though the indictment referred to them in the usual way as 'pined, consumed, and wasted' by witchcraft. Their present health is only temporary, because they still suffer such tortures, as everyone present has observed. And it's these tortures that would ordinarily tend to pine and to consume. Am I making myself clear?"

The jurors understood Stoughton's message clearly. When they came back into the courtroom, they delivered their verdict: guilty.

Calef had seen and heard enough. The court had overlooked the fact that no single act of witchcraft had been positively proven to have been caused by Burroughs, much less observed by two witnesses, except for the afflicted who could see into the Invisible World.

Calef rose from of his seat at the front, turned around and faced the crowd. "As long as men suffer themselves to be poisoned in their education, and be grounded in a false belief by the Books of the Heathen; as long as the devil shall be believed to have natural power, to act above and against a course of nature; as long as the Witches shall be believed to have power to commission him; as long as the devil's testimony, by the pretended afflicted, shall be received as more valid to condemn than pleas of not guilty to acquit; as long as the accused shall have their lives and liberties confirmed and restored upon them, upon their confessing themselves guilty; as long as the accused shall be forced to undergo hardships and torments for their not confessing; as long as teats for the devil to suck are searched for upon the bodies of the accused, as a token of guilt; as long as the Lord's Prayer shall be profaned, by being made a test, who are culpable; as long as witchcraft, sorcery, familiar spirits, and necromancy shall be used to discover who is a witch; so long as the innocent suffer as witches, God will be daily dishonoured and his judgements can be expected to continue."

"Remove him," Hathorne bellowed. The guards escorted Calef from the courtroom while the sheriff's deputies led Reverend George Burroughs back up the center aisle toward the exit.

But Burroughs got in one last proclamation. "I will die due to false witnesses," he shouted as they ushered him out of the building and back to the Salem Town jail.

Burroughs's statement had rattled Reverend Hale. Was Calef right? Was John Proctor's letter stating the truth? Were the magistrates themselves fallible? Were these trials being mishandled? John Hale had to do something. He rushed over to talk to Ann Foster before the next case was heard. In her own trial, she had accused Burroughs of attending the great witches meeting and had said that he would be the King of Hell. Hale recalled during Goody Foster's examination on July 16, that she wasn't totally convinced of her testimony and was being led through her testimony by suggestions from the magistrates. "You are one that brings this man to death," Hale pointed out to her. "If you have charged anything upon him, that is not true, recall it before it be too late, while he is alive."

"I have done nothing wrong," Foster claimed.

48

MIKE LEANED OVER and gently nibbled on Kerry's exposed neck. She purred like a kitten. She and Mike had awakened before the alarm this morning and had enjoyed some 'quality' time together.

"I need to get ready for work," Kerry said half-heartedly.

"Why don't you call in sick?" Mike teased.

"I can't do that when it's my own business and you know it," Kerry said, slapping his hand away, as it wandered underneath the covers.

"Then rearrange your appointments for another day and come sailing with me. It's supposed to be another gorgeous day," Mike suggested eagerly.

"Hon, you know I wish I could, but I can't. My clients need me."

Kerry threw back the covers and walked toward the bathroom. Mike's eyes devoured her voluptuous form as she made her way across the room. Kerry paused at the door, leaned seductively against the frame, and whispered, "Care to join me in the shower?"

Kerry didn't wait for an answer; she didn't need to. She heard

Mike fall out of bed, and, then, curse loudly when he stubbed his toe on a chair as he dashed toward the bathroom.

Mike could hear the water already running. He was about to reap the benefits of having the bathroom renovated a year ago. Besides having had all new appliances and fixtures installed, Mike had made a point of having the shower enlarged. It now boasted multi-level jets, a hand-held wand, and an over-sized shower head that could easily accommodate both of them. He had justified the larger shower on the grounds that, when they showered together, it would save time and water. Kerry had quickly pointed out it would actually take longer and use more water. But she wasn't really complaining.

Forty-five minutes later, they were in the kitchen of their two-storey, three-thousand-square-foot condominium situated on the edge of Frenchman's Bay. Their sailboat was practically sitting in their front yard. Having their boat so close by facilitated the frequent impromptu outings they enjoyed at all hours of the day. Kerry particularly enjoyed their sunset cruises. It was a relaxing time for her, away from the hustle of downtown. She would often prepare a dinner basket to take with them. They would sail on the lake and enjoy a barbeque while they watched the sun set. Most nights, they relied on the boat's engine to return them to harbor, since the winds usually calmed once the sun had set.

"If I don't leave now, I'll miss my train," Kerry said, gathering up her briefcase, her packed lunch and her car keys. She leaned over and gave Mike a passionate kiss. "Thanks for this morning," she teased.

"My pleasure." Mike grinned eagerly. "Let's do it again, soon."

"One-track mind." Kerry opened the front door. Mike followed her out.

"I'm heading down to the dock to make the most of this weather while I can. Last chance to change your mind," Mike said hopefully.

"Don't rub it in! I have three more months before I retire, then we can play all day long. Damn, it's going to be a long three months," Kerry replied miserably.

"What time will you be home?"

"The usual; around six," Kerry answered, tossing her briefcase and lunch onto the passenger seat of her silver Mercedes-Benz SLK Roadster.

"I'll have supper ready," Mike said. "Have a good day."

"You, too," Kerry shouted as Mike started for the marina.

Kerry started the car, pulled out of the driveway and headed for the Fastrax station, which, thankfully, was only fifteen minutes away. While stopped at a red light, Kerry reached into her briefcase for her comm; it wasn't there. "Damn, I must have left it on the bedside table," she cursed. She pulled a U-turn and headed back to the condo. *I'll just catch the next train and I'll still make my 9:30 AM appointment,* she thought.

49

KELLEN BEDDAR PULLED into the four-level parking garage, found a vacant spot, parked his blue Hyundai Veloster Turbo and turned off the engine. "Come on, Shelby, time to go," he said to his sister who was snoozing in the front seat.

"All right, already," Shelby mumbled, as she pulled herself out of the car. She had been up most of the night looking after her fiancé, who was fighting the current strain of the flu that was making its rounds.

"You can sleep on the way into the city," Kellen suggested.

Shelby Beddar was a twenty-three-year-old registered nurse and had been working at the downtown City Hospital for the last two years. She was five-foot-five, with long honey-blond hair that fell loosely about her shoulders. She had beautiful pale-blue eyes and a warm, friendly smile. Unless she was sleep deprived that is.

Kellen was two years older and seven inches taller. He had an athlete's physique, short-cropped brown hair and brown eyes.

Kellen grabbed his RCAF messenger bag off the back seat and locked the car. He was given the Royal Canadian Air Force bag as a Christmas gift. Proceeds from each bag sold went toward helping war veterans, like his grandfather.

Kellen made his way over to the stairs, with his sister straggling behind. "If you want to grab a coffee, you'd better pick up the pace. We have only ten minutes before the next train gets here," Kellen prodded. He had seen the express train pull out of the station just as they had entered the parking garage.

After quickly grabbing a coffee, as was his regular routine, Kellen took up his usual position at the west end of the platform, waiting for the train. He looked over his shoulder and saw Shelby sitting on a bench behind him, her head resting against a pole, her eyes closed.

Kellen and Shelby preferred the platform's west end and therefore the west end of the train. Because, when the train arrives in Union Station, they'd be close to the station's western exits and as a result, would have few commuters to contend with while exiting the station. And, once out of the station, they wouldn't be far from their final destinations.

Kellen had started working at his uncle's law firm after graduating from university. Even though he had had to start as a first-year associate at the Good, Beddar, Best Law Firm, he was gaining some valuable experience. He just had to be patient; he would work his way up to be a partner one day. Besides being ambitious, he had big dreams. To begin with, he would buy his first house; it would be something small and close to the law firm, so he could save on the daily forty-eight minute commute time. And before the month was out, he was going to ask his girlfriend of three years, Becky Lake, to marry him.

Kellen's thoughts of partnership, houses and Becky were rudely interrupted as the train rolled into the station. "Come on, Shelby, time to board," he shouted to be heard over the rumble of the train. When the train finally came to a stop, the doors slid open.

The waiting commuters quickly and quietly made their way on board. A few stragglers darted up the last few stairs to the trains platform and jumped aboard just as the doors were closing, all of them gasping to catch their breath. *What a way to start the day,* Kellen thought.

"Made it," Kerry mumbled. She looked around and promptly

found a vacant seat. *Not as packed as the express train,* she thought, sitting beside a very pregnant woman.

Kellen and Shelby found a vacant set of four seats on the lower level of the bi-level car. Shelby claimed the two by the window, leaning her head against the wall and throwing her feet up onto the seat facing her; she closed her eyes and easily fell asleep. Kellen took the vacant seats across from Shelby and put his bag on the seat beside her.

After the doors had closed, a voice over the public address system announced the next stop as the train pulled away from the station and headed west into the city.

Before Kellen pulled out his tablet to check his activities for the day, he looked around the car at the other the passengers. Some were slouched against the windows, trying, like his sister, to catch a few more zzzzs. Others were reading. Still others were having their morning coffee and muffin en route. A few were carrying on quiet conversations. As much as he disliked having to ride the train twice a day, he had to admit that it was a very civilized way to travel.

Tuesday, August 5, 1692

50

DARIC STOOD EIGHT feet from the magistrates; the accusers were to his right. His was the next case called to the bar.

Daric was wearing a white shirt with brown pinstripes, a brown tweed vest, and trousers. His shirt looked more beige than white right now. His chocolate-brown tie had been bartered several days ago for a loaf of bread. His highly polished black shoes were covered in dust, dirt, and other matter.

"You understand that you have been charged to be guilty of witchcraft?" Judge Stoughton asked curtly.

"I am not a witch or wizard and have done nothing wrong," Daric replied.

"You're not from around here, are you?" Judge Sewall asked warily.

"No, I'm not."

"Where exactly are you from?" Judge Hathorne interjected.

Dani and Daric had talked a bit about what they could say at their trial that wouldn't cast them under further suspicion. They realized that they didn't have a lot of leeway for explaining their sudden appearance.

"I'm from up north. My sister and I were trying to get away from all the fighting. We had just arrived in Salem when we were almost run over by a cart," Daric said, hoping his words would explain how they had suddenly appeared under the prison cart.

Sheriff Corwin stood up and declared, "I was driving the cart. I never saw you."

"We were standing among the crowd, when my sister got dizzy and fell forward into the path of the cart. I rushed to her aid." *Come on, it's a reasonable explanation.* Daric was hoping his response would put an end to the current line of questioning.

Before further questioning could resume, one of the afflicted girls cried out, "He's pinching me!" The others immediately reacted, joining the cries of the first. All, that is, except for Susannah Sheldon. She couldn't take her eyes off Daric.

Hathorne motioned to the guards. They stepped forward, grabbed Daric's hands and, holding them firmly, stretched his arms out, away from his body.

Dani sprang up from her seat, wanting to help her brother, but she was forcibly shoved back onto the bench. "Don't move!" Constable Neale barked.

Dani gave him a withering glare. Ever since she could remember, she felt overly protective of her younger brother. Even now, when he towered over her and could hold his own in a scrap, she still had that impulse to go to his aid.

"Mary Warren, who hurts you?" Hathorne asked.

"He does; he hurts me," Warren replied, pointing directly at Daric.

"You are to look straight ahead at all times," Hathorne ordered Daric. "You will not torment these poor creatures further."

"Why do you hurt these children?" Stoughton asked.

"Why would I hurt them? I don't even know them," Daric responded sarcastically.

Steady Daric. Dani prayed he would have some patience. *You don't need to make matters worse.*

"Whom do you employ, then, to do it?" Stoughton continued the questioning.

"No one," Daric said firmly. "Like I said, we just arrived in town when we were immediately arrested. We did nothing wrong. No one said anything. They just threw us in irons and dragged us off to jail."

Reverend Case had noticed that Sheldon was staring at Daric and hadn't moved or said a word. Case bent down and whispered to Sewall, who promptly looked over at the girl.

Case said loud enough for all to hear, "The devil has struck her dumb so that she cannot testify."

Reverend Noyes seized this opportunity to preach to the masses. He stood abruptly and bellowed, "Be sober, be vigilant, because your adversary the devil, as a roaring lion walks about seeking whom he may devour."

There was a great gasp among the crowd in the courtroom; they were nervous and frightened. They were looking suspiciously at the person sitting next to them, wondering whether they might be the devil himself.

The gavel banged several times on the table. Gradually, the crowd settled down and the trial was able to continue. The banging seemed to have snapped Sheldon out of her stupor. She suddenly realized she was the center of some unwanted attention. She swiftly pulled herself together.

"Which of you will go and touch the prisoner at the bar?" Stoughton asked. The court, once again, was relying on magic to produce evidence in this grand jury trial.

Sheldon lurched forward. She wanted to get as close to Daric as she could. But before she could take three steps, the other girls fell down into fits. Sheldon turned and scowled at her friends; their antics were putting a crimp into her plans.

"Look away from these girls, in case you make their afflictions worse," Hathorne instructed Daric.

Daric promptly turned his head to the left in response to Hathorne's instruction. He sensed someone approach, but saw no one.

Sheldon approached the handsome young man in the strange clothes. When the prisoner's hand was extended to perform the touch test, Sheldon latched onto his arm with both of her hands and rolled to the ground, yanking Daric with her. Her unexpected action had caught both guards by surprise, causing them to lose their grip on Daric.

As Daric lay in a heap on top of Sheldon, she whispered, "What's your name?"

"Daric," he replied, as he was being hauled back onto his feet.

Sheldon could have sworn she had felt a spark between her and Daric when she had looked into his beautiful blue eyes. She was infatuated with him. She wanted to know more about him. She wanted him as her own. But he was accused of witchcraft, however falsely; it was a situation she would have to remedy. He would be hers one day, of that she was sure.

Sheriff Corwin handed each guard a piece of rope. One piece was tied around Daric's left wrists, the other around his right. The guards, standing to either side of Daric, pulled on the ropes and hauled Daric's arms out, away from his body.

Dani had a quick flash of memory, triggered by seeing Daric standing there with his arms extended. It reminded her of better times when Daric was young and all he wanted was to be a pilot. He would run around the yard with his arms held out and pretend he was an airplane, sound effects and all. Hathorne's booming voice brought her back to reality.

"Take the rest of the girls to the prisoner," Hathorne ordered so the touch tests to continue.

The guards carried the other girls, one-by-one, over to where Daric stood. One of the deputies directed Daric's hand toward the girls and placed it firmly on their arms.

"They are well," Hathorne stated quickly, as he directed the girls be returned to their places.

"There's your evidence," Stoughton declared. "Do you still profess your innocence?"

"What would you have me say, that I looked into the eyes of the devil and I gave him my soul?" Daric posed sarcastically.

No! Dani moaned. *What were you thinking?*

"There you have it. He is a wizard," Case announced loudly. "He admitted conspiring with the devil."

"No, I was being facetious," Daric explained.

"Did you not just say you gave your soul to the devil?" Stoughton asked coldly.

"I know you think you understand what you thought you heard, but that's not what I actually meant!" Daric said scathingly.

Despite Daric's arguments, it didn't take long for the jury to return a verdict of guilty.

51

DANI'S CASE WAS the last to be heard this day. All the prisoners tried before her today had been found guilty. Dani didn't delude herself into believing that she would receive a verdict different from that already dealt to the others.

Dani walked proudly down the aisle and took her place in front of the magistrates. She was flanked by two guards. She looked to her right and watched the girls for just an instant. Dani knew the court theatrics would begin at any moment, of that she had no doubt.

"As with your brother, you understand that you have been charged to be guilty of witchcraft?" Judge Stoughton asked curtly. "How do you plead?"

"Not guilty," Dani replied.

The afflicted girls stared in awe at the young woman standing before the bench. Her strange clothes were cut differently than their own, making her look slimmer and shapelier; they weren't like the baggy, drab-colored dresses and petticoats worn by the women and girls around Salem. Dani was still wearing her nurse's uniform: the ankle-length, deep-blue chambray dress with a white collar and cuffs. Her outfit was missing the apron which she had sacrificed for bandages to aid Andrew Carrier.

"To save the court time, as it is getting late," Stoughton said, "do you concur with your brother's story?"

"About us fleeing from the north and being thrown in jail for doing nothing wrong? Of course I agree with his story, because it's the truth," Dani asserted.

The first witness was called to the stand to testify. Dani remembered seeing her talking with the jail keeper yesterday.

The witness walked down the aisle and stood beside Dani. Their eyes met. Dani could see bitterness and fear in her eyes and was at a loss for a reason why.

"State your name, young woman," Stoughton barked.

"Mary Lacy Jr.," she replied.

"What do you have to testify?" Hathorne asked.

"She's a witch. I saw it for myself," Lacy proclaimed.

"Saw what?" Judge Corwin jumped in. He had been sitting by quietly, letting Stoughton and Hathorne carry most of the weight of the questioning, but curiosity got the better of him.

"She saved the Carrier boy's arm with magic. The doctor said it had to come off. The witch told him no. Then she used her magic to cure him," Lacy declared.

"What do you say to this? Are you guilty or not?" Stoughton asked.

"Yes, I saved his arm, but I'm not guilty of being a witch or of using magic. I can explain," Dani said. But Dani never had a chance to offer her defence.

Susannah Sheldon had been glaring at Dani with contempt as she stood before the bench. As far as Sheldon was concerned, Dani was the enemy. And she couldn't care less that Dani was Daric's sister. Sheldon needed to make sure Dani didn't interfere with her plans; so she screamed as loudly as she could, fell to the ground and started writhing on the floor. As if on cue, the other girls dropped, screaming and writhing as well.

"Why do you torment these poor creatures?" Stoughton barked angrily.

"I do not torment them," Dani retorted.

"Whom do you employ, then?" Hathorne badgered.

"I employ no one," Dani replied firmly. She remembered this line of questioning from her examination and from the trials earlier today; it had led nowhere.

"Susannah Sheldon, who hurts you?" Hathorne asked.

Dani turned to her right to watch the theatrics.

Sheldon was struck dumb; she could only moan in pain as she pointed directly at Dani.

"Turn your head away from them," Hathorne ordered Dani. She complied, turning back to the bench. The screaming gradually diminished to a chorus of low moans.

Dani wanted to make sure she could instill some doubt within those who attended her trial today, in the hope that maybe, just maybe, someday, it would help the accused who came after her. She stared deeply into Hathorne's eyes and held her gaze while she asked, "Why is it that, when I look at you, you are not stricken as well?"

There was no answer from the bench.

"And if I were a witch, why would I want to reveal myself by using magic in this courtroom?" Dani asked. "That's as bad as holding a smoking gun."

"What does a smoking gun have to do with anything?" Reverend Case jumped in.

"In a murder case, if I were caught holding a smoking gun, it would certainly establish my guilt," Dani explained.

"We're not talking about murder, here," Case snapped back.

"Aren't we?" Dani asked bluntly, glaring at Case. She held her stare until he lowered his eyes; then she again addressed the bench. "Then tell me why you are hanging people who profess their innocence, yet you let confessed witches live? Is it not written in the Scriptures that thou shall not suffer a witch to live? So why is it they still do?" Dani's hypermnesic brain would serve her well, as she tried to drive her point home.

"What I have witnessed here today is neighbors blaming neighbors for their ill-fortune and accusing them of witchcraft. You blame a dead cow or a sick child on your neighbor when in fact it could simply be God's punishment. He certainly has plenty of reason to punish us, but we may never truly know the reason why.

Dani paused for effect before proceeding. She seemed to be having an impact; people were actually listening.

"Is it not true that the devil delights in plaguing people?" Dani asked the judges.

"Of course, he does. Everyone knows that," Case said, exasperated.

"With good and evil so apparently present in this world, to question the devil's reality is inevitably to doubt God's," Dani continued.

"No one here doubts God's existence," Case said tersely.

"Then isn't God ultimately in charge?" Dani asked, baiting the hook.

"Of that, there is no question," Judge Gedney said flatly, finally making some comment in these proceedings.

"Then God, in effect, has allowed the devil to inflict these trials. God has, in fact, permitted some individuals to torment the innocent."

Dani turned to look upon the six young girls, the ones who in her opinion were the cause of the witchcraft hysteria.

Sheldon immediately collapsed on the floor, again, followed closely by the others.

"Bring them over, one-by-one, and have her touch them," Hathorne instructed the guards. They ushered the afflicted toward Dani for the touch test. Predictably, they were instantly cured.

"Despite your grandstanding and your emphatic arguments and your insistent profession of innocence, here is the undisputed evidence," Stoughton declared in a booming voice for all to hear.

The outcome was inevitable: the jury came back with a guilty verdict. As Dani was led down the aisle, she could see doubt in the eyes of some of those in attendance. *Maybe my testimony will have some impact, will raise some reasonable doubt,* she thought, as she left the courtroom.

52

REVERENDS MATHER, LAWSON, Hale and Higginson all sat in the back of the now empty courtroom. They were lost in their own thoughts, reflecting on the day's proceedings. Finally, Reverend Lawson broke the silence. "It would appear that specter evidence, along with malicious stories, is the same evidence previously used to convict one accused, and is now used to convict them all."

"Evidence of incidents years ago, maybe even twenty or thirty years ago, about overturned carts, the death of livestock, cross words between relatives, or unexpected accidents or deaths occurring after some senseless quarrel," Higginson added.

"As I said before, there are far too many people being accused of witchcraft, people who have, up until this time, led righteous lives," Hale voiced.

"The evidence for all witchcraft cases should be as clear as the evidence used for other capital crimes. Magical tests, such as the touch test or witch marks, should not be considered lawful," Mather stated bluntly.

"Witch marks are a useless piece of evidence, for who among us is unblemished and could pass such a test?" asked Hale.

"And not all touch tests end the afflicted girls' fits. Time, more than touch, seems to be the cure," Lawson added.

"Even if it did work, is it still not sorcery?" Hale asked.

"Some would say that it was a scientific fact that a witch's touch could reabsorb the venomous and malignant particles that were ejected from the eye," Higginson clarified.

"Nonsense," Mather blurted out. "There's no way. If it were true, why are others not poisoned by the suspect's glance, especially the tender, fearful women in the courtroom?"

"That's what that young woman was trying to ask. And the magistrates gave no answer, if I recall," Lawson said, amazed. "It was as if they didn't hear her question or wanted to simply ignore it. Either way, I thought it was a well-crafted position."

"I'd also like to point out that the court today overlooked the fact that not one single act of witchcraft had been proven positively as having been caused by the suspects, let alone as having been observed by two reliable witnesses. The only witnesses were the afflicted girls, who are also the only ones who can see into the Invisible World," Hale stated candidly.

"And even the evidence given by the afflicted girls assumes that the accused and their specters are one and the same. The magistrates may as well have condemned for murder a man who kills his own shadow," Higginson said.

"It is a terrifying and deadly charade that is being played out here," Lawson muttered.

53

DARIC HAD WAITED anxiously at the cell bars for the return of his sister, staring down the aisle toward the stairs. To him, the wait seemed like an eternity. His mind was running amuck, playing out different scenarios, none of which were reassuring. What if she didn't return? What if she were sent to another prison? What if they decided to use her to set an example for others and opted to burn her at the stake?

"Why don't you take it easy? She'll be back soon enough," John Proctor said. John had been watching Daric since he returned from his trial, and Daric hadn't moved from that spot.

Daric wheeled around to face John, still clenching the bars tightly in his fists. "How do you know? How can you be so sure?"

Suddenly, Daric heard the creaking of the wooden stairs. *Someone's coming.* He strained to see who was descending into hell as he had so eloquently referred to as his new home.

"Thank God," he muttered. It was Dani. She was being escorted by Constable Neale.

"Told you," John muttered, but he doubted Daric heard him. Daric was too overcome with relief. Everything around him, except of course Dani, had faded from sight.

Once the cell door was locked and Neale had left the cellblock,

Daric made his way toward the back end of the cell, to their usual meeting place.

"Dani?" Daric called. She appeared instantly.

Dani had known her brother would be anxiously awaiting her return, but she hadn't expected to see a glistening tear running down his stubbled cheek.

"Hey," Dani whispered, "are you okay?"

"I'm fine, now," Daric said, as he collapsed onto the straw-strewn floor. "You had me worried. It seemed like you were gone for so long and, then, my mind started wander. Needless to say, it wasn't a pleasant experience."

"I'm sorry to have . . ."

"Never mind that. Tell me what happened," Daric interrupted. He hated when his emotions surfaced. He always thought it made him look weak, so he quickly changed the flow of the conversation. He was eager to hear about Dani's trial.

"What do you think happened?" Dani grunted in frustration. "It was the same thing that happened all day. The suspect gets called to the stand. The girls fall down screaming in pain. They point accusing fingers at the defendant. And then the verdict comes back guilty. That pretty much sums up my trial."

"Crap," Daric muttered.

"In my case, it was Susannah Sheldon who started the drama. I don't know what she has against me, but when she started screaming, the others joined in."

"The one who pulled me to the ground?" Daric asked, mystified.

"One and the same. But I did get in my two cents worth," Dani said proudly.

"You didn't do anything that would alter history, did you?" Daric asked warily.

"No, I just made a few observations and asked a few questions. Unfortunately, it did nothing to help my case, but I was hoping my actions might raise some doubt for future trials. So not to worry," Dani explained. "And by the way, what were *you* thinking!"

"What?"

"Telling them you had sold your soul to the devil, is what," Dani snapped.

"Actually, I said *gave* not sold," Daric said, trying to deflect his sister's wrath.

"Don't play semantics with me; you know you'll lose," Dani sneered.

"Okay, I'm sorry. I guess I wasn't thinking."

"That's apparent," Dani scoffed.

"So, now what? What happens next?" Daric asked nervously.

"Now that we've been found guilty, we'll be executed," Dani said miserably.

"We both know that can't happen. If we ever want to get back home, we need to get out of here. And to do that, we need to be able to touch our bands, something we haven't been able to do," Daric grumbled.

"And from what we've witnessed so far about the executions, the prisoners are taken one-by-one to be hanged. That scenario won't work for us. We need to come up with something so we can go to our executions together. Then, we'd be close enough to have a chance of escaping this hellhole," Dani concluded.

Present Day—Tuesday

54

EDDIE HAD GONE over the Fastrax train schedule for what seemed like the hundredth time.

"Get on with it," Harry barked. "What are you waiting for?"

"Just give me a minute! This is delicate work, but you wouldn't understand that, now would you?" Eddie jeered.

You'll get yours, you little shit, Harry thought as he glared at Eddie.

Eddie was having second thoughts about the commitment he had made to Richard Case. *I can't do this. I can't kill hundreds of innocent people.* His apprehension resulted from the research he had been doing last night. He had discovered that Fastrax trains had two diesel locomotives in a push-pull configuration. Twelve bi-level cars were between the locomotives. Each car had a seating capacity of one hundred sixty-two passengers. Over the course of a day, Fastrax made two-hundred-forty trips and carried some 185,000 passengers. Ninety percent of its ridership occurred during rush hour.

Richard had left explicit instructions that Eddie was to target a rush hour express train. He knew it would be packed with people, pressed into the cars like sardines in a can. But Eddie just couldn't bring himself to do it. He figured if he stalled long enough, there would be no express trains left to target. And with rush hour almost over, the trains wouldn't have as many passengers. Maybe he could live with that.

Eddie watched the 567 Fastrax train on his monitor. It had just made its last scheduled stop and now was heading into the city; its estimated arrival time was 9:10 A.M. Eddie worked his fingers nimbly over his keyboard and watched the results on the monitor. Just like that, with a couple of quick keystrokes, it was done. He hoped he'd be able to live with himself afterwards.

While Eddie had been focussing on his screen and struggling with his restless conscience, Richard had been occupied, too.

After loading his scuba gear, Richard climbed into his graphite-grey Audi Q7 SUV and left his elegant estate at 8:15 A.M., heading toward the Delaneys'. He didn't actually need his SUV, because Richard was making sure he'd be picking up just one passenger, but the Delaneys didn't know that. Not yet, anyway. So Richard had to maintain the charade.

Richard had the radio on for the entire trip, waiting to hear the breaking news. He had left clear instructions for Eddie to execute the plan at precisely 8:25 A.M. Timing was critical. Richard checked the dashboard clock; it showed 8:48 A.M. "Damn," he cursed, slamming his hand against the steering wheel. "Can't that damn kid complete one simple request?"

55

"MOTHER! MOTHER! ARE you in here?" a small voice echoed off the limestone walls.

"Dear God, that's Sarah," Martha moaned, as she pulled herself up off the filthy floor and made her way through the crowded cell toward the bars. Her worst nightmare was coming true.

"Here, Sarah," Martha called from deep within the cell.

Sarah frantically scanned the shadowy depths behind the bars, searching for her lifeline. Once Sarah saw her mother, she ran to her, desperately reaching through the bars to hug her. She hadn't seen her for over two months. Tears were streaming down Sarah's cherubic face.

Sarah Carrier was Martha's seven-year-old daughter. Her face was smeared with dirt. Her clothes were wrinkled and hadn't seen a bar of soap for what she could only assume was weeks. Her hair, poking out from under her cap, was knotted and tangled, meaning it had not seen a comb in a while, either. What else could Martha expect of her poor husband, who had to manage the farm, the household, and three frightened children all ten years of age or younger?

"Open the door quickly. Please!" Martha begged the jail keeper, Dounton, who had opened the men's cell first. He had ushered Thomas inside, locking the door behind him. Now Dounton made his way over to the women's cellblock. "Back away from the door," he grunted. Martha, reluctantly let go of her daughter, but Sarah wouldn't release her tenacious grip. "Sarah, please, let him open the door," Martha pleaded. Sarah hesitantly stepped aside, but staying within feet of her mother. She didn't want to let her mother out of her sight for fear she would lose her again. When Dounton opened the door, Sarah bolted into the arms of her mother, sobbing uncontrollably.

With her arms tightly around her daughter, Martha carried her precious bundle back to her corner of the cell. She gently cradled Sarah as she sat down. She leaned back against the cool stone wall. "It's all right, Sarah, I'm here. I'm not going anywhere," Martha cooed.

After several minutes, Sarah relaxed her grip and looked up with bloodshot hazel eyes and her tear-stained face. "I missed you," Martha whispered, gently cupping Sarah's cheeks.

"Who is this little one?" Dani asked.

"This is Sarah, my second youngest," Martha said, looking tenderly at the girl resting quietly in her arms. "Thomas is here, too. That's four of my five children," Martha said sadly.

Dani couldn't image what Martha was going through. If their roles had been reversed, Dani didn't know whether she would have had Martha's strength and courage. She couldn't help but admire her friend.

"Would you mind holding her for a moment? I'd like to check on my boys," Martha said.

"Sure," Dani replied, smiling warmly at the child who only stared suspiciously at Dani.

"Sarah, this is my friend, Dani," Martha explained. "She's going to sit here with you for a moment. I need to check on your brothers. I'll be right back, I promise."

Sarah's pleading eyes tore at Martha's heart. She gently pried Sarah's hands from around her waist and placed them in Dani's. "I'll be right back." Martha stood and walked to the bars.

"Richard?" Martha called. It took only a moment before all three of Martha's boys were standing across the aisle from her, peering through the bars. Even though only feet separated them, the distance could have been the span of an ocean; the results were the same. She couldn't reach out and comfort them as her motherly instincts craved. But she and her children would have to be strong if they were going to get through this.

"Is everyone okay?"

"We're fine, Mother," Richard said firmly, but there was a slight tremble in his voice.

"I need you to look after each other, you hear me?" Martha said. "Your father will see to our needs as best he can, but he still has to tend to the farm and take care of your baby sister."

"We'll take care of each other," Andrew chimed in. He had been moved back to the men's ward, when his health had ceased to be a concern. Andrew had his arm around his younger brother's shoulder, pulling him into his side for reassurance. They were good boys, Martha thought, realizing at the same time they were all too quickly growing up to be young men. They would need the extra strength that would occur with adulthood in the days to come.

"Thomas, you listen to your brothers. They know what to do. Okay?"

"I'm scared," Thomas whimpered.

"I know you are, but I need you to be a big boy now. You did like I told you to do, didn't you?" Martha wanted to make sure her children followed the explicit instructions she had left them before being arrested. For some reason, Martha feared her arrest was only the beginning.

"Sarah and I did exactly like you told us," Thomas said as he puffed out his tiny chest. "I told them that I had been a witch for only a week and that you had come to me as a talking yellow bird carrying a book for me to sign. And that you had baptised me in the Shawsheen River and had said that I was yours forever and ever.

"That's a good boy," Martha said appreciatively.

"Sarah said what you told her to say, too," Thomas added.

"I am so proud of both of you." Martha smiled feebly.

"Mother, why did you tell them to lie?" Richard asked, bewildered.

"A confessed witch has never been executed, so far. I thought it was the best chance that I had to keep my children alive," Martha explained. Richard nodded in understanding.

"I have to go back to Sarah. I promised her I wouldn't be gone long," Martha said regretfully. "We'll talk again later. Take care of each other." Martha stared for a moment longer at her three boys, trying to etch their images into her mind forever. She didn't know what tomorrow would bring. She just prayed that her children wouldn't have to endure the cruel fate that had been dealt to her.

Present Day—Tuesday

56

ALEX BEKKER COULD not believe his eyes. He was watching his monitor when suddenly the signal indicators started to change. "This can't be," he muttered, as he put down his coffee mug.

Alex Bekker had been a Rail Traffic Controller for over ten years and had never experienced anything like this before. It was like something out of an old Twilight episode. He tapped his keyboard to return the signals to their original settings, but something was wrong: terribly wrong. The computer wasn't responding. He could see on the monitor that commands were being given, and that commands were being executed, but they weren't coming from him.

"Oh, dear God! No!" He watched as Fastrax train #567 approached Blain's Bend, but he knew it was going too fast. *That curve will not handle a train going at that speed.*

Bekker snatched up the radio and started to call train #567. He prayed there would be enough time to slow the train down. The signals would normally alert the train crew to reduce its speed, but the signals had been tampered with. The crew of #567 would not realize the signals were wrong. They would proceed as the signals indicated and enter Blain's Bend too fast.

"Come on, pick up!" Bekker shouted hysterically.

* * *

Locomotive Engineer, Jack Turner, had been working for Fastrax for thirteen years. "After shift, I'm taking the wife to Vegas for a couple of days. She wants to see Donny and Marie. Me, I just want to gamble." He laughed jovially.

The In-Charge Locomotive Engineer, Matt Kline, had been with the company for seven years and was looking forward to his vacation, too. He glanced at the signal indicators ahead, checked the train's instruments and then turned to Jack. "Me, I'd rather be on a beach on some tropical island somewhere, with a Margarita in one hand and a beautiful native girl in the other."

Matt heard the radio squawk. "That's unusual," he said. Reaching for the receiver, he turned up the volume.

"Hit the emergency brake!" the voice over the radio screamed.

"What the . . ." But it was too late.

* * *

Kerry Kennedy was reading the latest book from her favorite author, Clive Cussler. She glanced up from the page she was reading and saw the pregnant lady reading the newest issue of *Parenting* magazine. Kerry took a moment to peer out the window. Recognizing where the train was, she knew they would be at the station shortly. She bookmarked her place and put her novel back into her briefcase. She still preferred the feel of a real book in her hands, not those fancy e-readers everyone seemed to have these days. As far as she was concerned, they could have them.

Kellen had been reviewing the case documents on his tablet for his morning meeting when he suddenly heard the grinding of metal. Looking up from his tablet, he noticed the car had started to tilt to the left. Then the lights flickered on and off. Screams erupted from startled passengers. "Shelby!" he shouted, throwing his body on top of his dozing sister as the car rolled onto its side. Between the grinding screech of metal, the shattering of glass windows, and the piercing cries from passengers, the noise was deafening. He held on tight.

"Kellen?" Shelby cried out.

"Hang onto to something and don't let go!" Kellen yelled.

The car continued under its forward momentum, but on its side. It seemed like everything was happening in slow motion. Bodies tumbled every way: crashing into each other, into the seat benches, into the metal handrails. Debris flew like mortar fire. *Please, let it end!* Kellen prayed.

Suddenly the forward end of the car nose-dived. Then, it finally came to a complete stop, resting at a hundred and thirty-five-degree angle. Everything that wasn't secured rushed to the lower end of the car, culminating in a pile of broken glass, bodies, and baggage. There was a tremendous explosion that shook the entire car. Then everything went dark.

Tuesday, August 12, 1692

57

TODAY HAD TO be the worst day by far. The sun wasn't even up and the temperature was already intolerable. The prison continued to bulge at its seams as people from all over New England were packed into the already overcrowded cells. They came from Ipswich, Andover, Topsfield, Haverhill, Reading, Beverly, Boston, even as far away as Wells, Maine.

Chief Justice and Lieutenant Governor William Stoughton signed and sealed the warrant. He handed it to Sheriff Corwin, who accepted the document. Corwin left Beadle's Tavern and made the short walk to the Salem Town jail. Of all the duties he had to carry out as sheriff, this was by far the one he enjoyed the most. He couldn't wait to see the expressions on the prisoners' faces when he read the warrant aloud.

* * *

"Listen up!" Sheriff Corwin bellowed. "I have a warrant here, so pay close attention." He began to read it out loud:

To: George Corwin High Sheriff of the County of Essex, Greetings

Whereas Elizabeth Proctor and John Proctor of Salem Village, Martha Carrier wife of Thomas Carrier of Andover, John Willard of Salem Village, George Jacobs Sr. of Salem, George Burroughs of Wells, and Dani and Daric Delaney of residence unknown, currently of Salem prison, all of the County of Essex in their Majesties' Province of the Massachusetts Bay in New England attended a Court of Oyer and Terminer held by adjournment for our Sovereign Lord & Lady King William & Queen Mary for the said County of Essex at Salem in the said County on the 5th day of August and were severally arraigned on several indictments for the horrible crime of witchcraft by them practised and committed on several persons and pleading not guilty did for their trial put themselves on God and their country whereupon they were each of them found and brought in guilty by the jury that passed on them according to their respective indictments and sentence of death did then pass upon them as the law directs execution whereof yet remains to be done:

Those are therefore in their Majesties' name William & Mary now King & Queen over England to will and command you that upon Tuesday next being the 19th day of August between the hours of eight and twelve in the afternoon of the same day safely conduct John Proctor, Martha Carrier, John Willard, George Jacobs Sr., George Burroughs, Dani and Daric Delaney from their Majesties' jail in Salem aforesaid to the place of execution and there cause them and every one of them to be hanged by the neck until they be dead and of the doings herein make return to the Clerk of the said Court and this precept and hereof you are not to fail at your peril and this shall be your sufficient warrant given under my hand and seal at Boston the 12'th day of August in the fourth year of the Reign of our Sovereign Lord & Lady William & Mary King and Queen.

Signed: William Stoughton, Chief Justice and Lieutenant Governor

As Corwin finished reading the warrant, Dani noted that the

second part had not mentioned Elizabeth Proctor. Dani guessed that Elizabeth had been granted a stay of execution until after the birth of her baby.

Corwin hung around just long enough to hear the wails of despair resonate throughout the cellblock before he left.

So, it's done, Dani thought. She did a quick calculation in her head and determined she and Daric had been incarcerated in Salem for twenty-five days. *Seems longer.* They would be hanged on August 19th; just one week from today. They had to think of something fast.

Present Day—Tuesday

58

"I DON'T UNDERSTAND," Quinn muttered for the hundredth time. "Everything was working fine when I left the lab last night; now, nothing works."

"You can figure that out when we get back from New Zealand," Sandra said. "Give me a hand, Quinn. Can you pull down our bags?"

"Sandra, you don't understand," Quinn said, tapping his comm. "With my system down, I can't track the movement of our kids. I won't know if they're in danger or if they've jumped to another time period," Quinn said helplessly.

"That is a problem, Quinn, I realize that. But think about it realistically for a moment. Even when we do know, there's nothing we can do about it," Sandra reasoned. "And knowing they're in trouble only makes me worry all the more."

"I suppose you're right," Quinn replied, as he walked to the closet to join Sandra. She was standing on the tips of her toes, trying to pull their soft-sided luggage from the upper shelf in their large walk-in closet.

After Quinn had taken the two bags down from the shelf, Sandra said, "Just put them on the bed." She was rummaging in her dresser drawer.

"What's the temperature going to be like in New Zealand? I'm not sure what to pack," Sandra wondered out loud. She pulled out some of her lingerie. She wore the same type of undergarments in all seasons, so it was the easiest place to start with the packing. It was the same for Quinn as she took some boxers out of his dresser drawer.

Quinn replied absent-mindedly. "It's their late fall; I'd leave the shorts at home. Besides, we won't have time . . ." Just then, Sandra's comm rang on the bedside.

"Quinn, can you get that; I'm kind of busy here," Sandra shouted with her head buried in the closet.

After a very brief conversation, only some of which Sandra could hear, Quinn said, "Just a sec . . . Sandra, you better take this." Quinn's voice carried a note of concern.

"Tell them we're going out of town . . ."

Quinn interrupted. "I did, but they insisted."

Sandra made her way out of the closet and walked over, taking her comm from Quinn. "Yes?" she said. She listened for several moments, then disconnected.

"The Bayshore East Fastrax train just derailed about ten miles out from Union Station. I need to get to the scene immediately," Sandra explained, relaying what she had been told.

"I'll stay and help," Quinn offered.

"No, you go and get that mineral. I want my children back home." Sandra gave Quinn a kiss, snatched her spare medical bag from under the bed, and dashed down the stairs, grabbing a jacket on her way out.

Quinn finished packing his bag, throwing in his swimsuit, a couple of t-shirts and an extra pair of khaki pants. He grabbed a windbreaker, picked up his bag, and headed downstairs and out the front door. Sandra had just reached the dock. Quinn knew it would be the quickest way for her to get to the scene.

59

I DON'T KNOW how much more of this I can take, Dani thought. The heat was unbearable. And the overcrowding of the cells stifled any natural air movement. The stench hung in the air like a thick blanket, only adding to the horrendous conditions. The small two-foot-by-two-foot window just below the upper storey's floorboards offered very little in the way of light or fresh air.

Dani and Daric had shuffled over to their quiet spot for their usual evening conversation. They had decided earlier to meet after most of the inmates had turned in for the night. But no one could really sleep in this extreme heat.

"I have an idea," Daric whispered excitedly.

"I hope it's a good one, because we're running out of time," Dani moaned pitifully.

"I need you to go back into that hypermnesic brain of yours and retrieve all the information you can about witch tests. I seem to recall some medieval water test."

"Yeah, death by drowning was used as a capital punishment in Europe during the Middle Ages. Some thought the only true way to test to see whether someone was a witch was to use what they called the Ordeal by Water test."

"Explain it to me," Daric said eagerly. An idea was brewing.

"It was believed that the accused who sank was considered innocent, whereas the accused who floated was guilty," Dani explained, gaining momentum. "Some argued that water, being so pure an element, would naturally repel the guilty, in this case a witch. And others argued that witches would float because they had renounced baptism when they entered into the devil's service."

"Okay, can we skip the theory for a moment? Just tell me how this water test worked." Daric was becoming impatient.

"Well, normally, the accused witch would have a rope connecting her to the assistants, who would be sitting in a boat. The rope was used to pull the accused up if she didn't float," Dani explained. "Some also thought the test was a no-win situation. If the accused drowned, she was innocent, and, if the accused floated, she was guilty and was hanged for being a witch. Either way, the accused ended up dead in the end."

"Great!" Daric exclaimed.

"What?" Dani was taken aback by Daric's enthusiasm.

"If we both die in the end, then it won't be too difficult to persuade them that this is the test we want to take."

"Excuse me? Is the heat getting to you?" Dani asked sarcastically. "You do know what you just said: that we would both die?"

"No, we won't," Daric replied, smiling mischievously. "We tell them that the water test is the only way to truly prove our guilt or innocence. We tell them we have to do it together, based on some excuse we'll make up. Then, when we are under water, out of sight from everyone, we swim over to each other, we touch our bands and, presto, we escape from this hellhole."

"You know, that just might work. But, first, we need to be able to talk to someone who we can convince and then have them persuade someone in authority to make it happen." Dani moaned after hearing the obstacles that she had just uttered and that they had yet to overcome.

"We can do it," Daric said reassuringly.

"And we have only six days to make it happen or we'll be swinging in the breeze atop Gallows Hill. Even though a fresh breeze would be very welcome right about now, I, for one, am not planning on going up that damned hill. I'll think of something; leave it to me."

"I was hoping you'd say that," Daric whispered, as a faint smile edged his lips.

60

DANI WAS TRYING to devise a compelling argument to persuade the powers that be that the water test was the only way to truly determine someone's guilt or innocence. She wanted to be ready when an opportunity presented itself. She was all too aware that time was not on their side. They had only five days left.

Dani heard the creaking of the wooden stairs. *I wonder who's coming.* She could tell it was only one person on the staircase, thankfully, meaning no more prisoners would be crammed into the already packed cells. So it wasn't the sheriff.

Dani knew it wasn't the sheriff's wife, because the steps weren't moaning loud enough for her weight. The sheriff's wife came often to barter with desperate prisoners, looking to get some prized possession in exchange for a meager piece of bread or, if one were lucky, a morsel of meat. And it wasn't Dr. Barton who regularly checked on the health of the prisoners. He provided what little aid he could, all at a cost which was zealously added to the inmates' bills. And it couldn't be the ministers who came to badger the condemned into confessing; those who still proclaimed their innocence were usually excommunicated. Some ministers would pray with the accused, but most would refuse, for fear of being associated with a witch.

The prison didn't receive many visitors except for the occasional family member who brought supplies to their loved ones. As Dani peered down the aisle, she noted that Martha was also taking an interest in who was coming down the stairs. They recognized the figure as soon as it entered the prison block.

"You spiteful little wench," Martha bellowed when she saw Susannah Sheldon enter the prison block. She jumped up and hurtled over bodies to get to her quarry. Martha reached through the bars, trying to get her hands on the vile creature.

"Leave me be," Sheldon said nervously, as she slipped past, only inches out of Martha's extended reach. "Witch," Sheldon muttered, her courage bolstered when she was far enough away and had the bars safely separating them.

Martha's rage slowly subsided when she considered it wasn't just Susannah Sheldon's testimony that had put her behind bars. Feeling deflated, she returned to her spot in the cell.

"What was that all about?" Dani asked, curious about Martha's uncharacteristic outburst.

"She was at my examination," Martha explained, her tone icy. "She told the magistrates I bit and pinched her and that I had said I would cut out her throat if she didn't sign my book."

"That's ridiculous," Dani blurted out.

"And then she told them the devil whispered to me. Of course, the afflicted girls were the only ones who could see this. Then she went on to testify that I had murdered thirteen people whose ghosts, according to her, were at my examination!"

"Murder?" Dani gasped.

"Relax, I murdered no one," Martha assured her. "It was during the smallpox outbreak two years ago. When my children and I came down with smallpox, the village quarantined our entire family. My children and I recovered, but my father died on Christmas day. I lost both of my brothers, one brother-in-law and two nephews. The village lost seven of its members. That's thirteen. They blamed me for the contagion, saying I had sickened them by supernatural means."

"That's crazy. Why would you inflict your own family?"

"They believed I had targeted the men in the family so that my husband would be first in line to inherit the family estate." Martha continued relating her story to Dani.

Meanwhile, Sheldon had made her way over toward the men's side of the prison block. "Daric?" she whispered. She was hopeful he would answer.

Daric had seen Sheldon come down the stairs. He had also been listening to part of the conversation between Martha and Dani. Needless to say, he wasn't receptive to Sheldon's visit. She was the one who had cried out against his sister. But, being the curious type, he didn't think there would be any harm in seeing what she had to say, so he made his way toward the bars.

Sheldon's face beamed when she saw Daric. She was ecstatic he had answered her call. "Hi," she said timidly.

"What brings you here?" Daric asked, as politely as he could under the circumstances. He had grown rather fond of Martha and seeing her fury had disturbed him. If it hadn't been for her and her husband, Dani and he would have starved by now. He knew their kindness was in gratitude for Dani's help with Andrew.

"I want you to plead guilty," Sheldon explained. "That way you won't be hanged. You can be afflicted like me. A few of my friends like all the attention they're getting. Me, I like the fact that people are listening to us; they believe everything we say." Sheldon paused for a moment, thinking, and then she continued. "Mary Lacy Jr. had been arrested like you. Then she convinced the magistrates that she was being tormented by the devil and they set her free. All she does now is testify against others who have been accused of being witches."

"And why would I do that?" Daric asked, desperately trying to rein in his anger. Had he heard her correctly? Did she think this was all a game?

"So we can be together, of course," Sheldon said enthusiastically.

An uncomfortable silence followed.

Sheldon was getting nervous. She was an attractive girl. Why would he not want to be with her? "I would be a good wife for you. I would give you lots of children. We could be very happy together."

Daric just stared blankly at her. He couldn't believe what he was hearing and then . . .

"So, that's all I have to do. First, plead guilty, and then pretend I'm being tormented. That will get me outta here?" Daric asked, repeating Sheldon's plan.

"Yes, and I can help you," Sheldon said. Her plan was going to work, after all. She would be taken care of and be with the handsomest man in the colonies. She would be the envy of all her friends. And her children would be beautiful. What more could she possibly ask for?

"Daric! What are you thinking?" Dani protested. She moved closer so she could listen in on their conversation. Sheldon flung her head around and gave Dani a cold-hearted glare.

"Okay," Daric said shrewdly, totally ignoring his sister's contemptuous interjection. "But, first, I need to confess to a magistrate. Can you get Judge Sewall to come here, so I can tell him my story?"

"Yes, of course," Sheldon said eagerly, turning her attention to her future husband.

"But don't waste time," Daric urged. "You know they're going to hang me on Tuesday."

"I know and I won't let that happen," Sheldon said adamantly. "We're going to be happy together, I promise." With that said, Sheldon ran up the stairs to fulfil her mission.

Daric looked over at his sister and winked. Then it dawned on her. This was part of their plan: to convince someone about the water test.

"Brilliant," Dani whispered. She had thought Sewall was a reluctant cog in the wheels of justice at the Court of Oyer and Terminer. If she could convince him, they would have a chance.

Friday, August 15, 1692

61

"WHAT DO YOU think it's like?" Martha asked sombrely.

"What?"

"Death."

"It depends on the method really," Dani said thoughtfully. "For instance, drowning is supposed to be quite pleasant in the end; you know, when water fills up your nose . . ."

"No, I mean after," Martha interrupted.

"Well, my mother said that you shouldn't be afraid because it's just like life was before you were born." Dani started to give her opinion and was interrupted again.

"Well, when I was born, I had an umbilical cord wrapped around my neck," Elizabeth interjected.

"Really?" Martha moaned.

"I like to think about the first laws of physics: no energy in the universe is created and none is destroyed," Dani philosophized.

"What?" Martha asked, bewildered.

"It means that every bit of energy inside us, every particle, will go on to be a part of something else: maybe burn as a new star in the galaxy ten million years from now, or maybe be a microscopic organism like an amoeba, or maybe even live as a sea dragon. Every part of us now was a part of some other thing: a raging storm cloud, a distant moon, a woolly mammoth, a howler monkey. Thousands upon thousands of other things that were just as terrified to die as we are. We gave them all new life, a good one, I hope." Dani finished and looked at the glazed and fearful expressions on the faces around her.

Oops, she thought.

Both Martha and Elizabeth looked at Dani as if she were from another world, which, for all intents and purposes, she was.

"What I'm trying to say," Dani carefully tried to backtrack, "is that I believe in life after death. When you think about the number of years that have already passed and the very short period of time our own existence occupies within those thousands of years, don't you think there has to be more to life?"

"I suppose," Elizabeth muttered.

"It's what makes me think that I can endure whatever this life throws at me, because there will be no end to my existence. I believe that life will begin anew," Dani said serenely.

Martha looked at Dani, pondering what she had just said. *Could she herself endure what was about to come?*

* * *

It was late when the sheriff's wife came downstairs into the cold damp cellar. When the sun set this late in the summer, the nights were cool, feeling even colder within the confinement of the stone walls of the prison—a cruel contrast to the insufferable heat during the day.

Ann Dounton, a matronly woman, walked to the back of the men's cell where Daric was sitting. In her right hand she held a lantern. On her left arm she balanced a loaf of bread and a jug of water on top of a woollen blanket.

She put the lantern down and said to Daric, "This is all yours, for that," pointing at his travel band. To her, it was just a fancy bauble; to him, it was his lifeline. But he couldn't help but look longingly at the items she was offering. He took a moment, before replying, to glance into the next cell. Dani was curled into a tight ball in a desperate attempt to ward off the dampness. He remembered how close he had come to losing her in London and vowed to never let that happen again. She was all he had.

Before Daric could reply to the offer, a faint voice said, "Don't even think about it."

A slow grin spread across Daric's face at the tenacity of his sister. He had his reply, not that his would have been any different. He shook his head at the sheriff's wife.

"No bother," she said. "I suspect I'll have both of them in a few days." She picked up the lantern, turned and headed back up the stairs.

"Actually, I was holding out for a one-inch-thick medium-rare porterhouse steak with a bottle of cabernet-sauvignon," Daric chuckled.

"Make that two."

62

DARIC HAD SLEPT little during the night. He kept hearing the scratching of vermin among the straw-strewn floor, looking for whatever tiny crumb they could find. He had also been finding it a challenge to count the passing of days, with no sun or moon for reference. The tiny cell window offered little in the way of light. Today, however, he could just catch a glimpse of the sun. It was still east of its apex, so it wasn't quite noon yet. All he was sure of was they had only a few days left. Would Susannah Sheldon come through for them? Or would they have to think of something else?

Daric's mental wanderings were abruptly halted when his attention was drawn to the sound of someone descending the stairs. First, he spotted a figure in a long dark cloak and a wide-brimmed hat. It was a man, of that he was certain. The man was holding a handkerchief over his nose, masking his face. Then he saw Susannah Sheldon appear. They walked to where Daric was sitting at the back of the cellblock. Dani was directly across from him, closely watching their approach.

"I understand you wanted to see me," the man said as he

removed his hat.

Judge Sewall; things are looking up. Daric stood up to face the magistrate. "Actually, I asked you to come here so you could speak with my sister," Daric said, as he nodded to the cell across from him.

Sewall, caught unaware, turned to face Dani. "I remember you. You're that outspoken young woman who was in court the other day," Sewall said cordially. He recalled being impressed by her passionate arguments.

"What are you doing?" Sheldon protested. "You're supposed to confess; that was the plan!"

"Yours, maybe, not mine," Daric said bitterly.

"Thank you for coming on such short notice. As you're aware, we don't have much time," Dani said sadly.

"What can I do for you . . ." Sewall drew a blank. Her name slipped his mind.

"Dani."

"What can I do for you, Dani?" Sewall repeated.

"I have an overwhelming belief that you're not completely satisfied with the way the witch trials are being conducted," Dani said bluntly.

Sewall took an impulsive step backwards. *Is she reading my mind?* he wondered.

"Believe me, you're not the only one," Dani stated.

"What are you saying?"

"A few weeks back, John Proctor wrote a letter. He expressed his concerns about the way confessions were being extracted by torture, how the property of the accused was being seized before any conviction, and how magistrates were so quick to accept spectral evidence alone as proof of guilt before sentencing innocent citizens to death."

"I don't recall any such a letter," Sewall said loftily.

"It was addressed to several Boston ministers. He hasn't received a reply," Dani responded.

"What do you expect me to do about it?" Sewall asked guardedly.

"We don't believe the spectral evidence that was used against us in court, since no one except for those afflicted girls could verify it." Dani's tone had hardened gradually, as she turned to stare at Sheldon with blazing eyes. Sheldon unconsciously cowered. Dani continued.

"Have you heard of the Ordeal by Water?"

"Why, yes I have. It's also used for capital punishment," Sewall remarked.

"Exactly," Dani said encouragingly. "My brother and I would like to undergo that test. We believe it's the only true test to prove our guilt or innocence."

"You don't know what you're asking," Sewall said.

"But I do. We have three days left before our execution. If the water test proves we are guilty, then hang us. But if we are innocent, is it not worth saving our lives? Don't the Scriptures say that the innocent shall be spared?"

"For what you're asking, there's not much time," Sewall balked.

"I know we're asking a lot, but it's our lives that are at stake here. Please."

"I'll make no promises, but I'll see what I can do," Sewall conceded.

"Thank you," Dani said, as Sewall turned and walked away. Sheldon was on his heels.

* * *

What harm would there be to act on her request? Sewall thought as he walked down Prison Lane, heading toward Beadle's Tavern. *It might just put to rest a lot of the reservations people were having about the outcome of these witch trials. Should the water test prove their innocence, it would finally put this whole business of spectral evidence in the trash where it belonged.*

63

SANDRA TOSSED HER bag onto the boat's passenger seat. She untied the bow line and then the stern. She flipped the bumpers inside and hopped into Daric's boat. Sandra was no stranger to running a boat. She held a Pleasure Craft Operator Licence, and she'd been handling boats of all shapes, sizes and configurations for years. Aside from Daric's home built twenty-four-foot fiberglass speedboat with its one-hundred-fifty-horsepower inboard Mercury engine, the Delaneys owned two Sea-Doo Jet Skis, a thirty-four-foot Sea Ray Sundancer cabin cruiser and two Pelican kayaks. But right now, Daric's boat was the only one in the water. *Thank God, it's also the fastest,* she thought.

"Not today, Bear," Sandra said firmly. Bear had bounded down to the dock with Sandra, her tail wagging eagerly. Bear loved a boat ride almost as much as she loved riding in the car, with her head stuck out the window. In the boat, she had the extra pleasure of biting at the wake along the side of the boat, often getting smacked in the side of her head when the boat hit a rogue wave. But that never seemed to bother her.

Bear sat forlornly on the dock as Sandra started the engine. With one last look and a wave to Quinn on the front lawn, Sandra pulled away from the dock and slammed the throttle wide open. As she rounded the peninsula, she prayed the loons weren't nesting yet, because the wake from the boat was sure to swamp their nest. Although she berated boaters who had no concern for wildlife, her focus right now was on the billow of black smoke she could see on the other side of the lake. *Thank God, the water isn't too choppy this morning,* she thought, *or this could have been a very uncomfortable ride.*

She tapped her comm. "Call Chief Bill Brown," she yelled over the sound of the engine.

Bill's anxious voice came over her comm. "Sandra, where are you? What's your ETA?"

"I'm coming in hot, Bill. I should be there, on scene, in a few minutes. I need a place to beach the boat close to the accident site. Can you have someone direct me in?"

"I'll have someone there ready to assist you," Bill replied promptly.

"Who's on scene now?"

"We have only one Fire Company on-site. They're dealing with the fire. Every available person from my division is either here or en route. There's more help on the way, but I'm not sure how far out they are. You'll be the first medical person on scene," Bill informed her.

"How bad is it, Bill?" Sandra asked hesitantly. Being rush hour on a Tuesday morning, it couldn't be good. The train would have been packed with commuters.

"It's not good, Sandra. The engine rolled, taking the first four cars with it. Then the engine burst into flames."

"Yeah, I can see the smoke," Sandra confirmed.

64

DANI HAD FINALLY figured out how to count the passing of days. The sheriff and his wife lived above the jail. She could catch the light and some movement through the floorboards. When all was quiet, then night had fallen, the day had ended, and another day in purgatory would follow. It was always the same routine.

Dani had determined that two days had passed since she had talked to Sewall. Time was not on their side. She and Daric had stopped taking handouts from Martha. She had five mouths to feed, including her own. And her husband was finding it more and more of a challenge to visit the prison while trying to manage the farm and their youngest, who did not travel well. He had to make arrangements with his neighbor to look after her; then he had to borrow a horse and make the twelve-mile return journey from Andover to Salem Town. His visits were becoming less frequent and his bundles less abundant.

Dani had asked Martha to give whatever food she could spare to Elizabeth, who was now feeding two. Dani had already traded her hat and overcoat to the sheriff's wife for food. Now she had nothing left to barter.

Dani lay curled in a ball in the dusty corner of the cell. Her idle mind was playing tricks with her, taunting her. She wondered whether they had run out of options, wondering why their father hadn't brought them back home, or whether he ever would. What if this was the life they were destined to live?

"Hey," Daric whispered, rousing Dani from her melancholy thoughts.

"Hey," Dani replied miserably.

"What's with you?" Daric asked. He wasn't used to seeing his sister look so despondent.

"What if our plan doesn't work?" Dani asked bleakly. "What if Sewall doesn't come through? What if we're dragged up that damned hill and flung from the ladder, twisting at the end of a rope until we gradually suffocate to death? What if . . ."

"Hold on a sec," Daric interrupted. Now he realized what had his sister so depressed. He was, too, just listening to her. "We're not going to dangle from any rope, trust me. Even if Sewall doesn't come through, I'll toss you my travel band and you can get out of here."

Dani bolted upright. "Like that's going to happen! Why would you even suggest that?"

"Think about it. There's no sense in both of us dying. This way you can at least escape."

"Why me? Why not you?" Dani asked. Even though she was determined that they were not splitting up, she wanted to hear his reasoning.

"Get real, sis. You've always been the favorite, aspiring, wonder child. You have an exciting future ahead of you. But me, I've always been the goof-off, always falling short of everyone's expectations. No one will miss me," Daric said dejectedly.

"I would," Dani said sincerely.

Daric looked at his sister and smiled warmly. "As I said, there's no sense in both of us cashing it in."

"Don't even go there. It's not going to happen. We came here together. We're going to leave together—end of discussion."

"But . . ."

"There's no but about it. I won't hear of it. We're in this together, to the very end, and hopefully that will be back home where we belong," Dani said decisively.

65

"YOU WOULD DO well, if you are guilty, to confess and give glory to God," Reverend Case said to Martha Carrier. The ministers had descended upon the accused, trying to convince them to confess, for they were putting their immortal souls at risk.

"If you would expect the mercy of God," Case badgered, "you must look for it in God's way, by confession."

"I have already made peace with God," Martha said coldly. "He will open his arms to receive me for I have done no wrong and I will take comfort in that."

Case turned from Martha, seeing a lost cause. He shouted so all could hear as he started his sermon with Ephesians. "My brethren, be strong in the Lord, and in the power of His might. Put on the whole armour of God that ye may be able to stand against the wiles of the devil. For we wrestle not against flesh and blood, but against principalities, against powers, against the rulers of the darkness of this world, against spiritual wickedness in high places."

"The Lord should open the eyes of the magistrates and ministers," Martha interrupted. "The Lord should show His power to discover the guilty."

Case snapped around and glared at Martha. He was unprepared for this rude interruption of his sermon. He took a moment to compose himself and, then, continued. "Wherefore take unto you the whole armour of God, that ye may be able to withstand in the evil day, and having done all, to stand."

"Reverend Noyes, will you pray with me?" John Proctor whispered, so he would not interrupt the sermon.

Noyes looked over his shoulder at the decrepit excuse for a man and turned his head back around in disgust while taking a few steps to distance himself from the accused witch.

"Stand therefore, having your loins girt about with truth, and having on the breastplate of righteousness," Case continued. "And your feet shod with the preparation of the gospel of peace. Above all, taking the shield of faith, wherewith ye shall be able to quench all the fiery darts of the wicked. And take the helmet of salvation, and the sword of the Spirit, which is the word of God."

After the reverends departed, Dani made her way over to sit with Martha and Elizabeth. Sarah was resting in Martha's lap. If her plans worked out, this might be the last chance she would have to talk to them.

"I admire the way you stood up to Reverend Case," Dani said.

"Actually, it's thanks to you." Martha smiled at her.

"What?"

"What you said the other day about death. I gave it some thought. And I think I can endure what this life will throw at me," Martha said soberly.

"You could plead guilty, renounce yourself as a witch. It will save you from the hangman's noose." Dani knew she was walking a fine line.

"If I do, then these ludicrous trials will continue and others will die," Martha persisted. "I realized that if I take a stand, I'll be fighting for the greater good. Struggles and sacrifice come with a price; freedom is never free."

"The needs of the many outweigh the needs of the one or the few," Dani recited from an old sci-fi flick she remembered. She was humbled by Martha's strength.

"Exactly. You understand," Martha grinned. "I can give them

my body, but I know my immortal soul will not be lost."

"If you could see into the future, how many do you think would take the stand you're taking to make a difference, to bring about change?" Dani treaded lightly.

"I don't know," Martha reflected. "I would hope at least a few."

"But what if the future sees us losing our family, our homes, our lives? And to save it all, we would only have to lose our very souls, by confessing," Elizabeth added.

"That, I cannot do," Martha said defiantly. "We need to stop this insanity. We need to make sure history doesn't forget what happens here."

"It won't." Dani said *Of that I can promise you, my friend.*

66

IT WAS LATE in the afternoon when Dani and Daric were led from the Salem Town jail, down Prison Lane. They were being escorted by Sheriff Corwin and his deputies, Neale and Starling. Behind them were Reverends Noyes and Case.

The procession turned right onto the main street and then travelled southwest, heading out of town, drawing the attention of onlookers.

Dani and Daric looked at each other; each wondering the same thought: *Did they get their wish?* They had been down this road before. It angled toward Salem Village and Boston and ran along the North River, which curved abruptly as it ran between bedrock hills. Dani looked to her right and noticed the river level: the tide was in. The last time they had followed this route, it was morning and at low tide.

The group turned right and headed toward the docks. Dani saw a figure leaning against an overturned bateau, or rowboat, by the docks. He was clothed in a dark robe and was wearing a wide-brimmed hat. When she got a little closer, she recognized Judge Sewall.

Tied to the end of the dock were two bateaux. These were flat-bottomed and double-ended rowboats, approximately twenty-five feet in length and five feet wide. Each boat had three benches and one set of wooden oars. The wooden boat's shallow draft worked well in the rivers and its flat bottom profile allowed for a heavy payload and good stability.

Sewall pushed himself off the overturned boat and approached the group. He nodded to Dani and then faced Sheriff Corwin. "I'd like to accompany you," Sewall said.

"Be my guest," Corwin responded, pointing to the boat at the end of the dock.

Dani was led to the end of the dock where she was helped into the boat. Reverend Case sat in the bow, Judge Sewall in the stern, and Constable Neale took the middle bench to man the oars. Dani was on the floor in front of him.

Daric was put in the boat closer to shore, with Reverend Noyes in the stern, Sheriff Corwin in the bow, and Constable Starling manning the oars.

Both constables pushed away from the dock with the end of their oars and began to row. As the boats moved out to the deeper channel of the river, Case said, "I'll take that," as he reached down to remove Dani's bracelet.

"No, wait!" Dani implored, looking into his soulless brown eyes. "If I don't survive this ordeal, then take it off my dead body. But give me the courtesy of keeping my few possessions until the very end."

Sewall shook his head at Case, who leaned back in his seat. "As you wish, makes no never-mind to me. I can wait another few minutes," Case chortled wickedly.

When the boats arrived at their appointed destination, Case motioned to Constable Neale. Earlier, Case had given Neale explicit instructions. After several protests from Neale, he finally relented. Neale reached down and grabbed the end of a thirty-foot length of rope and proceeded to tie Dani's ankles together, as he had been instructed to do. "This is so we can pull you back on board when you fail this water test or, should you succeed, we'll be able to pull you back from the watery depths," Case explained.

When Neale was finished with his task, Case said to Dani, "Stand up." Dani stood carefully, not wanting to rock the boat.

"The water will be very cold," Sewall warned.

"Back home, my brother and I used to jump off the ice floes in April. This won't be that cold," Dani said good-naturedly.

"I pray God clear you if you are innocent, and if you are guilty, discover you," Sewall prayed. Then without warning, Case leaned forward and gave her a shove. She tumbled over the side of the boat, heading for the water, but not before screaming, "Daric!"

Daric caught a quick glimpse of Dani as she splashed into the frigid waters of the North River. "Quick, pull her up! You forgot to take off her manacles; they'll drag her to the bottom!"

Daric froze when he saw the cold sneer on Case's face. His disdain was palpable. Daric knew then that Case had no intention of ordering the deputy to pull Dani up from the dark depths of the river. Without wasting another second, Daric dove overboard. He had to rescue his sister.

"Pull him back up," Case bellowed across to the other boat. Corwin and Starling quickly seized the end of Daric's rope. They both stood, planting a secure stance before hauling back, hand-over-hand, on the rope. There was some resistance as they slowly pulled in the line.

Daric noticed his forward momentum had slowed significantly. He was being drawn back toward the surface. He swam harder, kicking vigorously to push himself deeper into the murky water. Then he realized; he was being dragged back towards the boat. He reached around for his right ankle and struggled frantically to untie the knot. His lungs demanded oxygen. If he was feeling the urgent need for air, so would Dani. He had to hurry.

When Dani hit the water, she landed on her side, knocking the wind out of her. She quickly realized something about this water test was not right. She had limited movement of her hands and none whatsoever with her feet. Usually a very buoyant swimmer, Dani was sinking like a rock, deeper into the dark abyss, with no way of stopping her descent. She tried to reach around to her ankles to grab the rope, hoping to pull herself back to the surface. But the weight of her manacles and the numbness flowing through her fingers were hampering her efforts. *I can't go like this,* she scolded herself, *I have to be there for Daric.*

After what seemed like minutes, but were in fact mere seconds, Daric freed himself from his tether. He heard a splash from above and could only assume that whoever had been pulling on his rope had toppled overboard when there was no longer any resistance on the line; it gave him a small sense of satisfaction. But now he needed to find Dani; time was running out.

Daric swam to his right, at a hundred and twenty-degree angle, going deeper as he narrowed the gap between the two boats. Knowing the boat Dani had been in was about fifteen feet from his boat, he figured, if he could find the line, he could follow it down to Dani.

The frigid temperature of the North River was making Dani's whole body numb. She could no longer feel her hands or her feet. She could see nothing around her but darkness as she sank deeper. Dani had an odd sensation she was floating in outer space; it was a serene feeling of being free of all tethers, including gravity. That was the last conscious thought she had before blissfully closing her salt-stung eyes and drifted away.

Daric couldn't see a thing in the murky water, except for his hands in front of him. With the sky being overcast, there were no rays from the sun to shed any light into the depths below.

Dani, where are you? Daric pleaded. He groped into the empty abyss, searching in desperation for his only salvation. His hand hit something firm; it was the rope. Hand over hand he hauled himself down into the depths, his injured ribs objecting fiercely to the strain. He pushed the pain aside and desperately prayed he would find his sister at the end.

Daric's strength was rapidly evaporating, due to the cold and lack of oxygen in his system. Then his hand touched something cold, but soft. It wasn't moving. *Damn!* He wasted no time checking for a pulse. If he lost his struggle to survive, Dani would be lost, too. He reached into the darkness, searching for Dani's left wrist and, more specifically, her bracelet. He was becoming frantic. Finally, his right hand felt the bracelet. He heard a faint but audible clink through the water; then everything went black. His last thought was he hoped that the bracelets had actually made contact and it wasn't Dani's manacles that his travel band had touched.

Present Day—Tuesday

67

RICHARD PULLED UP in the Delaneys' driveway. He parked in front of the large four-car garage that doubled as winter boat storage. He got out of his SUV and walked to where Quinn was standing on the lawn. He was staring out over the lake at a boat racing away from shore. Richard would know that silhouette anywhere.

"Where's Sandra going in such a hurry?" Richard asked, as he approached Quinn watching the boat turn the corner of the peninsula.

"There's been a train derailment. Sandra was called to the scene. It doesn't sound good," Quinn said sadly.

"That's terrible. I hope it's not too serious," Richard responded. He was well aware of the situation and its seriousness, but he thought he should play dumb. "Are we still going?" he asked.

"Yeah, we're going. Actually, Sandra insisted. But first, I have a couple of things I need to do. Walk with me," Quinn said, as he headed out toward the gazebo.

Bear was bounding out in front of them as they made their way across the lawn. Richard noticed that Quinn looked miserable as if he had just lost his best friend. "You don't look so hot. Is everything all right, besides the train wreck, of course?" Richard asked.

"Something happened to my system. Everything is down," Quinn explained. "Maybe we should delay our trip, so I can get my system up and running again."

"No," Richard jumped quickly, maybe too quickly, because Quinn gave him a startled look. "I mean, didn't you just say Sandra wanted us to go? Let's get that mineral first; then, I'll help you get your system back online."

"I guess you're right," Quinn agreed. He opened the door to the gazebo and made his way to the lower lab, with Richard on his heels. Bear was leading the way.

"So, if your system is down, what are we doing here?" Richard asked, somewhat perplexed. Had he missed something? Was all his planning in jeopardy?

Quinn reached over and picked up a small dog collar. "First, I need to write a note to Daric and Dani. Then secure it to this collar and put the collar on Bear, along with these travel bands," Quinn replied as he gestured toward the jewelry case sitting on the metal table containing two small bands. "I was able to link these bands to the ones the kids are wearing."

"What'll that do?"

"The next time the kids initiate time travel, Bear will be swept right along with them. When they reach their next destination, Bear will be there, too. And in this collar will be a message from home," Quinn explained. "Just give me a second while I write something that will fit into the collar."

"But how will Dani and Daric know to look for a message?"

"Because, Bear has never worn a collar before. The kids will realize that and, then, investigate, or at least Dani will," Quinn explained.

Quinn took a special piece of waterproof parchment that he had previously treated. He wasn't sure where Dani and Daric would land in their next jump through time, so he wanted to make sure his note would survive in almost any situation. He scribbled out his message and when he was finished, he secured it to the inside lining of the collar.

"Bear, come here, girl," Quinn called as he knelt down. He went to place the collar around Bear's neck, but she swiftly pulled away.

"Come on, Bear. Don't you want to go see Dani and Daric?" Quinn got the response he was expecting. Bear's tail wagged furiously as she scanned the interior of the lab. She raced to the exact spot where Dani and Daric last stood before they vanished. She started sniffing around.

"Bear, you need this first. Come here, girl." Bear eagerly walked to Quinn, who quickly slipped the collar around her neck and held tight so she couldn't pull away.

"Awrooo." Bear voiced her displeasure.

"I know you don't like this thing. And I'm afraid you'll like these even less. Richard, hand me the bands, will you?"

Richard picked up the box; removed the bands and handed them, one at a time, to Quinn. He fastened one travel band around each of Bear's front legs. When Quinn finished, he released her. Bear awkwardly walked away, lifting and shaking each paw.

"Okay, let's go load the gear," Quinn said, having completed his task. "Come on, Bear, let's go." On the way to the house, Quinn watched Bear and smiled. She was prancing like one of those high-stepping horses, as she tried to get free of her new accessories. "It's all for a good cause, girl," he tried to assure her.

Once inside the house, Quinn left Bear a bowl of fresh water and a dish full of kibble. He also put out a few of her favorite treats. Quinn wasn't sure when Sandra would be home and he wanted to be sure Bear would be content until she was.

"Be a good girl," Quinn said as he closed and locked the back door.

Richard had already gone to the SUV and opened the rear hatch. Quinn tossed in his carry-on bag. "Let's load the equipment," Quinn said as he entered the garage.

In the first stalls, the garage housed two of the Delaneys' cars. The third stall held the cabin cruiser. The empty last stall was where

Daric's boat had been stored. Mounted along one of the end walls were the two kayaks. Along the back wall was a large set of storage lockers, which was where Quinn was heading.

Quinn opened the locker and pulled out one of the folded dive duffle bags. Then he pulled out his Hollis Bio Dry FX100 drysuit, including hood, gloves, and socks. He folded them carefully and placed them in the dive bag. Quinn preferred this drysuit over all others because it had an easy self-donning front zipper, plus it was lightweight and durable.

Next, from the top shelf, Quinn pulled a black dive mask and his regulator and tucked them into the duffle with his other gear. He reached into the locker and pulled out his thermal wear known as woolies, folded it, and placed it in the bag as well. Then he reached down and removed a smaller square bag with the word Predator etched in gold lettering across the front. The bag contained his Neptune Space Predator full face mask.

"Why the dive mask and regulator if you're taking your full face mask?" Richard asked

"It's a spare. When you're cave diving, it's a requirement to have redundant equipment," Quinn explained. "Did you pack woolies?"

"No," Richard replied naively.

Quinn opened another locker and pulled out another full face mask bag and some woolies. "Here, you can use Daric's," Quinn said as he handed the items to Richard.

"The full face masks are equipped with a built-in underwater communication system, so we can stay in contact while we're diving," Quinn explained. "Why don't you go pack those with your gear? I'll be right there."

"All right," Richard said, before leaving the garage. Quinn finished packing his gear which included fins, a five-inch titanium dive knife with sheath, a canister light, two flashlights, and a set of flares. Last but not least, he packed two dive computers.

Quinn took a quick look around the locker to make sure he hadn't forgotten anything. Satisfied, he closed the door and carried his gear to the SUV.

"You made arrangements, at our destination, for the items I had specified, right?" Quinn asked.

"Everything will be there and ready when we arrive," Richard replied.

"Then we're all set," Quinn said as he hoisted the bag into the SUV.

"We'll be back before you know it," Richard said optimistically, when he noticed Quinn staring out across the lake.

I hope she'll be okay, Quinn prayed, thinking about what Sandra would be facing.

Part V

Running Out of Time

68

QUINN CLIMBED INTO the passenger seat of Richard's SUV and immediately reached for the radio in the raised center console. He turned it on. The *Bang and Olufsen* Advanced Sound System automatically activated. Two acoustic lenses rose from the dashboard, allowing the system's 1,000-watt sound through its fourteen speakers to deliver the highest calibre listening experience to every seat of the SUV. Quinn didn't have to search for a station carrying the tragic news: they all had it.

"We have breaking news. A Fastrax commuter train, #567, travelling westbound into the city, derailed just moments ago. Emergency responders are being dispatched to the scene as we speak. From our news chopper overhead, they have spotted black billowing smoke in the area. It appears to be coming from what we believe would have been the front of the train. It could be a fire in the locomotive. We don't have many details at this time, but we'll keep you posted as we learn more."

Their drive to the airport was in silence, except for the news flashes resonating, one after the other, from the radio.

"We have been advised that all trains in the area of the accident have been suspended indefinitely, as the derailed cars and rescue operations are blocking the adjacent tracks."

"As of yet, there has been no word as to the cause of the derailment, but speed could have been a factor. Fastrax train #567 was approaching Blain's Bend when it derailed; why it derailed, we do not know at this time. But we can tell you this: the 567 Fastrax train had two new diesel locomotives in a push-pull configuration. There were twelve bi-level cars, each having seating capacity for one-hundred-sixty-four passengers. But during rush hour, those trains are jammed; standing room only. Commuters are packed into those cars like sardines in a can. So we could be looking at well over two-thousand commuters onboard that train."

"Dear God," Quinn groaned.

Richard had also been paying close attention to the news bulletins as he drove toward the airport. After all, he had a vested interest in the tragedy. He was listening for why the train might have derailed, but he knew it was too early for a determination to have been made. Days, weeks, even months of investigations lay ahead before the cause of the accident would be pinpointed. And when they finally figured it out, it wouldn't matter.

"We are now getting new pictures from our news chopper over the scene. Smoke continues to surge out of the west end of the train. We've been told that's where one locomotive would have been, but it looks more like a crumpled pile of twisted metal. I can't see how anyone in that locomotive could have survived. Wait . . . the fire crews have just arrived on scene . . ."

Quinn stared out the window, oblivious to the passing landscape. He was thinking about all those poor commuters; what they must be going through, the families they had left behind that morning on their way to work, some never to return home. He was no fool. From the reports of the devastation, he knew there would be fatalities. The only question was: how many?

"We have just learned that each Fastrax train runs with a three-person crew: two commuter train operators drive the train and

handle related operations. That would mean that two crew members were in that demolished locomotive. The third crew member is a customer service representative who would be in the accessibility car, in the middle of the train."

"We can see that the locomotive and the following four cars have left the tracks and have detached from the rest of the train and are flipped over onto their sides. The locomotive has uncoupled from the four cars . . . it appears to have plowed a deep borrow into the ground before finally coming to rest. The four jack-knifed cars behind have skidded over four-hundred yards ahead of the rest of the train and have plunged down an embankment, stopping within feet of the lake. There are four more cars leaning at a thirty-degree angle beside the tracks. The last four cars and the rear locomotive remain sitting upright on the tracks."

"What the hell happened?" Quinn raged at the sheer absurdity of the situation. "This type of accident should never have happened with today's technology. It's inexcusable!"

"You're absolutely right," Richard replied sombrely. As he spoke, however, he was thinking sadistically to himself that he knew exactly what had happened.

69

IT ALL SEEMED to be happening in slow-motion; it was so surreal. The train car's lights had flashed and then had gone out. Kellen could feel the car rolling over and hear the screeching of metal as the car continued its forward momentum. Windows began breaking; glass started flying everywhere. Seconds later, gravel started streaking in through the shattered windows, pelting passengers like bullets. Chaos erupted. Seats broke free of their moorings, smashing into passengers, pinning them helplessly underneath. Books, laptops, purses were flying through the air. People were hurled in every direction. He held steadfastly onto his seat. *Please make it stop!* he prayed. His other arm was locked tightly around his sister's waist. He felt something hit his head, momentarily stunning him, but he was able to maintain his grip. He was hanging on for dear life, and he knew it.

There was screaming, shouting, crying. Then everything stopped. An eerie silence ensued, followed almost immediately by an explosion in the car directly ahead of them. Kellen ducked instinctively, hoping the devastation might finally be over. After a few moments, he cautiously raised his head and surveyed the situation. Their car had come to rest on its side; it was set at a severe angle, its front end much lower than its back.

Something was running into Kellen's left eye. It stung. He reached up to wipe it off. When he pulled his hand away, it was covered in blood. He felt Shelby shifting beneath him. He released his hold and rolled off her.

"Are you okay?"

Shelby moaned. "What the hell happened?"

"I'll explain later, we have to get out of here. Now. Come on!"

He grabbed his sister's hand and pulled her up.

Shelby pulled back from Kellen's grip. She took in the car's interior and immediately choked back a sob. It looked like a war zone. Bodies were strewn haphazardly throughout the confines of the car. Unsuspecting passengers, who only moments before had been tapping out texts on their phones, scrolling through their emails, turning the pages of their newspapers, now lay in battered, twisted heaps, many with broken limps in positions for which human anatomy had not been designed. The car had been bent; there were broken windows, dislocated seats, and debris tossed aimlessly about.

"We can't leave." Shelby's training as a nurse had prepared her for handling emergencies such as this. She had to act. "We have to help. It could be a matter of life or death for some of these people. Now, tell me," she said, "what just happened?"

"I think the train jumped the tracks and then flipped onto its side," Kellen replied. He looked around for the nearest route to escape. Through one of the broken windows, which now seemed to function more as a skylight, he could see black smoke rising above their car.

"I thought I also heard an explosion and I definitely smell smoke," Shelby said tensely.

"The smoke is probably a result of the earlier explosion. I can only assume it was the locomotive." Kellen grew nervous; he had picked up the odor of fuel. *Spilt fuel; that can't be good,* he thought.

"But our car was right behind the locomotive!" Shelby fired back.

"Exactly my argument for getting out of here!" Kellen replied. He was fighting a sense of panic. The black smoke seemed to envelop the car, like a death shroud.

"Look around you," Shelby snapped back. "We can't just leave these people. Besides, I don't think we're in any immediate danger; it's not our car that's on fire."

"But the fire's right in front of us." Kellen stated bluntly. Then, reluctantly, he admitted, "You're right; we can't leave. It wouldn't be right; not if we can help. I just wanted to make sure you were safe."

"I know, and thanks." Shelby reached up and gently touched his forehead. "Are you okay?" she asked. Her first concern was her brother.

"Just a scratch," Kellen replied. "How can you be so calm?"

"I may seem calm to you, but inside, I'm terrified." A faint smile crossed her lips. "Let's see what we can do to help."

"Okay, but be careful. I'm not sure what's really nailed down in here," Kellen groaned; he had just pushed a seat out of their way. "Or how much time we have," he added, as smoke had begun drifting in through one of the broken windows.

"Thank God this wasn't an express train with wall-to-wall bodies," Shelby muttered. She carefully lifted someone's purse to see the face underneath. It was gone. She set the purse back down and moved on.

70

"KELLEN, SEE IF you can find the first aid supplies in this car," Shelby shouted, to be heard over the cries of the passengers. "They should be by one of the doors," she added, as she bent over a body and felt for a pulse. She didn't really expect to find one, based on the extent of the injuries she could see. *What a shame,* she thought. He was so young and good looking, too. She felt like she should do something; anything. Putting something over the body would have helped ease the feeling of abandonment that had gripped her, but putting a coat over a body that wouldn't know the difference as opposed to giving it to someone in shock made no sense. There was no question about where their aid and their limited resources had to be directed. She knew that the more injured passengers they could reach, the more they could potentially save or, in the very least, make as comfortable as possible. She hurried on to the next victim.

Clambering through the debris was like making his way through an obstacle course, with items constantly shifting, Kellen feared that he might further injure someone. Visibility was poor, too. The air was dense with settling dust and was now becoming mixed with drifting smoke. And the cries of the injured passengers were starting to wear on his nerves. He had to try to move faster; these people needed help. So he decided to use the handrails like monkey bars, testing them first, before swinging from one to another until he reached the upper end of the car. Kellen found a first aid kit just where Shelby said it would be, next to the washroom, by one of the doors.

"Here," Kellen huffed, trying to catch his breath as he held out the kit for Shelby. He coughed to clear some dust out of his throat he had ingested during his quick return.

"No, you keep it," Shelby instructed. "Go see if you can help the ones who are screaming the loudest. I'll focus on the ones who can't speak for themselves."

"All right, but I can only do some very basic first aid," Kellen reluctantly admitted.

"That's better than nothing," Shelby said reassuringly. "Now go. Do what you can. Holler if you need me."

Kellen scanned the car. Amongst all the wails of pain and cries of fear, one key question crossed his mind. *Where do I start?* He didn't have far to go.

"Here, hold this," Kellen stated, instructing a commuter to apply pressure on the lacerated arm of a fellow passenger. The wound was long but not deep; nevertheless, it would need stitches. "Help should be here soon," he said encouragingly. "Just keep pressure on that wound."

"Kellen, I could use a hand over here," Shelby called urgently.

"Coming." Kellen was getting pretty good at maneuvering through what he had termed the debris field. "What can I do?" he asked, as he knelt beside his sister.

"I need you to put your arms around his upper body and when I say go pull against me," Shelby explained. "He has a dislocated shoulder: I'm going to pop it back in place."

Kellen placed his arms around the man, being careful not to touch his injured shoulder. "Are you ready?" Shelby asked the injured man, who was gritting through the pain. He simply nodded. Shelby looked up at Kellen and got an affirmative nod from him, too.

"Okay, on three. Ready? One, two . . ." Shelby yanked the man's arm, and at the same time Kellen leaned back against the force. There was a popping sound.

The man in Kellen's arm's slumped in relief. He looked appreciatively at Shelby and then quipped, "I thought you said you were going on a count of three. What happened to three?"

"It's a diversionary tactic. You were so focussed on the countdown you would've tensed up on three, making the whole procedure much more painful," Shelby explained. "Sorry for the deception."

"No, it worked," the man said gratefully. "Thank you, both of you," he repeated, as his two heroes move on to new patients.

Shelby was bending down to check on another passenger. "Damn," she muttered. This was the second deceased body she had been checked a second time. *If we could at least put something over the bodies we've checked,* she thought, *we could avoid wasting precious time.*

Kellen had already sacrificed both sleeves of his new white dress shirt for bandages. This time he needed to rip another injured man's shirt sleeve from the undamaged arm. Kellen fashioned a crude sling to cradle the broken limb. It was not pretty, but it worked. It would help keep the arm immobilize until the victim could get some professional help.

Shelby has been concerned with one particular passenger she had helped earlier, who had a laceration just above the right knee. Based on the amount of blood loss, she was pretty sure it was an arterial bleeder. She had previously instructed the injured lady's friend to make sure she kept pressure on the belt that Shelby had used as a tourniquet. Shelby checked her watch. It was time to release the belt and check the color on the lower part of the leg. She didn't want to totally stop the circulation.

"Okay, how are we doing over here?" Shelby asked, as she returned to check on the lady's wound. Shelby was please the blood flow had decreased: the tourniquet was working.

"It hurts," the lady sobbed. "Am I going to die?"

"Not if I can help it," Shelby said decisively. "Help will be here soon and your friend is doing a fantastic job. Just keep doing what you're doing; don't stop. I'll come back and check on you again in a few minutes."

Shelby really hoped that what she told them was true; that help would be here soon. Several lives depended on it.

Suddenly, there was a groan of metal against metal, and the car shifted. Screams erupted.

"Kellen!"

"Shelby!"

71

SANDRA TURNED OFF the engine and immediately hit the power tilt button on the dashboard of Daric's boat. When she had told Police Chief Bill Brown she was coming in hot, she wasn't kidding. She ran the boat up onto the sand beach, forcing one of Bill's men, who was there to meet her, to leap out of the way. The boat finally came to a stop almost completely clear of the water.

As they scrambled up the slippery embankment, what Sandra beheld brought her to her knees. What had once been a beautiful red and white locomotive was now a pile of broken and twisted metal. The four cars behind the flaming locomotive were flipped on their side. The first car had uncoupled from the locomotive and had jack-knifed. The second car had plowed directly into the locomotive and looked more like a crushed beer can; the trailing two cars were still hooked together. The shouts and screams she could hear coming from the chaos confirmed that some passengers in those mangled cars were still alive; there was hope.

Fire crews were struggling to put out the fire that had engulfed the locomotive. The flames were licking dangerously close to the first passenger car. As far as being a rescue operation; there was no need. *No one could have survived that,* she thought. The fire crews' main goal would be to keep the fire from reaching what remained of the first four passenger cars. Sandra hoped that the locomotive's black box would be salvageable because she wanted answers to how this disaster could have happened in the first place.

When Sandra reached the top of the embankment, she immediately saw her friend, Police Chief Bill Brown, running toward her. "Sandra, thank God you're here. We've set up a unified command post. Come on, follow me." He gasped, as he tried to catch his breath.

"Bill, I've never seen anything this catastrophic before. I've been trained for this type of emergency, but I've prayed I'd never ever have to use it," Sandra said bleakly, as she took in the entire disaster scene.

"Same here," Bill echoed.

Sandra could never have imagined this type of destruction. The rest of the train looked like a toy that had been discarded by an angry child, tossed and scattered over a large area.

Sandra saw a hastily erected command tent on a small knoll up ahead, in the direction they were sprinting. It was beside a Fire Services truck, likely belonging to the Platoon Chief from the closest fire station, which would have had the first emergency responders on site.

From the tent's elevated location, Sandra surveyed the devastation below. She was soon interrupted by Chief Brown as he started the introductions between his continuing gasps for air.

"Sandra, this is Platoon Chief William Hockley. And Chief, this is Dr. Sandra Delaney, head of Emergency Services at Mount Albert Hospital."

Platoon Chief William Hockley was five-foot-ten-inches, one hundred and eighty pounds. He wore a grim but determined expression on his weather-beaten face. He removed his helmet, wedged it under his left arm, and extended his right hand, "It's very fortunate that you happen to be here so soon, Dr. Delaney."

"I just live on the other side of the lake," Sandra said, shaking Hockley's hand. "When I got the call, I jumped into my son's boat and came across." Sandra paused for only a moment. As the word son rolled effortlessly off her tongue, it stabbed painfully at her heart. Oh, how she missed her kids. Ever the professional, it was time to push personal feelings aside. She'll deal with those later. Refocussing, she continued, "And call me Sandra, please."

"Okay, Sandra. I received an update of the situation, while I was in transit, from my men who were already on site and were assessing the situation. They said the fire is not an immediate threat. We have other emergency crews on their way here, and we'll start the extraction of passengers from the train once we secure and shore-up the cars," Hockley stated concisely. He handed Sandra a red emergency vest with the initials DIC in reflective lettering on the back.

"Thanks," Sandra said, as she slipped on the vest. As head of Emergency Services she would be responsible for all the medics who would be attending the scene. The Doctor-In-Charge vest showed all medical responders who was calling the shots in their given area of expertise.

Hockley was following protocol under the Incident Management System. If there was a fire, Fire Services was to be in command of the operations, including rescue and extraction. If there were no fire involved in the accident or emergency, command fell to Emergency Paramedic Services. If that were the case the command would have fallen to Sandra, who was currently the only doctor on site. Only when the last patient has been removed would the overall responsibility be shifted to Police Services because the site would then be treated as a crime scene.

"I have my men currently securing the scene," Bill announced. "We've already cleared a direct route into the site so emergency vehicles can get in as close to the action as possible and get out quickly," Bill explained, while pointing to a small park area at the base of the knoll and to the right of the command post.

"I'll set up the triage area down there, too," Sandra added. "It's not ideal, but it'll have to do. There's enough open space over there for the air ambulances to land and it will be an adequate staging area for evacuating patients."

"The worst damaged cars are down the embankment, toward the lake," Hockley stated.

"And that's where the critical trauma cases will be. We'll need to focus our efforts there, first," Sandra explained, as the enormity of the situation sank in. "You do realize, that if that train was packed with rush-hour commuters, there could be over two-thousand people on board."

"We're definitely going to need more help," Bill mumbled.

While Sandra walked down to the triage area, she called Mount Albert Hospital. She instructed them to call in as many staff as they could and to notify the other local hospitals that they will be receiving patients, and lots of patients. She also asked them to send the Emergency Support Unit, which carries enough supplies to stock forty ambulances, which will keep her well equipped to handle almost anything thrown her way.

72

WHEN SANDRA ARRIVED at the small park, Emergency Paramedic Services or EPSs had just finished setting up a couple tents. Moments later an ambulance pulled in and rolled to a stop. She overheard instructions being shouted to the people who were emerging from the back it.

"There may be a few medics and EPSs here, but we're probably the only doctors on site. There'll be a lot of people here who need our help. This is not first come, first served. Your primary job is to prioritize the patients." The man speaking was yelling to be heard over all the commotion. Sandra guessed he must be the senior member of the team.

"Over here," Sandra hollered, as she waved her arm high in the air. She waited only a few seconds before everyone had gathered around before proceeding.

"Glad for the help," Sandra said. "I'm Dr. Delaney, DIC, doctor-in-charge. They told me to expect two attendings, five ER residents, and a surgical resident from Mercy Hospital. Who's the surgical?"

"I am," a female member of the team replied loudly. Dr. Fletcher was short, about five-foot-two, with brown shoulder-length hair.

"I'll be in the tent, you're in the field," Sandra explained. "You'll be the roamer," Sandra said, tossing a yellow emergency vest at Dr.

Fletcher.

Sandra then turned her attention to the man she had guessed to be the senior attending. "And you must be Dr. Morris, You're here with me."

Dr. Morris was Mercy Hospital's ER Residency Doctor. He was usually the one giving orders, not taking them. He was surprised by Sandra's bluntness, but not by her professionalism.

Sandra's attention was momentarily drawn away from the group as she hollered at some passing EPSs. "I need all this blood organized by type." "Where was I? Oh, yeah. Vests," Sandra mumbled to herself as she finished handing out the emergency vests. She reached down and grabbed a large bag that had been resting on the ground by her feet. "Each of you take a packet of tags. Each packet contains four colors. Green is for minor injuries. Yellow is for more serious injuries but not immediately life-threatening. Red is for critical patients who will not survive without treatment and transport. Black is for the dead or expected dead."

"Wait; expected dead? You're telling us to black tag a living patient?" one of the first-year ER residents asked.

"You want us to decide who lives and dies?" another first year ER resident questioned, horrified at the prospect of having to play God.

"We decide whose life you can save," Dr. Morris answered impassively. "And to prevent the next EPS or doctor from wasting time that could be better used elsewhere. Nothing in your training has prepared you for this."

"Do this, you'll save more lives than you'll lose. So grab your bags and tags. Let's move it folks. Oxygen tanks upright," Sandra yelled, as she left the group from Mercy. "Where are those gurneys? Line them up over here."

"Remember your training; good luck," Dr. Morris said encouragingly to his first-year ER residents.

Dr. Morris started to followed Sandra, who was now busy stringing up IV bags to the aluminum tent braces. He paused for a moment to assess the scene again. He couldn't believe the devastation. *How could this have happened?*

73

PLATOON CHIEF WILLIAM Hockley was standing in the command post tent on the small rise just east of Blain's Bend. It gave him a vantage point over the entire tragic scene below, a point from which he would coordinate Fire Services' rescue operations.

Hockley heard voices increasing in volume behind him. As he looked over his left shoulder, he was hoping to see more help arriving. He did. A small smile appeared on his face for the first time since he had heard about the tragedy. "The cavalry is here," he mumbled.

The three men who approached were all about the same build and height and all three wore jackets with the word 'Hockley' emblazoned across the back. They were his brothers, and all were captains of their own stations.

"Hey, Bill," one brother uttered before he was abruptly cut off.

"I told you, when we're on duty, it's Platoon Chief," Hockley reprimanded the youngest of his three brothers.

"Sorry," Barry Hockley muttered awkwardly.

"We need to get the reinforcing struts and shore up those cars on the track; they look like they're about to fall over," Hockley shouted, for all to hear who were within earshot.

"I'm on it," Barry said to the Platoon Chief. "Truck 55, grab those struts, some low pressure air bags and grab the rotary saw. We might have to cut our way into those cars. Come, on. Hurry it up! Time's awastin'," Barry yelled, running toward the truck. His men immediately sprang into action to execute his orders.

"The worst of the injuries will be down by the water in those four cars," the Platoon Chief growled. "Bruce, take your men and start at the water's edge, the first car. Brad, you and your men start on the forth car and work your way forward. Make sure you secure those cars from sliding, first."

"You got it." And off they both went.

The Platoon Chief saw another company's fire truck roll into the staging area. Before anyone could get out of the truck, the chief bellowed, "Get an aerial on that engine and lock down those flames. Then check the batteries for chemical leaks. I also need a body count. And find that black box. The investigators will want to look at it." There were no questions from the truck's crew. They drove toward the blackened ruins of the locomotive and to whatever grisly secrets were smoldering in its bowels.

Having given his men their assignments, Hockley could finally place several important calls. A 7-9-9 call went out for air ambulances; unfortunately only two were available. Another call went out to activate the Emergency Operations Centre, which coordinated all statements to the press. He also called Dispatch and requested more support from neighboring districts; they were going to need as many hands on deck as they could muster.

74

"HAVE SOME OF your men check on all the passengers in the last four cars, the four still sitting on the tracks." Police Chief Bill Brown was shouting orders to a new group of seven police officers who had just arrived. "If anyone's hurt gather them in that area over there." Bill pointed to the park that was now the make-shift triage area. "Their injuries should be fairly minor. For those who are uninjured, take their name, contact information, put them on buses, and get them where they need to be. Fastrax is sending the buses you'll need."

As the group of officers left to carry out the chief's orders, another group of police officers just reported to the command post. Bill didn't waste any time giving them direction. "I'll need anyone with medical or first-aid training to report to the DIC until more EPS personnel arrives," he instructed the new arrivals. Two officers immediately broke from the group and headed toward the triage area.

"Okay. You, you and you: go check in those last four cars. Collect all the emergency supplies and equipment you can find. There should be first-aid kits, backboards, automated external defibrillator—whatever you can find on board–and take it down to the triage area. They need it now!"

No sooner had Bill finished barking out his orders than the three officers he had singled out were dashing off toward the back of the train. "Damn, they're quick." His comment caused the remaining two officers to stand more erect, puffing out their chests, exuding pride in their comrades and their squadron.

"There're bound to be fatalities, just by looking at that wreckage," Bill acknowledged miserably to no one in particular. "We'll need a temporary morgue."

Bill looked at the remaining two officers standing in front of him. He could see them both cringe. No one liked this duty, but it was a necessity; they had to make sure no one tampered with the bodies. He surveyed the immediate area for a place they might be able to use as a morgue. He spotted a school on the far side of the park and a small warehouse on the near side. Being Tuesday, the school would be full of students: not a good place to store dead bodies.

"You two: go check out that warehouse over there," Bill ordered. "If no one's home, break in. We don't have time to be polite. Do whatever you need to do to secure that area. It's now a morgue; no visitors allowed. As soon as they start tagging bodies, any passengers with a black tag will be directed your way," Bill instructed. "You'll also be responsible for identifying as many bodies as you can. Questions?"

"No, sir." They snapped to attention and took off running toward the warehouse.

"We'll need contact information on everyone," Bill groaned. It was going to be a daunting task.

75

MIKE KENNEDY HAD used the small diesel engine to navigate the "Kerry Blue" Catalina sailboat out of Frenchman's Bay and into open water. Without having Kerry on board as his extra set of hands at the helm, he wanted to make sure he had plenty of open space to unfurl the sails without worrying about colliding with anything or anyone.

Once Mike had secured the lines around the sail winches, he walked along the upper deck toward the helm. He glanced at the weather station and made a slight course correction to get the full benefit of the warm southerly breeze. *Another beautiful spring day,* he thought. *Too bad Kerry couldn't be sharing this with me.*

Mike made himself comfortable at the helm and settled in to enjoy a leisurely cruise. He always enjoyed the sound of the Kerry Blue cutting through the water and the feel of the breeze on his face. Today he had the added benefit of being entertained by the diving antics of a flock of black cormorants searching for breakfast. The notion of breakfast reminded Mike of the small pot of coffee he had perked before leaving his private slip. A steaming cup of java would go great about now. He could almost taste it

Mike engaged the autopilot and went down into the cabin to pour a cup of coffee. While he was there, he would check the fridge.

Watching those birds get their fill of fresh fish made Mike's stomach growl, demanding attention, too. He couldn't blame his grumbling stomach entirely on the birds; the fresh air always made him hungry.

There had to be some leftovers from yesterday and sure enough there were. Kerry regularly made more than enough for the two of them, and now he was grateful that she had, because he didn't think to pack anything this morning before he left the house. After all, he had been a little preoccupied. A smile crept across his tanned face as he recalled how his day had begun.

Mike took two ham and cheese sandwiches from the fridge, a couple of napkins off the counter along with his trusty travel mug. With his hands full, he headed topside.

Mike checked the immediate vicinity for other vessels; there were none. He glanced at the weather station to confirm the winds were holding steady out of the southwest at thirteen knots. He knew they would pick up later in the day, making the afternoon a more invigorating cruise.

Mike was still sipping his coffee and finishing his first sandwich when he turned on the satellite radio for a little music. He was finding this outing much too quiet, and the quiet was making him miss his usual travelling companion all the more.

"The engine fire was caused by eleven-hundred gallons of spilled diesel fuel that firefighters are still working on getting under control."

"What?" Mike muttered to no one, as he reached over to turn up the volume.

"They've moved in the aerial apparatus to apply a steady stream onto the charred remains of the locomotive."

"Fire? Where?" Mike sputtered aloud. He scanned the skies looking for the telltale signs of fire. Thick black smoke rose in the western sky: the winds blowing wispy tentacles in his direction as if something alien were trying to reach out to him. "I wonder if that's what they're talking about."

"Eye witnesses said they saw cars flying off the rails, then sliding across the ground and disappearing down the hill toward the lake.

They weren't able to tell us whether any of the cars actually went into the water; they were too far away to see."

"What are you talking about? Cars? Rails? Lake?" Mike blurted. He was waiting impatiently for the news reporter to fill in the blanks.

"We don't know how many people were on the train, even though Fastrax uses a state-of-the-art electronic fare payment system called PAYGO."

"Kerry!!" Mike cried, as he bolted to his feet, his heart bounding in his chest. He checked his watch and fell back down into his seat.

"The PAYGO system electronically registers all passengers using this smart-card technology, replacing the need for tickets, tokens, passes or cash. When a passenger taps their PAYGO card on a fare payment device, the electronic chip embedded in the card calculates the fare and deducts it from the passenger's account. But the transit fare system doesn't communicate every transaction instantly to a central computer. As a result, we won't know how many passengers were on this train for another four hours when the system is next updated."

It took Mike a minute to slow his heartrate after taking in several deep breaths. His initial reaction had been one of terror until he realized that Kerry would have already been at her office; she couldn't have been on that train.

"Earlier reports indicate four cars have slipped down the embankment and are lying on their side, close to the water's edge. Emergency crews will be conducting a search and rescue operation in that area looking for survivors."

Mike adjusted his bearing to head toward the accident site. Maybe he could provide some assistance from his vantage point.

"The dead are being transferred to a temporary morgue that has been set up at a nearby warehouse. It's too earlier to tell how many will be making that journey."

As he made his way westward in the direction of the black smoke, he was still feeling uneasy. He wasn't sure why. He knew

Kerry was at the office. Mike checked his watch again. She had a morning appointment; she had to be there. But just to be sure and to set his mind at ease, he tapped his comm and speed-dialed Kerry's number.

It rang and rang and rang and rang.

76

KERRY COULD BARELY hear the faint but distinct ringtone of her comm. When she tried to reach the device strapped to her left wrist, she couldn't. She could hardly move at all. And she was having trouble seeing: everything was dark and blurry, and her eyes were stinging. She slowly wriggled her right arm out from under her body and wiped her eyes. When she pulled her hand away from her face, she saw blood. *That explains the burning sensation,* she thought. She felt around her. As she moved her hand slowly over the object on top of her, she abruptly pulled her hand back. *Oh my God, it's that pregnant lady.*

"Hey, can you hear me? Are you all right?" Kerry shouted at the lady, hoping to be heard over the cries from frightened and injured passengers. She got no response and there was no movement. She tried desperately to free her other arm because she couldn't reach around far enough with her free hand to check for a pulse. *Now what?* Panic crept into her very core. She could smell smoke; and where's there's smoke there's fire.

"I need help! Can anyone hear me?" Kerry yelled as loud as she could. She was wedged into a corner, trapped, and couldn't see the rest of the car. She had no idea whether anyone on the car could help her, or how long she would be trapped there. Kerry could tell by the screaming that there were injured passengers, but she had no idea how many and how badly. Were they all trapped like her?

"Hang on, I'll be right there," a strong male voice shouted. A moment later a very handsome face, covered with sweat and a streak of blood running down the left side, peered down at her and asked, "Are you hurt?"

"I don't think so. Just a cut on my head, I'm assuming from the blood running into my eyes," Kerry replied, unaware that the gash to which she was referring was much larger than she thought. "But I can't move. The lady on top of me is pregnant and I can't tell if she's all right."

"Let me," the young man said. He reached over and felt for a pulse. "She's alive. Do you know how far along she is?"

"No, but I'd guess in her third trimester," Kerry offered.

"Shelby, can you come over here," Kellen yelled over his shoulder. The earlier shifting of the car had rattled everyone, but it didn't last long. Kellen and Shelby were able to return to helping those who they could. But this time they were maneuvering more cautiously through the train, not wanting to chance another slip of the car.

Kellen turned back to Kerry. "My sister's a nurse at City Hospital. She'll know what to do. I hope you don't mind, but I don't want to move her off you until my sister checks her out first," Kellen said apologetically.

"I understand," Kerry replied, as calmly as she could manage under the circumstances.

A few minutes later Shelby made her way over to her brother. The smoke seemed to be dissipating, which meant the fire was under control. *One less problem to worry about,* she thought.

Shelby's face was streaked with blood from wiping her brow, and she looked as if she had the start of a wicked bruise on the lower part of her right jaw. "What ya got?" she asked, as she knelt beside her brother.

"This lady is about eight or even nine months pregnant. She has a pulse, but I didn't want to move her until you're sure it's safe to do so," Kellen explained.

"Good call." Shelby was proud of her brother's calm, considering their situation. Most people would be frantically crawling over everyone to save their own necks. Come to think of it, passengers in the car were somewhat calm considering their circumstances. Everyone was doing what they could for their fellow passengers; tended to the wounded, holding makeshift bandages over lacerations, comforting those with fractures, reassuring each other that help would soon arrive. These Good Samaritans amazed Shelby, considering chaos was all around them.

Shelby checked the pregnant woman for vital signs and then placed her ear over the bulging belly to check the baby. She felt some movement and looked up. The lady was regaining consciousness.

"My baby," she cried, grabbing her stomach.

"It's okay, everything's okay. You're safe," Shelby tried to assure her. "What's your name?"

"Joy, Joy Crow."

"Well, Joy Crow, it's your lucky day. I just happen to be a nurse. My name is Shelby and this here's my brother Kellen. And directly under you is . . .

"Kerry," she supplied, as she tried unsuccessfully to shift to a more comfortable position.

"Now, Joy, I want you to do something for me. Can you move your feet?" Shelby asked.

"Yes," Joy said after twisting her ankles around.

"Can you move your fingers and toes?" Shelby continued her diagnosis, looking closely at Joy's face and saw several minor lacerations, probably caused by flying debris. The cuts would have to be cleaned out at some point, but that wasn't her primary concern at this moment.

"Yes," Joy replied again.

"Then I'd say it's okay to get you off poor Kerry." Shelby gently pulled on one arm, Kellen took the other, and together they helped Joy sit up. Kellen turned to Kerry and helped her up. Kerry, once freed, immediately started shaking her left arm to get the circulation back.

"Thanks. Look, I'm a psychiatrist and have some medical training," Kerry said, once the tingling in her arm had stopped. "Why don't I go and see if I can help some other passengers. Shelby, why don't you stay with Joy? I'll yell if I come across something I can't handle."

"I'll go with you," Kellen volunteered. And the two of them started to work their way slowly through the debris-scattered car, checking on each person they came to. "And be careful of the broken glass; it's like walking on an ice rink."

About the time Kellen wondered when outside help would arrive, he saw the end of a ladder extending up above one of the broken windows. "Help! We need help in here!" he yelled. He made his way over to the window just as a firefighter had reached the top of the ladder. Hey!" Kellen bellowed.

"Hey," replied the firefight. "Can you tell me the situation inside?" he shouted into the window.

"We have several wounded, mostly broken bones and cuts, and at least twenty-five dead on this level. We haven't been able to make it upstairs yet," Kellen shouted in response. He sounded overwhelmed. "And we have a very pregnant woman," he added.

Kellen had barely finished speaking when he heard a voice louder than all the others coming from the far end of the car. "Aug-ggg! Something's wrong!" Kellen was pretty sure he recognized the voice. It sounded like Joy's.

77

IT TOOK THIRTY minutes for Richard and Quinn to get to the airport. They spent the entire trip listening intently to the devastating news on the radio. Every local station was reporting on the derailment of the Fastrax commuter train #567. Reports were still vague as emergency crews worked desperately to save as many lives as possible.

Richard pulled the Audi Q7 SUV in front of his personal hangar, where his private jet sat on the tarmac, fully fueled and ready for takeoff, as he had ordered.

The all-steel hangar was two-hundred feet wide, one hundred-fifty feet deep and forty feet high. It had no passenger waiting area because Richard never waited for anyone. It did, however, have a small office, located to the right of the hangar's massive door.

The office door opened and a tall, burly man walked out, wearing a crisply pressed black suit, a black tie, and blinding white shirt. He didn't look like a typical office manager; he had the air and build of a bodyguard. The man took a couple of strides toward Richard, then stopped and stood sharply erect on the hangar's glossy white epoxy floor. He seemed to be waiting for someone to give him his next orders. Quinn assumed that would be Richard.

"I'll be right back," Richard said, as he turned off the Audi's engine, abruptly putting an end to the continuous news reports. "Why don't you unload our gear, Quinn?" he said, getting out of the SUV.

Quinn nodded solemnly. He felt numb after listening to the reports of the catastrophe. He thought he should be doing something to help. But, at the same time, he recognized that they had the best medical help already on site. Sandra would do everything in her power to help those poor passengers.

Quinn got out of the SUV, whose luxurious interior he had been unable to truly appreciate under the circumstances. He opened the rear hatch and pulled out the two heavy dive bags. Both were immediately snatched away by one of Richard's staff.

As Quinn turned to follow the bags, he got his first real look at Richard's private jet. It was a G650 ER, Gulfstream's newest flagship and the industry's highest performance long-range business aircraft. Quinn had to admit it was a sleek-looking airplane. He had always had a fascination with aeronautics, ever since his first flight with his father in his own two-seater aircoupe. Quinn even helped Daric rebuild his 1950 Pratt & Whitney R-985 Wasp Junior aircraft engine.

As Quinn looked at the high swept wings, he noticed the absence of pieces that were standard on most aircraft. There were no vortex generators to disrupt the natural airflow over the wing. There were no leading-edge devices to improve slow-speed handling. And there were no exposed flap hinges and flap tracks to cause drag. Without these pieces, the aircraft would have improved speed, a greater range, and a quieter cabin. He was impressed.

Quinn shifted his attention to the aircraft's T-tail configuration. He wasn't at all surprised by what he saw. Written below the configuration was the aircraft's call sign: RBC, standing for Richard Barak Case.

"We're all set. Let's get aboard," Richard said, as he led the way up the stairs and into the aircraft. Quinn grabbed the remaining smaller bags out of the SUV and followed him. "Why don't you make yourself comfortable in the cabin? I'll join you as soon as we reach cruising altitude," Richard encouraged.

Quinn nodded as he glanced into the cockpit. He was awestruck by the sophisticated flight deck. There were ten touch-screen avionics controllers, drastically reducing the number of switches and dials normally seen in a cockpit. He would have to ask Richard about all that new technology, later.

When Quinn turned right to make his way back into the cabin, the man who had carried in the two dive bags earlier was blocking his way. He took the bags from Quinn and said, "Make yourself comfortable, while I stow these." Then he turned and walked down the aisle. *He's a stoic kind of guy,* Quinn thought.

Quinn made his way into the cabin and paused to drink in the sheer elegance, the sophisticated beauty and the exquisite functionality. Past the crew compartment and the galley, the cabin interior was divided into three distinct sections. The first section contained four high-back leather seats; two facing each other on each side of the center aisle. On the left side of the second section was a configuration of four seats around a table. On the right side was a cabinet, with a pop-up twenty-six-inch television including a variety of audio and video accessories. The third section contained a leather divan on the right side and two more facing seats on the left. The three sections of seating were arranged so that the aircraft could sleep six passengers. The handcrafted leather seats and divans were a soft cream color with chocolate brown piping. The tables and side panels were a high-polished acrylic, also chocolate brown. At the rear of the plane was the lavatory such as what might be found in a five-star hotel.

After Richard's employee had stowed the baggage, he exited the aircraft, securing the door behind him.

Quinn proceeded toward the back of the cabin, anxious to explore the interior further, when Richard's voice came over the intercom. "Time to buckle in, Quinn. We have clearance for takeoff."

Quinn found a seat in the middle of the cabin and strapped himself in. He was amazed at how quiet the interior cabin was. He couldn't believe he was on an aircraft, let alone that it was now taking off. As he waited for the signal that he could get up and walk about, he amused himself by investigating the area around him. He lifted a panel beside his seat, revealing an iPod. When he turned it on, the screen read Gulfstream Cabin Management System (GCMS). It was a personal control that passengers could use to regulate temperature, lighting, window shades and entertainment devices. "A very civilized way to travel," he muttered.

Quinn touched a button on the GCMS to lower the window shade to block out the sunlight. Then he reached for the controller and turned on the TV. Flashing across the lower part of the screen in a continuous red banner were the words "Breaking News".

"Rescuers continue to work diligently to extract passengers from the twisted wreckage of Fastrax train #567.

Quinn was so riveted to the television he hadn't realized the aircraft had reached cruising altitude and that Richard was now standing beside him. "What's the latest?" Richard asked, pulling Quinn away from the ongoing news coverage.

"They're still pulling survivors from the wreckage. They're using the jaws of life and hydraulic cutters to carve their way into the cars," Quinn announced sombrely. "So far, the death toll is eighty-seven; most of those were in the first few cars directly behind the engine."

"That's terrible," Richard uttered impassively. "Any news about Sandra?"

"Nothing." Quinn's worry was evident in his voice.

"Hey, let me get us a couple of beers," Richard offered, as he made his way back up the aisle toward the forward galley. "I would normally have had a crew of four on board, but we wanted this to be a clandestine operation and I figured the fewer people who knew about our plans the better." But that wasn't Richard's sole reason, only Quinn didn't know that.

Richard returned, handing Quinn a cold Guinness and taking the seat across the table from him. "Thanks," Quinn said, as he took a large gulp of the amber liquid. "So, tell me, who's flying this plane?" Quinn teased. He needed to try to lift some of the doom and gloom that was weighing heavily on his heart. He couldn't bear to think about what Sandra must be dealing with.

"This aircraft is equipped with precise, computer-controlled flight, the first of its kind. It has a data-concentrated network that acts as the central nervous system of the aircraft. The system is called Intelligence-by-Wire and uses wires, relays, circuits and servers rather than mechanical rods, pulleys and cables to manipulate flight controls. It links the active flight controls and touch-screen avionics with autopilot, autothrottles, autobrakes and an automatic emergency descent mode that protects against lost cabin pressurization. The aircraft virtually flies itself. The electronic system makes continuous corrections to keep the aircraft in an optimum aerodynamic position, which makes for a smoother flight and greater passenger comfort. And it's loaded with safety features, including redundant systems, stall protection at low speed, and buffet protection at high Mach," Richard recited proudly.

"I've never seen anything like it before," Quinn stated appreciatively. "So, when do we arrive in New Zealand?"

"We need to make a quick stop at the Bob Hope Airport in Burbank to refuel, and then it's a direct flight to Wellington."

"That's on the North Island," Quinn protested. "We want to be on the South."

"I couldn't find an airport close to the destination you gave me with a long enough runway to land my jet," Richard explained. "So, we'll have to land in Wellington. I've bought a small Piper Seneca V that we can fly from Wellington over to Nelson. It's only a twenty-minute flight to the South Island and Nelson is the closest airstrip," Richard explained.

"You bought a plane?" Quinn asked skeptically.

"I couldn't find a place that would rent me one," Richard smirked. "Besides, it'll give me a new toy 'down under' to play with."

Quinn shook his head in disbelief. Richard tossed money around like most people tossed trash. What did he care, as long as they reached their destination and got home, as quickly as possible?

78

CAPTAIN BRAD HOCKLEY and his men arrived at the fourth overturned car. They used a winch and cable to secure the car from sliding further down the embankment. Once secured, they promptly placed two twenty-foot extension ladders against the underside of the overturned car. Two firefighters rapidly ascended each ladder. They quickly determined that the car's passenger door was jammed shut. They called to their colleagues still on the ground, directing them to bring up the Jaws of Life. The requested equipment was hauled up the ladder in short order and was expertly used to pry open the crumpled passenger door and gain access to the car. Meanwhile, two other firefighters had climbed onto the top of the overturned car and gained entry through a busted out window.

Captain Bruce Hockley, who had been directed to the first of the four overturned cars, had made his way down to the water's edge. He had the foresight to bring along a three hundred foot length of rope that had been designed with special handholds. Spaced a foot apart, the handholds would allow the rope to be used as a ladder to help passengers up the steep and rather slippery embankment. Backboards to immobilize the critically injured were also on scene. Two of his men were working feverishly with heavy hydraulic cutters and spreaders to make an opening large enough to extricate injured passengers.

While he waited patiently, Captain Bruce Hockley realized the first car was precariously close to the water, only a few feet away from it. Assessing the angle of the car and the smashed out windows, Bruce feared the worst.

Bruce rushed up the embankment and spotted Police Chief Bill Brown making his way along the tracks with a handful of officers. "Chief, is the police dive unit on its way?" Bruce yelled. His shouting brought the Chief to an abrupt halt.

"Yeah, but it's still ten minutes out," Bill replied disheartened.

"What about that boat?" Bruce asked, pointing to the boat he had previously spotted down on the beach. He wondered whom it might belong to and when it might have arrived.

"It's Dr. Delaney's. She won't mind if we use it," Bill said confidently. He turned and shouted at two of his officers. "Smith, Ryan: get down to that boat, follow the current, and search along the shoreline for any survivors."

"On it, Chief," Ryan yelled. He and Smith slid down the bank, ran to the boat, and pushed it into the water. Ryan jumped onboard and got behind the wheel. After lowering the engine, he turned the key that Sandra had conveniently left in the ignition. He slowly backed away from the shore, swung the bow around into the current, and gave the engine a bit of gas. He guided the boat further down along the shoreline in order to turn around and slowly work his way back. Meanwhile, Smith proceeded on foot, searching along the shore, narrowing the gap between himself and Ryan. It was the quickest way to cover the most ground.

Before long, several uninjured passengers from the train and some residents from the nearby subdivision joined in the search.

79

THIS WAS THE one and only time Mike wished he had a motor boat. He was at the mercy of the wind and, right now, it wasn't blowing enough to get him to the derailment site as quickly as he had wanted. The smoke had dissipated; leading him to assume the firefighters had whatever was burning under control. What concerned him now was the number of people walking along the shoreline. They seemed to be looking for something. Then it hit him. They were searching for survivors or bodies.

Mike had pulled in the Kerry Blue's sails, lifted its running board and engaged the small diesel motor so he would have more manoeuverability. The magnitude of the destruction was gradually revealed to him as he got closer to the scene. What he saw shocked him. What lay crumpled just feet from the water's edge was all that was left of one of the train cars. "Good lord," Mike muttered. "How could anyone survive that?"

As Mike surveyed the water's edge from left to right, he noticed a police officer in a boat that was moving slowly and deliberately along the shoreline. Mike steered the Kerry Blue toward the officer's boat. "Hey," Mike shouted. "What can I do to help?"

"Check the area for survivors. We're not sure if any may have been thrown into the lake," Ryan hollered back.

"Got it. I'll head upwind and drift back toward you," Mike yelled. He was proceeding up the shoreline when something drew his attention away from the water and made him look up at the wreckage. He immediately saw someone who looked like Kerry being helped out of one of the overturned cars. Mike shook his head and looked again. *It couldn't be. She should be at the office,* he thought. There was one way to know for sure. "Kerry!" he yelled as loudly as he could. The woman turned and looked directly at him. He crumbled to his knees.

"Mike!" Kerry screamed back and waved to him. She wanted to reassure him that she was okay. But all Mike could see was that she was covered in blood; even her face was streaked with it. As his eyes remained fixed on her, he also saw that her clothes were torn in places; some pieces were even missing from her dress.

"I'm coming to get you," Mike shouted. He received no answer; worse, he could no longer see Kerry. She had disappeared. *What's happened to her?* he wondered. Driven by a growing fear, he turned the wheel and directed the Kerry Blue toward shore as quickly as the small diesel engine would take him. He shifted his focus momentarily from the water and looked for Kerry in the direction of where he had last seen her. There she was. She had been hidden behind some of the other passengers who had been extracted from the car.

"I'm coming to get you," Mike yelled again. Still there was no reply, but he could see Kerry was now making her way carefully down the embankment.

As soon as Kerry reached the beach, Mike tried once again. "I'm coming to get you," he yelled, as he reached over the stern of the boat about to release the dinghy from its davit. This time there was a response. He struggled to hear her reply against the general din all around him.

"No. Wait. I'm all right, just a little banged up." Although the words were hard to make out, they brought Mike a great sense of relief. Kerry was okay.

"You look like hell," Mike shouted, as the Kerry Blue continued toward the shore. He instantly knew his words had been inappropriate. He wished he had said something else or, better still, had kept his mouth shut.

"I couldn't hear you. What did you say?" Kerry shouted back. Mike felt another wave of relief wash over him.

"Nothing. It doesn't matter." Mike was about to say something more, but Kerry was shouting at him. "I'm going to see if I can help. There are so many needing medical attention. It's the least I can do."

The Kerry Blue was finally close enough to shore that, with only a little difficulty, Mike could hear what Kerry was saying. "Why don't you continue to help the police with their search of the water? I'll come back down here when I'm done. Okay?"

"Are you sure? You don't look so great." Mike still couldn't believe that Kerry had been on this train. She should have been on an earlier one.

"I'm fine. Honest. I'll see you in a bit," Kerry assured him. Then she blew him a kiss, turned, and climbed back up the slippery embankment aided by the rope ladder. She would look for someone in charge.

80

"YOU'RE DOING GREAT," Shelby assured Joy. "It won't be much longer, I promise. Is this your first?"

"Yes," Joy replied, between short panting breaths. "We'd been trying for three years and then it finally happened. Donald, my husband, was so happy."

Shelby had stayed with Joy while Kellen and Kerry assisted with the evacuation of the injured. The only passengers left in the car were Shelby, Joy and the twenty-five deceased. *Not the ideal setting for bringing a new life into this world,* Shelby thought.

Kellen popped his head down through the broken window that the rescue crew had used to remove the car passengers. "Okay, now it's your turn," he said, hanging upside down. Fire Services had tried to evacuate Kellen with the other passengers, but he had refused to leave his sister behind. He had argued that he had treated a lot of the injured and could help prioritize the evacuation, thus saving everyone precious time. His rationale had been hard to argue against, so they had allowed him to stay and assist.

"Kellen, we can't leave. Joy is about to deliver any minute," Shelby said urgently.

"Whoa! Okay, give me a minute. I'll get some help," Kellen said nervously, pulling his head out of the opening.

"No, wait! There's no time," Shelby shouted. Kellen poked his head into the car again. "Get down here and give me a hand," she pleaded.

"Okay, give me a sec," Kellen replied. He once again pulled his head out of the window and, from his perch on the side of the overturned car, shouted down to emergency responders who were on the ground. "There's a baby coming now! We'll need a stretcher before we can get them out."

Two rescue workers who were about to ascend the ladder paused, nodded and went in search of the necessary equipment. Kellen swung his legs around and jumped down through the window opening and made his way over the scattered debris and broken seats to kneel beside his sister. "What can I do?"

"Find something to wrap the baby in, preferably something clean," Shelby said. "And if you can find any water bottles, that would be helpful, too."

"Auuuuuuhhhh!" Joy's contractions were coming closer together. It wouldn't be much longer. Shelby moved from Joy's side and positioned herself by her feet.

"Okay, Joy. I need you to raise your knees and spread your legs. Your baby is about to make an appearance." Shelby was trying to remain calm and convey as much confidence as she could. But inside she was a nervous wreck. She had never delivered a baby before, except during training, and that had involved a doll, not the real thing. And so many things could go wrong. Maybe she should get some help.

"Kellen, try to find a paramedic," Shelby said, as calmly as she could. She didn't want to alarm Joy.

"I don't know, Shelby, they're all kind of busy right now," Kellen said hesitantly, as he looked up from his rummaging through the debris. He had witnessed the activity outside their car. "Even the firefighters have their hands full. They're still trying to extract the passengers in the cars behind us. Those cars were damaged, too, but not as horrifically as ours. But from what I've seen, there are a lot of seriously injured people needing immediate medical attention."

"I understand," Shelby admitted resignedly. She was only delivering a baby when life-threatening injuries were still being dealt with. She would have to do this on her own.

"So, Joy, I'd have thought you'd be on maternity leave. What are you doing on this train?" Shelby's attempt at a calming bedside manner could use a little work, she thought.

"I am on leave. My last day was this past Friday," Joy grunted through another contraction. "My leave of absence papers weren't ready. Auuugggg."

Shelby checked on the position of the baby. It wouldn't be long now.

"My boss, Cheryl Fergus, always leaves everything to the last minute. Auuuggg," Joy groaned and took a couple deep breaths before continuing. "When I asked her to put the papers in the mail she refused. She told me I had to come in and pick them up in person," Joy snarled.

Shelby couldn't believe Joy's boss could be so heartless and insensitive to someone in Joy's condition. Her boss couldn't possibly know what she was putting Joy through right now and all for what . . . to save postage? Shelby felt rage creep ever closer to the surface, but now wasn't the time for her to lose her temper. And boy, did she have a temper. Shelby liked a good fight, but she always fought for the underdog, against injustices, as she liked to say. Now, however, wasn't a good time to start a fight; she would have to wait.

Shelby could see the crown of the baby's head. "Okay, Joy, I need you to push."

Joy did as instructed. The baby was coming. "Kellen, I need those supplies!"

"Coming," Kellen yelled back, in order to be heard over Joy's screaming. He had scrounged up some first aid supplies, what had not already been used by other passengers. He had also retrieved his messenger bag and Shelby's knapsack–both contained water bottles. And in Shelby's bag was her gym towel, perfect for the baby.

"Here," Kellen said, as he placed the items beside his sister. "What can I do?"

"Go see what's keeping that stretcher. We're almost ready to get out of here," Shelby said, without looking anywhere but where she needed to focus her efforts. "Again, Joy, push."

"On it," Kellen said as he sprang to his feet and ran as best he could toward the window with the ladder propped outside. He climbed onto the edge of the seat and stuck his head out the window. "Can we get some help here? We need that stretcher, now!"

"I'll get it," replied Captain Bruce Hockley, the same fireman who had originally accessed the car. "Lawson, give me a hand."

Shelby carefully wrapped the tiny bundle in her gym towel and placed her in Joy's arms. "May I present your daughter? Joy, she's perfect."

Joy took the precious parcel from Shelby and looked upon her daughter's tiny red face. Shelby had cleaned her up as best as she could under the circumstances; to Joy she was the most beautiful baby she had ever seen.

"Thanks," Joy whispered hoarsely.

"You're welcome," Shelby replied. She had seen Joy's placenta and was concerned with the amount of bleeding Joy was still experiencing. She could only assume that the entire placenta hadn't been delivered. Shelby didn't want to alarm her; she just hoped help would arrive soon.

81

THE DOOR FLEW open, slamming into the adjacent wall. A voice boomed, "What the hell were you thinking? Do you know what you've done?"

"I didn't do anything," Alex Bekker protested adamantly, as he spun around to face his accuser.

"Then, what the hell happened?" asked Ray Bolton, Head of Operations. Never in his entire fifteen-year career had he ever experienced anything like this morning's tragic event. Heads would roll; there was no question of that, but whose? One thing was certain: Bolton would make sure his wasn't one of them. He had plans for his upcoming retirement and he wasn't going out with a black cloud hanging over his parade.

"I was sitting here watching the monitor like I always do, like I've done for the past ten years. Then suddenly, the signals changed. I hadn't touched a thing. But right there on my monitor, they changed. It was like they had a mind of their own," Bekker explained, pointing to the screen. Even to his own ears, his story sounded lame. But he was determined to press on. He had to convince Bolton that he had done nothing wrong. If he couldn't convince his boss, then this whole tragedy would be placed entirely on his shoulders.

"Look, the minute I realized what was happening, I tried to warn them. I picked up the radio and called the train. The second they picked up, I screamed 'hit the emergency brake', but it was too late. The monitor showed they had already entered Blain's Bend. I tried, I really tried. All those poor people," Bekker finished, sobbing quietly in his chair.

"Okay, Bekker, say I believe you. Tell me what you think happened then?" Bolton asked. He had calmed down somewhat since crashing into Bekker's office.

"It's the damnedest thing." Bekker thought for a moment as he wiped his runny nose on his shirt sleeve. "It was as if the Central Traffic Control System was receiving input from somewhere else."

"How could that be?" Bolton barked. "We have the most sophisticated and reliable system in the industry."

"It's the only logical explanation I have at the moment," Bekker offered. "But what I don't understand is why someone would want to derail a commuter train. Why hurt or try to kill all those people? Isn't that something only terrorists would do?"

"We'll have to wait for the results of the investigation for those answers," Bolton muttered.

"These trains should have had automatic braking systems. If they had, I could have stopped this from happening," Bekker moaned.

"Someday, maybe, but cost is always the driving factor in every business," Bolton explained.

"Damn the cost!" Bekker shouted. "How do you put a price on human life?"

82

AFTER A QUICK refueling stop in California, Richard took the Gulfstream jet to a cruising altitude of 45,000 feet, well above the commercial air traffic corridor. He set the cruising speed to Mach 0.85 and calculated they should arrive in Wellington just after sunrise. Taking his private jet would shave at least six hours off any commercial flight time, not to mention the delays and layovers associated with transferring flights and switching airlines.

Richard checked all his flight instruments one last time before leaving the cockpit. On his way through the galley, he picked up two glasses, a small bucket of ice, and a bottle of fifty-year-old Glenfiddich Scotch whiskey. It was one of the most expensive whiskies on the market, at $16,000 a bottle.

Richard found Quinn just where he had left him; still in front of the television, watching the latest on the train derailment. He could hear one of the survivors being interviewed.

"Everything seemed to be happening in slow motion—it couldn't end soon enough—the sound of scraping metal, the screaming, the crying, the shouting. And then there was an explosion. It sounded like it was at the front of the train."

"What's the latest?" Richard interrupted the broadcast as he placed the items he had been carrying on the entertainment unit beside the television.

"They're saying there are now one-hundred-eleven dead, thirty-two in critical condition and over three-hundred who have been sent to local hospitals with serious injuries," Quinn mumbled gloomily. "They said there are passengers still unaccounted for. They've been searching the shoreline looking for survivors who may have been thrown from the train. According to Fastrax's electronic fare system, there were over 1,450 passengers on board. If this derailment had happened with one of their express trains, that number would have been much higher, and so would have the fatalities."

"Do they know yet what caused the derailment?" Richard asked. *That damn kid was supposed to target the express train,* Richard reflected sourly.

"They're saying that speed could have been a factor, that the train took a curve in the tracks, the one they're calling Blain's Bend, at a speed greater than recommended," Quinn explained. "They were interviewing the Rail Traffic Controller a while ago, but I didn't catch all of what he was saying. He didn't seem to be making any sense."

Richard had his back to Quinn as he poured the scotch and listened carefully to what Quinn had to say. Richard had purposely positioned himself to conceal any unexpected reaction to the news regarding the investigation. He was relieved that the cause was yet to be determined. He should have left instructions with his man, Harry, to dispose of that Rail Traffic Controller; he was just another loose end that would have to be dealt with.

Richard turned around and handed Quinn a glass. "Here, why don't we give the news a rest for a while?" he said, switching off the television much to Quinn's chagrin. "You look like you could use a break."

Quinn reluctantly leaned back in his seat and accepted the drink from Richard. He raised his glass. The two men clinked rims. Each took a sip of the well-aged whiskey. "This is good," Quinn acknowledged.

"It should be," Richard replied brazenly.

They sat in silence for what seemed like an hour. Even though the silence had lasted only ten minutes, it was killing Richard. He couldn't stand it any longer.

"So, Quinn, tell me how close are you to finishing your project; to getting the twins back?" Richard was determined to use this opportunity to get as much information as possible from Quinn. He had to know if he wanted his plan to work.

"Hermes was working on the final computations for travel to the future when my system crashed," Quinn replied distantly, as his mind was pulled away from his concern over how Sandra must be coping.

"Right, I forgot. Do you know how long it will take to fix?"

"No idea. If it hadn't crashed, Hermes would have already finished his analysis. Then all we'd have to do is incorporate the chronizium and initiate time travel forward to bring my kids home," Quinn explained. "But if it was some sort of malicious virus that caused the crash, it could have corrupted my entire system. If that's the case, we'll have to start from scratch and that could mean months, maybe even years before I can bring Dani and Daric back home. By then, it may be too late."

Quinn was looking thoroughly dejected; Richard, on the other hand, was finding it hard to contain his elation. Quinn had just told him that Hermes could finish the task if the virus were removed from his system. As a result, Quinn was no longer necessary. Everything was falling precisely into place. Richard's plan was working perfectly. Now all they needed to do was find that rare mineral.

Richard glanced at Quinn and saw how miserable he looked. He had to keep Quinn focussed on what they still had to accomplish and, to do that, Richard had to bring Quinn back to the here and now.

"Quinn, this jet is equipped with two multichannel satellite communication systems. Why don't you give Sandra a call and see how she's doing?" Richard offered the despondent Quinn.

"Thanks, I will." Quinn glanced at his comm. "I'll call her in a couple of hours, when I know I won't be interrupting her work. She should be home by then; at least I hope she will be." Quinn turned and stared blankly out the window, lost in his own thoughts.

83

"DOCTOR DELANEY, HOW can we help?" Sandra looked over her shoulder and saw two officers standing behind her, anxiously awaiting her directions. They were standing at attention, uniforms immaculately pressed, highly polished shoes. She was sure that, by the end of the day, most of those fine clothes would have been damaged beyond repair and would have to be tossed in the trash. The same would be true of her own clothes. But these things happen.

"Chief Brown sent us. He said you could use a couple extra hands," one of the officers said. "We both have had medical training."

"Great. You can assist in triage zone three. That's anyone with a yellow tag. They'll need medical attention before being evacuated, but their injuries will not be life threatening. Anything you can't handle, defer to an EPS and move on to the next patient. The more you can treat, the more we can evacuate, and the better their chances will be," Sandra yelled over the sounds of wailing sirens that seemed to be coming from all directions and were getting closer by the minute.

"Got it," the officer replied. Without another word, the two men moved farther into the park, toward the tented zone designated 'Yellow Tags'.

"Put this one on the next ambulance," Sandra ordered, as she finished with her patient. While she stripped off her bloody gloves, she heard a new voice, louder than the others around her. "I have a lady here who just delivered a baby," the voice shouted. "We could use some help here," Shelby hollered, as she walked beside the stretcher carrying Joy and her newborn into 'Red Tags' zone.

"What's the problem?" Sandra asked, as she approached the stretcher, pulling on a fresh pair of gloves on her way.

"She's hemorrhaging. I can't stop it," Shelby explained.

"Did you deliver the baby?" Sandra asked, as she started to examine Joy.

"Yes."

"Were there any complications?"

"No, none," Shelby replied.

"Okay, we've got this." Sandra looked around for the EPS. "Get her on the next ambulance out of here. She needs to go directly to Mount Albert."

Two EPSs picked up the gurney and carried Joy and her baby toward a waiting ambulance.

Sandra pulled on yet another set of gloves. She bent over her next patient who had just been brought into the 'Red Tags' tent, which was serving as a field surgical theatre.

Shelby observed Sandra for a moment. Her clothes were covered in blood. Her hair was dishevelled. A dangling strand of hair was interfering with her vision until she brushed it away, leaving a red smear on her forehead. Shelby looked around the triage zones and couldn't believe how many people were in need of medical attention. No wonder she was having difficulty finding someone to help her with Joy.

"Look, I'm a nurse at City Hospital. What can I do to help?" Shelby offered.

"Fantastic," Sandra replied, never lifting her head up from the intricate work she was performing: trying to align the two ends of a compound fracture of a tibia bone. Suddenly it clicked in place.

Once the wound was dressed, the patient was ready for immediate transport to the nearest hospital, and another from a seemingly endless line of patients was brought in.

"We can always use the help," Sandra said, changing gloves again. "Can you help out in triage zone three? I just sent two police officers over there and I think they could use a little encouragement. This is overwhelming enough for the medical personnel. I can't imagine what they could be going through."

"No problem," Shelby said, before turning and making her way over to the triage area.

84

SHELBY HAD SOON been recalled from the 'Yellow Tags' zone to the 'Red Tags' zone, where critically injured patients were being treated. She spent the past three hours working beside Sandra, helping to stabilize trauma patients prior to their being transported to the nearest hospital. She had also been involved in handling several patients who had required resuscitation; some had made it, others had not. The latter had been moved to triage zone one; the morgue.

While working with Sandra, Shelby had also run into Kerry. Sandra had assigned her to provide whatever aid she could in triage zone four, the 'Green Tags' zone, reserved for the walking wounded. The zone was overflowing with patients, most of whom had arrived on their own, often holding a green tag. For the most part, their injuries had been minor: bumps, scrapes, lacerations, and the occasional dislocated shoulder. Kerry had lost track of how many patients she had treated. She couldn't recall how many lacerations she had stitched up, how many slings she had put into service, or how many bandages she had applied. She lost count long ago of the number of Tylenol she had dispensed to help patients manage their pain, and more times than not, she wished she had had something a little stronger to give to some of them.

As soon as patients were in a condition to be removed from the crash site, police, firefighters, paramedics, or whoever was handy, like Kellen, helped to get them moved. Patients in critical condition were put into two regional air ambulances and flown to hospitals with helipads. They loaded patients with less serious injuries into waiting ambulances, which drove them to local hospitals and, then, returned immediately to pick up more patients; the drivers never left their vehicles between pickups. And masses of patients with a wide range of lesser injuries were helped onto ambulance buses, supplied by a neighbouring region, and taken to various hospitals for the medical treatments they needed. The cycle of patients being picked up and delivered, picked up and delivered, went on non-stop for hours.

"Well, that's one thing I never want to experience again." Shelby sighed after the last patient had been evacuated from the triage area.

"I agree," Kerry muttered, as she walked over to see how her fellow passenger was faring.

"You know, if you stand back and look at it, it's almost like organized chaos–everybody's got their thing to do and they were all doing it. It's the one time where it works like a well-oiled machine. The only problem is having enough resources here. Hockley's new recruits, being paramedics, had a huge impact. And you two were a tremendous help, too. Thank you," Sandra said kind-heartedly.

"I meant to ask you earlier, but we were kind of busy," Shelby said to a very weary-looking Sandra. "Remember the lady with a newborn baby? Do you know how they're doing?"

"The baby is doing fine, thanks to you, as I recall. But I'm afraid the mother didn't make it. There was too much hemorrhaging. They couldn't stop it in time," Sandra said sadly.

"No!" Shelby moaned, slumping to the ground in despair and in utter exhaustion; all of her normally stoic defences were completely depleted.

Sandra placed a reassuring hand on Shelby's shoulder. "You did everything you could. No one's to blame here."

"Except her stupid boss who refused to mail her leave-of-absence papers to her, insisted she pick them up in person, and forced her onto that damned train," Shelby snapped.

"Shelby, I deal with death in my line of work all the time. Do you know how I get through it?" Sandra asked sympathetically.

"No," Shelby said, sniffling.

"We all know that each of us has only a certain amount of time that we will spend on this earth," Sandra said quietly. "Tomorrow's not promised. There is no way for any of us to know when the hands of time will stop and our time on this world will come to an end. It's what we do with our time that matters; it's what we do that will make our lives worthwhile."

"What are you getting at?" Shelby snapped.

"Shelby, Joy's life was very worthwhile, especially today. Because today, of all days, she brought a new life into this world, with your help."

Shelby finally looked up at Sandra after giving some thought to what she had said. Sandra was right; it was no one's fault. Things happened for a reason even if she couldn't understand why at the time. She suddenly felt bad for snapping.

"I guess some call it fate, or maybe it's a matter of being in the wrong place at the wrong time," Kerry chimed into the conversation.

"I think I believe more in fate than chance," Sandra mused. "And I'm sure it was fate that brought you two to my aid today. Thank you both, for all your help. Look, I've got to head over to the hospital now. Do you need a lift somewhere?"

"No, thanks," Shelby and Kerry said in unison. They had both made travel arrangements, earlier.

"Oh, I almost forgot. Before Joy passed away, she wanted you to know that she named her baby after you. Again, I'm so sorry," Sandra said, and then turned and walked away, leaving a heartbroken Shelby sobbing inconsolably in a heap on the blood-soaked ground.

Sandra stopped on her way out and spoke to Kellen, who quickly made his way over to comfort his sister. Sandra felt awful for having to leave so abruptly, but she had places to go and people to see before she could call it a day. Besides, she had her own demons that occupied her every waking moment.

85

IT WAS AFTER 10:00 P.M. when Sandra was finally dropped off at home. She glanced toward the lake and noticed the shadowy outline of Daric's boat reflecting off the moonlit water. She was grateful to have received a call from Bill at the hospital, offering to drive the boat back home. He had arranged for one of his officers to meet him at the Delaney Estate and take him back to the police precinct.

When Sandra approached the house, the motion sensor lights came on, casting a yellowish glow over the walkway leading to the back door. She had to smile as she recalled their first experience with this new technology, or at least it was new technology at the time. When they first installed the wireless floodlights, they had set the range to activate when a car pulled into the driveway, but that had proven to be a mistake. It didn't take them long to realize, especially after the lights flickered on and off several times during the night, that they had to narrow the sensory field. With the amount of wildlife living on the peninsula, every time an animal walked by, the lights would turn on and cast a blinding beam of light directly into the master bedroom for a full two minutes. In the middle of the night, those two minutes seemed like an eternity. And just when she thought she was about to doze off into REM sleep, they would come on again. Sandra was glad they wouldn't be disturbing her sleep tonight. She was dead tired; she wondered whether she would even notice if they did.

Sandra unlocked the kitchen door and was immediately greeted by a very lonely and starving family member. "Eeeheeeheee," Bear howled. It was a loud, high-pitched scream that Shibas were known to produce when they were either terribly unhappy or when they were extremely joyful over the return of a loved one. Bear's scream was one of joy.

"Well, hello to you, too, Bear." Sandra bent down to wrap her arms around Bear, who was more than willing to receive the affection. "Where were you when I needed a hug earlier today, eh?"

While scratching behind Bear's ear, Sandra noticed the collar. "What have you got here?" Then she spotted the bands around Bear's legs and she wondered. "Quinn, what are you up to?"

Upon hearing Quinn's name, Bear pulled away from Sandra and started searching the immediate area for her missing family member. "Sorry, Bear, he's not here," Sandra informed her. "Hey, you must need to go out. Come on, I'll walk with you for a bit. The fresh air will help clear my head."

Sandra opened the kitchen door and Bear was gone like a shot. "I guess you really needed to go."

Sandra strolled toward the shoreline and sat on one of the lounges while she waited for Bear to take care of business. She felt the stress of the day draining away. She couldn't help but reflect on the events of the day. A few hours ago, Fastrax authorities had determined that there had been a signal malfunction, which had resulted in the train's approach into Blain's Bend at too high a speed, thus causing the train to derail.

So much senseless loss. How could something like this happen, especially with today's technology? There has to be some way of preventing this type of catastrophe from repeating itself,' she thought.

Sandra picked up the hauntingly beautiful call of the loon echoing across the mirror-like surface of the lake. It was amazing how far sound could travel over water. She remembered when Dani and Daric were much younger and they used to have boat parties out on the lake. The sounds from the party made it seem like they were sitting right in their own back yard.

Sandra's reminiscing brought back the painful reality that her kids weren't home. She didn't know where they were or whether they were safe. She got up out of the lounge and headed back to the house. Twenty minutes later, Sandra opened the door and Bear rushed past her into the kitchen. "And I suppose you're hungry, too." Bear stared up at Sandra in anticipation, her tail rapidly dusting the hardwood floor.

Sandra could have cared less whether she had anything to eat right now. She was beyond being exhausted. *I wouldn't be long out of bed tonight,* she thought.

While Bear enjoyed her dinner, Sandra walked into the living room and went behind the bar. She knew exactly how she was going to put this day behind her: a little nightcap, scotch on the rocks would help her fall asleep tonight. She took a glass, dropped a handful of ice into it, and added a generous portion of amber liquid.

"What's this?" Sandra asked of no one in particular when she noticed a piece of paper on the bar. It looked like a note, probably from Quinn. She picked it up, along with her glass, and headed for the sofa, turning on the television as she passed. Bear had finished her dinner and jumped up beside Sandra on the sofa; she was looking for more attention.

"All done?" Sandra asked, scratching Bear behind the ear. As she lifted her glass to take a sip, the late evening news came on. "Ahh, that tastes good."

"The whole team responded superbly. Most of the injuries were muscular skeletal, so arms and legs and ribs. I'm very proud of how the staff at Mount Albert Hospital responded to this emergency. I'm also extremely grateful for the extra help and support from Mercy and the other hospitals that took some of our overflow."

Sandra was staring at an exhausted and bedraggled version of herself. "Bear, that's my interview from earlier this evening. I look a mess," she moaned. She realised she shouldn't be focussing on her appearance, given the circumstances, but it was part of the female DNA she told herself.

"A lot of passengers on that train were business people heading into the city to work. Fastrax, I know, also helped out today, mostly with transportation."

"What are the extent of the injuries?" (One of the reporters was thrusting a microphone in closer to Sandra's face.)

"Most of the injuries were fractures: rib fractures, leg and arm fractures."

"How many are in critical condition?" (Another reporter was butting in.)

"We currently have twenty-eight in critical condition. Eight went directly into the operating room after arriving here at the hospital."

"How many staff did you have to call in?" (Another reporter was shouting a question at Sandra.)

"Many of our staff came in of their own accord. Lots of trauma surgeons, orthopaedic surgeons and we called in extra nurses, radiologists, technicians and laboratory personnel to make sure we had a full team here. Everyone responded quickly. They really came through for us."

Sandra didn't need to hear the interview; she had been there. She turned her attention away from the television and to the note she had placed beside her, on the arm of the sofa. She was unfolding the note when her comm rang. She didn't even have to look; instinct told her the call was from Quinn.

"Hey, I was just about to read your note," Sandra said tenderly, as she turned the volume down on the television.

"No need to now. It just said we left the house shortly after you and, if all goes well, we should be back by late Thursday or early Friday," Quinn explained.

"That's great. Where are you now?" Sandra asked and then took another sip from her glass.

"We're somewhere over the South Pacific. I don't even know what day it is."

"That makes two of us," Sandra said, trying to stifle a yawn.

Quinn was referring to the International Dateline and whether they had crossed it yet. In Sandra's case, she felt that she had worked enough over the past thirteen hours to cover several days, all of them blurring together.

"I miss you already. Do you think you'll be able to find the chron . . . Oh my God, Bear just vanished! Quinn?" Sandra cried.

"Relax, Sandra, it's okay," Quinn tried to assure her. "I forgot to mention that the note also said I had linked Bear's bands to the kids' bands, so that the next time they jump into a different time period, Bear would join them there."

"But why would you do that? Isn't it bad enough that our children are lost in time? Now, you felt you needed to send Bear, too?" Sandra just couldn't understand Quinn's logic sometimes.

"Sandra, was Bear still wearing a collar?"

"Yes."

"Well, the collar contains a note for the kids," Quinn explained.

"But, Quinn, without Hermes, we have no way of knowing where they are," Sandra said anxiously.

"We can't do much about it, Sandra, even if we did know," Quinn reasoned. "I'll be home in a couple of days and I'll get Hermes up and running again, and then we'll get our kids back home. I promise."

"I knew there was a reason I married you," Sandra expressed tenderly.

Unknown—Day One

86

DARIC'S FIRST SENSATION was that of being wet. It made perfect sense because the last thing he remembered was diving into the North River to save his sister. But something was terribly wrong. It wasn't the icy grip of the North River he was experiencing; it was actually quite pleasant, like the balmy sensation of lying on the beach of a tropical island in the South Pacific. Save his sister . . . his mind snapped back to his first thought. "Dani!" he called in panic.

"Here," came the muttered reply from only a few feet away.

Daric finally noticed that he was half submerged in water. The upper half of his body was sprawled on a beach. *Glad I wasn't turned the other way around*, he thought. He pulled himself out of the shallows and rolled over to check on his sister.

"Are you okay?" Daric asked, as he looked her over carefully.

"Feeling a little waterlogged. You?"

"Fine," Daric replied, quickly scanning their new surroundings for any immediate danger. He couldn't believe their luck. It was like they had landed in a small piece of paradise. They were beside a river that was close to forty feet across. The beach they were on was about twenty feet in depth and thirty feet long. Along the river's edge was a small glade, covered in a soft green moss. There was a blanket of green lichen covering the rocks and also latching onto the trunks of the nearby trees. He could hear the soft roar of a waterfall off in the distance as it struggled to penetrate the thick lush forest. He assumed that the waterfall was the source feeding this river.

Beyond the glade were stands of large bamboo and a wide variety of ferns and palms. Spanish moss and various types of bromeliads clung from precarious perches atop the trees, creating a natural curtain and making it difficult to see more than five feet into the dense undergrowth. Daric knew there was wildlife around, for the air was filled with birdsong. It was as if each bird was competing, trying to be louder and more captivating than the others.

But the one thing Daric embraced above all else was the fragrant, moist, clean air. It was a far cry from the stench of the prison where they had been locked in for thirty-one days. He had wondered whether his sense of smell would ever fully recover.

"When you're finished daydreaming, I could use a hand here," Dani said, holding up her manacled wrists.

"Damn. I'm sorry, Dani." Daric crawled closer to his sister and held her wrists to examine the shackles. "I wonder why these and the rope around your ankles didn't disappear when we arrived here," he pondered for a moment, before reaching down and untying the rope around Dani's ankles.

"Maybe these materials are also available in this time period," Dani rationalized, "whenever that might be. Now, would you . . ."

Before Dani could continue, their attention was abruptly drawn to a rustling sound coming from the shadowy depths of the jungle directly in front of them.

"What is it?" Dani whispered.

"I don't know," Daric murmured. He started to get to his feet. He wanted to place himself between his restrained sister and whatever might be approaching. But just as he got one foot under him, a loud high-pitched scream echoed throughout the glade, sending the birds in the trees to flight. Their numbers were so great that the sky momentarily darkened as if the sun had disappeared behind a storm cloud.

"If I didn't know any better, I'd swear that was . . ." Something barrelled out of the underbrush knocking Daric flat onto his back.

"Bear!" Dani yelled.

"Eeheeeheee," Bear screamed. She was finally reunited with her two favourite humans. She gave Daric a thorough face wash with her tongue before jumping over to give Dani the same exuberant greeting.

"Bear, where did you come from?" Dani didn't even try to block or dodge the assault, but instead savoured it.

"Check out the bands," Daric said, pointing to Bear's legs. "Those were the ones in Dad's lab. Do you think he sent Bear here?"

"He must have. Bear, take it easy," Dani urged, as she struggled with the overly excited pet. "I'm happy to see you, too."

"I wonder why Bear didn't materialize beside us. We've only ever been a few feet apart from each other every time we've jump through time," Daric observed.

"I'm assuming Dad somehow linked Bear's bands to ours. His calibrations must have been off a bit," Dani speculated. As she reached up to put her arms around their loving pet, she noticed the collar. "What have you got here, Bear?" She removed the collar and started running her fingers over the inside lining.

"What are you doing?" Daric asked, watching his sister fumbling with the collar.

"Bear never wears a collar, so I'm thinking it might be a vehicle to carry a message to us," Dani explained.

"Well, Bear doesn't normally wear bands either, but I don't think it would be wise to remove those," Daric countered, just as Dani pulled out a piece of parchment.

"Aha," Dani sneered. "Told ya."

"Give me that," Daric said as he snatched the note away. He had more dexterity with his hands than Dani did at the moment.

"Hey," Dani protested feebly. Still shackled, she was also

wrestling with an excited Bear.

Daric unfolded the note carefully so as not to tear it. He couldn't believe what it said. "Dani, we've only been gone five days. You were right; time does travel at different speeds. Dad has been working on getting us back home."

Dani took the note back from Daric and read it for herself. Their father hadn't given up on them. In her heart of hearts, she knew he never would. The rest of the note read, *Hang tight and stay out of trouble; we'll have you home soon. BTW, thought waves determine travel destination.*

"That's not a lot of information," Dani remarked anxiously. "What kind of thought waves and whose? Do they determine time, location or both, and how do we control them?"

"I guess there wasn't a lot of room on that piece of paper for Dad to elaborate," Daric reasoned. "And maybe it really doesn't matter, because we'll be back home soon. All we have to do is sit tight and wait. But first, let's get you out of those manacles."

87

"OKAY, I THINK this will work," Daric announced as he sat down next to Dani, who had been patiently waiting for what seemed like hours. Bear had been quite content to stay glued to Dani's side while Daric went foraging for some makeshift tools he could use to remove Dani's manacles.

"Now, hold your wrist over this boulder," Daric instructed. He hoped he had finally found the shape and mineral composition of stone that would work. He had already gathered quite a collection of remnant shards scattered at the base of the makeshift anvil.

"My wrists were so raw from these cuffs. I remember the burning sensation I felt after I was pushed into the salty North River. Now, look at them; they're all healed," Dani remarked, as she placed her wrist over the large boulder Daric had previously rolled into place.

"My ribs are healed, too," Daric added. "They're as good as new."

"So I guess my theory still holds true, then."

"What theory is that?" Daric asked disinterestedly, as he placed the small pointed stone he had found in the river next to the rivet securing the cuff or cup-lock to Dani's wrist. A rivet had been inserted into each cup-lock and flattened with a hammer by a blacksmith. Daric figured he just had to dislodge the rivets and the cuffs would open.

"When we travel backward through time, whatever happened in our prior time period simply hasn't occurred. So the month we spent in prison never happened," Dani concluded.

"How can you say that?" Daric snapped irritably. "We saw those people being executed. We witnessed and were actually a part of those ludicrous trials."

"Yes, we were, but that was in 1692," Dani explained calmly. "But where we are now is prior to 1692. So, in fact, what happened in Salem hasn't happened yet. But that's not to say it won't."

"So, where do you think we are? And for that matter when?" Daric placed the sharp point of the stone back onto the end of the rivet.

"As I said, we are definitely prior to 1692."

"Aside from your crazy theory and the fact that our injuries have been healed, how can you be so sure?"

"Because every time we've travelled, we've always gone back in time. We started in the twenty-first century, jumped back to the twentieth, then jumped further back to the nineteenth, and this last one was the seventeenth. My guess would be that we are somewhere between 1400 and 1500s."

"Okay, genius, say that you're right. Do you have any idea where we might be?"

"Not yet, but give me some time to figure it out," Dani replied confidently.

"Turn your head; I'm going to give this a whack," Daric instructed.

Dani turned her head away from the impact area. A moment later, she heard a crack as the stone struck metal.

"Whoa!"

"What happened?" Dani turned back around.

"You should have seen the sparks fly when I made contact," Daric explained.

"You must have found chalcedony, commonly known as flint rock, which is great, because we'll need that if we want to start a fire," Dani said.

"First rules of survival I learned at Venturer Scouts: find water, build a shelter, and find food," Daric recited.

"Well, it looks like water isn't a problem," Dani said, referring to the crystalline river beside them.

"Neither is food. That river is teeming with fish. I just have to figure out how to catch some," Daric muttered. "Now, turn your head again. Before we can do anything, we need to finish getting you out of these.

88

"WE SHOULD BE arriving in Wellington in about three hours," Richard said, returning from the cockpit after checking the avionics. He took the seat opposite Quinn.

"Great," Quinn replied indifferently.

"So, tell me, Quinn, why did you want to create the ability to travel through time?"

"Learning about whether time travel could occur in principle may give us new insights into how the universe works, and even how it got here," Quinn answered.

"Why spend all your time and energy on a pipe dream?"

"For years, physicists have been interested in testing the boundaries of the laws of physics. I'm no different, just more persistent." Quinn smiled faintly.

Quinn stared out the window, admiring the intricate shapes of the billowing tops of the cloud cover. From up here, the sun was basting the white cotton tops in a golden hue. But on the underside, they would be seen as much darker and perilous, expelling violent flashes of blinding light, followed by thunderous crashes and torrential downpours. Quinn recognized the towering cumulonimbus clouds and understood what naturally occurred when they were around. He was relieved that they were flying above the raging storm that was playing out below. He didn't much care for turbulence.

Turning his thoughts back to Richard, Quinn posed a hypothetical question. "Richard, if you had my travel bands, and you could go anywhere in time, where would you go?"

"I'd travel back in time," Richard said with no hesitation. He knew exactly what he would do. He hadn't stopped imagining what he would do since he had devised his devious plan.

"I'd have thought you would have gone into the future, to see how humankind had progressed, then taken some advanced technology or medical cure and brought it back to the present in order to make a fortune from it," Quinn expressed, knowing what drove Richard's ambitions: the mighty dollar.

"I have all the money I could possibly want or ever spend. What I don't have is respect," Richard snapped.

"That, my friend, you have to earn. Money can't buy that."

"No, but changing the past can," Richard jeered.

"But you can't change the past."

"Sure I can. You know that retro movie; I think it was called Back in the Future . . ." Richard reached mentally for the title.

"Back to the Future," Quinn offered.

"That's it. I simply alter a piece of history and all will be right with the world."

"That absurd story where Marty McFly runs into himself is fiction, nonsense really. Nature has a way of protecting itself. Things can't make themselves impossible, something will always happen to prevent a paradox."

"A paradox?" Richard inquired.

"Let's say you want to go back to right a wrong. For example, you want to go back into the past and kill your grandfather because he was a sadistic murderer. The simple fact that you exist today means that you failed."

"That doesn't make any sense," Richard protested.

"Sure it does. You can participate in shaping history, you can see what transpires, but you cannot change history from the course it was destined to take," Quinn insisted.

"Well, I don't agree. I guess I'll just have to prove you wrong," Richard snapped irritably.

"Okay, say you're right, even though you're not, and you could change history, what would you change?"

"It's quite simple really," Richard began, staring out the airplane's window, as if the tale he was about to tell was playing out before his very eyes. He had heard this story so many times; it felt like he was reliving it personally.

"Back in 1189, my ancestor, who was travelling with Richard the Lionhearted on the third of the Great Crusades, was falsely accused of robbery by one of his comrades-in-arms. Do you know what the punishment was for robbery back then?" Richard asked bluntly.

"Cut off a hand?" Quinn ventured.

"Good guess. That, I think, my ancestor could have lived with. But you're wrong." Richard savoured that one word for a moment, relishing how good it felt as it rolled off his tongue. *Whoa, the great Professor Quinn is actually wrong for once in his impeccable life.*

Richard stood up and started to pace the aisle; he needed to gather himself before he continued with his abhorrent tale.

"King Richard, himself, ordered that my ancestor be first stripped and shaved. As if that wasn't humiliating enough, the order was carried out in front of his own men. King Richard then ordered his men to pour boiling pitch over my ancestor's head and down his body. Do you know what it feels like to have hot tar poured all over you?" Richard asked bitterly.

"Can't say that I do," Quinn replied, now feeling sorry he had ever asked the question, as he observed Richard's ire slowly build.

"I tried it once, when I was very young, to see what it would feel like, but only on my left hand. It was quite painful," Richard recalled. "I can only imagine the pain associated with having that pitch poured all over your body. Not to mention how painful it would be to get it off.

"Anyway, then five men were ordered to shake bags of feathers over my ancestor, to completely cover him. Do you know what they did next?"

"No, what?" Quinn muttered.

"They placed him on top of two beams, which were perched on the men's shoulders and they paraded him through camp. Then, in the end, he was left behind as the army moved on. They left him with no clothes to wear or weapons to defend himself with."

"But, Richard, even if you do travel back in time, you can't change history," Quinn insisted, still desperately trying to get his point across to the infuriated and pacing Richard.

"You are such a fool, Quinn. All I have to do is put the blame on someone else and history will right itself and unfold the way it should have," Richard said.

"This time you're wrong, Richard. History will unfold as it already has. Your ancestor may be saved from tar and feather-ing, but he will still die branded a thief, a criminal," Quinn stated firmly.

Richard spun around, glaring coldly at Quinn, fury etched in his face. "You lie!" My ancestor was a very close friend of King Richard, if you know what I mean. They had been more than just friends, for years. And then King Richard takes the word of some common soldier over that of his dear friend, exacts his form of justice, and leaves him to die." Richard continued. "My ancestor should have been fighting alongside King Richard for all those years, joining in all those tributes, honors, and awards he so rightly deserved."

Richard continued to pace as he ranted on. "I will make sure that happens." He stormed out of the cabin and headed for the cockpit. He strapped himself into the pilot's seat, his heart rate well above normal. "You just wait and see, Quinn. I'll show you, and in the process I'll take everything you hold so dear," Richard snarled nefariously, as he muttered to himself.

Quinn sat alone back in the cabin, trying to figure out what button he had pushed to throw Richard over the edge. He had never seen his friend so agitated before. Quinn knew Richard's education had been mostly bought and paid for and that Richard had barely cracked open a textbook, but what Quinn was conveying was basic physics. Richard should have known this.

Quinn shrugged. *Since light travels faster than sound, some people appear bright until you hear them speak,* remembering one of his favorite quotes from Einstein. He rested his head against the backrest of the seat and closed his eyes. It was going to be a long day.

89

THE PIPER SENECA V was crossing over the turquoise waters of Cook Strait. Quinn could see two Interislander ferries passing each other, one headed for Wellington on the North Island, the other for Picton on the South Island. Covering fifty-seven miles, the three-hour trip had been described as one of the most beautiful ferry rides in the world. Quinn had enjoyed the spectacular scenery on his last trip to New Zealand with Sandra. Just four months ago, they had travelled through Marlborough Sound, with its steep wooded hills and quiet bays, before passing through Tory Channel, the major arm of Queen Charlotte Sound. The Sound's calm and placid waters had been a marked contrast to the rough waters of Cook Strait.

As much as he had enjoyed the leisurely ferry ride, Quinn acknowledged that, for this trip, Richard was right. Time was of the essence and a twenty-minute flight was preferable to a three-hour ferry crossing. Ahead, the peaks of the Southern Alps jutted through the thick cloud cover, looking like the lower jaw of some long-forgotten prehistoric carnivore. The Southern Alps were the showpiece, the marvel of nature that drew tourists by the thousands every year. There were over one-hundred-thirty peaks that rise over 7,800 feet. Prominent among them was *Aorangi*, Maori for the Cloud Piercer, which was uninspiringly renamed Mount Cook, after the eighteenth century navigator.

An hour ago, Quinn and Richard had landed in Wellington and picked up the Piper for their trip to Nelson on the South Island. Richard had also instructed the Wellington airport manager to ensure the Gulfstream jet was fueled and ready for their return trip home. Richard had palmed him a wad of cash for his discretion.

Now they were on final approach to the Nelson Airport. Richard had just received clearance to land. *That was a quick flight,* Quinn thought, *seems like we just got airborne.*

After smoothly touching down, Richard exited the active runway. Turning right, he taxied the Piper to a small hangar where he had been instructed to park the aircraft. Shutting down the twin turbocharged two-hundred-twenty horsepower engines, Richard removed his headphones and placed them over the yoke.

"Why don't you get our bags while I check in," Richard said as he was leaving the aircraft. "The vehicle's over there," he added, gesturing to his left. Richard had made prior arrangements with the airport manager to acquire the dive equipment Quinn had specified and to provide them with ground transportation.

"On it," Quinn replied, getting out of the plane. He walked around to the left side of the aircraft and opened the passenger doors. The passenger section of the Piper had ergonomically designed seats of plush natural leather and high-grade carpeting that was color-coordinated to match beautifully. The expansive doors made loading and boarding the aircraft an effortless task. And the cabin was one of the widest available in this class of aircraft.

Quinn reached into the passenger section, removed their dive bags, and walked them over to the rental vehicle. He was just finishing his inspection of the rented equipment already in the vehicle, when Richard appeared at his side, carrying the rest of their luggage, the two lightest pieces.

"All there?"

"Everything I asked for," Quinn replied affirmatively. "You set to go?"

"Yeah," Richard said. "The Piper will be fueled and ready to take us back to Wellington, whenever we're ready to leave."

With the rented equipment filling the back of the vehicle, Quinn had no choice but to put their two large dive bags on the roof racks. When he was satisfied that the bags were secure, he jumped off the running board.

"All right, let's get going. We still have a long day ahead of us," Quinn announced with a note of impatience in his voice. He climbed in behind the wheel. Richard tossed his two smaller bags onto the floor in the backseat and settled in beside Quinn.

The rental was a Jeep Wrangler, a prototypical off-road vehicle. It was a later model than Richard had hoped for, but it had been modified without sacrificing the strength of the Jeep's distinct character. Modifications included fuel injectors for maximum performance, front and rear differentials for optimum traction, a touch-screen navigation system, and steering stabilizer for improved off-road handling. The exterior had a fresh coat of military green paint with matte black fender flares. Accessories included a front bumper with winch, a rear bumper with hitch and tire carrier, roof rack which incorporated a cargo basket, and auxiliary lighting. Overall, Richard was satisfied with the airport manager's choice of vehicle.

The Jeep pulled out of the airport and headed toward Blue Creek Resurgence, the place where, four months ago, Quinn had found the chronizium, the rare mineral needed to bring his kids home.

Unknown—Day One

90

DANI WAS RELIEVED to be finally free of the eight-pound manacles. Now that she had her freedom, her first priority was to take a bath and divest herself of the filth and stench of that desolate Salem prison. Daric had insisted on checking the perimeter to make sure they would be safe here. She had sent Bear along with him hoping to keep Daric out of trouble. So, now was the opportune time for her to enjoy a quiet, leisurely bath.

Dani took off what was left of her nurse's uniform, the same uniform she had been wearing since they'd left the year 1888. It was caked in filth. She would have preferred to discard it, but she couldn't. It was the only clothes she had and she would have to make do with it. So she placed the soiled dress on the beach. Next she removed her undergarments; they would be the first things she would wash. *What I wouldn't give for a bar of soap right now,* she thought.

With her undergarments in hand, Dani walked to the water's edge and stuck her toe in. The water was cool but not uncomfortable, a welcome relief from the warm humid air. She eased herself into the river and completely submerged. "Oh, this is heaven," she sputtered as she resurfaced and swam slowly back to the shore.

At the shore, she sat in the shallow water, scooped up some wet sand and began to scrub her clothes. After getting as much dirt as she could out of her garments without damaging their material, she stood up, strolled across the beach, and draped the clothes over a branch at the edge of the clearing so they could dry in the early afternoon sun.

As Dani turned and headed back to the river, she muttered, "Now, it's time for a little exfoliating." At the water's edge, she plunged in and disappeared into the cool depths. A school of fish darted out of her way as she swam to the bottom. She snagged two handfuls of sand and resurfaced. Without bothering to get out of the water, she vigorously rubbed the sand over her skin until it was a rosy pink. Then she worked on cleaning her hair, which, surprisingly, had not grown since she and Daric had left home. "But then again, it's been only five days," she reasoned. She plunged underwater once again to rinse the sand out of her hair.

A small fern frond parted. Dark eyes observed from the opposite bank of the river as a head emerged out of the water. The intruder sat in silence, riveted to what was materializing before him.

As the hidden intruder watched, the figure from across the river glided gracefully out of the water and onto the warm sandy beach. She was tall, one of the tallest females he had ever seen. Her hair glistened in the afternoon sunlight as if spun in gold. Water, in intricate rivulets, cascaded down her sculpted sun-kissed body. When she turned to the river and lifted her face toward the heavens, her voluptuous breasts, her slim waist, and her well-shaped legs were breath-taking. She was a vision of beauty.

The intruder let out a gasp when he realized what he had just witnessed: the birth of a goddess from the river. He quickly threw a hand over his gaping mouth.

Dani looked toward a sound she thought she had heard coming from the other side of the river. She scanned the shoreline with its dense foliage, but could see nothing out of the ordinary. She simply. "Must have been my imagination," she muttered, walking to her drying clothes. As she took them off the branches and put on her undergarments, she turned around to cast a careful eye one more time at the distant shore. All appeared normal.

The intruder, after waiting a few minutes to be sure he wouldn't be detected, slowly and cautiously made his way out of the area following the same path by which he had arrived. He paid particular attention to where he placed his feet; a snapping twig would reveal him to the already suspicious goddess. He had to get back and tell the others he had witnessed the birth of a goddess; soon all their troubles would be over.

91

WHILE DANI WAITED for Daric to return from surveying the perimeter of their secluded beach, she set off to do a little foraging on her own, but only in the immediate vicinity. She wanted to see what she could find that might be of use. She soon hit the jackpot, or so she thought. Dressed solely in her undergarments, which could pass as a modern-day bikini, she collected her treasures and returned to the beach.

She carefully picked through the many stone shards left from Daric's numerous attempts to remove her manacles. She selected one. It was a piece of obsidian, a black, glass-like volcanic rock found all over the world. Dani knew it would be perfect for her needs since society used obsidian in her true present day in surgical tools because of its naturally sharp edge.

Dani set to work. She pulled a narrow strip of cloth off the hem of her dress and put it in the palm of her hand. She placed the piece of obsidian on the cloth and wrapped the material around the larger end of the stone, so she could grip it securely without cutting her hand. Then she struck along the edge of the obsidian with a small hammer-like stone, flaking off little bits until one edge of the obsidian was tapered to a point. When she was satisfied with her results, she carefully removed the obsidian from the cloth. She wrapped the thick end of the stone with pieces of twine she had pulled off the ropes that had previously bound her feet. Before long, she had finished crafting a handle for her knife. She set it down beside her and repeated the process with another piece of obsidian. This time, she lashed the finished shard to the end of sturdy stick. She now had a spear to go with her knife.

Dani looked around the glade for any sign of Daric. He seemed to have been gone a long time. *Hope he's all right,* she thought. Then she remembered Bear had gone with him. Bear would keep him out of trouble, she hoped.

Dani thought about trying to start a fire, but decided against it. She was still feeling a little unnerved from earlier in the day when she had had a sensation of being watched. She was concerned a fire might reveal their presence if indeed others were in the area. She would have to wait until Daric returned to be sure it would be safe to do so.

Even without a fire, there was enough to do to keep Dani busy for hours. She started by getting one of the dried calabashes, also known as bottle gourds, she had found during her earlier scavenger hunt. Dani easily cut it in half with her newly-crafted knife. She scraped out the dried pulp and seeds and, using handfuls of sand, rubbed the interior of the gourd until it was perfectly clean and smooth. "Fancy looking cups, if I do say so myself," she said, admiring her handiwork.

After cleaning out a few more gourds, Dani reached for a long bamboo pole she had previously collected from the surrounding forest. She used her new knife to split the end of the sturdy pole into four parts. She tied twine at the base of the slits to prevent the pole from splitting further. Then she stuffed the split ends with the dried pulp from the gourds to force the tips apart, like four prongs and finished by shaping the points into barbs. She had just fashioned a very effective fishing spear. At least, she hoped it would be effective.

Dani heard rustling in the brush behind her only seconds before a blur of sesame red came thundering toward her. If she hadn't been leaning against the base of a tree, she would have been bowled over. "Bear," she exclaimed, "where have you been? Did you get lost?"

"No, we didn't get lost," Daric grumbled sarcastically. "I just wanted to make sure we'd be safe here. Except for what may lurk in the forest at night, we'll be relatively okay, that's if we want to stay here for a while," Daric said, falling down unceremoniously. He lay sprawled on the sand, exhausted from fighting his way through the thick undergrowth for the past four hours.

"Well, we do have fresh water and an abundance of fish. And I've found we have tubers, some berries and wild herbs, and a variety of fruit trees all around us, so we won't go hungry. All we need to do now is build a shelter," Dani remarked.

"Give me a minute, will ya?" Daric moaned. "While I was out making sure we'll be safe, you've been sitting here on your butt working on your tan. I'm hungry and thirsty and too damn exhausted to do anything about either right now." Daric lay spread-eagled on the ground, his eyes closed. He never noticed the smirk that crept across Dani's face.

"Come on, Bear, let's see where the best place would be to build us a home," Dani said. She got up, brushed away the sand, and headed off. She hadn't gone far before she heard a moan.

"All right, I'm coming," Daric protested. "Besides, you don't know what to look for."

"Oh, I don't know about that. A fallen log over a hollow in the ground would be Mother Nature's way of providing an adequate shelter," Dani retorted.

"I'm not sleeping under any log," Daric barked. "Come on, this way," he said, as he led them toward the sound of a distant waterfall.

92

DANI AND DARIC were following the river, walking along its banks. The thundering sound of the waterfall was getting louder and louder. Suddenly, they came to another glade. The air was filled with the mist given off by the water cascading down a fifty-foot high waterfall. The falling water formed a brilliant white curtain, in the midst of the shadowy depths of the surrounding forest.

Without a word, Dani and Daric stopped and admired the beauty before them. The incredible lushness of the surrounding trees and undergrowth matched the magnificence of the waterfall. "Wow," was all that Dani could say, as she became aware of the incredible explosion of life around her. Tropical birds, in a myriad of colors, dotted the branches overhead. A troop of howler monkeys let the intruders know their presence was not welcome. A small deer drinking at the river's edge nervously lifted its head and then darted into dense brush, disappearing from sight. Dani thought the place looked like one of those secluded lagoons she had seen pictured in travel advertisements for Hawaii. It truly looked like paradise.

"Bear, get back here," Daric yelled, when he saw her take off after the deer. His yell brought an abrupt end to Dani's thoughts about paradise.

Bear stopped. She looked at where the deer had disappeared into the forest, then back over her shoulder at Daric. Bear hesitated only a moment and then trotted back into the clearing. She paused as she approached the place where the deer had been drinking before it was frightened away. She hunched over and sniff the area. Bear thought a cool drink would be a good idea. She stretched her neck down and lapped up as much water as she could. Traipsing through the forest with Daric for hours had been hard work.

"Well, we can't stay here," Daric complained tiredly.

"Why not?" Dani protested.

"Well, for starters, it's too wet," Daric replied, referring to the constant spray from the falls. "And it's too noisy with those chattering apes."

"They're called howler monkeys," Dani corrected.

"Whatever." His exhaustion and hunger were making him irritable. Dani recognized the signs and decided not to press the issue.

"So, I guess we should head back to our original campsite," Dani offered.

"Give me a sec. I don't want to make this trip a total waste of our time," Daric said, making his way to the base of the falls. He paused for only a moment after reaching the falls. "I'll be right back."

Before Dani could ask where he was going, Daric had disappeared under a curtain of rushing water. "Daric?"

"Relax, I'm right here," he shouted, to be heard over the roaring falls. "I just wanted to see if there might be a good hiding spot back here and there is."

Daric had found a cavern buried behind the curtain of falling water. To his amazement, it was perfectly dry, starting a few feet back from the opening. If they needed to hide from trouble, this could be the perfect place. He would just have to stock it with whatever supplies he could gather. He figured after what they'd endured during their recent travels, it was better to be safe than sorry.

"Okay, let's head back," Daric said, after reappearing from behind the watery curtain. "There's a large cavern behind the falls. We can use it as a hideout if we need to. Once we get our camp settled, I'll start bringing up some supplies to leave in the cavern, in case of an emergency."

"Do you think we'll need to go into hiding?" Dani asked nervously. She still had an uneasy feeling that someone had been watching her earlier in the day, a feeling she hadn't yet shared with Daric.

"Never hurts to be prepared," Daric replied, as he led the way back to their private beach.

93

WHEN DANI AND Daric got back to their beach, they realized it was too late to build a proper shelter. They would have to sleep under the canopy of stars for a night, an eventuality that rather appealed to Daric. The skies were clear, so far, and they could only hope for a full moon or even a partial one that could cast some light into their little corner of whatever world they were now in.

"I'm going for a swim to see if I can fist a fish," Daric announced. He had already taken off his shirt and pants and was standing in only his boxers.

"You're going to what?"

"Fist a fish," Daric repeated. "You put your hand under water and wiggle your fingers while staying perfectly still. The fish will swim up and, when it opens its mouth to take the bait, you ram your fist into its mouth—hence fist a fish."

"I could catch the fish . . ."

"Yeah, right," Daric mocked. He knew Dani was no fisherman or fisherwoman, for that matter. Out here roughing it, he realized the majority of the work would rest entirely on his shoulders. But he could handle it, he thought, as he stood a little taller and threw out his chest.

"Then, I'll start a fire," Dani offered.

"No, thanks," Daric quickly shot back. "I remember the first time you tried to start a fire. It was a disaster."

"Fine, you don't want me to fish or build a fire. Then, what can I do?" Dani snapped. She was annoyed that Daric thought so little of her abilities, but she would show him! Besides, she had been only eleven when she had tried to start her first fire. How could she have known she should have built something to contain it first? She had learned a lot since then.

"Why don't you wash out my clothes? I see you've already done yours, so you know how to do that," Daric quipped.

"Fine," Dani bit back, as she bent down to pick up Daric's dirty clothes. She was so angry that she thought it better to distant herself from her brother; so she walked to the far end of the sand beach, with Bear on her heels. Bear had decided to stick close to Dani this time, less exertion on her part.

As Dani washed and fumed, she decided not to tell Daric she had already fashioned some dishes out of gourds, or that she had made a knife, a weapon, and a fishing spear. She would bide her time and wait to play out her cards when the time was right. She would show Daric just how capable she was!

94

WHEN DANI HAD finished cleaning Daric's clothes, she walked back up the beach. She was much calmer now. She saw Daric was still trying to 'fist a fish' and, so far, wasn't having any luck.

After hanging Daric's clean clothes on the same branches she had used earlier to dry her own, Dani sat on the beach to watch Daric, with Bear curled up next to her. Dani had to stifle a laugh a couple times when Daric swung his fist out of the water with nothing to show for his efforts. After five minutes of watching this comical routine, she asked, "Do you think there's catfish in the river?"

"Yeah, I suppose so, why?" Daric replied in frustration.

"Do you remember when we were younger and Nanny caught that catfish off the end of our dock? And Bear wouldn't have anything to do with it?"

At the sound of her name, Bear lifted her head off Dani's leg. "It's okay, Bear; we'll find something for you to eat," Dani said, as she continued to scratch behind the dog's ear.

It was getting late and Dani had wasted enough time watching Daric's failed attempts at providing dinner. She gently lifted Bear's head off her lap, stood up, and retrieved her fishing spear. Daric was so focussed on fisting a fish that he was oblivious to the on-shore activities.

Dani walked upstream from Daric where his antics wouldn't scare the fish away. She waded into the water, knee deep, and stood there, unmoving for close to half a minute. Then, with lightning speed, she thrust the fishing spear into the water. Pulling it back, she had secured her first fish: a catfish by the looks of the whiskers and the lack of scales. She knew that this one fish wouldn't feed the three of them, so she prepared for another strike, and another, and another.

With her abundant catch in hand, she walked back down the beach and deposited her fish on a boulder. She checked on Daric. *Still as stubborn as ever,* she thought. "Come on, Daric, time to call it quits."

"And just what do you expect us to eat for dinner," he barked, standing waist deep in the river with his hands on his hips.

Dani, with her back to Daric, bent down to gather up her prize. Wait for it . . . wait for it . . .Dani turned around and lifted her two hands. They were holding at least eight pounds of fish. She couldn't mask the grin on her face even if she had wanted to.

"Where the hell did you get those?" Daric grumbled, as he made his way out of the water and onto the beach. Dani placed her catch down on a nearby rock.

"It was easy, with my fishing spear," Dani explained, showing off her handmade tool. "So, you see, dear brother, I wasn't just sitting here on my butt all day working on my tan."

Ashamed for his remarks, Daric bowed his head and muttered his reluctant apology. "I'm sorry, Dani. I should have known better. You can be very resourceful."

"Apology accepted. Now, you can clean the fish, while I start a fire," she ordered.

"But . . ."

"No buts."

"But, what am I going to clean them with?" Daric asked hesitantly.

"Oh, you can use my knife," Dani said casually, as she handed over her handmade knife and savoured the stunned reaction on her brother's face. *I could never get tired of this,* she thought, and, then, reluctantly turned away to begin her search for just the right location to build a fire pit.

95

AFTER HAVING FOUND a suitable location, it didn't take Dani long to build the fire pit with rocks she had hauled from the river. Satisfied, she turned her attention to preparing for the pit's inaugural fire. She formed a nest-like tinder ball out of dried grasses, small twigs and bark and nestled it in the bottom of the pit. She gathered up sticks and placed them in piles beside the pit, separating them by size, so she could add them gradually to build a hardy fire.

"Here goes," Dani mumbled, as she knelt down in front of her tinder ball. She picked up the flint that Daric had discovered earlier. She held it with one hand as close to the tinder ball as she could; at the same time, she grasped the metal cuff from her manacle and struck it across the edge of the flint to create a spark. It only took a couple of tries before the tinder started to smolder. She bent down, cupped her hands, and gently blew until the tinder burst into flames. As the flames grew, she slowly added the smaller pieces of kindling, then the larger pieces. It wasn't long before she had a sturdy fire going.

"Nice job," Daric said, as he sat on the opposite side of the fire, out of the drift of the smoke. He placed the freshly cleaned fish on a rock beside his sister.

"You, too," Dani replied. She wasn't going to play the card by saying, if I caught dinner you clean it and cook it, because she knew if they both wanted an edible meal, it was up to her to deliver.

While Dani was cooking the fish, Daric went off to collect firewood so they would be able to keep the fire going throughout the night. Dani had placed each fish on the end of ripe pieces of bamboo and had planted the other end of the shafts into the sand, anchoring them with rocks, so that the fish hung over the flames. Dinner would be ready in a few minutes, fortunately, since both of them were famished. More correctly, all three of them were famished, she realized as she glanced over at Bear who had been keeping a close eye on the fish.

"Daric, try to breathe between mouthfuls. You're worse than Bear when she's wolfing down her cheese, without even letting it touch her taste buds," Dani chastised.

At the reference to cheese, Bear perked up as she recognized her favorite bedtime treat. "Sorry, Bear, I don't have any," Dani said, patting Bear on her head and coaxing her back down.

"What happened?" Daric asked hesitantly as he and Dani sat around the campfire after enjoying one of the best meals they could remember having had in a long time.

"What do you mean?" Dani asked, preoccupied with giving Bear a belly rub.

"In 1692. What happened to the others?" Daric asked, apprehensive about hearing the answer, but he was curious all the same.

"If memory serves me correctly . . ."

"As if it's failed you yet," Daric interjected. "You've got a mind like a steel trap."

"As I was about to say," Dani continued, "the others, as you put it, were executed. On August 19th, 1692, John Proctor, George Burrows, Martha Carrier, George Jacobs Sr., and John Willard were hanged at Gallows Hill."

"Damn," Daric muttered. "I wish we could have done something."

"Me, too," Dani said sadly. She had studied the trials in her first year at university and had been appalled at the injustice of it all, and at how society had so easily fallen right back into the same snare during the so-called McCarthy Era.

"What about Martha's children?" Daric asked anxiously. "Please tell me they escaped Martha's fate."

"The governor formally terminated the Court of Oyer and Terminer on October 29th. Unfortunately, eight more innocent victims did hang before that happened. But the Carrier children were eventually set free."

"Why was the court terminated, not that I'm objecting?" Daric asked.

"Those vile, so-called, afflicted girls went a little too far. They accused some of the richest and most powerful people in the colonies. They accused the mother-in-law of Judge Corwin. They also accused two sons of the former governor, even the wife of Reverend Hale. The straw that broke the camel's back, however, was when they accused Lady Phips, the wife of the governor; that's when their little game came to an end and their so-called supremacy was shattered," Dani said in disgust.

"But what about all that convulsion stuff? How do you explain that?"

"Today, or I should say in our era, it would be diagnosed as symptoms of hysteria, sort of like the symptoms that were observed in soldiers in military hospitals during World War II," Dani explained. "I believe that some girls may have actually been suffering, but I truly believe the rest were play-acting, enjoying the power and the attention."

"I don't understand how a court run by what appeared to be educated men could fall for such deception," Daric grunted.

"During that period in time, settlers were facing many hardships: a smallpox epidemic, random Indian attacks, war with the French, to name only a few. They even believed that God sent messages by way of comets and rainbows. And many believed that they could even be tormented by witchcraft the same way we can catch a cold today," Dani said. "It didn't take much to put doubt into an already skeptical mind."

"But ghosts, really?" Daric scoffed.

"Think about it. The so-called magic that the afflicted were claiming happened left little or no evidence, kind of like a poison. The only proof the court had available to them was circumstantial evidence, or spectral evidence."

"It's idiotic," Daric grumbled. "I bet not one of those judges regretted their involvement in those witch trials."

"One did: Judge Sewall. He was the only trial judge to apologize. The trials ruined his reputation. He spent years visiting families that had been wronged. I think we picked the right man to help us get out of jail," Dani acknowledged.

"I'm glad it was him and not that crooked sheriff or his uncle."

"Here's a tidbit I think you'll find interesting. Every single sheriff in Salem, since Sheriff Corwin, has died on the job because of health problems, especially blood disease, which is something that is very rare. Corwin died of a blood ailment one year after the witch trials. They no longer have a sheriff in Salem."

"Well, that's good news. I never did like that guy. He was too quick to seize the goods of the accused, even before they had been convicted. Poor John Proctor was wiped clean of everything that Corwin could carry or cart away. Hey, what about John's wife?"

"As I recall, she had a baby boy who she named after her husband, and she was actually able to retrieve some of their pilfered belongings," Dani said cheerily.

"I'm happy for her, though I'm sure her life would have been tough without John," Daric finished, while succumbing to an overpowering urge to yawn. "I think it's time we get some sleep."

"Do we need to put Bear on a tether?" Dani asked nervously.

"Why?"

"I don't want her roaming around the jungle. You never know what's out there or what she'll find or what will find her. Remember when she wandered off to explore when she was just a puppy? She found a furry intruder, and we spent the next several hours washing her with tomato juice. When it rains, she still smells of skunk."

"We'll put her right here between us tonight, so don't worry," Daric reassured her. "But to be sure, I'll loop some twine under her collar and tie it round my ankle to make sure she stays close by."

"You're sure we'll be safe? You never know what's lurking beyond the light of our fire," Dani repeated. She was exhausted, too. It had been a long day, but a productive one. However, she had been dreading the idea of closing her eyes. She did not feel well-protected from whatever might be prowling about in the forest at night.

"Hey, not to worry. We have a watch dog, remember? Our own warning system," Daric said, scratching Bear's left ear. "Right, Bear?"

Bear leaned in to Daric's hand, thoroughly enjoying all the attention she was receiving. "Come on, girl, time for bed," Daric said, as he lifted Bear and placed her in the middle of the palm fronds they had gathered to make a bed.

"I guess you're right," Dani conceded reluctantly, as she crawled on top of the palm leaves, next to Bear, who was circling around and sniffing every inch of the bed. Dani clutched her knife in one hand. She wanted it close by, just in case.

Daric put some more wood on the fire, banking it so it would burn for several hours. He would get up during the night to check the fire and restoke it if needed. The bright flame should keep any night stalkers away. He picked up the spear Dani had made and placed it beside him as he lay down beside Dani. *Can never be too prepared,* he thought.

"Good night," Daric said. There was no answer. Dani had already drifted into an exhausted sleep. "Well, then, good night, Bear," Daric said, redirecting his comment to their four-legged family member resting between them.

Bear lifted her head, gave Daric's hand a lick, and put her head down, her ears perked, listening to the sounds of the surrounding forest.

96

QUINN AND RICHARD DROVE through richly fertile valleys in the folds of the northern ranges. Even though everything was covered in a glistening blanket of moisture from the earlier rainfall, there was a gentle warm breeze in the air. They passed vast acreages of towering pines, all regimentally aligned, cloaking the slopes of the high hills.

Quinn pulled off the road into the small settlement of Tapawera, twenty-four-miles southwest of Nelson, by the banks of the Motueka River. The town had one school, a *4 Square* supermarket, two cafés, and a garage, all for a population of just under five-hundred people. It also had a campground just on the outskirts of town.

Quinn pulled up in front of the garage that shared its parking lot with the supermarket next door. He backed the jeep in beside a pumpkin-orange Volkswagen camper van. Whenever he could, Quinn always parked in the 'go' position.

"Why are we stopping here?" Richard asked impatiently.

"Jim, the guy who runs this garage, is an avid diver. I want to ask him about the amount of rain they've received recently. I need to know what to expect for our dive," Quinn explained. "I'll only be a minute."

As Quinn got out of the jeep, he couldn't help but stare at the strange vehicle alongside it. Besides being a garish color, it had the words Samwise Gamgee in bold green letters emblazoned across the sides; below the lettering were two crossed swords. He had to smile to himself: the color of the camper was about the same color as the character's hair in the movie. And it wasn't far from here that the Lord of the Rings had been filmed.

Quinn shook his head, turned, and walked into the garage. About five minutes later, he reappeared. He could tell by the scowl on Richard's face that he was getting rather impatient.

A young woman in her late twenties coming out of the supermarket caught Quinn's attention. She had two large grocery bags in her arms and stopped alongside the orange camper.

"Dart Ford is flooded," she said volunteered.

Quinn was flabbergasted. "How did you . . ."

"The duffle bags with 'Scuba Max' written across them," she replied, tipping her head in the direction of the Jeep's roof racks. "The little red seahorse was a sure give-away."

"Oh," Quinn muttered half-heartedly.

"I just came back from up there," she said. "I was planning on hiking up to the Granity Pass Hut, but the ford over Dart River was flooded, and you sure wouldn't want to be carrying your gear over that rickety footbridge."

"My friend, Jim," Quinn pointed over his shoulder to the garage, "said they've had about three inches of rain in the last twenty-four hours."

"That'd be about right," she confirmed, as she tried to juggle the bags of groceries into one hand, so she could open the vehicle's sliding side door with the other.

Quinn stepped forward to take one of the bags from her. "Here, let me help you."

"Thanks," she said with a pleasant smile. "Give it about an hour, and the ford should be clear enough to cross." She climbed into the back of the van to stow the grocery bags. She would normally have put her purchases into the appropriate cupboards in the van before driving away, but opted today to stow the bags until she got back to the campsite. After all, she had all afternoon to organize the van's interior, because her hiking was out of the question for today.

She climbed out of the van and slammed the sliding door shut. "Thanks," she said.

"And thank you . . ." Quinn responded, putting out his hand and realizing he didn't know her name.

"Jaclynn," she replied, extending her hand to meet his.

"Thanks, Jaclynn, for the information. Hopefully you can hike that pass tomorrow," Quinn said cheerfully.

"Here's hoping. Take care," Jaclynn said, as she walked around the front of the van and got into the driver's seat. She started the engine. As she pulled the van ahead and turned in front of the Jeep, she glanced over at the lone passenger inside. She cringed when she saw the pinched eyebrows and the scowl on the face staring back at her. She shrugged, then smiled and waved cheerfully as she drove out of the parking lot. "I wonder who shit in his corn flakes," she mused.

97

QUINN COULDN'T UNDERSTAND why Richard was so irritable. He knew Richard was usually the one in control and calling the shots, and when he wanted something, he wanted it *now*. But it wasn't like they could do anything about the weather. Richard's agitation seemed to have started the moment they had landed in New Zealand.

Quinn didn't want to waste any more energy thinking about Richard's mood. So he shrugged and walked to the Bushman's Café; he figured he might as well take Jaclynn's advice and wait an hour before proceeding to the dive site. Richard reluctantly tagged along behind him.

The door of the café screeched on its hinges as the two men entered. A prominent groove in the well-worn laminated floor formed a direct path up to the Formica counter. Across the front of the counter stood eight red leather, chrome-rimmed swivel stools that were bolted to the floor.

Behind the counter was a buxom woman who had to be in her mid-sixties. She faced her new patrons when she heard the protesting door swing open, demanding some WD40. She knew the screeching irritated some of her customers, but the noise was an effective door chime, and saved her from having to spend her hard-earned money to buy one. The noise was even loud enough to let her know she had customers when she was out back in the kitchen.

"I can't eat here," Richard complained rather loudly as he looked around the diner that seemed to have sprung out of a fifties movie. It was more like a greasy spoon than the café that the sign outside had advertised.

"Sure you can, son," the woman behind the counter interjected with a raspy voice. She sounded like someone who had been smoking most of her life. "It may not look like much, but it's clean, and I make the best food in town. Just ask anyone."

Richard looked around the diner. Except for himself, Quinn and the woman behind the counter, there was no one else in the café.

"Great, cause I'm starving," Quinn said cheerfully, sauntering to the counter and throwing his leg over one of the stools. After scanning the chalkboard menu posted on the wall, he knew exactly what he would order. "I'll have a cheeseburger, with fries and a coffee."

Richard plopped down on the stool beside Quinn. "Make that two," he ordered.

"A little early for burgers and fries, isn't it, boys?" the proprietor asked, glancing at the clock behind her: it read 9:30 A.M.

"Not according to our internal clocks. At home, it would be 5:30 P.M., time for an early dinner," Quinn quipped.

The woman took two cups from a shelf behind her and placing them on the counter. She reached for the pot of coffee, expertly filled the cups and positioned them in front of her new customers. "Here you go, boys, enjoy your coffee; I'll be back in a few minutes with your food."

"Thanks," Quinn said, reaching for the glass sugar dispenser. There were pairings of condiments all the way down the twenty foot counter: cream and sugar, salt and pepper, mustard and ketchup; all the essentials according to Quinn.

As promised, the woman came out of the kitchen about five

minutes later with two plates and placed them in front of her two hungry customers. Quinn had never seen a burger that big before. What must have been at least a ten-ounce burger that had been run through the garden: it was stacked with lettuce, sliced tomatoes and onions, with a large dill pickle set on the side. The rest of the plate was heaped high with home-cut fries.

"This looks great . . ." Quinn paused. He always seemed to wait too long to ask for names.

"Ruby."

"Thanks, Ruby. This looks wonderful," Quinn said cordially. "If I can't eat it all, can I have a doggie-bag?"

"Sugar, you'll finish that, trust me. It's too good to have as seconds," Ruby teased as she headed back to the kitchen.

"She's right; this is really good," Richard conceded half-heartedly.

"Umm . . . um," Quinn confirmed around a mouthful of food.

A few minutes later, Ruby reappeared. She picked up the coffee pot. "So, what brings you boys to my little corner of the island?" She refilled the cups, without waiting to be asked.

"We're heading to Blue Creek Resurgence for a little cave diving," Quinn said, swallowing another mouthful of burger.

"Well, you boys be careful up there. We've had a lot of rain lately," Ruby cautioned. "You should have come a few months back; you would have had better conditions for diving."

"This was kind of a last-minute trip," Richard explained. As far as he was concerned, the fewer people who knew where they were going and what they were doing, the better. His thoughts were interrupted by the screeching door hinge.

Ruby looked over and waved. "Be right with you, Tom." She looked at Quinn and Richard who were still enjoying their large meal. "I'll be back in a bit to see if you'd like some fresh-baked apple pie," she said, walking to meet Tom, not waiting for a response.

"She's got to be kidding," Richard moaned. "I'll be lucky to have room to finish this."

While savouring his cheeseburger, Quinn couldn't stop his mind from wandering back to a more memorable occasion many years ago. According to a Delaney family tradition, a family member who was having a birthday could choose the restaurant where the family would go to have dinner and celebrate the birthday. In the case of Dani and Daric, who shared the same birthdate, they had alternated year-to-year on who got to choose the restaurant. When they turned four, Daric picked a place. He had picked a new A&W that had opened only two months earlier. The A&W was one of those nostalgic drive-in diners, where customers used to park out front and place their orders through a speaker box. Soon afterwards, a young female server, wearing a blouse, short skirt and on roller-skates, would deliver the meal on a tray, hanging the dinner tray from the partially rolled down driver's side window. The dinner at the A&W was the first time Daric or Dani had experienced that kind of restaurant. It was also the first time Daric had ever eaten a cheeseburger, something that had since become a staple of Daric's diet. *Daric would love this burger,* Quinn reflected sombrely, as he swallowed his last mouthful.

"Are you finished yet?" Richard grunted, wiping his mouth and hands with a wad of napkins.

"Yeah," Quinn replied, being abruptly pulled back to reality. *Damn, I miss my kids,* Quinn thought miserably.

"Well, let's get going then." Richard got up from his stool, threw some cash onto the counter and left the café. Quinn stood, glancing down at the cash. He knew full well that there would be enough to cover their tab, plus a generous tip. One thing he could say about Richard was that he was never cheap.

"Thanks, Ruby," Quinn called as he walked toward the door.

"You boys be careful, now," Ruby cautioned. It was as if she was showing genuine concern for their well-being, which surprised Quinn; they had just met. Moments later, Quinn and Richard climbed into the jeep and left the small town of Tapawera behind.

98

THEY DROVE FOUR miles along a paved road, passing lush green pastures speckled with grazing sheep. Then Quinn turned right, pulling onto a dirt road. They passed verdant rolling hills, dotted with clusters of majestic pines. Signs of logging activity in recent years were still evident, but, thanks to New Zealand's policies to promote sustainable forestry, new saplings were already taking root and concealing the scars that the loggers had inflicted on the countryside.

Farther along, the road became crowded with overhanging trees, while the underbrush and large ferns worked diligently to consume the road that had carved its way through the foothills. After about thirty minutes, Quinn broke the silence. "She was right."

"What?" Richard muttered absentmindedly. He had been staring blankly out the passenger side window, lost in his own thoughts, oblivious to the passing apple orchards and harvested hop fields.

"Jaclynn; she was right."

"About what?" Richard grunted.

"The ford over Dart River; it's passable now," Quinn answered.

"Oh, that," Richard mumbled. He finally took stock of his surroundings, angry for not having paid attention earlier. He would have to negotiate his way back out of here. The narrow gravel road they were travelling, besides being extremely bumpy, was more akin to an old wagon trail, barely wide enough for a vehicle. It followed the path of the meandering river. He hoped they met no one coming from the other direction because there was no place to pull over to let them pass.

A few minutes later, Quinn drove the Jeep off the dirt road and onto a grassy area known as Courthouse Flat. Part of the area had been cleared as a camping site. Its expanse of green grass was broken only by the tiny golden buttercups dancing in the gentle breeze.

Quinn navigated the Jeep to the back corner of the flat and tucked it between some bushes. He wanted to be as inconspicuous as possible, given that his goal was to get in, complete the dive, and get out quickly, quietly and unobserved. That was the plan.

Quinn had good reason for wanting to be unseen. Even though no laws regulated what divers could or could not do, they were expected to follow well-established principles. One was that they would not disturb the environments in which they dove. Another was that divers would never, ever, remove fossils or artifacts from a cave, unless it was under the supervision of a museum or university. However, Quinn was here to find and to remove a rare mineral he labelled chronizium. He couldn't let anyone know what he was up to.

"My friend Jim said it's better to dive at Blue Creek Resurgence in the dry, summer months because the water level and flow in the cave system can be unpredictable at this time of year," Quinn explained. "But we don't have a choice, do we?"

"No, I suppose we don't," Richard agreed, looking around. The surrounding terrain was very remote and isolated. He saw only one road in and one road out: the one they had travelled. There was only one other car parked in sight; it was parked near the trail head. There wasn't a sound to be heard, except for the wind rustling through the tall grasses around the edge of the flat and the distant symphony of birdsong high in the trees above.

Quinn was anxious to get this dive underway, to get into the cave and find the chronizium he needed to bring his children home. Any delay could jeopardize their lives. He could only assume, from the last vital signs received from their travel bands that they were coping with their current situation. How was beyond Quinn's comprehension. He could only pray that their luck would hold out a little while longer.

99

DURING THE COOL hours of the early morning, Dani started crafting a few tools they would need to build their shelter. They had learned quickly last night that sleeping on the ground wasn't ideal, especially after various night crawlers had come to investigate the new arrivals in the glade.

Just as she had done the day before, Dani started by selecting a stone, one that was bigger and wider than the ones she had used to make her knife and spear. Using the same process, referred to as knapping, she hammered the stone with a larger rock, flaking pieces off the edges until it was the right shape and size for what she had in mind. Then she picked up a sturdy stick, approximately one-and-a half-inches in diameter, and, using some twine, lashed the stone securely to it. After briefly admiring her axe, she turned her attention to making a hammer.

Daric used the axe to chop down a variety of lengths of bamboo and placed the cut poles beside a tree at the edge of the glade. He came across a large walking palm tree with its five-foot stilt-like roots. He thought the roots would make a perfect frame for a wikiup or tipi. However, the tree was too far from the glade and inside would be a tight fit for the three of them. Besides, they needed to be off the ground; he reminded himself as he scratched his leg. But since he was already there, he chopped at the roots, which he would later use as supports for their shelter.

Meanwhile, Dani used her knife to cut moss into square mats. When she thought she had enough moss mats, she turned to cutting and gathering palm fronds from a nearby palla tree.

Dani and Daric spent most of the afternoon gathering materials for building a shelter. It was getting late by the time they had assembled everything they needed, but they were determined to get their shelter at least started before it got dark.

After a quick meal of fresh fruit and berries, Dani and Daric pooled their efforts and started hammering short bamboo poles into the ground until only two feet of each pole remained above the surface. When they finished, they had three rows of upright posts between two trees, which were about eight feet apart. Daric notched the top of each upright post and laid a ten-foot-long bamboo pole across a row of posts, nestling it into the notches. He repeated this procedure for the other two rows. Soon they had an eight-by-ten-foot frame to support a raised floor for their shelter. They laid the floor using smaller bamboo poles. Dani finished it by spreading fern leaves on the floor just as the sun was setting.

It had been a long day, but they felt satisfied with their progress. The raised floor would at least keep them off the ground for the night. They would work on the lean-to roof tomorrow. Thank goodness, it was another clear night. Maybe they had finally found a little piece of paradise for a change.

"Come here, Bear," Daric said, holding the end of twine he had used before to tether Bear.

"I don't think you'll need that," Dani said confidently.

"Why? You wanted her tied last night," Daric argued.

"Bear hasn't let us out of her sight since she arrived. Maybe disappearing right in front of her in Dad's lab spooked her," Dani speculated. "She may think it could happen again."

"Yeah, you're right. She has been sticking close by," Daric concurred. "Let's try out our new digs. I'm beat."

Daric picked up Bear and placed her on the raised floor. Only after she had repeated her investigation of the bed did she feel safe enough to go to sleep. She curled up between her two favorite people and drifted off, but always with one ear tuned into her surroundings.

Present Day—Wednesday

100

"WE HAVE ABOUT a mile hike up the trail to reach the cave entrance. It's going to take us a couple of trips, so why don't we take our dive bags first so we can check out how accessible the entrance is? If everything looks okay, then we can unload the rest of the equipment," Quinn suggested. Richard nodded in agreement.

After untying the dive bags from the roof rack, Quinn tossed them down to Richard. Hauling their own bags they followed the Blue Creek track toward Mount Owen. About halfway there, navigating their way through beech forests, they passed some derelict mine works. "Must have been some prospecting up in them thar hills," Quinn bantered, accent and all.

"Yeah," Richard grunted. "How much farther?"

"Almost there," Quinn reassured him. He nodded cordially to a few trampers as their trails met and crossed along the way. They were coming back down from the trail that led up to the Granity Pass Hut. *They must have been camping up there overnight,* Quinn thought, as he watched the water-logged trampers pass by.

Quinn was getting a little uneasy from the silent treatment he was getting from Richard. Walking through such a spectacular country, Quinn thought he would try to lighten the mood. "Richard, did you see that peak over there?"

Richard followed Quinn's pointed hand. "Yeah," he mumbled, negotiating his way across a narrow, hastily built wooden bridge.

"That's Mount Owen," Quinn said. "It's part of the Marino Mountains and stands at 5,625 feet above sea level."

"Great," Richard grunted; not caring one way or the other.

"I bet you didn't know that Mount Owen was where Peter Jackson filmed part of the Lord of the Rings trilogy. It was in The Fellowship of the Ring movie, at the part where the characters were being led by Aragorn. Do you remember, when they left Moria, they emerged onto a rocky plateau?" Quinn waited for an answer. None came.

"Well, that scene was filmed on the slopes of Mount Owen," Quinn concluded.

"Amazing tidbit of information. Thanks," Richard grunted again. "How much farther?" He heard the faint sound of rushing water. He was hoping they were getting close to their destination.

"Not much," Quinn sighed.

After another ten minutes of trudging through the rough cut trail and climbing over fallen trees, now moss covered in their early stage of decay, they came to the end of the trail. There was a flat area that acted like a balcony hanging over the stream below. Quinn put his bag down, walked to edge of the balcony and peered downwards. "Give me a minute to check this out," Quinn shouted back to Richard, who was sitting on his dive bag, trying to catch his breath.

"Whatever," Richard panted, as Quinn disappeared over the edge. Richard took stock of his surroundings and realized the entrance to the cave was well away from anywhere the average tramper would think to look and it was completely hidden from sight. 'That's good,' he thought.

Richard had been getting anxious ever since arriving in New Zealand. He wanted to get this over with, the sooner the better, as far as he was concerned. He had set his plan in motion and knew there was no turning back. Besides, the end result would be well worth all the effort.

Quinn carefully traversed the moss-covered boulders as he descended. According to Jim, back at the garage, it had rained most of the previous day. Quinn was eager to find out what effect the rain had on the cave system; visibility could be an issue. He immediately noticed the flow in the stream had increased and the water level was at least three feet higher than the last time he had been here, four months ago in the dry summer season. Not only did Quinn wonder what the flow might be like inside the cave, but the higher water level might also make the entrance chamber more cramped. Regardless, they had no choice. He headed back up top.

Quinn climbed over the edge ten minutes later. "We're good to go," he announced. "Let's go back and get the rest of the gear." Richard nodded in agreement as he got to his feet.

The trip took them twenty minutes to get back down to the Jeep. They met no one along the way.

Quinn walked to the rear of the Jeep. "I knew we would have to hike a mile to get to the cave entrance. So, I thought we could save our backs by using carts to haul our tanks up the path," Quinn explained, as he unlashed a couple of two-wheel carts, which had been strapped over the spare tire on the rear of the Jeep.

"Good idea," Richard mumbled.

Once the carts were removed, Quinn opened the jeep's back hatch and pulled out several coils of rope and a diver's reel. Then he reached back into the hatch and pulled out something and quickly shoved it into his pocket.

Richard was never really one for seeing what needed to be done or for pitching in. He usually hired someone to do any manual labor for him. So Quinn had accepted the fact that he would have to do the majority of the work on this trip. He really couldn't complain though. By using Richard's jet, they had cut their travel time down considerably.

True to form, Richard made no effort to help with the preparations for the hike up to the cave. Quinn had removed the tanks from the back of the jeep and strapped them onto the carts, using the bungee cords that had held the carts to the rear rack of the Jeep. He also strapped the coils of rope onto his cart.

After checking that he had not overlooked anything, Quinn locked the Jeep and slung a rather battered canvas bag over his shoulder. "Okay, Richard, it's time to head back up the trail," he announced.

Richard walked, without enthusiasm, to his cart and joined Quinn for the climb up the trail one more time. *This trip could take a while,* he thought.

Neither Quinn nor Richard said anything as they worked their way up the trail. Each seemed to be lost in his own thoughts. After about five minutes of hiking, out of nowhere Quinn shouted, "Sting!"

"Where?" Richard said, frantically swatting the air with his free arm looking around for the offending assailant.

"Not where; what?"

"Huh?"

"I was trying to remember the name of the hobbit sword. It's Sting," Quinn clarified, as he watched Richard stand down from his search for the unwelcomed intruder.

"What are you jabbering about?" Richard snapped.

"The crossed swords painted on Jaclynn's van; they were the short swords used by the hobbits. Frodo's sword was called Sting. It glowed blue when orcs were around," Quinn said triumphantly. The name had been eluding him for the past few hours.

"Who cares?" Richard snapped. "Let's just get on with it." He was struggling to pull his cart over a half-buried boulder in the middle of the trail, a boulder he didn't remember being there during his first trip. Looking up ahead, he could see he would have to negotiate several more protruding rocks. *Whoever cut this trail needs a lesson in how to use dynamite,* he thought.

Quinn turned around and studied Richard for a moment. Something was definitely bothering him. Maybe Richard was nervous about the upcoming dive. Although he was an experienced diver, Richard had never gone cave diving before. *That had to be it,* Quinn concluded.

Richard continued to struggle with the heavily laden cart and the exertion of the long uphill hike. The trek through the areas of beech forest, where the gentle breeze was shaking the raindrops from the branches, made it feel like it was raining all over again. And as he rubbed against the underbrush along the trail, his already drenched clothes sucked in even more moisture. *Maybe that kid had it right. Maybe we should have waited until tomorrow, too, instead of hiking through this wet crap today,* he thought.

The challenge of hauling the tanks along the forest path in damp clothes soon turned out to be the least of Richard's problems.

On arriving at the cave entrance and after taking a short break to recover from the climb, Richard assessed the cave entrance. It didn't inspire much confidence. He realized he would have to wade through a rapidly flowing stream, clamber over at least two larges sets of wet and slippery moss-covered boulders, and then lower himself ten feet down a small crack just to get to the entrance pool. And he would have to accomplish all that while carrying his dive equipment and tanks.

Richard turned around to confront Quinn with his dilemma. But before he could utter a single word of protest, he noticed Quinn had vanished.

101

IT HAD TAKEN most of the day, but their shelter was finally finished. Dani and Daric stood back to admire their hard work.

The raised floor they had built the previous day worked well during the night. It had kept them off the ground and out of the reach of tiny night crawlers. After a breakfast of freshly picked berries, Dani and Daric focussed their efforts on finishing their shelter. They began by fastening a bamboo pole horizontally between the two trees that stood at either end of the raised floor. They positioned long bamboo poles down from the horizontal pole, pasted the back edge of the platform and onto the ground. They secured the upper ends of the poles to the horizontal beam. This created a skeleton for the slanted roof, or lean-to. Over the sloping poles, they put layers of palm leaves, overlapping them to form a more solid cover. And lastly, Dani laid the moss mats on top of the leaves, providing insulation and making the roof waterproof.

"Maybe we should move the fire pit closer to the shelter," Daric wondered aloud. "If it were closer, it might provide more warmth during the cooler evenings. It might also keep predators, large and small, at bay. What do you think?" Daric finished.

"Sounds good to me," Dani answered.

Daric started transferring the warm rocks from around the fire pit to a new location, closer to the shelter. He used a stick to shovel the smoldering embers onto some green palm leaves and moved them to the new pit. Afterwards, he restoked the fire. Meanwhile, Dani gathered up the leftover moss from around the lean-to and deposited it beside the new pit to dry out. Once it had dried, they would store it under the shelter and use it to start another fire should the current one go out.

"I think we did a great job," Dani said proudly, surveying their campsite.

"Yeah, but what I wouldn't give to have my own soft bed. That platform is about as comfortable as sleeping on a rock. I think I'll gather more palm leaves for a little more padding," Daric complained, rubbing his sore shoulder as he wandered into the surrounding forest.

"I'm going to cool off," Dani said, turning and making her way down to the beach, with Bear on her heels. She dove into the river, wearing only her undergarments, which were very much like a bikini swimsuit. When she resurfaced, she noticed Bear running along the shoreline, darting in and out of the water, but venturing in only a few inches. She cautiously swam over. "What do you see, Bear?"

Minnows flitted about just under the glass-like surface of the river, or what was glass-like until Bear jumped in. Every once in a while, the minnows snagged a small bug that had unfortunately landed on the surface. "Are they teasing you, Bear?" Dani chuckled, as she watched Bear's head plunge down and snap at the water, frantically trying to catch the darting fish. It reminded her of when Bear was a puppy and she would bite at the waves as they rolled onto the shore.

"Hey, Bear, come on in here with me," Dani said, trying to coax Bear into the water. She was determined to teach Bear how to swim.

Bear's head suddenly snapped up, ears pitched forward.

She stared across the river at a point on the opposite bank. "AAARROOOO!"

Dani turned to see what had alarmed Bear. She caught just a fleeting glimpse of a young boy as he tumbled into the river and disappeared under the surface.

"What's all the yowling about?" Daric asked, making his way to the water's edge.

Dani waited a few seconds for the boy to resurface, but she saw only an eruption of bubbles. "He can't swim!" Dani screamed, springing into action. She swam as fast as she could to close the thirty foot gap between them.

"Dani, wait! You can't save him," Daric yelled urgently. "What if he's supposed to drown? We can't alter history, remember."

He wouldn't be here spying on us, if we weren't here, Dani thought, as she quickly narrowed the distance. When she reached the spot where she had last seen the bubbles, she dove under, kicking as hard as she could to power her way down to the bottom.

Dani could she the young boy's arms reaching up toward the surface. She was in time; he was still conscious. She wrapped her arm around the boy's waist and, holding tight, pushed off the bottom, propelling them both to the surface. When they broke the surface, the boy started coughing violently.

"Here, give him to me," Daric offered, realizing Dani, too, was struggling to catch her breath. Daric had immediately dived into the river and swam toward Dani as soon as he had seen her go under for the boy. He wanted to be close by, in case he was needed.

"Thanks," Dani sputtered, as she handed the boy over to Daric, who immediately wrapped his big arm around the small torso.

Daric swam back to the shore and carried the young lad up the beach and placed him gently on the edge of their shelter's platform. "Take some easy breaths. You'll be okay," Daric tried to assure him. But the boy looked at Daric oddly, his head cocked to one side. After coughing up more water, the next thing out of his mouth was, *"No puedo nadar."*

"So I can see," Daric replied in Spanish. "What's your name?"

"Titu Cusi," the boy replied, staring up at the extremely tall man with the sandy-blond hair, lightly tanned skin and piercing blue eyes. He was nothing at all like the other foreign invaders. Putting on a brave front, the boy asked, "What's yours?"

As Dani approached the shelter, she heard Daric and the boy carrying on a conversation in Spanish. *Well, that narrows down the number of possible locations where we might be,* she thought. She also thought how fortunate she and Daric had been to spend most of their family vacations immersed in different countries and cultures. The family would select a vacation destination and, then, for the next year they would learn the destination's language and history so they could truly experience what it would be like to live there. Their parents had firmly believed that in order to know a country, you must first know its inhabitants: what they think, how they live, and what they do.

"How's he doing?" Dani asked, as she neared the shelter.

Titu Cusi was eight years old. He had copper-brown skin, high cheekbones, soft brown eyes, and a slightly curved nose. He stared awestruck at Dani, who was standing before him, water running down her half-naked body.

"He's doing better, thanks to you," Daric replied.

"Goddess," Titu Cusi uttered, dumbstruck.

"This is Dani, my sister," Daric explained. "And I'm Daric. Dani, this is Titu Cusi."

"Well, hello," Dani said cheerfully, with her perfect smile, which only further convinced Titu Cusi that he was really in the presence of a goddess.

"You were here the other day, too, weren't you?" Dani probed. The reluctant nod of Titu Cusi's head confirmed her suspicions.

"I told my family I had witnessed the birth of a goddess from the river. They didn't believe me," Titu Cusi admitted dejectedly.

"Goddess," Daric blurted out as he laughed at the notion. "Hardly."

"Ignore him. Do you live around here?" Dani asked.

"Yes, and it's getting late. I should go before someone starts to wonder what's happened to me," Titu Cusi said, pushing himself off the shelter's platform.

"Are you sure? It could be dangerous out there all by yourself," Dani said anxiously.

"I know this area very well. I'll be fine," Titu Cusi assured her. He threw his arms around her and gave her a hug. "Thank you for saving me."

"Your welcome," Dani beamed back. "You be careful going home."

"I will." Titu Cusi turned and walked off, quickly disappearing into the dense forest surrounding the glade.

"You know you may have just altered history," Daric warned when he knew the boy was out of earshot. "Why did you interfere? You know we're supposed to only observe."

"I know," Dani retorted. "But, I looked at it this way; if we weren't here, he wouldn't be here and therefore he wouldn't have fallen in the river."

"But . . ."

"There's no but about it, Daric. I wasn't going to sit here and watch that kid drown and you can't tell me you wouldn't have done the same," Dani said defiantly.

"You're right. I would have gone after him, too," Daric admitted reluctantly. He couldn't have stood by and done nothing. He just hoped Dani was right, and that history has not suddenly been rewritten.

"I'll go catch us some dinner," he offered. Picking up the fishing spear that was resting against the tree, he headed down to the beach.

102

"I KNOW I shouldn't complain, but I'm getting a little tired of fish," Daric said, licking his fingers after finishing his last mouthful. "What I'm really craving is a cheeseburger with fries and maybe even a nice cold beer to wash it all down."

Bear immediately sat up. There was that word again: cheese!

"We should just be thankful for what we do have, like an abundant supply of food and water and, now, a roof over our heads," Dani scolded. "Remember, how we were able to survive in 1937 only through the generosity of others. And then there was London where we had nothing at all. We had to live on the cold, damp streets of Whitechapel for days until you were forced to steal for our survival. And what about Salem, where we were thrown into prison and wallowed in the filth and stench for over thirty days, praying for any mere morsel to eat?"

"Yeah, I guess you're right. I should be thankful for our little piece of paradise," Daric agreed reluctantly.

Was Daric right? Was this their little piece of paradise? Dani wondered, as she took in her surroundings. They had everything they needed. They were safe. No one knew they were in the area, except for Titu Cusi. And she was relatively certain that they wouldn't get into any trouble here. All they had to do was wait until their dad got them home, and he was working on doing just that. *It shouldn't be long now,* she thought.

"Besides, we're relatively safe and out of trouble here," Daric remarked. The fact that he had just voiced Dani's very thoughts was a bit unnerving. "It's only a matter of time before Dad gets us back home. Speaking of Dad, what do you think he meant when he said thought waves determine travel destinations?"

"I don't know. His note was pretty vague," Dani replied. "It could mean that our thoughts can determine where we end up, as in a specific location. Or it could mean the time period or era we travel to. Or it could be a combination of both. And is it your thoughts or mine that determines all of that? There seems to be more questions than answers."

"Do you think, if we touch our bands together and recite 'there's no place like home', that we'll be back where we started?" Daric asked jokingly.

"If it was that easy, Dad would have said so," Dani said aloofly, missing Daric's joke completely. "Besides, we always seem to be going backwards in time, never forward. Maybe that's the problem. Maybe that's what Dad's working on," Dani speculated, but her thoughts had drifted elsewhere. *I wonder.*

* * *

In the dead of night, a growl resonated between Dani and Daric. Daric lifted his head and looked out into the glade, then around the shelter. "What is it Bear? Did you hear something?" Daric whispered. He listened intently, but heard nothing other than the normal stirrings of the nocturnal animals foraging for food, the same noises he had heard for the past two nights.

Bear got to her feet. Her deep-throated growl gradually increased in volume. "What is it?" Dani voiced groggily.

"I don't know," Daric replied nervously, as he saw shadows moving outside the reach of their fire's light. "Who's there?" Daric called out, throwing an arm around Bear to keep her close. He could feel the vibration of her persistent growl.

The shadows slowly emerged out of the darkness and stepped into the light of the campfire. There must have been a dozen men, more like warriors. Each carried a painted wooden shield in one hand and a heavy club in the other, poised to strike at a moment's notice. They all wore the same knee-length tunics. Overtop, they wore heavy-quilted cotton armor, the pattern resembling a checkerboard. They had red bands with fringe wrapped around their legs, one below the knees and one above the ankles. On their heads they wore wooden helmets adorned with colorful bird feathers.

The group parted suddenly, allowing another man to step into the light. He was followed closely by a small boy. "Dani, Daric, it's me," called Titu Cusi.

"What's going on? What are you doing out here? Who are these people?" Dani fired off a round of nervous questions, as she and Daric got out of their shelter. Daric still maintained his firm hold on Bear.

The man standing with Titu Cusi moved closer. He wasn't dressed like the other visitors to their campsite. He wore a plain white tunic made of fine wool and he carried a spear that appeared to be gold in colour.

Dani was feeling somewhat uneasy as she continued to observe the man before her. She noted he was shorter than Daric as were all the other men around the campsite. Could this man be Titu Cusi's father? Although far from sure, she had a sense that he might be about the same age as she and Daric. She puzzled for a moment and realized that Titu Cusi would have been born when the man was in his early teens.

"My son tells me you saved his life," Titu Cusi's father stated, staring intently at Dani. Maybe his son had been right all along: maybe she was a goddess. But what was that strange four-legged creature with her? And the man beside her wasn't like the other dark-bearded foreigners invading their land. These two strangers had light-colored hair and blue eyes. They reminded him of the Chachapoyas, or Cloud Forest People, who were tall, fair-skinned, blond-haired and blue-eyed.

"Yes," Dani answered nervously.

"Please, come with me. It is not safe out here," Titu Cusi's father said. Dani sensed his words were not a request, but an order. "We need to move quickly and quietly. Kill the beast and let's go."

"No!" Dani bolted from the shelter and put herself directly in the path of a rapidly approaching warrior, bent on carrying out the order. Titu Cusi's father raised his hand. The warrior immediately stopped, only inches away from Dani and just moments from forcefully pushing her aside.

"She's not a beast. She's our pet. She's part of our family," Dani explained.

"As you wish," Titu Cusi's father said, while pointing for them to move along.

Dani and Daric looked at each other, weighing their options; they had none. They gathered up their meager belongings. Daric grabbed the twine and tied it to Bear's collar. "Want to keep you close, Bear," he whispered to her, while scratching her ear reassuringly.

Flanked by the warriors, Dani and Daric were led away through the darkness, away from their little piece of paradise.

They hiked for over two hours in complete silence, except for the odd grunt or groan that Dani or Daric uttered after tripping over a fallen log or kicking some protruding rock. It was difficult to see where they were going as they made their way through the dark forest under a moonless sky. Bear stayed glued to Daric's side at the end of her leash.

The group finally emerged from the dense forest and came upon a valley dotted with lights. It looked like a field full of fireflies.

Dani and Daric were led up several flights of stone stairs and ushered into a building. "You will stay here," Titu Cusi's father announced. "It is late. We will talk in the morning." And with that, he turned and walked away. Titu Cusi cheerfully waved goodbye and hurried after his father.

Daric had noticed that two of the warriors had been left behind, posted at the only entrance to or exit from the building. "Well, I guess we might as well make ourselves comfortable till morning," Daric observed. The stone building with its thatched gabled roof had only one room and one window. A piece of leather covered the doorway and the window. In the center of the room was a fire pit, which was the only source of light. It also provided some much needed heat. Around the fire were a couple straw mats covered with richly woven blankets; the only so-called furniture in the place.

"We don't have much choice, do we?" Dani grimaced, feeling apprehensive about their situation.

"Look, I think we'll be fine. You saved Titu Cusi's life. I would think his father should be grateful. If he wanted to hurt us, he could have done that back at the campsite," Daric reasoned. "Besides, Titu Cusi didn't look concerned."

"I hope you're right," Dani sighed. "Let's get some sleep. It'll be daylight soon."

Dani and Daric got as comfortable as they could on the mats, with Bear nestled beside them. Bear was soon fast asleep, but Dani and Daric couldn't sleep. They couldn't stop wondering what the next day might have in store for them.

103

LOCATED IN THE city of Cuzco, the *Qoricancha*, or Temple of
the Sun, had once been the holiest place in the Inca Empire. Its
thick walls had been constructed of precisely chiselled and fitted
grey stones. The walls' interior surfaces had been clad with banded
sheets of gold, now stripped bare. Only specialized priests and the
reclusive temple virgins, or *mamacuna,* had been allowed to walk
barefoot through the hallowed halls. But on this day, the priests
looked on, horrified, as a man in tattered leather boots strode arro-
gantly through its halls.

Diego de Almagro was a Spaniard, short and rather stocky. He
had ugly features, no doubt a result of a clash with local natives
twelve years before, when he had been permanently blinded in one
eye. He was courageous in battle, but he was often boastful.

Part way along the hall, Almagro turned and disappeared into
a well-guarded room. He stopped in front of two men sitting on
the floor. They had evidently been badly beaten during Almagro's
overnight seizure of Cuzco, the capital of the Inca Empire. Almagro said nothing as he observed the two men.

One was Hernando Pizarro, the lieutenant governor of Cuzco. At thirty-seven years of age, he was the second eldest of the Pizarro brothers. He was tall, heavily built, extremely arrogant, and the least liked of the brothers. The second man was twenty-five-year-old Gonzalo Pizarro. He had a black beard, was strikingly handsome, and had a reputation as a womanizer. He was an excellent horseman as well as a fine marksman with both the crossbow and the harquebus. And he was known to be the stingiest member of the Pizarro family, who had already achieved infamy for their miserliness.

"You can't keep us prisoner. We're the brothers of the Governor, Francisco Pizarro," asserted Hernando.

"Yeah, that's right," Gonzalo muttered through a split and swollen lip.

"You mean the man who's been my partner for the last eighteen years?" Almagro asked with a sneer in his voice. "The one who, on our very first expedition together, cost me my left eye? The man who sent me on a fool's errand, no doubt hoping it would be a one-way trip?" Almagro paused for a moment and just glared at the two Pizarro brothers in their blood-stained clothes.

"At the suggestion of your dear brother," Almagro resumed, "I left this city twenty months ago with five-hundred Spaniards, twelve-thousand native auxiliaries, and hundreds of horses on an expedition to the south. Your brother had promised I'd find wealthy cities, peasants, and fertile lands for the taking. But what did I find? The mountain passes were so clogged with snow we could barely get through them. We had endured frigid temperatures, starvation, and constant attacks from local natives. I lost over one-hundred of my men and over half my horses. Most of the native auxiliaries either died or fled. And when I returned here, what did I find? The new Inca emperor, Francisco's puppet king, has left Cuzco and started a rebellion. And hundreds of Spaniards are trapped in the city." Almagro paused.

"So, why didn't you come to our aid, if you knew your countrymen were trapped in the city?" Hernando snapped. "Why did you first seek out the emperor? We've heard you were in secret negotiations with him."

"I met with the emperor," Almagro acknowledged calmly. "I tried to reason with him, to get him to end the rebellion. He asked me how much gold it would take for the Spaniards to leave his empire. I told him that, even if all the surrounding mountains were made of gold and silver and if he were to give it all to the King of Spain, the king would not order the Spaniards from this land. Hearing that, the emperor told me to leave and to go wherever I wanted, because he and his people would die, if they had to, in order to rid their land of the foreign invaders."

"And who gave you the power to negotiate about anything in our brother's territory?" Gonzalo blurted out.

"If you hadn't stolen the emperor's wife for yourself, and if the two of you hadn't taunted and mistreated him, the emperor would never have rebelled," Almagro fired back. "You brought this mess upon yourselves."

Almagro stormed out of the room. He was no fool. He knew Francisco Pizarro, his old partner since 1519, no longer needed him to organize expeditions, no longer needed him to provide reinforcements and supplies. Francisco was content to rule over his new territory. His days of exploration and conquest were over. He had amassed a fortune, something Almagro had missed out on, having arrived in Peru in April 1533. He was not part of the one-hundred-sixty-eight men who had captured the reigning emperor, and therefore, he was not deemed eligible to partake in the division of gold and silver in Cajamarca; the treasure offered to the Spaniards in exchange for leaving the Inca Empire. The Spaniards never intended to walk away from such wealth. And in return for their opulence, they executed the emperor.

Almagro's thunderous footsteps echoed through the empty temple halls. He had long thought that their partnership had been an equal one. It was now, more than ever, clear he had been mistaken. Francisco's wealth and titles far exceeded Almagro's. And unbeknownst to Almagro, who was leading an expedition south of Peru, the King of Spain had recently granted Francisco an additional two-hundred-forty-five miles, which now encompassed Cuzco. When the king had originally split the Inca Empire into two, in 1534, he had awarded the northern part of the empire to Francisco and the southern part to Almagro. The position of the boundary between the two territories had not been clearly defined, leading both Francisco and Almagro to believe that Cuzco was in his territory. When Almagro had returned from his expedition and laid siege to Cuzco, he had unknowingly committed an act of war against his old partner, Francisco.

Almagro came to a large wood door at the end of a hall. He pushed against the dark vertical boards. The door swung open. He stepped outside where he was intercepted by Rodrigo Orgóñez.

Orgóñez was like most Spaniards: tall and black-bearded. At forty-seven-years-old, he was also a conquistador in search of his fortune and his own governorship. He had been loyal to Almagro for the past five years and was now his second-in-command. He had been instrumental in flushing the Pizarro brothers out of the former emperor's palace, which had belonged to Huayna Capac, the father of the current emperor.

"You need to execute the Pizarros, immediately," Orgóñez stated boldly. "That Hernando is a spiteful man and, when the chance comes, he will avenge this humiliation."

"We may still be able to use them," Almagro said calmly. "They're not going anywhere."

"Then let me take my men and attack Ciudad de los Reyes (the City of the Kings). Let me capture Francisco Pizarro. With his two brothers already in prison, Francisco's territory will be ours."

"I can't commit my forces to los Reyes," Almagro answered. "Doing so would leave Cuzco undefended and open to attack by the rebels. I think our best approach would be to start by capturing or killing the emperor and thereby crushing the rebellion."

"As you wish," Orgóñez reluctantly agreed. "Cut off the head of the snake and the body withers and dies," he jeered.

"Once we have dealt with the rebel leader, then we can turn our focus to *los Reyes* and my ex-partner, Francisco Pizarro." Almagro could hardly wait to confront his old partner.

104

"QUINN?" RICHARD WHISPERED nervously, looking around, trying to figure out what had happened to Quinn.

"Up here," Quinn replied calmly.

Richard turned around one hundred-and-eighty degrees and found Quinn half-way up a nearby tree, tying a rope around its trunk, just above a large branch.

"Don't do that," Richard barked.

"What?" Quinn asked innocently, as he shimmied down.

"Disappear like that. I was worried," Richard grumbled.

"Okay. Now, here's the plan. I'm going to take this end of the rope and secure it at the bottom of the cavern. I'll need you to use these," Quinn said, pulling several carabiners out of his pocket, "to attach the gear to the zip line."

Quinn fastened the end of a smaller-gauged rope to the carabiner and handed it to Richard. "Using this rope, slowly lower the gear down to me. When I signal, pull the line back up and fasten the next set to the hook. Got it?"

"Got it," Richard sighed. He was relieved he didn't have to carry the heavy tanks down the slippery slope. Besides, this process would save a lot of sweat and time.

Richard and Quinn spent half an hour lowering all their equipment into the cave. They spent another thirty minutes using another rope to lower the equipment the last ten feet to the entrance pool. Finally, with the help of the rope, they themselves descended to the entrance pool.

Quinn was reassured when he finally got to the entrance pool and saw that the water was very still and that there was sufficient space to perch on some rocks and get kitted up.

They slipped out of their wet street clothes and spread them carefully across some boulders at the cave entrance, hoping they would dry in the warmth of the sun, which had finally made an appearance.

"The trip back down the trail in an hour or so should be much drier," Quinn said encouragingly. But Richard was too busy to pay much attention to trivial nonsense. He was trying to slip into his thermal wear, which looked like a pair of long john underwear. The glacial water was a frigid forty-three degrees Fahrenheit. The extra layer of warmth was definitely a necessity.

The two men pulled on their Hollis Bio Dry FX100 drysuits, with hood, and followed by their heavy duty drysuit boots. Quinn reached into the canvas bag he had carried from the Jeep. He pulled out a pair of dry-gloves and handed them over to Richard. "Use these; they'll keep your hands warmer than your regular gloves."

"Thanks. I didn't realize the water would be this cold," Richard admitted reluctantly. He hated to be caught unprepared.

"Not a problem," Quinn muttered as he strapped his titanium dive knife to his right leg and his two dive computers to his left wrist. Redundancy is the key for cave divers; always have a backup system, he recalled his instructor saying. He pulled the remaining gear out of the canvas bag and put it into his drysuit's utility pockets.

Last but not least were the air tanks. They were called rebreathers, like the ones the astronauts used when they did space walks.

They were computer-controlled devices that let divers breathe their own air over and over again, by scrubbing out the toxic carbon dioxide. Quinn had learned early on that rebreathers were especially good for cave diving because they released no bubbles. In some cave dives, tanks that discharged bubbles could dislodge ceiling debris, which could drastically affect underwater visibility. But that wasn't a concern here.

Quinn instructed Richard to put on his Neptune Space Predator full-face mask, so he could test the communication system. "Can you read me?"

"Loud and clear, just like you were inside my head," Richard replied.

Once Quinn and Richard had finished getting all kitted up and had run through a full check of their equipment, it was time to go find what they had come halfway around the world to get. Quinn reached behind him and picked up a reel of white nylon line off the rock ledge.

"What's with the rope?" Richard asked.

"Laying line is the first rule of survival when cave diving. It's like leaving a trail of bread crumbs; it lets you know which way is out," Quinn explained. "It's not like you can just pop to the surface and have a look around any time you want."

"Ready?" Quinn asked.

"Let's do this," Richard replied affirmatively.

"Grab one of the deco tanks. We'll leave them at a decompression stop in case we need to use them on our way out," Quinn explained, as he clipped one of the tanks to his waist belt. "I figure our dive shouldn't take us any more than forty-five minutes, if the chronizium is where I found it on my last trip here."

"Good, cause this water is freezing," Richard complained, dangling his insulated feet and legs over the shelf into the water below. Although he was complaining about the cold, he couldn't actually feel it through his protective layers.

Quinn slipped off the shelf at the entrance pool. As soon as he hit the water, he recalled the first time he had ever gone diving.

He and Sandra had gone to Turtle Island while vacationing in the Bahamas. He remembered the first sensation he had experienced underwater: he'd been breathing and heard the rush of bubbles passing his mask. The next and more euphoric sensation had been that of weightlessness, of being able to float in three dimensions. It had not been long before he and Sandra had graduated from recreational diving to technical diving.

Quinn never got tired of the rush he always felt when he entered a cave for the first time, not knowing what lay ahead, what wonders of nature he might encounter, maybe something he had never seen before. Just turning a corner, he might discover a new passage. Or he might experience the thrill of being the first person ever to find something no else had ever seen before, like when he had discovered chronizium. The excitement he had felt about the chronizium gave him just a small glimpse into how Charles Darwin or Jacques Cousteau might have reacted to their discoveries.

Even Quinn's children had a natural affinity for water. That was one reason Quinn and Sandra had built their home on a peninsula, surrounded by water. The only family member who didn't share this love of water was Bear, even after all of Dani's coaxing.

Pulling his thoughts back to the task at hand, Quinn descended to fifteen feet. He turned on his dive light as the natural light slowly faded the deeper he ventured into the cave and the further he was from the cave entrance. When Richard arrived beside him, they proceeded toward the back end of the entrance pool and the tunnel down into Blue Creek Resurgence. The rocky pool dropped to forty feet, then took a sharp dogleg to the right. The stone boulders soon gave way to gravel as the tunnel plunged downward on a forty-five degree angle.

"Richard, it gets tight in here for a little while, so hang back and just follow me down," Quinn instructed through the masks' communication system. Richard held back, watching Quinn move ahead slowly.

Quinn had to frog kick his fins, since the slope didn't provide enough height for his usual flutter kick. But he was pleased to note that there was no discernable current in the water at this point as he descended past seventy-five feet. That was good news. *Maybe all that rain wouldn't be an issue.*

"Richard, are you still with me?" Quinn asked. He knew he was because he could see Richard's dive light bouncing around the pale colored walls. The reflected light made the space feel less cramped, unlike some darker cave systems that seem to absorb the light.

"Right behind you," Richard said tensely. The whole time Richard had been swimming down the slope, he had kept seeing small avalanches of stones and pebbles following him. He had found them somewhat distressing.

Quinn started laying a guideline when they had reached the dogleg, using the reel of white braided nylon line, which was about an eighth of an inch in diameter.

During Quinn's dive training, he had learned that fixed lines were placed throughout the main tunnels of a dive cave. However, the main lines of a cave didn't start at the entrance to the cave, but typically at a point beyond ambient light. This technique prevented open-water divers or untrained or uncertified people from viewing the line as an open invitation to enter the cave. And labyrinthine caves, like this one, that had smaller side tunnels, had additional lines. These lines didn't connect to the main line, but ended about five to ten feet off the main line and the main tunnel.

As Quinn worked his way along the main tunnel, he occasionally checked his dive computers. After securing the guideline, he attached directional markers to the line, which were plastic arrows that had an important function: they pointed the way out of the tunnel. Quinn had also dropped off their decompression tanks, which they may need to use when exiting.

When the two men reached a depth of one-hundred-fifteen feet, they came to a restriction. "Is this the end?" Richard asked. He clearly saw that the way ahead was partially blocked and that the sliver of an opening wasn't big enough to allow them passage. And he had noticed no side tunnels during their descent, which was also a good thing because it meant there was only one way out, so far.

"Not at all; we just have to push through that opening," Quinn said. "Follow my lead."

Quinn remembered that, at the bottom of the slope, the gravel accumulated and, depending on the amount of rainfall and water flow during the winter season, the slope could be anywhere from five feet to eighteen inches from the roof of the cave, the latter being their case.

Quinn moved forward, pushing his hands through the small opening. After enlarging it somewhat, he strained to pull himself through. Using his chest to push away more of the gravel in front of him, he inched forward; the metal cylinders on his back grazed the rock ceiling. In a couple of minutes, he was through.

"Come on, Richard. Just push through the loose gravel," Quinn encouraged.

Richard began working his way through the restriction. Suddenly, he felt like he was being buried alive. "What's happening?" he exclaimed with panic in his voice.

105

"IT'S ALL RIGHT, Richard. Take it easy. The gravel is just filling in behind you. It naturally piles up here. You're perfectly safe. Just keep pushing it aside," Quinn said, as calmly as he could. If Richard were to panic, his breathing would become erratic and he would consume a lot of air.

When Richard was finally through the restriction, he started to calm down. He noted, with considerable relief, that the cave was quite large. He also saw several passages leading off in different directions. "A person could get lost down here," he quipped, trying to regain his lost composure.

"Now, you know why we use the guideline," Quinn replied.

Once through to the larger chamber beyond the restriction, they took stock of their equipment before proceeding. "Okay, this particular intersection has to be carefully navigated, because, when we head back to the surface, there are six options to choose from, but only one leads to the entrance pool," Quinn said.

"Great; you didn't happen to bring a map with you?" Richard asked nervously.

"All we have to do is follow the guideline. We'll be fine," Quinn said. "Come on, it's not much farther."

At the first intersection, Quinn turned right, with Richard close behind him. The tunnel that ran off to their left was a dead end which Quinn had discovered on his previous dive.

The wonders of nature never ceased to amaze Quinn. He drank in the beauty before him. The rich golden color of the walls carried all the way up and ran along the ceiling of the cave. The floor of the cave had gradually changed from gravel to small sand-colored rocks. The clear blue water allowed him to see at least fifty feet ahead.

Quinn had been regularly checking his dive computers. They now indicated that he and Richard had risen to eighty feet. He knew they were approaching the end of Tunnel A and that it would soon join up with the main tunnel, but that wasn't where Quinn needed to go. He veered slightly to the left, swam ten feet, and stopped short of another tunnel entrance.

"This is Tunnel C," Quinn explained, his left arm pointing to the tunnel entrance in front of him. "A short way down, there are three fingers off this tunnel that aren't marked on any existing map."

"Then how did you know about them?" Richard asked.

"I was exploring here four months ago. That's when I discovered the chronizium," Quinn clarified. "Two of these fingers are dead ends; the third is where we're headed."

"Then let's go," Richard said impatiently.

"Let me go ahead and check it out first, to make sure it's still accessible," Quinn said. Then he drifted off down the tunnel to the right while Richard held back.

Quinn was laying line into Tunnel C when he came across a lot of fine sand that had accumulated about thirty feet in from the tunnel entrance. He promptly went to work clearing it away, resulting in the passageway slowly opening up in front of him. He didn't recall there being this much sand here before, but no problem, they could still proceed.

"Richard, follow the line in. I'm just ahead of you about forty feet," Quinn instructed. Within moments Quinn spotted Richard's light bouncing off the walls, even before Richard had reached him.

"Ahead of us is a large cavern with an air pocket. I tested it with a portable O^2 sensor on my last dive. We can get out of the water and warm up a bit while we look for the chronizium," Quinn offered.

"Lead the way," Richard urged. "I could use a little break from this ice bath."

Quinn moved ahead, continuing to lay line. Another twenty feet up the spur and his head surfaced. He shone his light around the cavern. *This is the place,* he assured himself.

Quinn pulled himself up onto the sandbar. He freed himself from his mask and shrugged the harness and cylinders off his shoulders as he waited for Richard to surface. It was a short wait, with Richard surfacing only a minute behind him.

"Pretty awesome, right?" Quinn remarked, as Richard adjusted to their new surroundings.

Quinn and Richard were standing on a ten-foot-wide sandbar. Further into the cavern, Richard could hear the sound of dripping water. Looking around him, nothing caught his attention; it was just another cave, and he was here on a mission. "So what are we looking for?" he asked impatiently.

Quinn ignored Richard's irritability for a moment as he took in his surroundings. He was in awe of the stalactites that hung from the ceiling; they made him feel as though he was standing inside the gaping jaws of a prehistoric creature. He recalled the rate of growth of a stalactite was one cubic centimeter every one-hundred years.

"Well?" Richard was losing his patience.

"Yeah, right," Quinn responded, as his mind snapped back to the task at hand. "We're looking for a rock, black, kind of like a volcanic rock, but shiny, and it has sort of an inner glow. I guess it really looks more like a star garnet."

"Volcanic black, but shiny, with an inner star, got it. I'll go right, you go left. Shout when you find it," Richard directed, as he moved off, panning his dive light along the ground.

Quinn shook his head and wandered to the left, panning his

light as he headed directly to the spot where he had found the chronizium on his last visit.

The two men had been searching for only a few minutes when something went terribly wrong. Quinn was the first to feel a vibration. He quickly glanced over at the water. He could see tiny ripples on the once glass-like cavern pool.

"Richard, take cover. Hug the wall," Quinn yelled, moments before a tremendous crashing sound filled every part of the cavern

106

HAVING HAD LITTLE sleep during the night, Dani was up early. She was nervous. She wondered what the day had in store for her and Daric. She walked to the room's only window. Dani looked out and was awed by what she saw.

The complex Dani was in was situated atop a high granite spur; she now understood why they had had to climb several flights of stone stairs in the dark the night before. She could see a river dividing the valley below; a village was on the eastern side of the valley and this elevated complex on the western side. The river meandered through the flat-bottomed valley, until it narrowed and descended the eastern side of the high snow-capped mountains that framed the valley.

The village below to the east of the river was laid out in a grid-like pattern. There were four long streets crossed by seven shorter ones. Each of the resulting blocks consisted of two walled compounds, with each compound containing four buildings around a common courtyard.

On the valley's north side there was a rising series of at least a dozen agricultural terraces that started at the bottom of the valley and climbed up the surrounding hills. These terraces flanked the stone stairway, making the complex appear like a fortress. Dani could see workers tending to the crops on the terraced fields. What the crops were, she couldn't tell from this distance.

"Come on." Titu Cusi's excited voice echoed in the sparsely furnished room, interrupting Dani's appreciation of nature's magnificence and her efforts to figure out where she and Daric were. Their surroundings had offered her no clues.

"Well, good morning, Titu Cusi. What's up?" Dani asked inquisitively. She looked over at her half-slumbering brother who had moaned in protest of the disturbance.

Titu Cusi was down on his knees, stroking a very excited Bear, who licked his face with exuberance. Titu Cusi was dressed in a wool tunic adorned with an elaborate interlocking geometric pattern embellished with golden thread. On his feet, he wore leather sandals and, on his head, a headband with three brightly colored feathers sticking up at the center of his forehead. "My father requests your presence, at once. So, we must go."

"All right," Daric grumbled, as he threw off his blanket, sat up, and reached for Bear's vine leash. It seemed to him as if he had just gone to sleep.

"Do you know what he wants?" Dani asked anxiously.

"Nope, but we shouldn't keep him waiting." Titu Cusi stood up, took hold of Bear's leash and led the way. Dani and Daric followed. The two guards who had been posted at their door during the night trailed behind them in silence.

Dani couldn't help but marvel at the intricate stone work they passed along the way. Huge stone boulders were fixed together without the use of mortar or mud. In fact, they were so precisely fitted that not even a knife blade could be inserted between any two boulders. The complex was surrounded by walls, some still being reinforced by craftsmen. Fountains carved from white granite were in several locations throughout the complex.

A small bundle of fur darted out from behind one of the

fountains. Bear took chase, yanking her leash out of Titu Cusi's hand. "Bear, no!" Daric yelled, as he dove after the end of the leash, snagging it just before Bear disappeared from sight. Daric pulled Bear back and held her close. He wasn't sure what had sprung from behind the fountain, but he thought it looked a lot like a guinea pig.

Titu Cusi led Dani and Daric toward a large building in the center of the complex's square. As they approached it, Dani noted that the building had an impressive double-jambed doorway. The roof was constructed from large wooden beams covered with thatch.

Inside the building, Dani, Daric and Bear continued to follow close behind Titu Cusi. As he led them through one hall after another, Dani was amazed by the intricately sculpted stonework and the finely hammered golden artifacts placed with reverence throughout. She had a strong sense that the building must be of some great importance.

After a few moments, the threesome, with Bear, entered a room bathed in the early morning sunlight. On a raised platform at the head of the room, sitting on an elegant gold-colored chair, was a man. Dani and Daric glanced at each other with raised eyebrows, the man gestured that they should advance. They moved forward slowly, hesitantly. After taking only a few steps, they realized they were in the presence of the man who had ordered them to this complex, the man who had proclaimed himself to be Titu Cusi's father. They stopped, unsure what to do or say.

Titu Cusi's father had copper-brown skin, high cheekbones, dark almond-shaped eyes, and an angular nose. He was wearing a soft vicuña wool tunic with a gold plate over his chest. A cape was draped over his shoulders, angled slightly off to the right side. He held a golden lance in his right hand; a golden dagger was stuck in his waistband. On his forehead was a red headband, decorated with a fringe of tassels. On his feet, he had gold-colored sandals.

Strategically stationed around the room were a dozen men. Each was wearing armor made of thin silver-colored metal plates; each had small bands of gold and silver adorning their heads. Daric assumed they might be bodyguards or elite guardsmen.

"Come," Titu Cusi's father said, gesturing them deeper into the room. Titu Cusi had run into the room, and was now sitting on the edge of the platform, scratching a very contented Bear behind her ear.

When Dani and Daric reached the raised platform, they stopped and waited, not knowing what was coming next.

"I am Manco Inca Yupanqui, the *Sapa Inca*, the supreme ruler of the Inca Empire. Welcome to Ollantaytambo," Titu Cusi's father announced with an air of authority.

Dani had been bothered by a niggling thought ever since she first met Titu Cusi. Now it all made sense. She immediately knelt, pulling Daric down with her.

107

"YOU'RE NOT LIKE the other *viracochas* who invade my land. Where do you come from and what are you doing in my empire?" Manco asked suspiciously.

"*Viracochas*?" Dani inquired. Although the Inca Emperor spoke perfect Spanish, this word wasn't familiar to her.

"The foreigners who raided my land and who captured, enslaved, tortured, and are killing my people. They plundered our temples and stole all they held. They even stole my beloved wife and queen," Manco growled. "They were given the name *viracochas* because, when they first arrived here, we thought they had come from *Viracocha*, the creator god. They were bearded people, very beautiful and white. They ate out of silver plates. They threw thunder like the sky. The beasts that carried them were very large and wore silver shoes. You're not like them and you don't dress like them. So, again, I ask: who are you and what are you doing in my land?"

"Lord," Dani said, while still on her knees, not looking directly at the emperor, "we were on a ship in rough seas when we crashed against a reef. Our ship sank. We are the only survivors. My brother and I have been fending for ourselves ever since. We were trying to live a quiet and peaceful existence."

"Until I found them," Titu Cusi said proudly, puffing out his tiny chest.

"You've travelled a long way," Manco said skeptically. He paused for a moment and glanced down at his son, who was sitting beside Bear, gently stroking her soft fur. Manco smiled and then looked back at the two strangers kneeling before him. This was something the foreign invaders had never done; shown respect for his title or position. "And your names would be?"

"I'm Dani," she said, risking a moment to look up at Manco; she saw a slight twinkle in his soft-brown eyes. "And this is my brother Daric."

Daric had not moved a single muscle since being hauled to his knees by his sister. She was weaving a fantastic tale, and he would let her take the lead on this, because, honestly, he had no clue what was happening.

"Please rise," Manco instructed, gesturing with his arm. "I owe you a great deal of gratitude for saving my son's life. I didn't believe him at first, when he told me of a goddess he had seen in the forest, who had risen out of the river. He can have such a wild imagination at times. But when he returned late yesterday soaking wet, I first suspected foul play, until he told me what had happened."

Dani and Daric stood up. "I'm just glad we were able to reach him in time," Dani said.

Manco clapped his hands. Immediately two women appeared in the doorway. "Now," was all Manco said before they disappeared through the same doorway. Dani and Daric looked at each other apprehensively.

A few moments later, the same two women reappeared. They paused for a moment and bowed their heads. "Please, go with them," Manco urged.

Daric bent down to retrieve Bear's leash, but stopped abruptly when he heard Manco say, "Leave her here." Daric, now at eye level with Titu Cusi, looked directly into his eyes. There was no malice there, only tenderness. Titu Cusi nodded his head. "She'll be fine, I promise. Go."

108

DANI AND DARIC followed the two women out of the so-called throne room. "What's going on?" Daric whispered. "Do you know where we're going?"

"I don't know what's going on," Dani replied quietly, "but I've figured out where we are."

"Where?" Daric asked softly.

"We're in South America. The Andes Mountains are to the west and we're on their eastern slope," Dani explained. "It's believed the Spaniards corrupted the name of the forest people, who were called Antis, to Andes . . ."

"Enough with the history lesson. Where and when exactly are we?" Daric interrupted.

"As to precisely where within the Inca Empire, I'm not sure, because the empire at its peak was pretty big. It included parts of what are now Ecuador, Bolivia, Peru, Argentina and Chile, an area roughly the size of Texas and New Mexico combined, close to 400,000 square miles."

"Dare to hazard a guess?" Daric pressed.

"I'd have to say somewhere in central Peru, because that would be close to where the Inca capital of Cuzco was located," Dani replied.

Dani and Daric entered another room. Each were led to a separate corner. On the floor in front of them lay a pile of fabric. The woman who had accompanied Daric to his corner reached up to unfasten his shirt. He quickly seized and held her hands. "Dani?" Daric yelped, looking over his shoulder for some help, or at least, some guidance.

"I know," Dani replied, as the woman in front of her started to unfasten her nurse's uniform, or what was left of it. "Just go along. I think we're getting some new clothes. And frankly, I'm glad."

"All right," Daric said, as he released the woman's hands. He shrugged and flashed her a charming smile, causing her cheeks to turn rosy-brown and prompting a tiny high-pitched giggle.

Dani was dressed with a large cloth, made from fine alpaca wool that had been dyed navy blue. It was wrapped around her body and pinned at the shoulder. A mantle was draped over her shoulders and fastened in front with a large gold pin. Dani looked at the woman and, with a questioning look on her face, pointed at the exquisitely crafted pin.

"*Tupu,*" the woman explained.

A belt, embroidered with gold thread, was tied around her waist to accentuate her figure. Then bands were tied around each of her legs, one band above and one below her knees. And leather sandals were strapped onto her feet.

The woman pointed at Dani's travel band and motioned that she wanted Dani to remove it. Dani shook her head no. The woman reached to remove the band. Dani pulled back her left arm and put her right palm up in front of the woman. Dani looked stern and shook her head as she said, "No." The woman looked a little uneasy, but she understood.

Finally came the finishing touches. Three bands of braided gold were placed around her head. An intricately crafted gold cuff-bracelet went above her right wrist; her travel band adorned her left. A gold necklace was hung around her neck. When the woman finished, she stood back and checked Dani over from head to toe. She smiled.

Daric had to persuade his attendant that he didn't want to be wrapped in a loin cloth; he preferred to keep his boxers. After several hand gestures back and forth, he won out. He was outfitted with a blue knee-length wool tunic; a cape, fastened by a large gold pin, was draped over his shoulders. He also wore leather sandals, a headpiece, a cuff-bracelet on his left arm, and a necklace. The woman assisting him had tried to remove his travel band, but he had stopped her; removal of his travel band wasn't negotiable.

When the two women were satisfied with their charges, they escorted Dani and Daric out of the room.

"You do realize that this stuff is real gold?" Dani whispered in awe.

"You're kidding?" Daric looked at what he was wearing and then glanced at Dani, appraising her attire. "There must be a fortune here."

"There is. The Inca use the precious metal only to indicate status, for celebrations and ceremonies in their temples, for religious statues, and for some tools and decorations. Gold holds no monetary value for them; it's just another rock from the mountains," Dani explained quietly.

As Dani and Daric were led back the way they had come, Daric continued to focus on the fine craftsmanship of the new cuff-bracelet on his arm. Without turning his head, he whispered to Dani, "Do you have any idea what the date might be or what year we're in?"

"The Inca don't use a calendar system or absolute dates. They measure time by sequence of events," Dani explained. "And they don't count their age in years, but by noting the different stages of life, such as their physical condition or their ability to work. But I could hazard a guess," she teased, throwing the same terminology back at Daric.

"Please do," Daric bantered.

"Manco Inca Yupanqui's reign started when Francisco Pizarro placed him on the throne as his puppet king shortly after having executed his brother, Atahualpa. According to the Spanish chroniclers of the time, that would have been in 1533," Dani recalled from early history lessons.

"So, we're in the mid-1500s, somewhere in South America, most likely central Peru, is what you're saying?" Daric recapped.

"That's about as close as I can guess right now," Dani said, just as they entered Manco's throne room and were startled by a high-pitched scream.

109

UPON SEEING DANI and Daric enter, Bear had let out a Shiba scream. She swiftly escaped the affectionate attention she was receiving from Titu Cusi and ran over to greet her favorite humans. "What have you got there, Bear?" Daric asked, as he examined Bear's new accessories. She was wearing a new gold collar and a gold chain-link leash interwoven with blue yarn, the same shade of blue he and Dani were wearing.

"These are all just a small token of my gratitude," Manco stated, explaining his gifts. "I have made you both honorary Inca nobles. You will have all the privileges that come with that distinction." Manco paused for a moment, looking down at his son; they exchanged grins. "I'd like you to stay in my empire. It would be safer for you, but only if you wish."

"Please, say yes," Titu Cusi urged excitedly, running over and throwing his arms around Dani. "Please, stay."

Dani looked over at Daric, who simply shrugged his shoulders, as if to say where else do we need to be? Dani looked down into Titu Cusi's upturned angelic face. "We would love to stay," Dani answered. "Thank you," she added looking up at Manco.

"Great. Now that that's settled, come, let's eat."

Manco gestured toward a pile of woven mats that had been

scattered on the floor. As they made themselves comfortable, a parade of beautiful young women entered, all of them carrying metal trays laden with food and drink.

"Quit staring," Dani whispered to Daric in English.

"But these women, they're gorgeous!" Daric exclaimed. He couldn't take his eyes off them as they entered the room, each one more stunning than the previous.

"They're probably the emperor's concubines. So, unless you want to create a scandal, I suggest you lower your eyes, now," Dani urged strongly. Titu Cusi, who was sitting beside Dani, giggled at the strange sounding words.

"Good point," Daric said, as he shifted his attention from the parade of attractive women. Reverting back to Spanish, he asked, "Lord, what is this place?"

"Manco, please, when it's just us," the emperor said, with a sincere smile. "This is Ollantaytambo, one of the royal estates of my great-grandfather, Pachacuti," Manco explained. "After the Spaniards invaded the empire and executed my brother, Atahualpa, they made me the new Inca king. It wasn't until much later that I finally realized that they were not *viracochas* or gods, but simple ordinary men driven by greed. I no longer wanted to be their puppet king, so I rebelled. After I escaped Cuzco, I gathered my chiefs from across every province and told them we were going to wage war against the Spaniards, no matter what the cost. I told them it's better to die on your feet, than to live on your knees." Manco paused.

"I brought thousands of warriors to the plains outside Cuzco to fight and win our capital back from the Spaniards. But when they attacked, we were no match for their superior weapons and armour, so we were forced to pull back. We relocated to Calca, thinking we would be safe there, but it was only twelve miles from the capital, still within easy striking distance. So, we moved deeper into the Yucay Valley. We're now over thirty miles northwest of the capital. I control the entrances to both the Yucay Valley and the tributary valley that leads up over the Panticalla Pass and down into the eastern jungles. This is a more defensible retreat," Manco explained. "And I can still orchestrate the war effort from here, through my spy network and my generals in the field."

While Manco had been talking, the women had spread out delicate green rushes before him where they had placed trays of gold, silver, and earthenware. Manco now pointed to what he wanted. One of the ladies picked up the item and held it in her hand while he ate.

Daric looked longingly at the trays spread out in front of them. He couldn't stop his stomach from grumbling after his nostrils got a whiff of the array of delectable food and drink. There were platters of corn, potatoes, quinoa, tomatoes, different varieties of beans and squashes, and assorted of nuts and fruits. Everything looked delicious.

"Help yourself," Manco encouraged. "It's really quite good."

Daric immediately reached for something that looked like roasted meat. He was tired of eating only fish and fruit. He took a bite and savoured it. He had no idea what he was eating. Its taste was rather like chicken, but its texture was chewy and rich, like duck. The skin was salty and delicious. "What is this?" Daric asked, licking the juices from his fingers.

"Conejillo de indias," Titu Cusi blurted out.

"They're epicurean delights, reared for eating not for cuddling," Manco chuckled.

Daric choked on the piece he was trying to swallow. He reached for a goblet and took a deep gulp of its golden liquid. *That didn't help,* he realized, as he forced the sour liquid down. He would have much rather spit it out, guinea pig and all, but he thought better of it. The image of a furry little ball dashing out from behind the fountain earlier in the day flashed before his eyes. He just hoped that it wasn't gracing his plate at this moment.

"And that is *chicha,* beer made from maize, also known as corn. It's a taste you have to acquire," Manco said exultantly. He couldn't remember the last time he had enjoyed such a good meal with such great company.

"Your Spanish is rather good," Dani said, deflecting the attention away from Daric's poor table manners.

"Once I realized that the foreigners were not going to leave, I felt it wise to learn the language, so we could communicate without the potential for misinterpretation," Manco voiced. "Over the past four years, I've been making sure that most of my administrators, military and nobles are trained in the basics of the language."

Dani ran a quick calculation; four years, then it must be 1537. Just then a man ran in, fell on the floor in front of Manco and started sputtering words between pants for breath, that neither Dani nor Daric recognized.

"Do you know what he's saying?" Daric whispered to Dani.

"No. I think he's speaking in the Incas' native language known as *runasimi*," Dani replied quietly.

After the messenger had finished delivering his message Daric asked curiously, "What did he say?"

"He says the enemy approaches from the southeast," Manco translated for them, since all of Manco's *chaskis,* or messengers had not yet been taught Spanish.

Manco stood up and bellowed, "Fetch my armor and horse!"

"Horse?" Dani asked, knowing that the animals were not indigenous to this region.

"We've learned a lot in the last four years," Manco proclaimed.

110

RODRIGO ORGÓÑEZ, AS instructed by Almagro, led a force of seventy cavalry and thirty foot soldiers, together with native auxiliaries. Orgóñez's goal was quite simple: capture or kill the leader of the native rebellion–Manco Inca.

The army travelled out of the city of Cuzco, along the stone road that led northward toward the Yucay Valley. When they reached the lip of the bowl-shaped valley that cradled the city of Cuzco, Orgóñez paused and looked back. Smoke was rising from the cook fires through the thatched roofs of high-gabled houses. Green hillsides and snow-capped mountains rose in the distance. The city was laid out in the shape of a reclining puma, the symbol of strength and power in the Inca culture. Near its heart was the central square, the site for public assemblies and religious ceremonies. Nowhere in the empire had Orgóñez seen a city with the air of nobility that Cuzco possessed. He was determined to make sure Cuzco never fell into the hands of the Pizarros. Once he finished off the rebel leader, he was going after Francisco Pizarro.

The army continued its march onto the upper ridge of the

valley, past the giant stone fortress of Saqsaywaman, with its colossal limestone walls and three imposing towers. The fortress, which represented the head of the reclining puma, was built on a rocky hill on Cuzco's northern edge. It was protected on three sides by steep slopes. The fourth side fronted a grassy plain and faced the city. The Inca had built a series of gigantic walls which they used for defence: three walls, one above the other were built of stones so large that no one could believe they had been placed there by human hand. The stones had been moved and positioned without the aid of the wheel or large beasts of burden, which had arrived only with the coming of the Spaniards. Even if the wheel and beasts had been available, it is doubtful that they would have been any real help in moving the huge stones.

As Orgóñez rode past the fortress, he couldn't help but remember the countless natives who had bravely defended it. When they could no longer keep it from falling to the enemy, they had felt that they had disappointed their emperor. In their despair, they had chosen to leap from the high walls and the towers rather than face sure death at the hands of the attacking Spaniards. Most died on impact; those who survived were clubbed or stabbed to death. Soon afterwards, the sky above the fortress filled with majestic black condors with their white fur-like collars and the ugly red-headed vultures, all waiting to descend to feast upon the flesh of the dead.

Orgóñez's forces worked their way down into the narrow, flat Yucay Valley and followed the winding blue-green river. When they realized they had to ford the river, they regrouped and proceeded across in single file, so they could test the river's depth as they advanced. Just as the first of the cavalry were about to reach the far shore, a shout went out, "We're under attack!"

Orgóñez saw sling throwers on the other side of the river. They were hurling rocks at his men, who were defenseless in the water, their hands pulling on the reins, trying to control their frightened horses. While the rocks were not lethal unless you got hit directly in the face, they could injure a horse. And Orgóñez had no horses to spare.

"Move, now!" Orgóñez shouted to his men who were still waiting to cross. "Get over there and kill those natives."

The remaining cavalry still on shore lunged into the river, eager to provide aid to their compatriots. The once easy flowing river now looked more like a set of rapids, churned by the charging horses. Once across, the cavalry didn't take long to crush the opposition. The natives' sticks and stones were no match against twelve-foot lances and steel swords slashing down from above.

As Orgóñez's forces resumed their march though the valley, they had to cross the winding river five more times. Each time they were met with the same resistance. Each time the results were the same. And each time, the troops continued to push forward. When the valley became more constricted, the native scout stopped.

"What's going on?" Orgóñez yelled, annoyed with yet another delay. They had already travelled thirty miles.

The scout looked up at Orgóñez sitting astride his horse and then turned and simply pointed. Orgóñez followed his arm. There, in front of them, on the top of a massive stone spur jutting out from the valley wall, as if suspended in mid-air, was the temple fortress of Ollantaytambo.

"Oh my God," one of the foot soldiers muttered.

The sight was overwhelming; actually, it was horrifying for the Spaniards. Protected by the valley's high walls, the temple was located against a very steep hill. The only visible entrance into the temple fortress was a single stone doorway that had been filled in with rocks. A stairway leading toward the top of the fortress was flanked by a dozen high terraces with large, well-built stone walls. On top of the enormous terraces were thousands of native warriors.

Orgóñez's men, who were gathered on the plain below, saw that many of the warriors were holding boulders above their heads, ready to hurl them down the minute the Spaniards attempted to rush the fortress. Looking more closely, they soon noticed that, standing with the usual native warriors, was another group of warriors. Orgóñez's native auxiliaries called them the Antis.

111

THE INCA PEOPLE believed that their emperor was descended from the sun god, Inti. And, on days like today, it was easy to see why. As Manco stood proudly beside his warriors, he had on his gold chest plate, emblazoned with the image of the sun. His gold helmet adorned his head. His gold halberd–or axe–was clutched in his right hand. A gold shield was strapped to the side of his horse. All the gold shone brilliantly in the early afternoon sun, making Manco look like the sun itself

Flanked by his elite guards, Manco was ready to lead his warriors into battle. Many of them were his regular Inca warriors. Many others were the Antis who were standing shoulder-to-shoulder with his warriors and whom he had enlisted for their unique skills.

The Antis were tropical rain forest people, who lived at the eastern boundaries of the Inca Empire that extended to the edges of the Amazon. To the Inca, this was the land of the Antisuyu quarter, one of the four quarters of the empire and the place where civilization ended and savagery began.

Over the years, the Incas made several attempts to conquer parts of the rain forest, but the environment had proven to be too alien. Once within the forest, the Inca generals had found that they lacked familiar points of reference on a visible horizon. Their disoriented armies had thrashed about futilely, in the dense and unfamiliar terrain.

Eventually the Inca realized they couldn't defeat or assimilate the Antis. This realisation led Manco's grandfather, Tupac Inca, to form a military alliance and trade relationship with the forest people. The Inca would provide copper and bronze tools, finely woven cloth, and salt in exchange for hardwoods, honey, beeswax, tropical bird feathers, animal skins, oils, fats, and other products of the tropical forest. Inca colonies were established along the warm, forested foothills of the eastern Andes. The colonists planted and harvested crops and continued a mutually beneficial relationship with the Antis.

Many of the Antis painted their faces with dyes made from tropical plants and fruits. They often had tropical bird feathers protruding from the skin around their noses and mouths. They sometimes integrated feathers into their headbands, adding a bright palette of color to their jet black hair. But what Manco was most interested in was their expertise and precision with the bow and arrow, a weapon never mastered by the Inca warriors.

"What are they waiting for?" Daric asked of no one in particular as he peered down on the invading forces. He and Dani had joined Manco at the wall overlooking the valley below. It was easy to pick out the hundred or so Spaniards in the mass of bodies standing on the plain; the sun glinted off their steel helmets and chest armor. They also noticed that each foot soldier was carrying a wooden shield, about two feet in diameter, in one hand and a twelve-foot, steel-tipped lance in the other.

The cavalry carried larger shields. Made from animal hides stretched over a wooden frame, they were much lighter than the shields carried by the foot soldiers. The ferocious, thousand-pound horses bearing the cavalry also wore padded armor, making them more difficult to kill.

Daric knew that the armaments of the Spaniards were far superior to those of the Inca. The Inca weapons were similar to those that would be used for hunting: knives, spears, and battle axes made with copper or stone blades. For the most part, Inca weapons were designed for hand-to-hand combat between equally armed foot soldiers. Even the quilted cotton amour and wicker helmets the Inca wore were no match for the flesh-slicing weapons of the Spaniards.

Suddenly a cry went up, "Santiago!"

"Look!" Dani shouted. She reached over to grab Daric's hand and, then, thought better of it, in case the travel bands should touch. She just stepped a little closer.

112

"I DIDN'T COME thirty miles and lose over one-hundred native auxiliaries to turn around and go back empty-handed," Orgóñez grunted, as he stared at his second-in-command.

"But that place looks impenetrable," Caso groaned. Ricardo Barak Caso had served beside Rodrigo Orgóñez as cavalrymen under Diego de Almagro for the past five years. Just recently, after Orgóñez had been promoted to be Almagro's second-in-command, tensions had grown between the two conquistadors. Caso was a black-bearded, hardy six foot tall, forty-five-year-old who had come to the New World seeking fame and fortune. He was thin-lipped with a pointed jaw, broad nose and wide-set cold brown eyes.

Glancing at his cavalry, Orgóñez observed a look of sheer terror on most of their faces. "Well, it doesn't look like any of those young men are brave enough to charge the fortress to test its defenses, so it's up to us," Orgóñez announced to a reluctant Caso. "On three: one . . . two . . . three . . . Santiago!" the two conquistadors yelled in unison as they spurred their horses and bolted from the ranks. The soldiers, completely stunned by the audacious act they were witnessing, froze in formation.

Orgóñez and Caso raced for the wall and didn't stop until they were pressed against it. Two Inca defenders ventured too close to the two attackers and suffered at the end of the steel-tipped lances. Soon, the sky filled with arrows that rained down on Orgóñez and Caso. Both men quickly turned their horses around and dashed back toward their forces.

Their bravery had not gone unnoticed by their men. Having felt shamed, a group of younger riders broke away from the rest of the cavalry and charged the fortress, heading directly for the entrance-way. They were followed closely by a group of foot soldiers, both native auxiliaries and Spaniards. As the Spaniards attempted to clear the stones from the only entrance, a barrage of stones and arrows assailed them.

"Damn, those archers are accurate," Caso admitted begrudgingly, as he watched a multitude of native allies fall under the sharpened bamboo points that arced through the sky before plummeting to earth.

"Call them back, before they all get massacred," Orgóñez yelled.

* * *

"Keep it up," Manco shouted encouragingly, as he observed the devastation below. Besides the native auxiliaries, several horses had also succumbed to the hail of arrows and boulders.

Suddenly, the attack broke off and the enemy began to pull back. A huge roar went up among the Inca. They had defeated the enemy. They had pushed them back. But Manco knew that now wasn't a time for celebration, for the battle had not yet been won.

Bolstered by the Spaniards' retreat, the Inca warriors started making their way down from the high terraces, intent on annihilating the foreign invaders and claiming victory.

113

RODRIGO ORGÓÑEZ, BEING a keen military strategist, quickly sorted through his options. He knew from experience that fighting the Inca on level ground would be a sure victory because the Inca didn't stand a chance in hand-to-hand combat against charging horses and slashing swords. He just had to get them down from that damned fortress. As he looked up toward the west, he realized that they were doing just that; they were coming down to him. *So this isn't going to be a total loss,* he thought. He saw the emperor, the sun glinting off his golden amour, was still at the top of the ridge. As he watched, Manco raised his right arm, the one holding the gold halberd, and, then, Manco, astride his horse, proceeded to descend. "This is perfect," Orgóñez muttered.

"Where's Manco going?" Daric blurted out. "He can't win against that army, not with those primitive weapons."

Dani had been carefully studying Manco throughout the morning and early afternoon. She had concluded that he was a very shrewd and perceptive young man. He was planning something, she was sure of it. But what?

When Manco had raised his halberd, Dani had been watching closely, trying to figure out Manco's plan. She had noticed that he had cast his gaze downward, over his right shoulder. From where she was standing, she couldn't see what he had been looking at from his higher vantage point. She now moved closer to the wall. Dani peered over. She caught a quick glimpse of a banner waving twice before disappearing. It was a signal, an acknowledgement of an order. She waited a few moments and then realized what was happening. "Brilliant," she muttered. "Simply brilliant."

Dani moved over to stand beside Daric, who was just about ready to take off after Manco. "Relax and watch," Dani whispered to him.

Daric looked at his sister in disbelief. "Relax? Can't you see what's about to happen? It'll be a blood bath!"

"Just watch," Dani said calmly, looking at the plain below.

Daric turned back to the battle. He couldn't comprehend how Dani could be so composed, given the circumstances. Daric saw Manco as he reached the plain and engaged the enemy. Fighting beside him were his elite guards, determined to protect their emperor at all costs.

Daric recognized the two horses charging toward Manco; they were the two that had initially stormed the walls. Then he noticed water spurting from under the hooves of the thundering horses. "Hey, where's all the water coming from?" Daric asked, bewildered.

"Genius," Dani muttered, astounded by Manco's resourcefulness.

"What is?" Dani pressed.

"Manco realized his warriors were no match for that army," Dani explained, never taking her eyes off the battle below. "So he devised a secret weapon. And at just the right moment, he signalled for it to be engaged."

"What weapon?" Daric was becoming exasperated.

"Look," Dani said, pointing to the source of the water. "Manco had his engineers build a series of canals alongside the Patacancha River. He signaled to have them opened, flooding the plain below. Manco realized that he couldn't win a battle against a charging cavalry, so he devised a way to diminish their maneuverability, leveling the playing field, so to speak."

Orgóñez's and Caso's forward progress had slowed considerably when they had been forced to engage several Inca warriors. But Orgóñez was determined to get to the rebel leader who had been so kind as to deliver himself almost into Orgóñez's hands.

Manco was only half a football field away, but Orgóñez was finding it extremely difficult to control the speed and direction of his horse. Looking down, he immediately realized why. The plain was flooding. "Damn!" he cursed. If he didn't call a retreat soon, they would all die. Manco had taken the one great advantage Orgóñez had over him and had neutralized it.

"Pull back!" Orgóñez ordered, yelling to be heard over the cacophony of the battle: the natives' conch shells and clay trumpets heralding the attack, the terrified neighing of horses, the sounds of metal clanging, the screaming of men battling and dying, the splashing of water swirling all about. "Pull back!" By now, the water had risen to the horses' bellies.

Orgóñez's forces disengaged and pulled back. They made a determined march out of the valley. Close behind were hordes of Inca warriors, who continued to attack throughout the rest of the day and into the night.

114

RODRIGO ORGÓÑEZ HAD ordered a disgruntled Caso to bring up the rear with his men as the Spaniards and the remaining native allies made a forced retreat out of the Yucay Valley. The quarter moon, darting in amongst the scattered clouds, provided little light to guide their way, prompting Orgóñez to order that torches be lit. The injured were carried on makeshift litters; the mortally wounded were left behind to die.

"Look out!" someone yelled from within the ranks. Suddenly there was an outburst of shouting and screaming. Torches bounced and swayed erratically in the dark. Deadly silence fell once again, punctuated by the moans of the wounded, the muffled mumblings of frightened men, and the clattering of steel hooves on the stony ground.

"If those Incas keep bolting out of the darkness without warning, striking and then retreating again, without us even seeing them, we'll all be dead before dawn," one of Caso's men complained.

"Just keep moving," Caso ordered. They had lost another ten native auxiliaries in the most recent attack, the fifth since they had left the valley. It was only another seventeen miles to the city of Cuzco, and Caso was determined to push his men all night to get there.

* * *

The sun was just about to breach the eastern horizon when Orgóñez and his army rode into Cuzco. It had been a long, hard, and demoralizing night. Orgóñez headed directly toward Almagro's palace, which had belonged to the former *Sapa Inca*, Huayna Capac and father of the current emperor. Orgóñez had to give Almagro's his report, and he had asked Caso to join him.

Orgóñez explained the battle and the ensuing retreat to Almagro while they shared a warm meal. "Manco knew exactly how to use his location and its resources to every advantage, from his fortified hilltop fortress to his redirection of the river. He had us at a disadvantage right from the beginning."

"So, I guess you now know what it feels like from Manco's perspective, since he's been fighting an uphill battle for the last four years," Almagro scoffed. He was extremely disappointed in Orgóñez's results. The Spaniards had superior weapons, forces, and tactics, yet they had failed to capture the rebel leader.

"One thing I'll say about those warriors," Caso reluctantly admitted, "is that, when they taste victory, they'll continue to chase you like demons possessed. And those Antis were fearless. Some of them kept shooting arrows even when they were dying."

After Orgóñez had recapped his losses for Almagro, he made a request. "Let me try again. I know what to expect and I know how to defeat him. Just give me more men and a dozen harquebuses, then I can't fail."

"We have a more pressing problem," Almagro announced. He could not criticize Orgóñez's determination; he was one of the most capable men Almagro had under him.

"What could be more pressing than ending this rebellion?" Orgóñez grunted.

"Francisco Pizarro has sent a force of five-hundred troops, who are currently marching toward Cuzco, most likely ordered to take back the city and to free his brothers. I need you to prevent that from happening," Almagro stated bluntly.

115

AT THE END of last evening's celebrations, Manco had shown Daric and Dani to their new lodgings. According to Daric, they all looked the same: one room, stone walls, woven mats for beds. Before Manco had bid them goodnight, he asked them to join him for the mid-day meal.

Later that morning, Dani and Daric had made their way to the temple's most ornate room, which they had dubbed the throne room the day before. Sitting comfortably on the floor with Manco and Titu Cusi, the four of them were enjoying a meal of meat, fruits and vegetables. Considering his experience with the roasted guinea pig the day before, Daric decided it was wiser to ask before diving into any dish he didn't recognize.

"The venison is delicious," Daric muttered around a mouthful. "And I'm really getting to like this beer. What did you call it?"

"*Chicha*," Manco replied, as he fed a piece of meat to Bear. "Why do you call her Bear, when she looks more like a culpeo or fox?"

"When she was very young, she had a flatter nose in a rounder face. She looked like a little bear," Dani explained, as she watched

Bear enjoy the attention she was receiving.

"So this is where you've been hiding," said an angelic voice.

"Come, join us," Manco beamed in delight. "I'd like you to meet our new friends."

A young and gorgeous woman entered the room. She walked directly to Manco and placed a kiss on his right cheek before sitting beside him.

Daric was spellbound.

"This is Dani and her brother Daric," said Manco, starting the introductions. "And this is my *coya*, my queen and sister, Cura Ocllo."

Dani snapped a quick look at Daric and they both mouthed the word, *eww*. Fortunately, Manco and Cura Ocllo didn't notice the exchange.

Cura Ocllo was a petite woman, less than five feet tall. She had long brown hair and warm brown eyes that seemed to denote a hint of merriment. She was wrapped in a soft white vicuña wool cloth with gold embroidery. She wore a gold headpiece that looked like a small crown. She also wore gold accessories, all indicative of her position in the empire.

"I'm very pleased to meet you, my queen," Dani said cordially.

"I'm not too sure what's expected of me, when I meet a member of royalty, especially such a beautiful one. I don't want to be disrespectful," Daric admitted, embarrassed.

"Relax, Daric, a simple hi, how are you, will do just fine," Cura Ocllo said charmingly. "Manco told me what you did for Titu Cusi and that you are joining our empire. I am pleased."

"Thank you," Dani acknowledged.

"How many children do you have?" Cura Ocllo asked, as she slid a slice of cactus fruit into her mouth.

Daric couldn't help himself this time; he spewed his *chicha* out of his mouth, miraculously avoiding spraying anyone.

"Daric!" Dani scolded. "Our apologies. Where we come from, we don't marry our siblings."

"Oh," Cura Ocllo said, baffled. "It's how we preserve the purity of the royal blood lineage. Only those born of our union may rule as Emperor of the Incas."

"I have only half royal blood," Titu Cusi admitted sadly. "My mother is another wife of my father."

"You will always be a son to me," Cura Ocllo said lovingly, while ruffling the lad's hair.

A messenger ran into the room and knelt before Manco before relaying his news. Dani watched carefully and noted the look of alarm on both Manco's and Cura Ocllo's faces.

After the messenger had delivered his news, he promptly left. "This can't be good, whatever it is," Daric remarked.

"It's not all bad. My spies have learned that both Pizarro and Almagro want Cuzco, which Almagro now possesses. They tell me he has over six hundred Spaniards and about four thousand native allies," Manco explained. "If they fight and kill each other, all the better for us."

"They also tell me that there's a second Spanish force of nearly five hundred men approaching Cuzco from the north. If either group attacks Ollantaytambo, I don't think we could win that battle." Manco paused for a moment, weighing his options. There was no question in his mind. "We must move," he announced.

116

"WHAT THE HELL was that?" Richard exclaimed, trying to see through the cloud of settling dust.

"A tremor most likely," Quinn said, as calmly as he could. He knew New Zealand had over 10,000 earthquakes per year; it was just that he had never been here or, for that matter, in an underground cavern when it had happened.

Quinn took a quick survey of their situation. He noticed that a couple of stalactites had crashed down into the cavern. Miraculously they had missed their dive gear, which had been left on the sandbar. *That could have been disastrous,* Quinn thought.

"Well, let's find that mineral and get out of this cave before we get trapped in here or get knocked senseless by more falling rocks," Richard said with some urgency. Then a wickedly wonderful idea came to him. *Perfect,* he reflected.

"Good idea," Quinn replied, as he resumed searching for the chronizium.

While Quinn focussed intently on his search, Richard began to move in closer. He knew that once Quinn had found the chronizium, Quinn would be expendable; Richard would no longer need Quinn's help.

As he made his way toward Quinn, Richard bent down and picked up a length of stalactite that had fallen during the tremor; he grasped it like a club in one hand. He was soon standing, unnoticed, behind Quinn. Richard was poised and waiting for just the right moment. He didn't have to wait long.

"Richard, I found a small shard, but I don't . . ."

Richard slammed the stalactite down onto the back of Quinn's head. Quinn never saw it coming.

Quinn fell face first onto the sand bar. Blood oozed out of his left ear. Richard was unsure whether Quinn was alive or dead, but he couldn't have care less.

"You're such a trusting idiot, Quinn," Richard mocked. "You invented time travel and never even stopped to wonder about all the possibilities. You never imagined that someone might want this scientific breakthrough for themselves." He reached down and pulled the chronizium out of Quinn's lifeless hand.

Richard walked to his dive gear and kitted up. "Just to be on the safe side," Richard jeered. He pulled over Quinn's rebreather unit and opened the valve; there was an audible hiss. Richard then slid into the water and disappeared.

Richard followed the guideline that Quinn had so carefully laid on their way into the cave. On his way back out, Richard reeled the line back onto the diver's reel. He didn't want the guideline to lead anyone into the secluded cavern and the possible discovery of Quinn's body. If or when it was ever discovered, it would look like a diver had wandered into an unchartered cave and had been killed by falling rocks. No one would suspect foul play.

117

RICHARD WAS CAREFULLY making his way out of the cave system. He was desperately hoping that the tremor had not dislodged anything that would block his route. In hindsight, he realized he should have waited until he was out of this underwater labyrinth before he had dealt with Quinn. But, so far, he had noticed nothing different. He paused momentarily at the deco tanks and checked his dive computer. Realizing that decompression wasn't needed, he clipped the two tanks onto his belt and continued swimming toward the cave entrance.

A faint light filtered through the water directly ahead of him. "Daylight at last," Richard muttered. He hauled himself out of the water and onto the ledge. He removed his dive mask and rebreather unit. Next, he pulled up the two deco tanks and placed them on the ledge beside him.

"Damn," Richard sputtered. It had finally dawned on him that he would have to cart all this equipment back to the jeep. It would take a couple of trips and time he didn't have to spare. But there was no other alternative. He had to cover his tracks.

Richard pulled on his clothes and tossed his dive suit and thermal wear into the dive bag. He clipped the two deco tanks onto the carabiner before working his way to the top. Using the pulley system Quinn had rigged, he hauled the equipment out of the mouth of the cave; a process he repeated three times. After everything was up, he removed the rope from the tree. "Leave no evidence behind," he told himself.

For the next two hours, Richard struggled to move all the gear back down the trail from the cave to the Jeep. It was grueling work, especially for a man unaccustomed to such strenuous exercise. It was all he could do to load the gear into the Jeep.

Richard took one last look up the trail. Why, he wasn't sure, but he did. Then he climbed into the Jeep and settled himself behind the wheel. It felt good to finally sit down. He reached into his pocket and fished out the key he had earlier retrieved from a pocket in Quinn's pants. He put it into the ignition and, after a short pause, started the jeep and drove away from Courthouse Flat.

It took Richard an hour and a half get to the Nelson airport, bypassing the little town of Tapawera. He pulled up beside his fuelled Piper Seneca V aircraft and turned off the engine.

The airport manager had been expecting Richard and walked out of his office, clipboard in hand, to greet him when he saw the Jeep pull up. "Where's your buddy?"

"He decided to stay and visit a friend of his in Tapawera and then he's grabbing a flight out of Christchurch," Richard said confidently. He had remembered, from his search for an airport where he could land his private jet, that Christchurch had domestic flights to the North Island and a few international flights, mostly to Australia. It was a plausible story and the airport manager was buying his lie.

Richard threw his dive gear into the passenger section of the Piper and secured the rear door. He opened the pilot's door and was climbing into the cockpit when he heard a shaky voice behind him.

"But what about the rest of the equipment?" the manager asked nervously.

Richard spun around and stared coldly at the manager who could tell instantly that Richard didn't take kindly to being delayed.

According to the manager's inventory sheet, he knew he couldn't afford to replace the missing equipment he had rented for the two men. The gear was all expensive high-end stuff, exactly what Richard had asked for.

Richard glared at the cowering airport manager. Then he reached into his pocket and pulled out a wad of bills, which he tossed at the man. "Here, this should cover it," Richard replied while grinned slyly. "Now, if you wouldn't mind stepping back, I'm kind of in a hurry."

"Sure, no problem," the manager replied mechanically, as he counted the roll of money in his hands.

* * *

Two hours later, Richard was at cruising altitude in his Gulfstream G650 ER jet. He was on his way home. He had programmed the navigation computer and placed the controls on autopilot and he was now sitting in a comfortable lounge chair sipping on a scotch. In his left hand, he was slowly turning over the piece of chronizium, examining it for the first time. "So you're the magic bean," he muttered.

118

IT HAD TAKEN a day and a half to pack up everything. There were thousands of porters, pack trains of llamas, herds of alpacas, Anti archers, Manco's elite guard, his wives and his children. From atop his royal litter, Manco gave the signal for the procession to move.

Dani and Daric had originally declined the offer of being carried in a litter until Cura Ocllo explained that it was customary for nobles to travel that way. Not wanting to offend their hosts, Dani and Daric relented. Bear rode on the litter beside Dani and seemed to enjoy the ride.

The litters they travelled in were lavish vehicles. There were two long horizontal poles, which rested on the shoulders of the litter bearers. The pole ends were covered in silver and hammered into the shape of a puma's head. An elegant low-walled wooden box was mounted between the two poles. On the floor of the box, there was a seat covered with soft cushions. Overhead, a cloth canopy protected the riders from both the sun and the rain.

When Dani remarked how smooth the ride was, Cura Ocllo explained that members of the Rucana tribe were the only men allowed to carry the highest Inca nobility. They were specially trained from an early age to provide the smoothest ride possible.

Amongst the procession walked all the expertise needed to keep the empire running: priests, astrologers, weavers, farmers, herders, stone masons, accountants, architects, and quipu readers. The quipus readers were important because the Inca didn't have a written language; instead they used quipus, knotted string devices, to record everything from population counts to harvested crops to songs commemorating heroic kings. The readers were proficient at how to prepare and read quipus.

The expedition was heading north. It advanced along the road that followed the banks of the Patacancha River, a tributary of the Yucay, in the bottom of the Urubamba Valley, also known as the Sacred Valley. After several hours, the expedition arrived at a point where the road split into two; the only two roads out of the valley. One road continued down the valley to a city where it climbed up over the mountains and eventually ended at Machu Picchu. The other climbed out of the valley and led toward the Panticalla Pass. The expedition turned toward the pass.

As the procession climbed higher, Dani looked back over the broad vastness below. Smoke still rose above the thatched roofs of the houses. Terraced fields with crops of corn now lay abandoned. Snow-capped mountains stretched into the distance, and the winding Yucay River glistening in the early morning sun. The spectacular panorama disappeared from view the moment her litter turned a bend in the road.

After continuing along the ascending road for five hours, the procession crossed the Panticalla Pass. The snow-capped summit of Wakay Willka (Mount Veronica) loomed to the left of the pass. To the right, was an endless expanse of clouds blanketing the area below for as far as the eye could see, appearing to swallow the bases of the surrounding mountains. This was the entranceway to the land of the Anti.

Manco Inca and his procession worked their way down through the moist cloud forest, past an abundant variety of tree ferns, tangled moss-covered vegetation, and orchids in enough colors to satisfy any painter's palette. Hummingbirds flitted from flower to flower, gathering nectar, wings moving so fast they were almost indiscernible, making the little birds appear as if they were suspended in mid-air.

Following the Lucumayo River, the expedition reached the Amaibamba Valley. In the distance were herds of guanacos and vicuñas, which only the emperor was allowed to hunt and which were prized for their fine wool. "Let's take a break here," Manco announced. He needed time to figure out where to go to next.

119

IT HAD BEEN a long journey yesterday before Manco had called a halt for the day. Wasting no time this morning, the expedition was on the move early. With every step, the new day grew brighter, since sunshine often arrived suddenly as it crested the surrounding mountain peaks. The spreading rosy glow of dawn swallowed the stars.

Before long the group came to a stop. Daric jumped down from his litter and walked ahead to see the reason for the delay; after all, they just got started. "You can't be serious?" he exclaimed, when he saw what was ahead of them.

The mountain road that Manco had been leading his group along ended abruptly at a steep canyon. In front of them was the Chuquichaca Bridge. It was a two-hundred foot long suspension bridge. It was constructed of rope suspended between four stone towers, two on either side of the canyon. The walkway between the ropes was made of sticks and woven grasses. Far, far below the bridge was the Urubamba River, glinting in the hot sun like a giant golden snake.

Manco looked at Daric, amused by his new friend's nervousness. "I assure you, it's quite safe."

The procession moved across the suspension bridge as it swayed and bounced under their weight. Once across, Manco instructed native work crews to remain behind to block the passageway into the valley. The work detail started by carefully dislodging boulders from above and rolling them down onto the trail. Next, they toppled trees, creating a tangled barrier that effectively obstructed the trail. Manco hoped that these small defensive measures would keep the Spaniards at bay, or, at least, delay them.

Manco led the rest of the procession up into the Vilcabamba Valley. He had decided the previous night that he would settle at Vitcos, a royal estate of his great-grandfather, Pachacuti. It would become the new capital of his dwindling empire. Although Vitcos was only seventy miles from Cuzco, the terrain between them was steep and rugged.

At the end of the Vilcabamba Valley lay Vitcos, an extensive complex of royal residences perched on a hill at the end of a narrow outcropping, surrounded by steep cliffs on three sides. Vitcos overlooked the deep valleys to the east and to the west. It had a spectacular view of a series of mountain peaks to the south.

The large royal estate opened onto a small plaza within Vitcos: that was where Manco was headed.

120

RICHARD PULLED HIS SUV into the Delaney driveway. He got out and walked up to the house. He leaned forward and rang the doorbell. A few moments later the door swung open.

"Richard, you're back," Sandra said, as she peered over Richard's shoulder searching for Quinn. When she saw that Richard was alone, she turned her concerned eyes toward their long-time family friend. "Richard, where's Quinn?"

"Sandra, come on inside," Richard urged, leading her by the arm into the living room.

"Richard, where's Quinn? Did he go straight to his lab?" Sandra persisted, as Richard motioned her to sit down on the sofa.

Richard took a seat beside her. "Sandra, there's been an accident," Richard began.

"What kind of accident? Where's Quinn?" Sandra's voice escalated with each word, as panic took hold.

"We were diving for the mineral when there was an earthquake," Richard explained. "I barely escaped with my life."

"Richard, where's Quinn?" Sandra was getting more angry than frightened with Richard's failure to answer her question.

"He got trapped in a cave-in. There was no way he could have survived."

Sandra stared at Richard in disbelief. "No. No. It's not possible."

"I was there, Sandra. I saw it. I barely escaped being crushed myself." Richard cringed, immediately regretting the use of the word crushed.

Richard wasn't ready for what happened next. Sandra sprang on him. She started pounding his chest, hard and screamed, "How could you have left him behind? Why didn't you stay and try to help him? How could you leave him there?"

Richard grabbed Sandra's flailing arms to stop any further pounding on his already aching body. "Sandra, listen to me, for a minute, please!" Sandra calmed a bit, gently sobbing.

"There was nothing I could have done, if I had stayed. It could take weeks, even months, to reach his body," Richard explained, as he cradled Sandra's hands.

"No. No, it can't be," Sandra sobbed. Her head fell against Richard's chest and she openly wept. Richard held her and let her cry. All he could do was be there for her in her grief.

Then suddenly Sandra bolted upright. "My children," she cried out.

"Sandra?" Richard was confused.

"Without Quinn, Dani and Daric have no way of getting back home! Oh dear God, I've lost them, too."

121

RODRIGO ORGÓÑEZ HAD proved his worth to Diego de Almagro three weeks earlier. He had defeated the five-hundred troops that Francisco Pizarro had sent to liberate his two brothers from prison. In an almost bloodless battle, Orgóñez and his men had attacked at night, surprising Francisco Pizarro's troops. Most of the defeated army had opted to join Almagro's side in what was sure to be the prelude to a civil war.

In the days following Orgóñez's success, Almagro granted Orgóñez permission to go after Manco Inca one last time. He also incurred Orgóñez's wrath–actually, the two men nearly came to blows–when Almagro informed Orgóñez that he had released Hernando and Gonzalo Pizarro. Orgóñez's reaction was immediate and very loud. "You did what?" he shouted. "Are you crazy?"

Orgóñez's explosive outburst didn't surprise Almagro; in fact, he was expecting it. "I know you don't approve," he replied calmly, "but I made them promise to uphold the peace and I took them at their word."

Almagro's calm voice did nothing to allay Orgóñez's concerns and fears. There was no doubt in his mind that Hernando would seek revenge for the treatment he had suffered at the hands of Orgóñez and his men when Hernando and Gonzalo had first been captured. Orgóñez also knew that the Pizarros would be the last people on earth to either forget or forgive. But only time would tell whether Orgóñez's assertions were correct.

Even though Orgóñez remained troubled by the release of the Pizarro brothers, he carried on with assembling the men and other resources he would need to go after Manco. At the same time, Almagro came up with and implemented what he saw as a brilliant plan. He installed Paullu Inca on the imperial throne in a bid to fracture the Incas' loyalties and further weaken the rebellion. Paullu was about the same age as Manco Inca and the two men shared the same father, Huayna Capac. Paullu's mother, however, was not of pure royal lineage, meaning that the throne was rightfully Manco's.

Almagro's plan placed Paullu at the head of the native auxiliary army and he was poised to join Orgóñez in leading the expedition against Manco. Almagro felt that Paullu could play an important role since he had already demonstrated his ability to handle native forces. In the recent battle against Francisco Pizarro's troops, he had led ten-thousand native auxiliaries and had helped to sway the defeated natives over to Almagro's side. And he hadn't forgotten Paullu's role in his expedition to Chile. If it hadn't been for Paullu, Almagro and his men would not have survived that expedition.

As soon as preparations for the expedition were completed, Rodrigo Orgóñez, with Paullu Inca and Ricardo Barak Caso, led their troops out of Cuzco and down into the Yucay Valley. They encountered no resistance, this time, as they forded the river or as they marched past the now vacant temple fortress of Ollantaytambo.

The army left the valley and headed up north toward the Panticalla Pass before coming to an abrupt halt. "It's going to take us hours to clear this mess," Caso grunted, referring to the blockade along the trail.

"This is Manco's work," Paullu announced.

"Start clearing the path," Orgóñez ordered, as he dismounted.

Caso was proven right. It took several hours of hard work to clear the trail. By then, it was too dark for the forces to resume their journey. They would have to camp and wait until morning.

1537—Day 30

122

"THAT'S IT, TITU Cusi," Dani encouraged. "Keep calm; breathe nice and easy. I'm right here if you need me, but you're doing just fine."

Dani was standing chest deep in the river beside Titu Cusi, who was learning how to tread water. He was slowly swinging his arms horizontally back and forth underwater while his legs were moving underneath him.

"This is kind of fun. It's like I'm walking in water," Titu Cusi observed cheerfully. "I'm not even tired. I think I could do this for a long time."

"That's the idea. Treading water can be very useful when you're tired and too far from shore to take a rest," Dani explained. "It's also an important skill to have to help keep you in one place, if you need to be rescued."

"Like I did," Titu Cusi said.

"That's right," Dani replied. "If you'd known how to tread water, I wouldn't have had to search for you underwater and would have gotten to you much sooner."

"But, if I knew how to swim, I wouldn't have needed rescuing in the first place," Titu Cusi teased.

"Yeah, that's right, and you've made great progress over the past two weeks with your swimming." Dani smiled down at his beaming face. "Come on, let's rest for a bit. We can practice again in a little while."

"Okay," Titu Cusi said, as he started to swim toward shore, where two of Manco's elite guardsmen had been stationed to watch over and protect the swimmers.

After reaching the shore, Dani and Titu Cusi lay down on the bank. They soaked up the heat from the afternoon sun while enjoying some peace and quiet. Lying next to Dani was Bear, exhausted from chasing the minnows; they lurked just under the surface and had darted away every time Bear had tried to catch one.

"I don't think I'd like to be a ruler," Titu Cusi stated candidly, breaking the tranquility of the moment.

"Why do you say that?" Dani asked, as she sat up and looked at her small companion.

"I don't think I would like all the jobs that go with it," Titu Cusi said, with child-like honesty.

"Then, what would you like to be?" Dani asked. Watching Titu Cusi's face, she could see his brow furrow as he contemplated her question. After a few moments, his face brightened. He turned and looked up at Dani.

"I'd like to be a storyteller," Titu Cusi announced excitedly.

"That's interesting. What kind of stories?" Dani probed.

"Interesting stories," Titu Cusi stated, "not like the stories we're forced to learn about our ancestors; they're so boring."

"But, Titu Cusi, those stories are very important; they're the history of your people," Dani explained. "If those stories had not been passed down through the generations, you would know nothing about your culture, your traditions, your customs."

"So?" Titu Cusi grunted.

"Let's take now, as an example. What if no one was left to tell the story about how your people fought to rid their land of the foreigners?" Dani asked. "What your people are going through right now would be lost in time forever."

"So?" Titu Cusi said, a little less bored this time.

"It's important that we learn from history, Titu Cusi," Dani said, "because if we don't, we are destined to repeat it." Dani recalled saying the same thing in a Salem prison not so long ago. She looked over at Titu Cusi. He was still lying down but, she was pretty sure he was listening to what she had to say. She decided to test that theory.

"And in most cases, history gets recorded by the victors, who generally glorify their own side of the story. Would you want that? Would you want the Spaniards to record your history?"

"No!" Titu Cusi bolted upright. "I'm going to tell our side of the story!"

"And I'm sure you'll be a fine storyteller," Dani said, ruffling his hair. "Come on; it's getting late. We should get back."

Dani knew she was treading a fine line by talking to Titu Cusi about his future, but she was sure she wasn't interfering with his destiny. At most, she might be helping steer him onto the path that he would eventually follow. She knew that he would someday tell his people's side of the story to a Spanish friar and would ask him to record it. As a result, the valiant struggles that Titu Cusi's people made against a superior adversary would not be lost forever.

123

"WELL, THAT WENT much better than last time," Dani said glee-fully, holding Titu Cusi's hand as they entered the temple of the royal estate. Bear darted past and headed for Manco. Dani's mood quickly changed when she noticed the somber expression on Man-co's face.

"What's wrong?" she asked sincerely.

"It's my brother, Paullu. I've sent him messages asking him to join me here and to fight against the Spaniards, but, in every response, he's declined my offer." Manco could not forgive his brother for refusing to join his fight against the invaders. He felt betrayed. Ironically, history was repeating itself. Manco's older brothers, Huascar and Atahualpa, had gone to war against each other after their father died, to determine who would rule as the next emperor.

"And a messenger just told me that the Spaniards have declared Paullu the new emperor."

"Can they do that?" Dani ask incredulously.

"Of course not; not legally anyway. I'm the only legitimate Son of the Sun," Manco replied. "But Paullu is ambitious and would rather live the life of an emperor in the capital than as a fugitive here in the jungle. In effect, Almagro has divided the empire and essentially weakened our position. It's probably exactly what he had in mind when he gave Paullu the crown."

Titu Cusi had walked over and sat beside his father, hoping to provide some comfort. Manco looked at his son; tousling his damp hair, he asked, "So, how did the swimming lessons go?"

"Better. I can keep my head above water now for a long time," Titu Cusi gushed. "And I can swim better than Bear; she won't even go into the river."

Upon hearing her name, Bear turned her attention away from the morsels of food that Manco had been slipping her. "Where's Daric?" Dani asked, moving further into the room and sitting down on a woven mat.

"He's practising," Manco replied absentmindedly.

"Practicing what?"

"He's learning how to use the *porra*, the *warak'a* and the *allus*."

"You'll need to explain that to me. I don't know those words," Dani said.

"The *porra* is a heavy club designed to crack open a human skull. It's a long wooden handle with a ball of copper on the end of it, with five protruding points," Manco explained.

"And the *warak'a* is a cord made of wool. You put a stone in the center and swing it around really fast. I can knock a gourd off a log from twenty paces," Titu Cusi boasted proudly.

"Like a sling." Dani understood. "And the *allus*?"

"It consists of three round stones sewn into leather bags attached to a cord. When you throw it at a horse, it tangles the horse's legs so they can't move. And if you throw it at a soldier, it will bind his arms to his body, making him virtually defenceless. None are lethal weapons by any means, but it's all we've got," Manco said resignedly.

"Hey, I'm starved. Is it whatever-mealtime-it's-supposed-to-be about now?" Daric bellowed as he entered the chamber.

124

AT DAWN, THE Spaniards and their native auxiliaries had resumed their advance up the Vilcabamba Valley, eventually finding Vitcos at the upper tributary of the river. It was an expansive complex of royal residences situated on a hilltop overlooking deep valleys.

On Orgóñez's signal, the Spaniards and the native forces moved swiftly. They charged up the hill, meeting little resistance. When the forces entered the complex, pandemonium broke out. Native men, women, and children panicked and tried to flee, as the Spaniards, with their swords drawn, ran into the houses and palaces. Some were looking for the rebel leader, Manco. Others were searching for gold, silver, jewelry . . . whatever kind of treasure they could get their greedy hands on.

Manco and everyone else living in Vitcos had been caught completely off guard and had had no chance to mount a defence. How the Spaniards had got so close without an alarm being sounded was inconceivable. But they had.

"Lord, you must flee," a priest urged Manco. "Now, before it's too late. You must save yourself because without you the rebellion will die. Hurry, please, you must go now!"

"Okay, but then you follow with the rest," Manco reluctantly commanded. He knew that with his capture or death the empire would be lost. At least this way, he could live to fight another day. So he grabbed Cura Ocllo and, having no time for their royal litters, allowed his wife and himself to be unceremoniously whisked away into the jungle on the backs of the empire's fastest runners.

"Sit perfectly still," Dani whispered to Titu Cusi, who was holding tightly onto Bear. She had wrapped her arms around his tiny body, trying to conceal him. Daric had placed his body over his sister's and had struggled to pull some blankets over all of them. Dani and Daric could have escaped using their travel bands, but they immediately dismissed the idea for two reasons. First, they didn't want to leave Titu Cusi alone and second, they had no idea where they'd end up. They knew if things got worse; they still had that option. But for now, they hoped they might be overlooked in the dark, back corner of the room.

Above all the yelling and screaming coming from outside, they could hear footsteps approaching. Not the gentle sounds made by sandals, but the clatter by heavy leather boots. "Well, what have we under here?" a male voice jeered, as the tip of a lance peeled back the blankets, exposing the hidden group.

Daric slowly stood up, trying to shield Dani and Titu Cusi behind him. Dani peered up into the face of the Spaniard and couldn't contain the gasp that escaped. She was staring at a bearded 'Uncle Richard'. She would know those wide-set cold brown eyes and thin-lipped pointy jaw anywhere. And it seemed as though he kept popping up wherever they travelled through time. But why?

"Out you get," the Spaniard ordered, nodding toward the doorway. He could tell by their fine clothes that they were people of some importance.

Dani stood with her back toward the Spaniard, helping Titu Cusi up off the floor. When her hand reached out to his, he put an elegantly carved bone knife, which had been tucked into his belt, into Dani's hand. She quickly hid it under her robe. The trio, with Bear in tow, walked slowly toward the door and out of the building. They were aghast at the pillaging and destruction they saw before them. Piles of plunder littered the central plaza. Thatched roofs were ablaze. Anyone who raised arms now lay dead on the ground.

"What have you got there, Caso?" Orgóñez asked, as he looked over the elegantly dressed trio.

Dani instantly recognized that Caso was Spanish for Case as in Uncle Richard. Looking over at Daric, she could see he had realized the same.

"That's Titu Cusi, Manco's son," Paullu offered. "The other two, I don't know, but they definitely aren't Inca. Their coloring is more like the Chachapoyas."

"They're my attendants," Titu Cusi boldly announced. There was no concealing the fact he was Manco's son, not in front of his own kin. So he would do the next best thing he could think of; he would try to keep Dani and Daric close to him.

"Well, aren't you the lucky one?" Caso sneered, as his cold brown eyes seemed to undress Dani where she stood. His lustful gaze didn't go unnoticed by either Titu Cusi or Daric. Instinctively, they both moved a little closer to Dani, determined to keep lecherous hands away.

"Where's your father?" Orgóñez demanded.

"I don't know," Titu Cusi said belligerently, earning him a swift backhand across the face from Caso, knocking him backwards into Dani's arms.

"Hey!" Dani protested, putting a protective arm around Titu Cusi's head. "That's not necessary. The emperor was here, but he was in his palace when you attacked. If you haven't found him, then he's probably escaped."

"Go find him," Orgóñez growled at Caso.

* * *

Three hours later, Caso and twelve members of the cavalry returned empty-handed. "There was no sign of him. He's disappeared," Caso reported.

Although Orgóñez was disappointed that his expedition to Vitcos had failed to capture Manco Inca, he didn't consider it a total loss. Vast quantities of treasure had been seized and were being loaded onto the backs of llamas for the trip back to Cuzco. A large stash of Spanish weapons, armor and clothing had been discovered and would be distributed to the desolate conquistadors who, in some cases, were still wearing the clothes they had been wearing when they had first arrived in South America. And, most importantly, Manco's son had been captured and was now lying on one of the royal litters, clutching a stupid fox he called Bear; his two attendants on either side of his litter. Orgóñez was confident Almagro would be able to use the kid to draw Manco out of hiding.

When satisfied nothing more could be achieved at Vitcos, Orgóñez led his forces out of Victos and headed back through the valley toward Cuzco.

"Maybe we should have stayed in Ollantaytambo," Daric muttered to Dani. "At least there we had a fighting chance." Manco's confidence that Vitcos would protect him had cost him dearly.

125

"NO, SANDRA, YOU haven't lost the twins," Richard assured the distraught woman. "I have the mineral, the . . . what did Quinn call it . . . the chronizium. I have it. Quinn said that's what he needed to bring the twins home."

"But, Richard, Quinn is the only one who knows how to do that," Sandra said dejectedly. "Without him, you won't have a clue where to start."

Richard had to bite back his anger at her slight. He knew Sandra had not intended to denigrate him; he accepted that she was upset and grieving.

"Sandra, Quinn hasn't been working on this project alone. He's had help," Richard continued. "Hermes has been helping Quinn all along. Between the two of us, we should be able to figure out how to get the kids back home."

"But there's something wrong with Quinn's system. It went down just before you left for New Zealand. He was going to look into what the problem was when he got back," Sandra sighed, trying unsuccessfully to stifle a sob.

"Well, I have an associate who can fix anything. Why don't you let me see if he can figure out the problem?" Richard said encouragingly.

"Do you really think he can?" Sandra asked hopefully. "Do you think you can get my children back?"

"I'll do everything in my power, I promise."

Sandra collapsed sobbing into Richard's arms. Maybe all wasn't lost. Maybe, just maybe, there was a chance. Even if only a small one.

Richard was very reluctant to release Sandra from his embrace, but the sooner he got into Quinn's lab, the sooner he would be in possession of those miracle bands. He gently lifted Sandra's head off his chest and tenderly held her cheeks in his hands. Looking into her tear-stained face and bloodshot eyes, he still thought she was the most beautiful woman he had ever seen. And now, with Quinn out of the picture, he was determined to make Sandra his own again, as it had been back in high school. But the timing would have to be just right or he would risk driving a wedge between them forever. He could wait. He would wait. *A little while longer,* he told himself. *A little while longer.*

126

AFTER SITTING WITH Sandra until she had finished crying herself out, Richard led her up to her bedroom. While she was changing, he grabbed two sleeping pills from the medicine cabinet.

"Here, take these," Richard said, as he placed the pills in Sandra's palm and handed her a glass of water. "They'll help you sleep."

"I don't think I need them," Sandra protested weakly.

"They'll help you rest," Richard insisted, gently guiding Sandra's hand containing the pills closer toward her. She reluctantly succumbed to Richard's persistence and swallowed the pills. Richard took the empty glass and put it on the bedside table.

"I'm going to run home, grab a couple of things, including a change of clothes, and then I'll be back," Richard said.

"Why don't you get some rest yourself, Richard? You look exhausted," Sandra said, stifling a yawn.

"Maybe, you're right. I could use a couple of hours sleep. I'll come back first thing in the morning," Richard responded. Then he pulled the covers up and tucked them under Sandra's shoulders. He leaned in and gave her a peck on the forehead.

"I'll pick up the spare key from the kitchen, in case you're still sleeping when I come back in the morning. I'll pop up and look in on you to make sure you're all right, before I head out to the lab,"

Richard said.

"No! Please, wake me when you get back. I want to help if I can." Sandra's protest fell on deaf ears. Richard sat on the side of the bed and watched as her heavy lids gradually closed and her breathing slowed.

Fifteen minutes later, Richard exited the house through the kitchen door. He paused for just a moment and looked around. He would have to figure out what to do with this place when all was said and done. But that could wait for later. Right now, he had other more urgent matters to take care of.

Richard climbed into his SUV and pulled out of the driveway. As he was driving along the narrow dirt road, a deer darted out in front of his vehicle. With his reflexes slowed by fatigue, he failed to brake immediately; the Audi's sensors, however, activated the emergency braking system, narrowly averting a collision. The deer stared at the SUV for a moment and, then, bounded into the forest that lined both sides of the road.

"Damn it!" Richard exploded, his heart pounding wildly in his chest. "I'm going to burn this whole bloody place down, the entire peninsula."

1537—Day 32

127

ORGÓÑEZ AND HIS forces had made good progress since leaving Vitcos, but Cuzco was still at least a day's travel ahead of them. So, with darkness starting to fall, Orgóñez ordered his troops to stop and camp for the night.

The journey had been tiring; especially for the prisoners Orgóñez was taking back to Cuzco. Among them were Dani and Daric. Their hands had been bound with cords, making it difficult for them to maintain their balance as they trudged along the cobbled roads. Daric had stumbled more than a dozen times; Dani, too, had acquired a few bruises.

Guarded by two heavily armed Spanish invaders, the prisoners had been corralled together, their hands finally untied. Daric had found a secluded corner where he thought he might be able to protect Dani and Titu Cusi. Later that night, however, Caso and a few of his men found the trio, wedged between two trees and propped against a rocky ledge.

"Come on, sweetie, let's have some fun," Caso slurred lecherously, followed by a wicked chuckle. His men laughed right along with him. They had all been drinking around a campfire and were now looking for a little entertainment.

"Leave her alone," Titu Cusi ordered, getting to his feet, and facing off against the seven larger men before him.

"Well, will you get a load of him?" snorted one of the soldier. "He thinks he's the emperor."

"Like he said," Daric said firmly, as he got to his feet and positioning himself in front of Dani, who remained huddled on the ground, clutching Bear to her chest. "Leave her alone."

"I know I can't touch the brat, but that doesn't mean I can't show you some manners," Caso grunted. He pulled back a fist and took a swing at Daric, who easily dodged the sloppy blow.

"Hold him still, will ya," Caso ordered his men, who quickly lurched forward and seized Daric's arms.

Caso had pulled back his arm to deliver another punch that Daric knew he wouldn't be able to evade. All he could do was brace for the impact. But none came.

"What's going on here?" Orgóñez demanded, as he maintained a firm grip on Caso's arm. Orgóñez had gone looking for his second-in-command to talk about tomorrow's departure. When Caso was nowhere to be found, Orgóñez knew exactly where to look.

"Let go of me!" Caso bellowed. "We're just having a little fun."

"Get back to your fires. The fun's over," Orgóñez growled, releasing his grip.

Caso held Orgóñez in a stone-cold glare for a moment. They both overheard one of the drunken men mumble as he turned away, "But we didn't get to have any fun yet."

Caso grudgingly followed his angry men back to their fires where they eventually settled down for the night. That was the last attempt anyone made 'to have a little fun'.

128

LATER THE FOLLOWING day, Orgóñez and his men arrived at the ridge overlooking their journey's end. Before going on, Orgóñez ordered a halt. The men welcomed the break in what had been an arduous march. They looked down onto the bowl-shaped valley ahead of them. At its center was Cuzco, the royal hub of the empire. It was nestled against low hills, tucked into the end of a long, forested valley; snow-covered mountains graced the horizon. All major roads converged here.

Cuzco was divided into two sectors, upper and a lower, demarcating the social hierarchy of the empire. Houses in the lower sector were rectangular, with one room and one story, and were arranged around common courtyards. They were built of fieldstones or adobe bricks and had thatched roofs. Their doors and windows were in the traditional trapezoidal shape. In contrast, the buildings in the upper sector were constructed of finely cut and fitted stones and included numerous palaces for the nobles. Meandering through much of the city were two rivers, their banks and bottoms paved so that the water ran clear and clean; even when water levels rose, they didn't overflow. Several cantilever bridges spanned the rivers at various points throughout the city. A large central plaza was the site of frequent celebrations and religious ceremonies. After what seemed like only a few minutes, Orgóñez signalled his men to move on. Before long, they had descended from the ridge and entered the city. They made their way through the narrow streets, which were just wide enough to accommodate mounted rider riding in single file. When they reached the central plaza, the group came to a halt.

"Take our guests to the prison. I want a twenty-four-hour guard detail on those three," Orgóñez ordered, pointing at Dani, Daric and Titu Cusi, who was keeping a tight grip on Bear's leash.

A dozen men stepped forward and herded the Victos captives toward a gray building with beautifully sculptured walls. Dani, Daric and Titu Cusi, with Bear in tow, were separated from the other prisoners and were taken to a large chamber where they were left under guard.

Titu Cusi walked to the far wall and slumped down into a corner by himself. He looked miserable. Bear, sensing the boy's melancholy, trotted over and sat beside him.

Daric walked around the chamber looking for anything that might help them out of their current predicament. Dani walked over and sat beside Titu Cusi. She was worried about him. He hadn't uttered a word since entering the city. "I know this isn't the best of circumstances, but at least we're unharmed and safe for the moment. So, don't worry," Dani said calmly.

"This place is *Qoricancha*, our Temple of the Sun, the holiest place in the empire, or at least it used to be," Titu Cusi said tearfully. "They've destroyed it."

Dani looked around the interior of the room and could see protruding naked pegs, a sure sign that there had been something hanging on the walls. "I'm so sorry." It was all she could think of to say.

"There used to be a strip of gold two hand-spans wide and four fingers thick halfway up the wall," Titu Cusi explained. "The gateway and doors were covered with sheets of gold. And up there," Titu Cusi said, pointing to a spot on the wall where the sun was filtering in through a window, "hung a large image of the sun beautifully molded and set with many colorful stones. And right below it was a garden where the earth was lumps of fine gold, and the planted stalks of corn that filled the garden were also gold–the stalks, the leaves and even the ears."

"We call gold 'the sweat of the sun' and we call silver 'the tears of the moon'," Titu Cusi went on. "The invaders have melted down most of our treasured possessions and shipped the gold and silver back to their lands. No one thought to ask about their significance. No one appreciated the artistry. They destroyed everything, and for what?" Titu Cusi's voice had gradually increased in volume as his anger built.

"The greed of these men controls them so much that they'll stop at nothing to get more," Titu Cusi growled. "They kept coming to batter and humiliate my father to get him to reveal where there was more silver and gold, more than what they had already taken from the empire."

Titu Cusi looked pleadingly at Dani, his brown eyes brimming with tears. "When will it end?"

"I don't know, honey," Dani said sadly. She wrapped a loving arm around the distraught child. "But what I do know is that no matter how bad things get, there is always hope, and with hope, anything is possible."

In fact, Dani did know. She knew that in six years, Titu Cusi would witness the murder of his father and that he would barely escape the same fate.

129

"AM I INTERRUPTING anything?" a short, squat man asked, as he entered the prison chamber. He slowly walked over and stood in front of his prisoners. Looking down at the young lad, he said, "You must be Titu Cusi, Manco's son."

Titu Cusi looked into the face of the ugly, one-eyed man in disgust. "That's right," he said defiantly, as he stood. He might be only an eight-year-old, but he had the maturity, bravery, and hutzpah of a future emperor. "And who are you?"

"I'm Diego de Almagro, governor of Cuzco, and your host," Almagro replied, looking at the other two occupants of the room. "And you are?"

"I'm Daric; this is my sister, Dani, Titu Cusi's attendants." Daric displayed the same defiant tone that Titu Cusi had voiced and he continued the same ruse that Titu Cusi had played in Vitcos.

"Welcome to Cuzco. Please sit. Let's talk." Almagro gestured for them to return to the woven mats on the floor. He slowly and painfully made his way down to the mats to join them. "I have taken ill recently and don't get around as easily as I used to," he explained.

Within moments, several women entered, carrying trays of food and drink. They placed the trays on the floor and immediately left.

"I know this isn't what you're accustomed to, but it's the best I can do under the circumstances," Almagro stated apologetically. "I hope you haven't been mistreated," he added, looking at Titu Cusi and, then, nervously at Dani. She truly was a vision to behold, just like Orgóñez had said.

"You mean like you mistreated my father," Titu Cusi snapped.

"That wasn't me. I was–and still am–friends with your father," Almagro asserted. "When I came back from Chile, I sought him out before coming back here to Cuzco. I sent him letters, telling him how appalled I was at the mistreatment he had received at the hands of the Pizarros. I told him I wanted to bring those responsible to justice."

"I heard on the way back here that you had released two of the Pizarro brothers," Dani said coldly.

"That couldn't be helped. I had no legitimate grounds to keep them detained," Almagro quickly explained.

"Just another lie," Titu Cusi grunted. "They were the ones who abused my father, yet they received no punishment, even though you had promised you'd punish them."

"You don't understand. Your father had to agree to cease his rebellion and return to Cuzco with me, but your father refused to do so. If he had returned with me, I could have petitioned the King of Spain for a pardon on his behalf."

"My father had learned over the past four years that the Spanish invaders could not be trusted. He had been lied to. His older brother had been lied to. Even after providing everything that was asked of him, you murdered him anyway," Titu Cusi growled.

"Again, that wasn't me; that was Pizarro," Almagro explained. He was determined to place the entire blame for the rebellion on the Pizarros. But, first, he needed to negotiate a truce with Manco. Only then could he write the king and report these atrocities and be in a position to ask that he be granted governorship over the entire empire, not just the worthless southern portion he had been granted already. He wanted Francisco Pizarro's northern realm as well.

"So, what are you planning to do with us?" Daric asked, nibbling on a piece of fruit and slipping a peanut to Bear.

"Right to the point, I like that," Almagro said. "I'd like Titu Cusi to . . ."

"Almagro!" Orgóñez shouted as he burst into the chamber. "There's an army approaching, led by Hernando Pizarro and his brother Gonzalo."

"Are you certain?" Almagro asked nervously.

"I told you the Pizarros would never keep their word, especially that arrogant Hernando," Orgóñez retorted bitterly.

"Then we must prepare," Almagro declared. "My apologies; we'll have to finish this conversation at another time." He got up with Orgóñez's help and they left the room, Orgóñez yattering the whole time.

"This can't be good," Daric muttered.

1537—Day 35

130

AT DAWN IN the middle of a swampy area of the plain called Las Salinas, about two miles west of Cuzco, two armies faced each other, about to do battle.

On one side of the plain were the forces of Hernando Pizarro, who was charged with recapturing the capital city of Cuzco. Under him were eight hundred Spaniards and several thousand native allies. He had split his two hundred cavalry evenly and had positioned them on each flank; they were in full armour and bearing lances and swords. His five-hundred foot soldiers were positioned in the middle, wearing armour and carrying shields and swords. In front of the foot soldier stood a row of one hundred harquebus men, holding their primed three-foot guns ready to fire at any given order.

Hernando Pizarro's forces were under the command of three men. Hernando himself was in command of one of the cavalry corps. The second corps was commanded by Alonso de Alvarado, whose liberation forces had previously been defeated by Orgóñez and who had seen most of his men go over to Almagro; he was itching for retribution. Gonzalo Pizarro was leading the infantry.

On the opposite side of the plain were Almagro's force of five-hundred men: two-hundred forty cavalry and two-hundred-sixty foot soldiers, whose weapons included six cannons. In addition, there were six thousand native warriors, equipped with *warak'a* or slings and *porra* or clubs, under the leadership of Paullu Inca. He had been instructed to position his warriors around the perimeter. He had also been ordered to kill any Spaniard who tried to flee the battle, regardless of whose side they were on. Almagro did not tolerate deserters.

Almagro, being too sick to lead the impending battle, had placed Rodrigo Orgóñez in command. Orgóñez commanded one corps of cavalry while Ricardo Barak Caso led the other. One of Caso's men commanded the infantry.

Although sick, Almagro had no intention of missing the battle. So, he had some of his men carry him on a litter to a nearby hill which overlooked the plain. From here he would have an unobstructed view of the battle as it unfolded.

On a nearby hill, natives from the city and the surrounding areas gathered to watch the bearded invaders kill each other in their own civil war. Many hoped that the battle would be the beginning of the end of the foreign invaders. Among the observers were a few of Manco's spies.

Orgóñez dismounted. The sun glistened off his curved morion helmet and body armour. With the reins of his horse in one hand, he walked the length of his troops and, as he walked, he tried to bolster the morale of his men. "This battle is a disservice to both God and His Majesty. We tried to negotiate with the Pizarros," he shouted. "They made many promises they failed to keep and, without a doubt, they have promised those men who now fight alongside them a great deal of wealth to be shared among the victors. If only those brave men could know that the Pizarros have no intention of rewarding the victors, then this battle could be averted. But that will not happen, because those men, our countrymen, have been bribed with visions of riches beyond their wildest dreams.

We know that the Pizarros are the ones responsible for the Inca rebellion and for the deaths of hundreds of our comrades. So, we fight on the side of justice. We know that victory will be ours!" A thunderous roar went up as Orgóñez ended his speech.

On the other side of the plain, another pep talk was being delivered. "Almagro is a traitor!" Hernando bellowed from astride his horse. "He seized Cuzco, which belongs to Governor Francisco Pizarro, and in the wake of battle, he imprisoned me and my brother, Gonzalo. We were treated brutally. It's because of Almagro that we are here today. He's responsible for inciting this war with our fellow countrymen. This is more for a point of honor than for past injustices. We need to punish those who follow the direction of a traitor. By order of the governor, we are here to regain control of Cuzco. When we are victorious, there will be many provinces and wealth to be divided among you, and only you!" A roar erupted from the soldiers; many of the cavalry soldiers had to tighten the reins on their startled horses.

131

AFTER THE ROUSING speeches from their respective commanders, the men on both sides of the plain shuffled nervously, silently waiting for the order to be given. Swords had been unsheathed, lances had been lifted and poised, visors on helmets, if they had them, had been lowered, and banners were fluttering in the light breeze.

Hernando Pizarro looked over at his brother. Gonzalo gave him a nod to show his men were ready. Hernando glanced over at Alvarado and received the same signal. Hernando squinted in the sunlight across the plain, focussing on Orgóñez. Staring directly at him, Hernando raised his sword, held it up for just a few seconds, and then swiftly lowered it to signal the start of battle.

Thunder exploded and blue-gray smoke filled the air as one hundred harquebus men pulled their triggers. Invisible lethal lead balls streaked across the plain toward Orgóñez's men. Hernando's crossbowmen released a volley of metal-tipped arrows.

Orgóñez watch in horror as groups of cavalrymen and their horses went down. Foot soldiers fell suddenly, some looking down at the holes in their armour and wondering how they had got there, others clutching and pulling on shafts protruding from their armour. Orgóñez was certain that Hernando's troops would have raced around their flanks and made an all-out dash to seize Cuzco, therefore avoiding combat. He was wrong.

Orgóñez yelled over at Caso, "Charge and break up those harquebusiers!"

"Do you want me to get butchered?" Caso yelled back. He was no idiot; he knew that following the order was tantamount to committing suicide. Caso got only part way across the plain before another volley of arrows and lead was fired directly at him and his men. He could see they didn't stand a chance against that superior fire power. He spun around and raced back to join the rest of the forces; his men following his lead.

Orgóñez would deal with Caso's insubordination when the battle was over; right now, they had to win. Orgóñez raised his head to the sky, muttered a prayer, and cried out, "Santiago!" as he charged alone at the enemy. He slashed at a harquebusier and stabbed a foot soldier as the two armies narrowed the gap between them.

The sounds of metal clanging, horses neighing, harquebuses exploding, men shouting, and the wounded wailing filled the battlefield.

Almagro could see from his vantage point that his army was losing against the superior weaponry of Pizarro's men. He could see that his men were struggling bravely to hold their ground, but were slowly being pushed back. He had seen enough to recognize the outcome.

"Take me back," Almagro instructed his litter bearers. They whisked him away from the battle scene to seek temporary refuge in Saqsaywaman, the fortress above the city. It would be only a matter of time before he would be sought out.

Orgóñez led another charge, spurring his horse forward while shouting: "Keep going. Push them back. We can win this!" The thunderous, almost deafening sound of several harquebuses rolled across the plain. Orgóñez was thrown to the ground as his horse fell from under him. Orgóñez was now at a disadvantage, having to fight on foot. He continued to attack; he continued to spur his men on.

Caso had watched Orgóñez's horse go down, taking Orgóñez with him. He watched as Orgóñez kept battling the enemy. He noticed seven of Pizarro's men close in and surround him. They stabbed him, attacking all at once. The barrage was too much for Orgóñez to defend against; he went down. On the ground, Pizarro's men continued to assault him. Caso watched in horror as one of Pizarro's men pulled Orgóñez's beard back and slit his throat. But the man didn't stop there; he severed Orgóñez's head. Then he grabbed a lance and stuck the bloodied head on the end, thrusting it into the air, amongst the loud cheers from Pizarro's troops.

Caso knew it was time to save his own neck. He turned his horse and raced back to Cuzco. He would claim his prize and then leave. But first, he had to fight his way off the battlefield.

Once Orgóñez troops saw their commander's head at the end of a lance, they broke from the fight and scattered.

Paullu Inca, recognizing that he was battling on the losing side, abruptly switched sides. He ordered his warriors to attack Orgóñez's men, instead of Hernando's.

The entire battle had lasted only an hour.

132

ALMAGRO'S MEN CHARGED back into the city of Cuzco in an attempt to collect some of their precious property and, then, escape before Hernando's forces arrived. Dani and Daric heard shouting in the streets outside their prison. They walked to the window to see what all the commotion was about. They saw bloodied soldiers running everywhere; it was bedlam, with men pushing and shoving, arms laden with stolen wealth. Those who were empty-handed ran into buildings and, mere moments later, reappeared clutching as many looted items as they could carry. Maybe this was the diversion that Dani, Daric and Titu Cusi had been waiting for.

"Get Bear and Titu Cusi," Daric whispered to Dani. "Let's use the chaos out there and make a run for it."

Daric walked over to the doorway and peered out. No one was there. The guards had vanished. He turned and called just loudly enough to be heard, "Let's go."

Daric led Dani and Titu Cusi down the hallway. As they passed other chambers, they released the prisoners. One prisoner they released was Manco's half-brother Cusi-Rimac. He had been fighting alongside Manco since the beginning of the rebellion and had successfully ambushed a Spanish escort, killing all but two of them.

The escaped prisoners crept quietly through the temple, meeting no resistance at all along the way. When they reached the main entranceway, Daric cautiously surveyed the scene outside. There was pandemonium everywhere. The soldiers were clearly fleeing from something, Daric thought, and it was probably best to do the same.

Daric turned to Titu Cusi, knelt down to his level, and looked him directly in the eye. "Do you know where your father is?"

"Yes, he's in Vilcabamba. He told me that's where our next move would be," Titu Cusi replied confidently.

Daric looked over at Cusi-Rimac. "Do you know where that is?" Cusi-Rimac nodded yes. "Great. We need to take him back to his father. You lead the way."

"You're coming too, right?" Titu Cusi asked anxiously.

"Of course we are," Daric replied. "We'll be right behind you. We have to make sure Bear stays with us and we don't want to slow you down."

"Let's go," Cusi-Rimac ordered as he grabbed Titu Cusi's hand. They raced out of the temple and across the courtyard, followed by the other escaped Inca prisoners, with Dani, Daric and Bear bringing up the rear.

By this time, Hernando's men had entered the city and were chasing down Almagro's remaining troops. Hernando's men were using this opportunity to settle old scores; others to increase their wealth by stealing whatever Almagro's men were trying to haul away. The whole city had become the new battlegrounds. One of Hernando's men had brought the lance carrying Orgóñez's head into the city and had stuck it up in the middle of the courtyard for all to see.

Dani and Daric ran down the narrow city streets, darting into open doorways when they heard someone approaching. In all the confusion, they became separated from the others and didn't see where they had gone.

"We're in the middle of a bloody war!" Daric exclaimed, amidst the shouting of commands, the screaming of the injured, the thunder of hooves racing across the stones, and the blasts from the harquebuses.

"We'll never find the others in all this confusion; so, let's get out of here while we still can," Dani suggested, as they ran for cover into a building.

"Don't you think that's what we're trying to do?" Daric snapped.

"No, I mean out of this time period," Dani clarified.

"What if we land in a worse situation?" Daric warned uneasily, looking to make sure the coast was clear before they ran out.

"What could possibly be worse than a war?" Dani shot back, as they ducked into another building, just as a group of cavalry rounded the corner.

"Just what I was looking for," an evil-sounding voice sneered.

Daric and Dani turned and were confronted by Caso. He reached out and grabbed Dani by the arm and forcefully yanked her to his side. Daric moved to intervene, but quickly thought better of it when he saw that Caso had his beefy arm wrapped around Dani's torso and was pressing a knife against her throat. "What do you want?" Daric asked, knowing the answer.

"I've got what I want," Caso replied coldly. "And unless you want to feel the end of this blade, I suggest you get out of here." He pointed the knife at Daric, waving it in front of his eyes.

Just then, Bear sank her teeth into Caso's leg, holding on tightly. Bear was by no means a large dog and she wasn't one to start a fight. But she was very protective of her family and she could tell by the tension in the room that something was amiss.

Caso's hold on Dani eased as he swung his blade down at Bear. Daric seized the moment. He grabbed Dani's arm and yanked hard, pulling her out of the Caso's clutches. Daric didn't hesitate for a second; he reached over and touched his band onto Dani's, and they disappeared.

"Bear!" Dani screamed just as everything went black

133

EDDIE'S RELATIONSHIP WITH Harry Bennett had taken a one-eighty-degree turn after Richard had left for New Zealand. The unexpected turnaround was part of the reason that the two men were now sitting in front of the fireplace in Eddie's living room, playing a game of chess and enjoying a couple of cold beers. "It's your move, Harry," Eddie announced.

"I don't know why I let you talk me into playing another game," Harry grumbled. "You've won the last three."

Eddie had used his time wisely during Richard's absence and had gotten to know the house staff. He had been astounded to learn that the staff consisted of two people. There was Harry, who served as Richard's manservant, chauffer, and bodyguard. And then there was Vashti Barinov.

Vashti Barinov was Richard's cook and housekeeper. The poor woman got up before dawn to make sure that Richard's clothes were pressed and laid out for the day and that his breakfast was cooked and on the table when he entered the dining room. She alone looked after the entire mansion.

Richard had purchased Vashti when she was only twenty-two-years-old and had trained her from the very beginning on how he wanted his household run. She had no money; she had nothing to her name. Everything she needed Richard provided: food, shelter, even the clothes on her back. She had access to a closed-in yard for any fresh air she might like to have, but she never had any leisure time to avail herself of it. In fact, she hadn't had a day off in over fifteen years. She hadn't even been in contact with her family back in Russia: not that she didn't want to, but because Richard had threatened to kill her family if she ever tried to contact them. He had told her, as far as they were concerned, she was dead to them, so just move on.

A knock came to the door. "I'll get it," Eddie said, leaping up and running across the living room. On opening it and seeing who had knocked, he said jovially, "Here, let me help you."

Vashti was a big-boned woman, about five-foot-six-inches tall and one-hundred-sixty pounds. She wore her brown hair up in a bun and her sad brown eyes reflected her despondent soul. She was wearing a white stud-fastened chef's jacket, black trousers and sensible black shoes; carrying a large silver tray loaded with food and drinks.

"Thanks, Eddie. You're a dear," Vashti meekly. It was probably the first time anyone had ever offered her any help.

"My pleasure," Eddie replied. "Come on in; we're just finishing up."

"You mean cleaning up," Harry grunted. He inhaled deeply and admitted, "That smells wonderful."

"Just what you boys ordered: cheeseburgers, fries, and a beer. Hope you don't mind, but I made myself some, too," Vashti said shyly, as she entered the room.

"Fantastic, please join us," Eddie encouraged, as he placed the heavy tray on the mahogany coffee table and gestured for Vashti to take the seat on the sofa beside Harry. Eddie pulled up one of the leather wingback chairs.

While they enjoyed their dinner, Eddie asked cautiously, "Do you know when Mr. Case will return?"

"I would suspect any day now," Harry answered around a mouthful of food. "This is delicious, Vashti. I wish this was on the menu more often, instead of all that fancy rich food Mr. Case always orders."

"Sure would make my life a lot easier," Vashti admitted.

Suddenly the door flew open. "Well, well, well, what do we have here?" Richard thundered.

134

"IT'S REALLY NOTHING, Mr. Case." Harry jumped up off the sofa and ran to stand beside his boss. "We were just having dinner."

"Do you take me for an idiot? I can see that," Richard boomed.

Vashti swiftly collected the plates and bottles, placing them on the tray which she snatched off the table and quickly left the room. Richard's cold hard glare sent a shiver up her spine. She would probably pay dearly for this indiscretion; Harry would, too. She prayed it wouldn't be too harsh.

"Leave us," Richard grunted to Harry. "Have my SUV fueled and cleaned before morning."

"Yes, Mr. Case," Harry said, as he darted from the room.

"So, Eddie, what kind of mischief have you been up to while I've been gone?" Richard asked warily, making his way into the room.

"What kind of mischief could I have possibly gotten into while locked in this room?" Eddie countered.

"Don't get smart with me kid," Richard warned, as he sat in a leather chair. "What's the latest news on the train derailment? Do they have any leads yet?"

"They're all running around in a maze, searching for the exit, but only finding dead ends," Eddie said proudly. "There's no way in hell they can ever trace that hack back to this location. Last I heard, they're thinking it must have been terrorists, but it's not clear which ones they may have in mind."

"Good," Richard grinned. "That'll keep them busy and misdirected for months, maybe even years."

"Tomorrow morning, you're coming with me. I need you to remove your virus from a terminal and assist me with completing my plan," Richard announced, as he rose from his seat.

"What plan?" Eddie was curious. He had provided Richard with a computer virus, had crafted materials to lift fingerprints, had manufactured a set of duplicate fingerprints, and had derailed a commuter train, without knowing Richard's true plan. Eddie knew only that Richard had promised to reunite him with his dead parents when it was all over. Richard had sworn he could bring them back to life. Eddie was just hoping Richard would keep up his end of the deal.

"You're on a need-to-know basis, and right now, you don't need to know," Richard scoffed. "Get some sleep. We're leaving early in the morning." With that Richard left the room, locking the door behind him.

"Nice to have you home, Richard," Eddie muttered bitterly under his breath.

Author's Notes
Part IV

Before beginning to write my three books, I decided the books' stories would involve different periods of history. I also decided how each story would start and end. These decisions have led to a number of challenges. One has been to find historically accurate material for each period. Another has been to weave the material into adventurous and informative stories that readers can enjoy as they take this journey with me. The search for reliable material, especially, has taken a lot of time and effort, even more than I had anticipated when I began to write.

In the first book, we ventured to 1937, where the Delaney twins encountered Amelia Earhart working on her first attempt to circumnavigate the globe. Suddenly, with Dani's life hanging in the balance and Daric desperately trying to save his sister, they unexpectedly found themselves in the cold damp streets of East End London in 1888. Befriended and taken in by a generous young couple, the twins endeavoured to blend into their new situation. Splashed across the front page of every newspaper are the alarming headlines of gruesome murders occurring in the East End. Dani and Daric never realized, until it was too late, how close they came to confronting Jack the Ripper.

Their abrupt exit from 1888 London brought Dani and Daric to the current part of their journey through time: to 1692, Salem, Massachusetts, and the notorious witch hunts.

When I started my research into the Salem witch trials, my first epiphany was that there were two Salems: Salem Village and Salem Town. Salem Village, today known as Danvers, was a three-hour walk from Salem Town and was the poorer of the two communities. It was also where the witchcraft hysteria began, with the resulting trials taking place in the town. I sometimes had difficulty differentiating between the two [communities] when the reference material I was reviewing simply stated that such and such occurred in Salem.

The reference material included many official documents, which I like to use in relation to specific historical events. Such documents, however, posed a challenge, because they were written in the language of the seventeenth century.

While seventeenth century language has much in common with current-day language, it sometimes unveils significant differences. Spelling, grammar and structure are from time to time different. The overall result is a different manner of speaking and writing, a manner that is on occasion challenging to understand. So, when I found passages that I wanted to include in my story, I have at times used current-day language, so that the original meaning can be more easily understood by the reader.

During my research, I came across some unique names. I found that it was not uncommon to give children bizarre names; among many such names were Increase, Cotton, Truegrace, Reform, Hopedfor and Restore. I also found a lot of names, such as Mary, Martha, Elizabeth, Sarah, John and George which were widely used at the time. And there was also the practice of giving children their parents' first name; while this practice is not that uncommon today, in the seventeenth century it also applied to giving female children their mothers' first name.

While I am on the subject of names, there was also the spelling to consider. I found that different documents would spell the same individual's name differently. Even original court documents had different spellings, depending on who had authored them. In such situations, I used the spelling that was inscribed on the stones that make up the Salem Witch Trials Memorial. The Memorial, located in Salem, was dedicated in August 1992 to the victims of the witch hunts.

During the writing of the Salem story, I took actual dialogue from a court transcript of one of the accused's testimony and attributed parts of it to another character in my story. The meanings and words are historical fact, but, in a couple of instances, I took some literary licence as regards to who actually said the words. As for people and places, the records show that Reverend Increase Mather attended only one trial, that of Reverend George Burroughs; I placed him, however, sitting quietly in a corner of Beadle's Tavern, observing three examinations, those of Ann Forster and the two Mary Lacys. There were some other minor deviations from the historical events and descriptions set out in official documents, but, as in all my stories, I tried to stick to the facts.

Writing this Salem story was challenging because I had difficulty believing that people—including well educated people—actually believed that the spirit world was the one and only source of all their hardships

I acknowledge my debt of gratitude to those who have dedicated themselves to documenting and explaining the events and conditions associated with the Salem Witch Trials, especially the events of 1692. As always, I have tried to respect historical facts, while, at the same time, interweaving my characters—the Delaneys, Richard Barak Case and others—into the fabric of history.

I hope you enjoyed the journey . . . ***Until Next Time.***

Author's Notes
Part V

You will find that this book has a larger portion of the content dedicated to the Present Day storyline than you have seen in the previous book. Since there are a few plots running at the same time within each book, it was time to bring the Present Day storyline more into focus, and to ensure that Book III wasn't over weighted, but fairly balanced.

In the Present Day plot, I needed to create a distraction; one that would prevent Sandra from travelling to New Zealand, so Richard could execute his diabolical plan. Sandra being the head of Emergency Services at Mount Albert Hospital, gave me an idea: I needed a tragic event that force her to remain behind. So Richard convinced Eddie to derail a passenger train. While doing my research on this particular subject, an Amtrak train actually derailed in Philadelphia. I felt somewhat ghoulish reading the reports and watching the news footage of the train derailment; all in an effort to educate myself so that I could write a more realistic account of the events in my story. I know that including any tragic event in a story can bring real-life events to the forefront. But I also learned, while doing my research, that speed has been a factor in many train derailments, not only in North America, but globally.

But it shouldn't be—we have the technology. Legislation needs to be put in place so that all trains, regardless of whether they are commuter trains or freight trains, would have a mandatory Positive Train Control. According to the Association of American Railroads, PTC is a technology that can automatically stop or slow a train before a tragic event occurs, such as train-to-train collisions, high-speed derailments or train travel on tracks that are off-limits due to repairs or maintenance. The Rail Safety Improvement Act of 2008 stated that by 2015, PTC must be installed on all rail lines that carry passengers or certain hazardous materials. While it's not certain that PTC would have prevented the Amtrak train accident or the Fastrax one in my book, it is designed to automatically slow trains as they approach bends in the track such as the one where the high-speed derailment occurred.

When I picked the Inca Empire for one of the historical pieces in this book, I was primarily drawn to this period because of romanticized rumors of lost gold; how the Inca were stashing away golden relics from the Spaniards in an attempt to preserve some of their cultural heritage. When I started to research the Inca Empire my first epiphany was that they had no formal means of recording their own history; they had no written language. Most documentation about the Inca had been written by the Spanish, so needless to say it may be bias regarding actual facts. But with nothing else of record to go on, I was left to use what was available to me. I found that picking a specific period in time to use as the basis for my story was quite a challenge. First, there was the famous Machu Picchu believed to be the royal estate of Pachacuti, the ruler credited with the vision to expand the Inca Empire. Then there was the civil war between two brothers, Huascar and Atahualpa, both believed to be the next *Sapa Inca* after the death of their father, Huayna Capac. At this time, the Inca Empire was fractured; it was the opportune time for the Spaniards to invade. After the death of the two warring brothers, the Spanish conquistador, Francisco Pizarro, appoint younger brother, Manco Inca, to the throne as his puppet king. Manco Inca realize, before too long, that living under the atrocity of these bearded foreigners was not what he wanted for his people, so he escaped and organized a guerrilla resistance that lasted almost forty years.

In the historical storylines in my books before this specific period, I was able to document precise dates of events. But the Inca did not use a calendar system or absolute dates. They measured time by sequence of events. They did not count their age in years, but by noting the different stages of life. The only dates available were those of the events involving the Spaniards, such as the Battle of Las Salinas that actually occurred on April 26, 1538. However, for the purposes of my book, I had to condense the timeline in which the events unfolded. And the attack on Ollantaytambo, which I wrote was led by Rodrigo Orgóñez, was, in fact, actually lead by Hernando Pizzaro and took place prior to his imprisonment in Cusco under Almagro.

I fear that dates may also be a challenge going forward with Book III, but I guess; only time will tell.

I acknowledge my debt of gratitude to those who have dedicated so much of their time and effort into the relentless quest of documenting Inca history. Except for what I have noted above, I have tried to respect historical facts, while at the same time, interweaving my characters—the Delaneys, Ricardo Barak Caso and others—into the fabric of history.

I hope you enjoyed the journey . . . *Until Next Time.*

Bibliography

1. Time Travel

- Gott, J. Richard. *Time Travel in Einstein's Universe: The Physical Possibilities of Travel Through Time.* Mariner Books, 2002.

- Kaku, Michio. *Physics of the Impossible: A Scientific Exploration into the World of Phasers, Force Fields, Teleportation, and Time Travel.* Doubleday, 2008.

- Magueijo, Jaao. *Faster Than the Speed of Light: The Story of a Scientific Speculation.* Basic Books, 2003.

- Nahin, Paul J. *Time Travel: A Writer's Guide to the Real Science of Plausible Time Travel.* Johns Hopkins Univ Pr; Revised ed. edition, 2011.

2. Salem Witch Trials

- Calef, Robert. *More Wonders of the Invisible World.* n.d. http://www.piney.com/ColCalef1.html. 2016.

- Kallen, Stuart A. *The Salem Witch Trials .* San Diego, CA: Lucent Books, 1999.

- Kent, Kathleen. *The Heretic's Daughter.* New York: Little, Brown and Co., 2008

- Library, University of Virginia. *Boyer, Paul, and Stephen Nissenbaum, eds. The Salem Witchcraft Papers: Verbatim Transcripts of the Legal Documents of the Salem Witchcraft Outbreak of 1692.* 2003. http://

etext.virginia.edu/salem/witchcraft/texts/transcrip.

- Roach, Marilynne K. *The Salem Witch Trials: A Day-By-Day Chronicle of a Community Under Siege* . Rowman & Littlefield Publishers, 2004.

- Upham, Charles W. *Salem Witchcraft: With an Account of Salem Village and A History of Opinions on Witchcraft and Kindred Subjects* . Cedar Eden Books, 2016.

- Wilson, Lori Lee. *The Salem Witch Trials (How history is invented)*. 1999.

3. **Ancient Inca Civilization**

- Baquedano, Elizabeth. *Aztec, Inca, and Maya* . DK Children, 2005.

- George, Charles and Linda. *Life During the Great Civilizations - The Inca* . Blackbirch Press;, 2005.

- Hagen, Craig Morris and Adriana von. *The Incas (Ancient Peoples and Places)*. Thames & Hudson, 2012.

- Jones, Dr. David M. *The Complete Illustrated History of the Inca Empire*. Lorenz Books, 2012.

- MacQuarrie, Kim. *The Last Days of the Incas*. New York: Simon & Schuster Paperbacks, 2007.

4. **Present Day Storyline**
   - Transportation Safety Board of Canada, *Railway Investigation Report, 2016 http://tsb.gc.ca/eng/rapports-reports/rail/2012/R12T0038/R12T0038.asp*
   - Xlisulas Limited: *Cave-Diving in Blue Creek Resurgence 2014*

   https://www.youtube.com/watch?v=Iwr_Flnp7ps

   - Tech Dive New Zealand: *Drive Reports: bc070110,*

bluecreek070410, bluecreek180211

http://www.techdivenz.com/reports.html

- Waitomo Glowworm Cave: https://www.waitomo.com/discover/magic/the-history-of-waitomo-glow-worm-cave

Acknowledgements

Again, I'd like to express my deepest gratitude to Hugh Willis who signed up for this *Next Time* journey, not realizing it would take five years. If it wasn't for you, I would not have had the confidence to put myself out there. I am forever thankful.

For technical assistance, I'd like to thank Jason Yoshida, Deputy Fire Chief and Gary Lewis, Superintendent/Manager, Professional Standards for Emergency Medical Services for their expertise regarding their departments' respective roles as emergency responders in the event of a train derailment.

I'd also like to thank Roman Mizanski, owner and head instructor of Innerspace Divers Supply who tried to explain, with a passion and extreme patience, the requirements for cave diving and the type of equipment recommended.

And a special thank you to my niece, Jaclynn, for taking the time out of your vacation to drive to Courthouse Flat to provide me with environmental details. You just happened to be in New Zealand in the same season as my storyline.

I am also grateful to Kerry Mills and Michael Dunn for their expertise in sailing and for letting me borrow the 'Kerry Blue'.

Thank you to Lynda Orrell, Emergency Room Nurse (retired) and to Diane Cole, Registered Nurse in the Neuro/Trauma Intensive Care Unit at St. Michaels Hospital for their technical medical assistance.

And a special thank you to all my beta readers; your feedback kept me writing.

The adventure continues with

NEXT TIME BOOK 3

RACE AGAINST TIME

Read on for an exciting glimpse into the next book in the Next Time series coming out soon.

Part VI

Race Against Time

1

QUINN SLOWLY OPENED his eyes. Except for a sliver of light filtering through a crack in the cavern wall, there was only pitch black. He began to pull himself up, but immediately regretted it. His head throbbed incessantly. "Oww," he moaned. He figured he must have been struck by a piece of stalactite loosened by the tremor they had felt moments ago. He called out. "Richard?" And again, he regretted it.

"This is worse than a hangover," Quinn groaned, reaching up to hold his aching head. He felt something moist and sticky. "Richard, are you okay?"

Quinn felt the ground around him until his hand recognized the shape of his dive light. He clicked it on and quickly scanned the cavern. Richard was gone. And so was Richard's equipment.

"The coward," Quinn muttered. "A little tremor and he runs for the hills."

Quinn pulled his hand away from his head and noticed blood on his fingers. He looked down and saw the large chunk of stalactite lying close by. "No wonder my head hurts," he grunted.

Quinn went to retrieve the piece of chronizium he had spotted before the tremor, but it was gone. "I didn't come all this way to go back empty-handed," he muttered. "Okay, Quinn, start looking. You need to get out of here, too, before something else falls on you." Quinn, on his hands and knees, searched the area where he had found the first shard, when the beam from his dive light bounced off something shiny. He reached over and picked it up. "That's it!" he exclaimed, as he examined the mineral. This piece was larger than the first one he had found and subsequently lost.

Quinn tucked the chronizium into his utility pocket. "Time to get out of here," he said, making his way over to his equipment. He checked the gauge on his rebreather unit.

"You bastard!" Quinn shouted in the empty cavern. "Richard! How could you?"

Quinn now realized he had been duped. He hadn't been struck by any falling object. Richard had clobbered him over the head when his back was turned and had taken the chronizium and left after bleeding Quinn's air supply. With no air in his rebreather unit, there was no way Quinn could get out of the cavern, definitely not the same way he had come in. And who knew how long it would be before someone would stumble upon this cavern … days, months, even years. He didn't have that kind of time to wait. He had to find a way out.

2

QUINN CHECKED HIS equipment over to see whether there was anything he could use to help get him out of this death trap. He picked up his mask and put it on.

"Richard? What do you think you're doing?" Quinn shouted into the mask's communication system. He waited a few moments. He didn't really expect a reply, but he had to try. Quinn checked his dive computer and realized that too much time had passed since the tremor. Richard would be out of range of the communication system by now.

"Damn!" Quinn tried changing the frequency on the mask's communication system and called out to anyone who might be within range, but the only reply he received was static.

Quinn took off his mask and set it down beside him. He reached for his rebreather unit. As he had noted earlier, the gauge's needle was showing "empty"; even so, he remained hopeful. The two tanks on the Poseidon Discovery MKVI Rebreather unit, which he had specifically asked for when he was renting his diving equipment, were independent of each other. Richard, who had never used a rebreather unit before, would have been unaware of the backup air supply, so when he opened the valve to empty the tanks, he had only emptied one tank before leaving the cavern. Unfortunately, when Quinn checked the second tank, there wasn't enough air for him to get back to the surface. "Another dead end," he muttered. Quinn took stock of his drysuit. His five-inch titanium dive knife was still strapped to his right leg. In his utility pockets, besides the piece of chronizium, were a spare dive light, two flares, and a handful of glow sticks. On his left wrist, Quinn had his two dive computers. One contained a virtual dive map he had preloaded prior to their dive. It had a backlit display specifically for cave diving and a built-in digital compass that could be used both during a dive and on the surface. His other dive computer was a redundant system, but it also functioned as a watch.

Quinn never went on a dive without packing his dive tool pack. It was like a Swiss army knife, with multiple stainless steel hinged tools, only they were designed for repairing dive equipment.

Having taken stock of his meager resources, Quinn focussed his attention on the rebreather unit. He removed the two tanks from their harness and pulled off whatever rubber hoses and nylon straps he could; they weren't cumbersome to carry and might come in handy if he ever got out of here.

Sitting with his salvaged gear beside him, Quinn tried to stay calm and come up with a plan on how to get out of the cavern and get back to the surface. As he considered the number of discouragingly unworkable ideas that came to him, he turned off his dive light to conserve its batteries. In the total darkness, he saw a sliver of light coming through a crack in the back wall of the cavern. He stood up and moved slowly and carefully toward the light. "Could I be so lucky?" he wondered aloud.

3

AS QUINN CAUTIOUSLY made his way to the back of the cavern, he was guided by the thin shaft of light seeping through the crack in the wall. "I don't remember any light in here before, other than from a dive light," he said out loud, in a futile attempt to break the eerie silence that engulfed him. "Maybe the tremor caused the crack."

The crack was only a few inches wide, not nearly wide enough for Quinn to squeeze through. He placed his face against the wall and gazed through the opening. The light was coming from the other side of the cavern wall, but he couldn't identify its source. "I'm too far underground for that to be daylight," he reasoned. He tried to squeeze his arm through the crack to determine how thick the wall was, but the opening was just not wide enough. He took another look through the crack and tried to estimate the wall's thickness.

"Maybe, just maybe," Quinn said with a hint of optimism. As he headed back over to his meager collection of supplies, he checked his dive computer on his wrist. Enough time had passed for the oxygen that Richard had released into the cavern to dissipate, most likely through the same crack that was now offering Quinn at least a glimmer of hope.

As Quinn stood contemplating his next step, a rough plan began to form in his mind. "This might just work."

Quinn turned on his dive light and set to work. He collected scattered chunks of stalactite from the cavern's floor and piled them in an area as far from the cavern's back wall as possible. When satisfied with his small barricade, he returned to his supplies. He picked up the back-up cylinder and headed once again toward the fissure in the wall, stooping to pick up a piece of stalactite on his way.

At the fissure, Quinn placed the cylinder gently on the sandy ground and started to pound the wall around the crack with the piece of stalactite. He succeeded in chipping away a few chunks of limestone from the crack, creating a small cradle that could hold the cylinder.

Quinn picked up the cylinder. He paused for a moment to check his dive computer again. Still okay, he confirmed. He slowly opened the air valve and then wedged the cylinder into the newly formed cradle. He hurried away from the tank and crouched behind his barricade.

"Okay, Quinn, you've got only two shots at this. Let's make the first one count," he muttered, trying to give himself some much needed encouragement. If this doesn't work, he would have only one flare left for a second and final attempt. He just hoped that he didn't blow himself up in the process. He pulled a flare out of his utility pocket and examined it. It looked okay. He took one deep breath, pulled the cap off, and ignited it. He immediately tossed it at the oxygen tank and took cover. There was a deafening explosion and a blinding flash of light, followed immediately by complete silence and total darkness.